ETERNAL EMPIRE

WESLEY WONG - LAUREN SPENCE - STEPHEN MAYER
COLOR FLATTING ASSISTS

SPECIAL THANKS

MARY BEAMS
ROMMEL CALDERON
LANE FUJITA
ERIN GOLDSTEIN
KAREN HILTON
TIM INGLE
ED LOPATEGUI
LEAH LY
LAUREN SPENCE
GIANCARLO YERKES

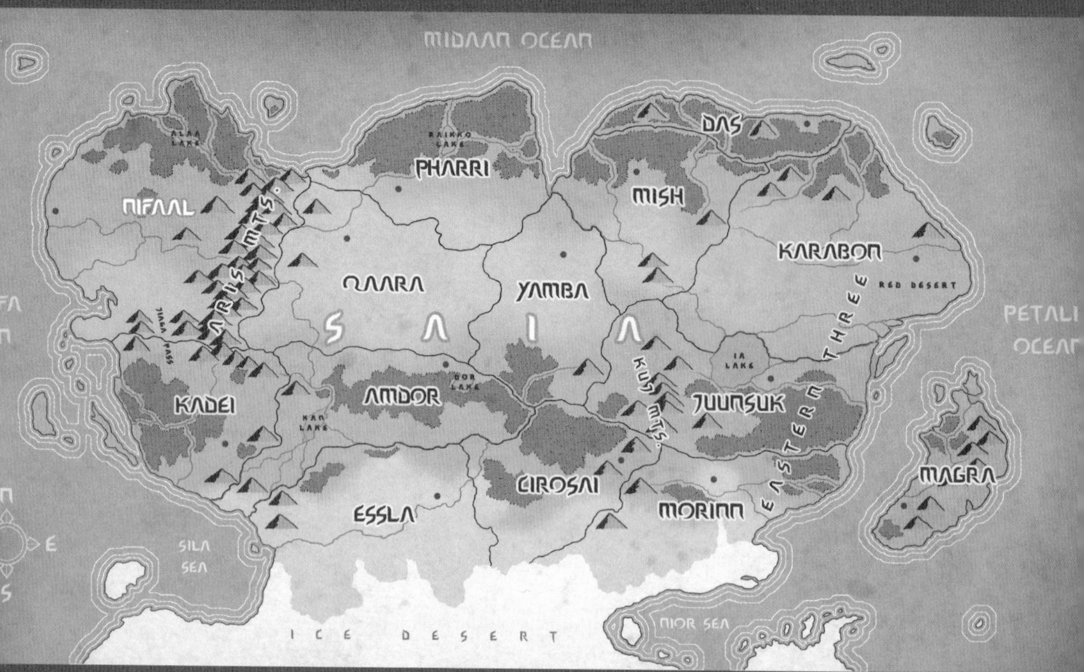
MIDAAN OCEAN
DAS
PHARRI
NIFAAL
MISH
KARABON
ARIS MTS.
QAARA
YAMBA
RED DESERT
BONTIFA OCEAN
PETALI OCEAN
S A I A
EASTERN THREE
KUJ MTS.
JUUNSUK
KADEI
AMDOR
CIROSAI
MORINN
MAGRA
ESSLA
SILA SEA
NIOR SEA
ICE DESERT
N
W
E
S

IMAGE COMICS, INC.

ROBERT KIRKMAN Chief Operating Officer - ERIK LARSEN Chief Financial Officer
TODD MCFARLANE President - MARC SILVESTRI Chief Executive Officer - JIM VALENTINO Vice President

ERIC STEPHENSON Publisher / Chief Creative Officer
COREY HART Director of Sales - JEFF BOISON Director of Publishing Planning & Book Trade Sales
CHRIS ROSS Director of Digital Sales - JEFF STANG Director of Specialty Sales - KAT SALAZAR
Director of PR & Marketing - DREW GILL Art Director - HEATHER DOORNINK Production Director - NICOLE LAPALME Controller

IMAGECOMICS.COM

ETERNAL EMPIRE, VOL. 2. First printing. OCTOBER 2018. Published by Image Comics, Inc. Office of publication: 2701 NW Vaughn St., Suite 780, Portland, OR 97210. ISBN: 978-1-5343-0687-5.

SARAH VAUGHN

STORY
SCRIPT

JONATHAN LUNA

STORY
SCRIPT ASSISTS
ILLUSTRATIONS
LETTERING
DESIGN

6

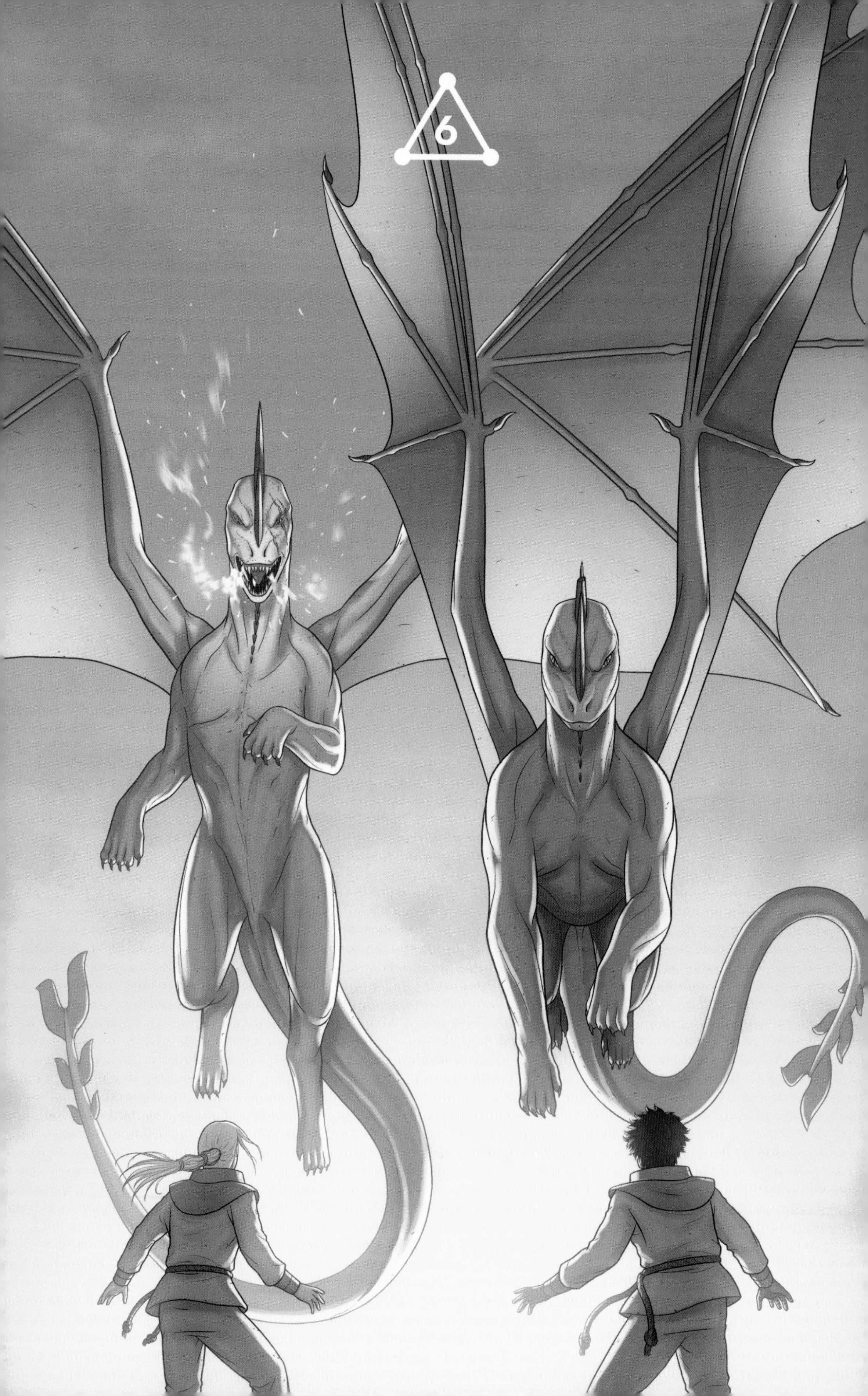

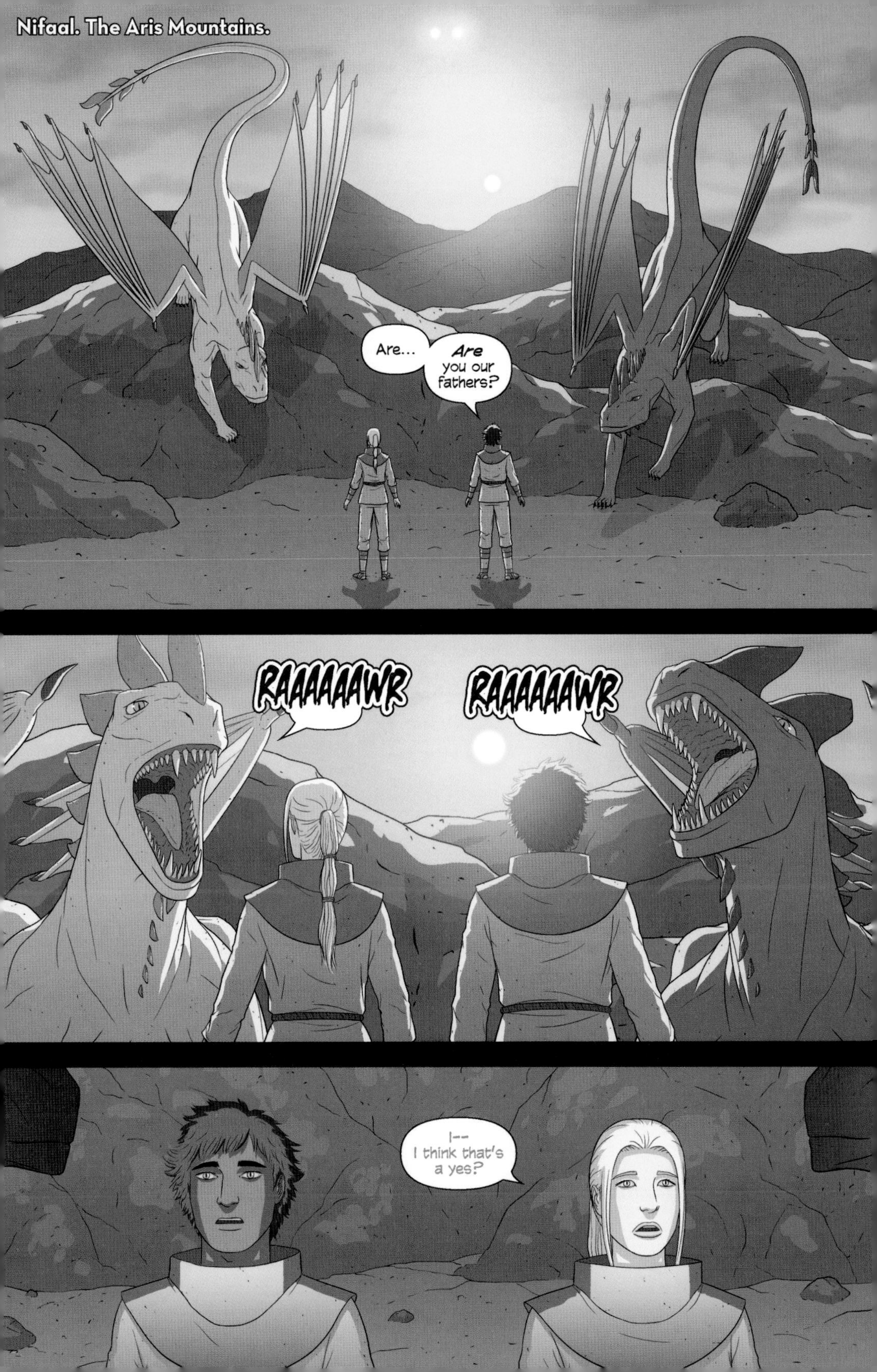
Nifaal. The Aris Mountains.
Are...
Are you our fathers?
RAAAAAAWR
RAAAAAAWR
I--
I think that's a yes?

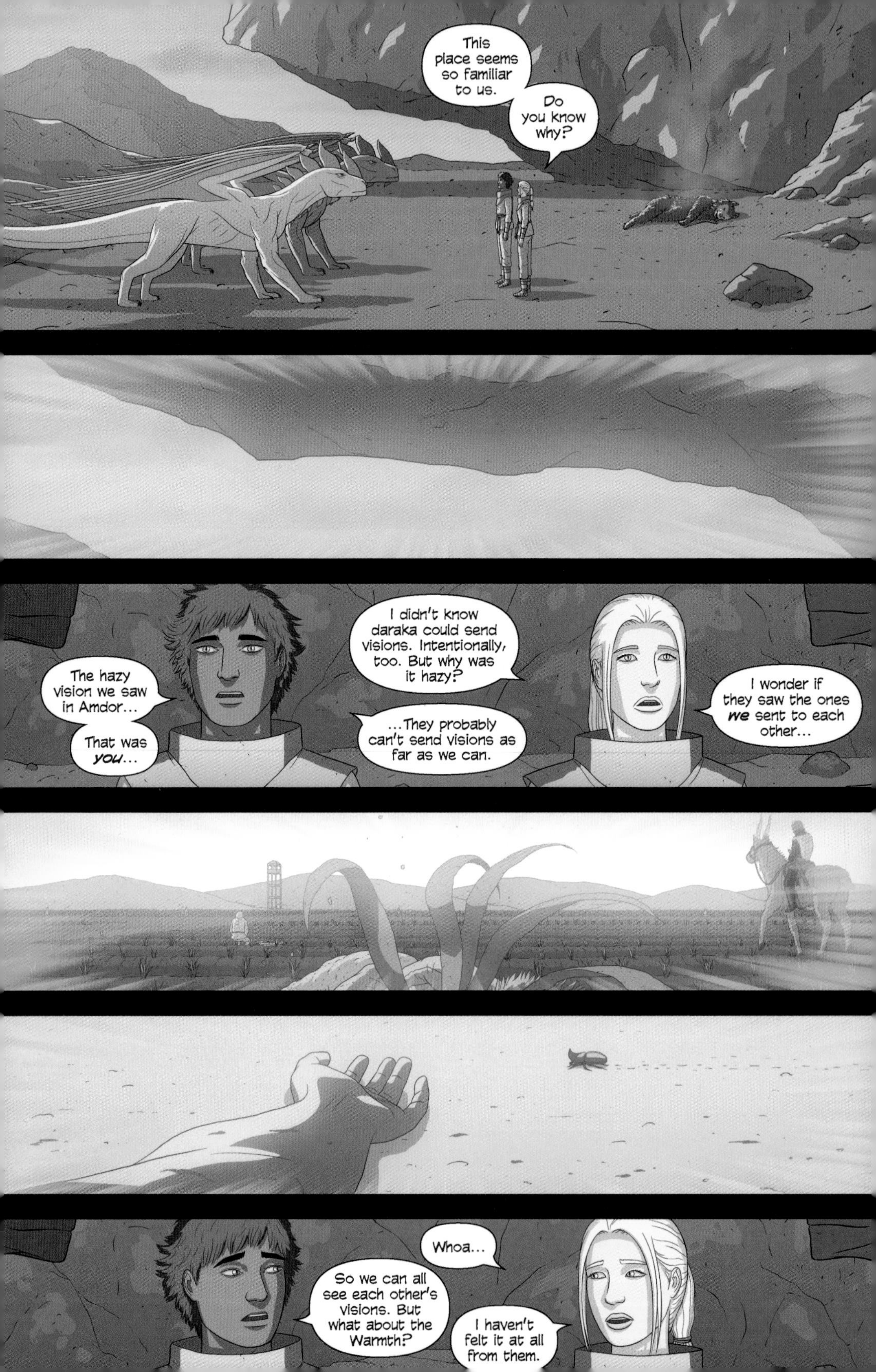
This place seems so familiar to us.
Do you know why?
The hazy vision we saw in Amdor...
That was *you*...
I didn't know daraka could send visions. Intentionally, too. But why was it hazy?
...They probably can't send visions as far as we can.
I wonder if they saw the ones *we* sent to each other...
Whoa...
So we can all see each other's visions. But what about the Warmth?
I haven't felt it at all from them.

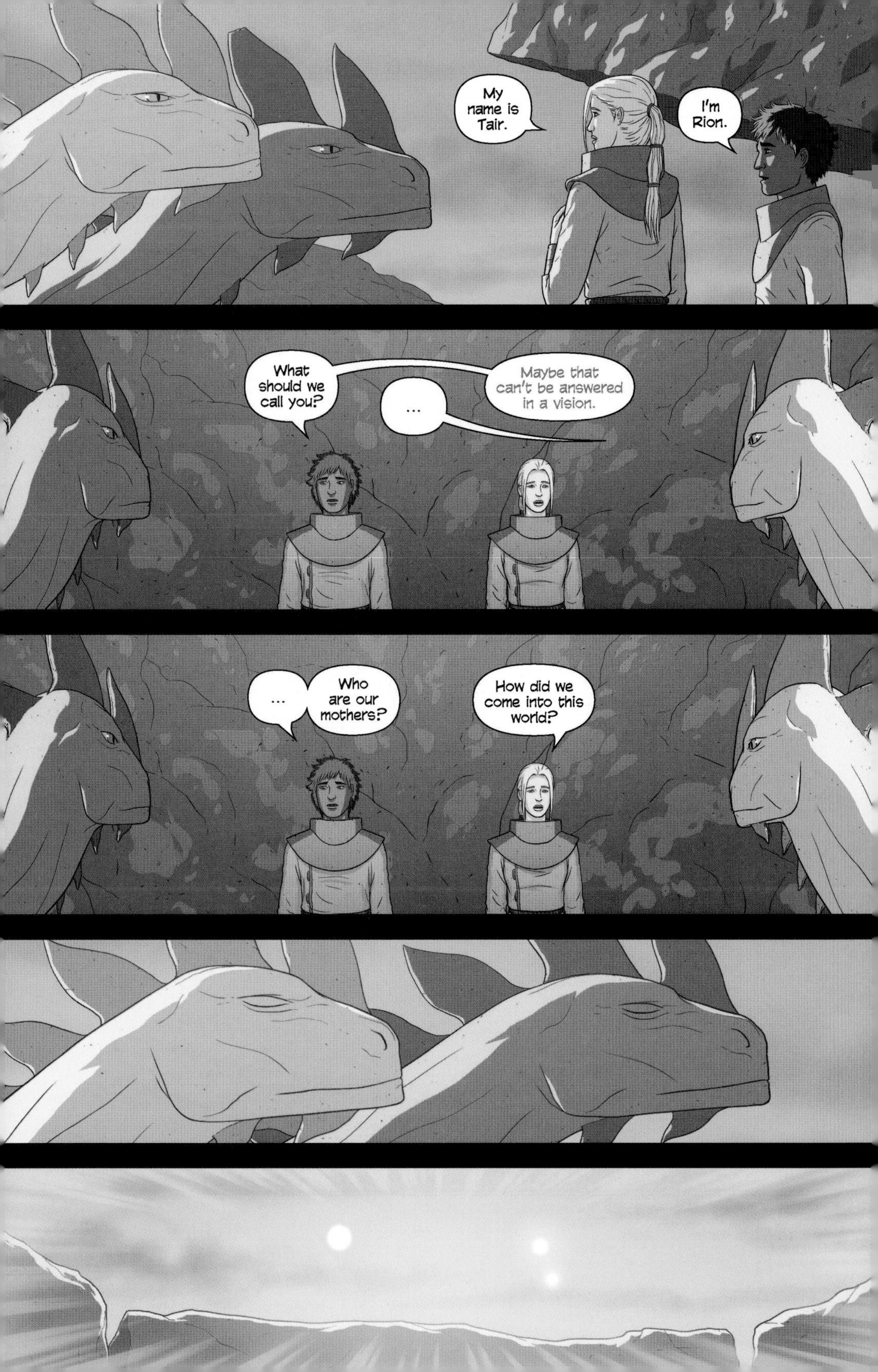
My name is Tair.
I'm Rion.
What should we call you?
...
Maybe that can't be answered in a vision.
...
Who are our mothers?
How did we come into this world?

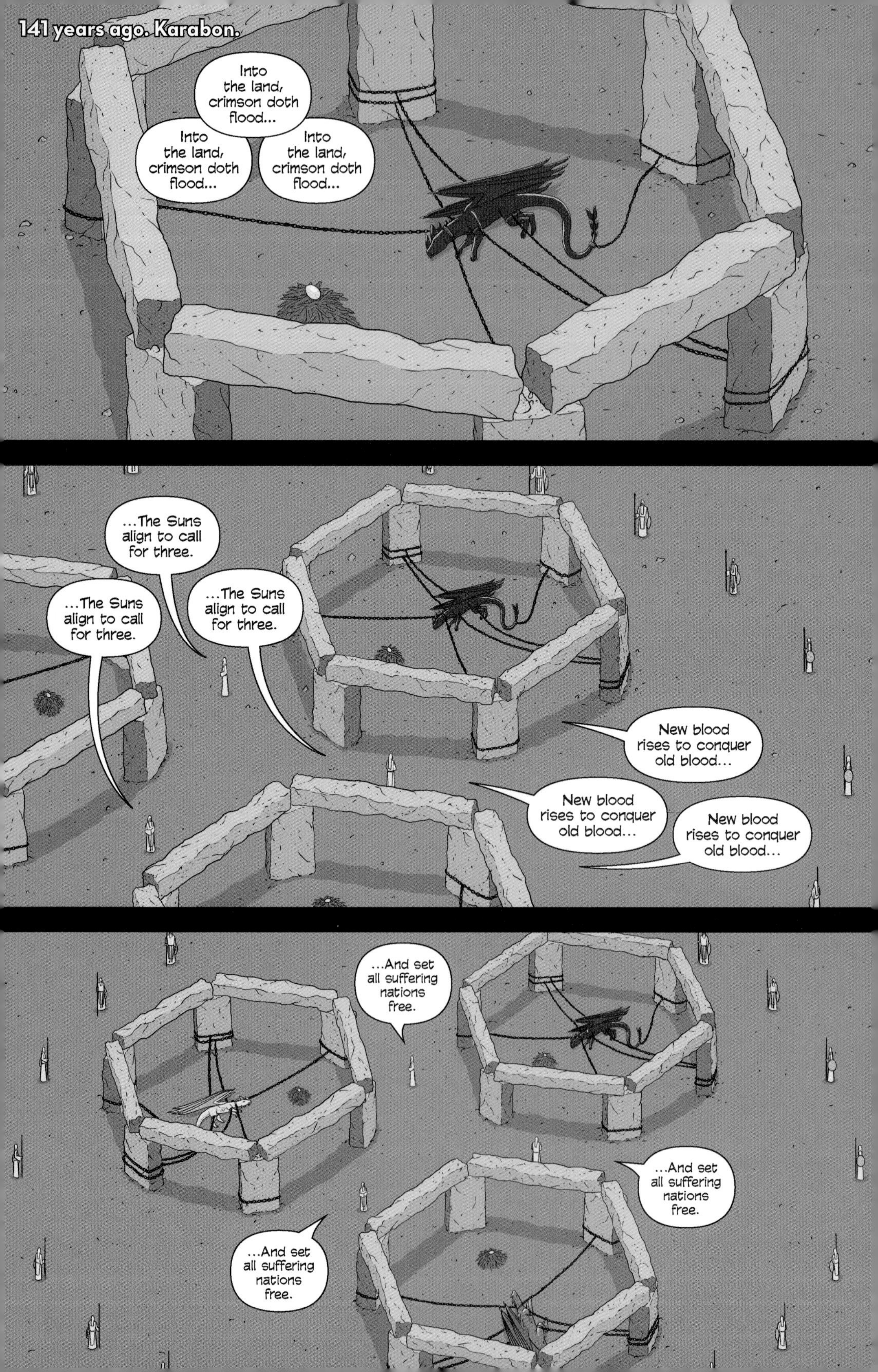

141 years ago. Karabon.
Into the land, crimson doth flood...
Into the land, crimson doth flood...
Into the land, crimson doth flood...
...The Suns align to call for three.
...The Suns align to call for three.
...The Suns align to call for three.
New blood rises to conquer old blood...
New blood rises to conquer old blood...
New blood rises to conquer old blood...
...And set all suffering nations free.
...And set all suffering nations free.
...And set all suffering nations free.

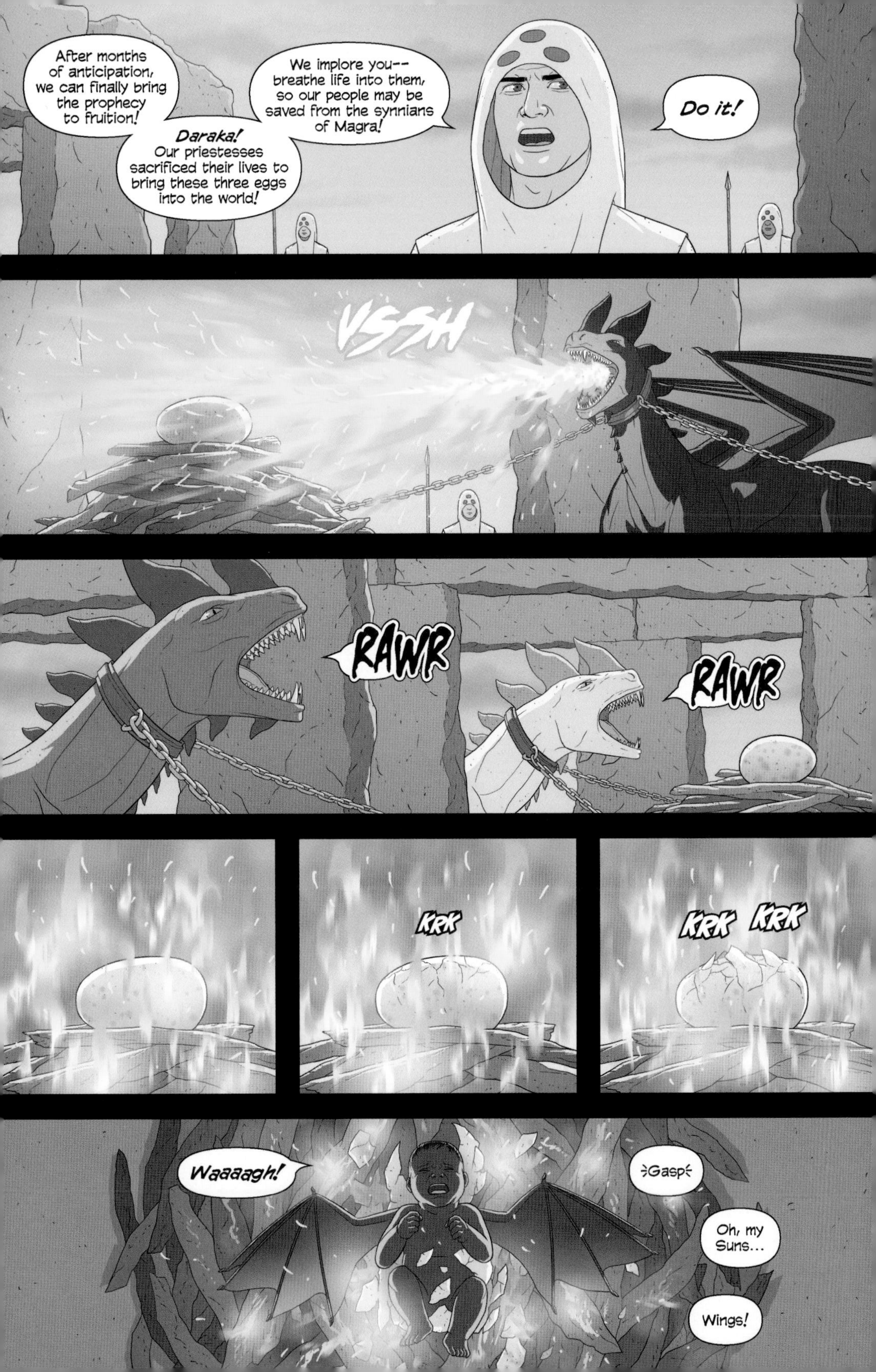
After months of anticipation, we can finally bring the prophecy to fruition!
Daraka! Our priestesses sacrificed their lives to bring these three eggs into the world!
We implore you-- breathe life into them, so our people may be saved from the synnians of Magra!
Do it!
VSSH
RAWR
RAWR
KRK
KRK KRK
Waaaagh!
Gasp
Oh, my Suns...
Wings!

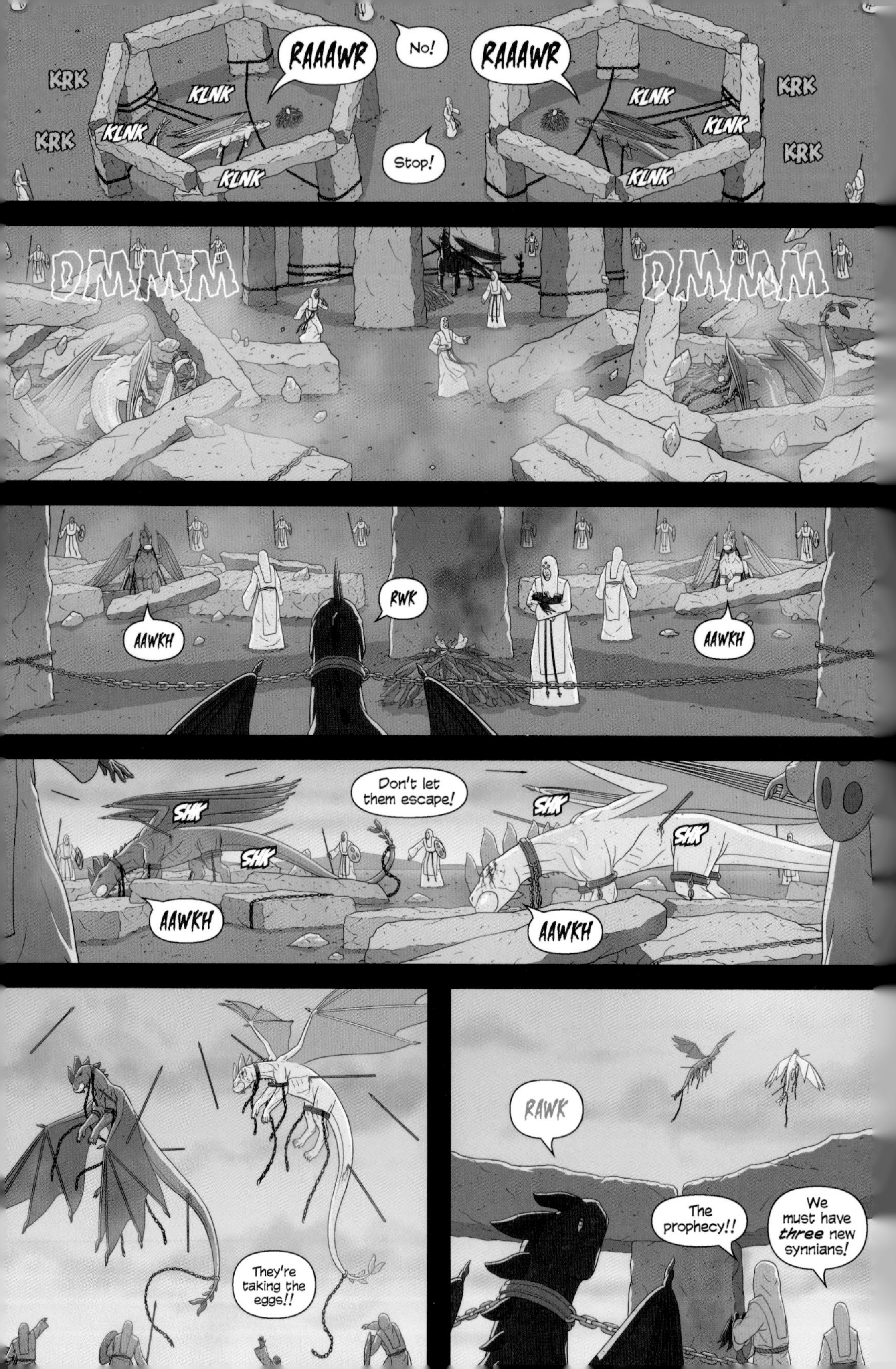
KRK
KRK
KLNK
KLNK
KLNK
RAAAWR
No!
Stop!
RAAAWR
KLNK
KLNK
KLNK
KRK
KRK
DMMM
DMMM
AAWKH
RWK
AAWKH
Don't let them escape!
SHK
SHK
SHK
SHK
AAWKH
AAWKH
They're taking the eggs!!
RAWK
The prophecy!!
We must have *three* new synnians!

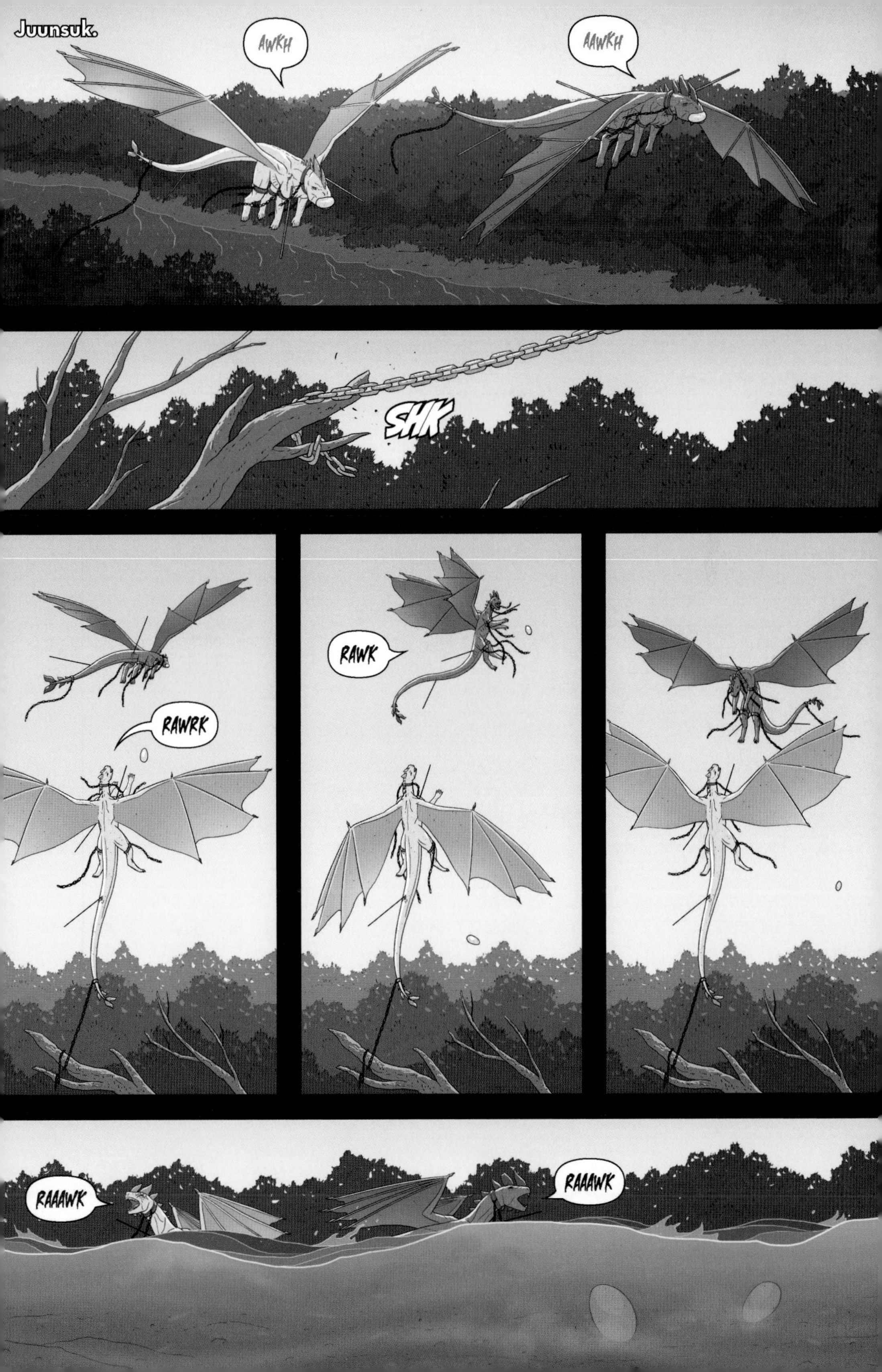
Juunsuk.
AWKH
AAWKH
SHK
RAWRK
RAWK
RAAAWK
RAAAWK

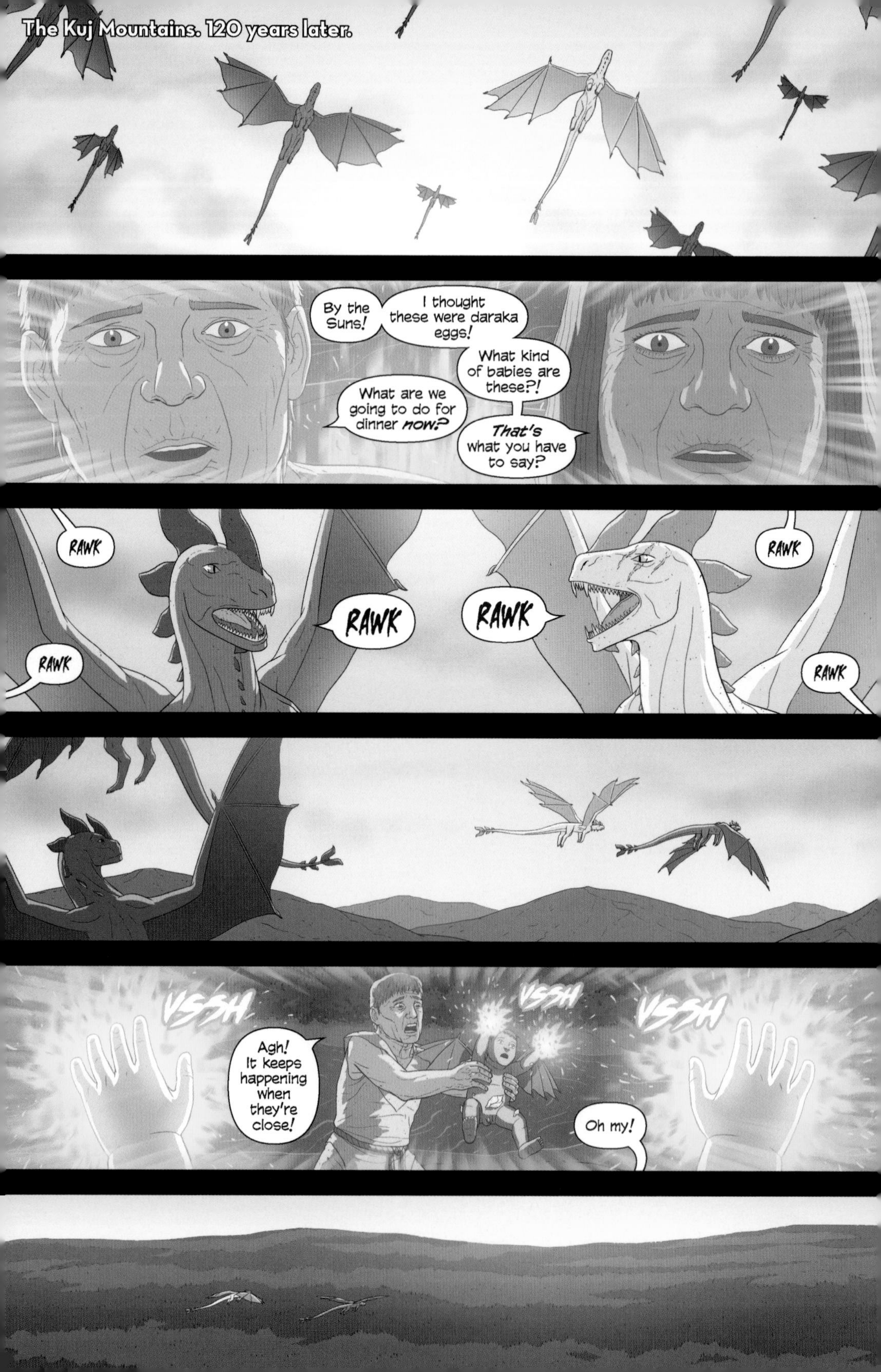

The Kuj Mountains. 120 years later.
By the Suns!
I thought these were daraka eggs!
What kind of babies are these?!
What are we going to do for dinner *now?*
That's what you have to say?
RAWK
RAWK
RAWK
RAWK
RAWK
RAWK
VSSH
VSSH
VSSH
Agh! It keeps happening when they're close!
Oh my!

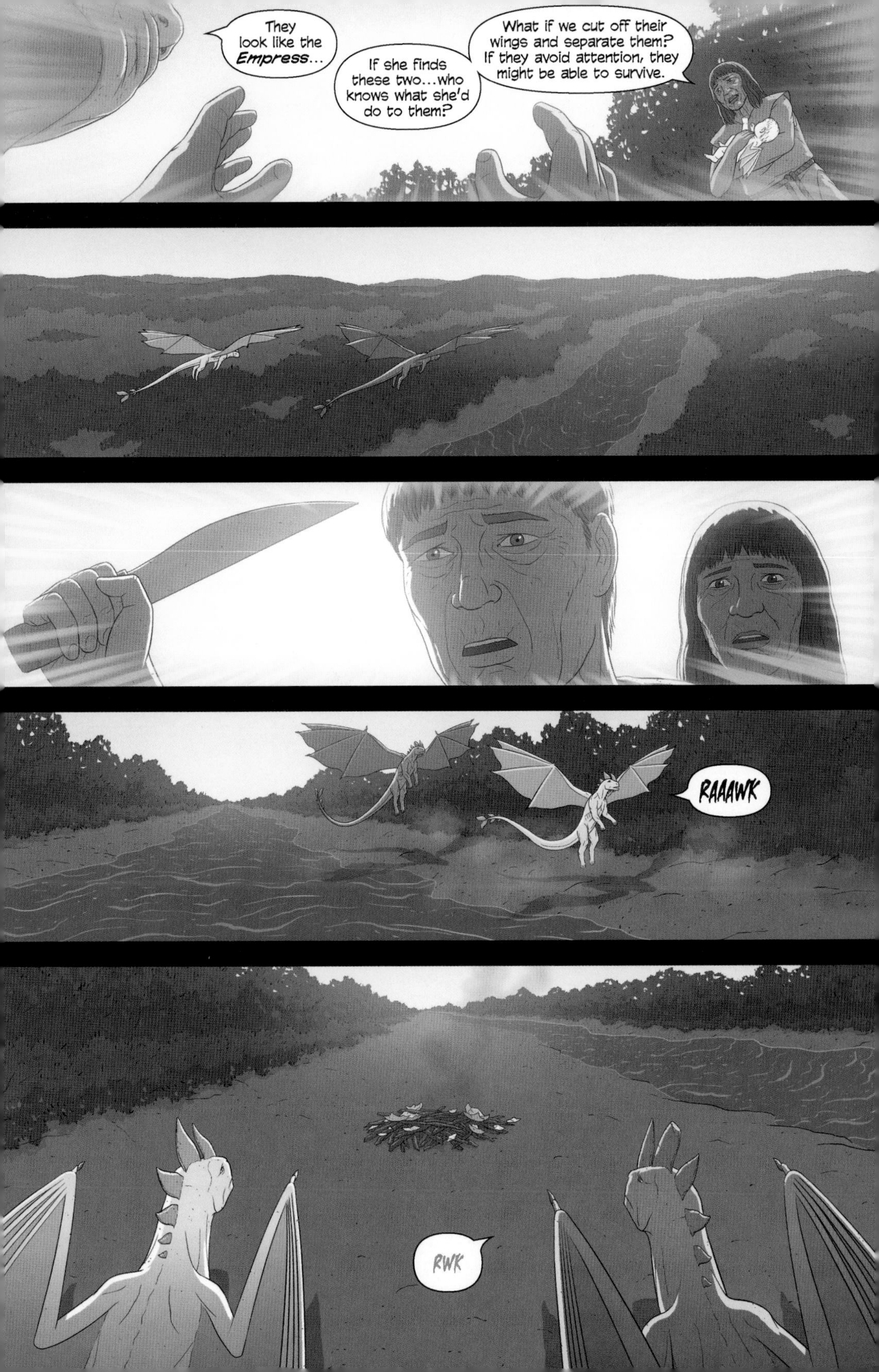

They look like the *Empress*...
If she finds these two...who knows what she'd do to them?
What if we cut off their wings and separate them? If they avoid attention, they might be able to survive.
RAAAWK
RWK

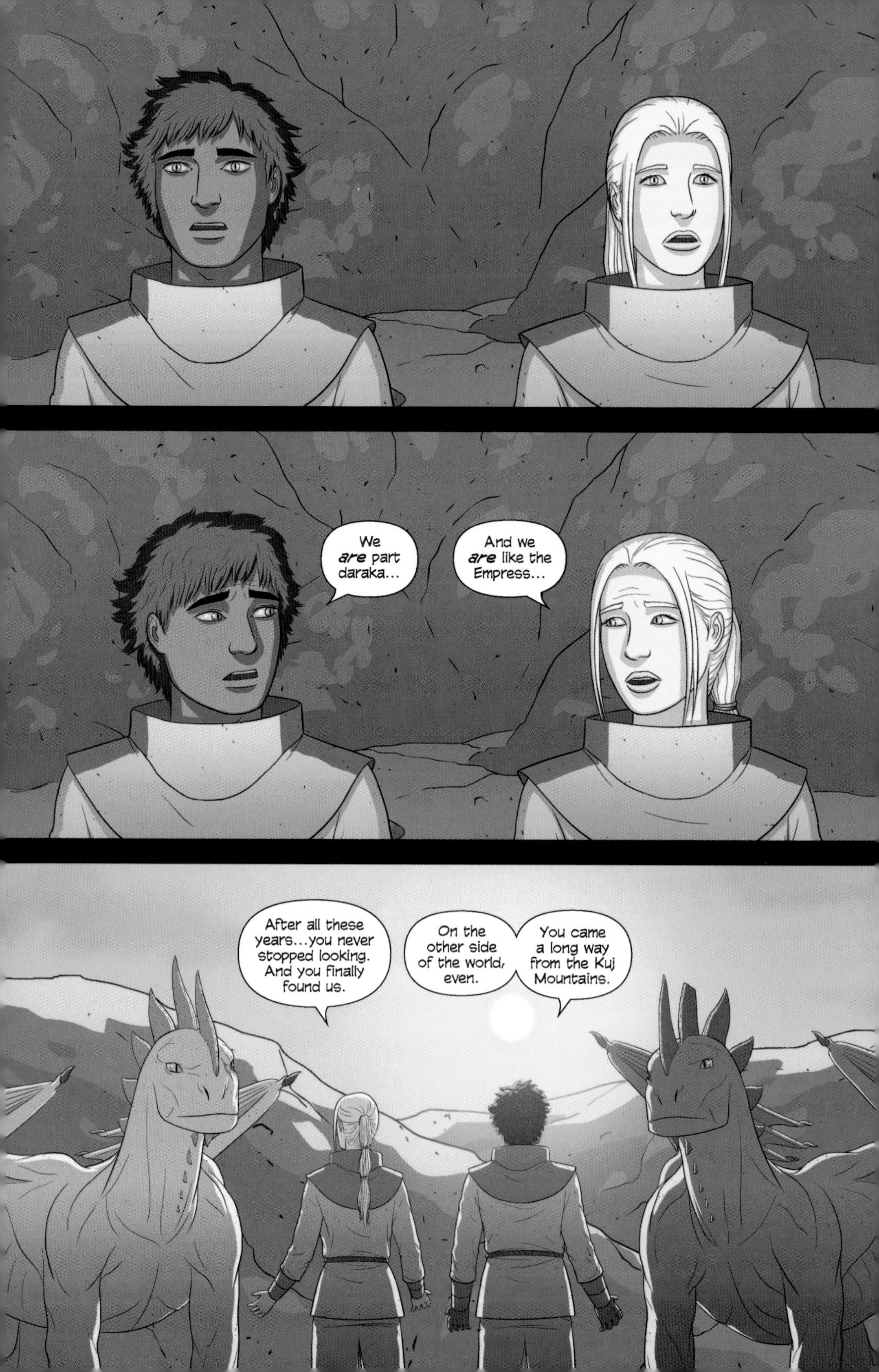
We *are* part daraka...
And we *are* like the Empress...
After all these years...you never stopped looking. And you finally found us.
On the other side of the world, even.
You came a long way from the Kuj Mountains.

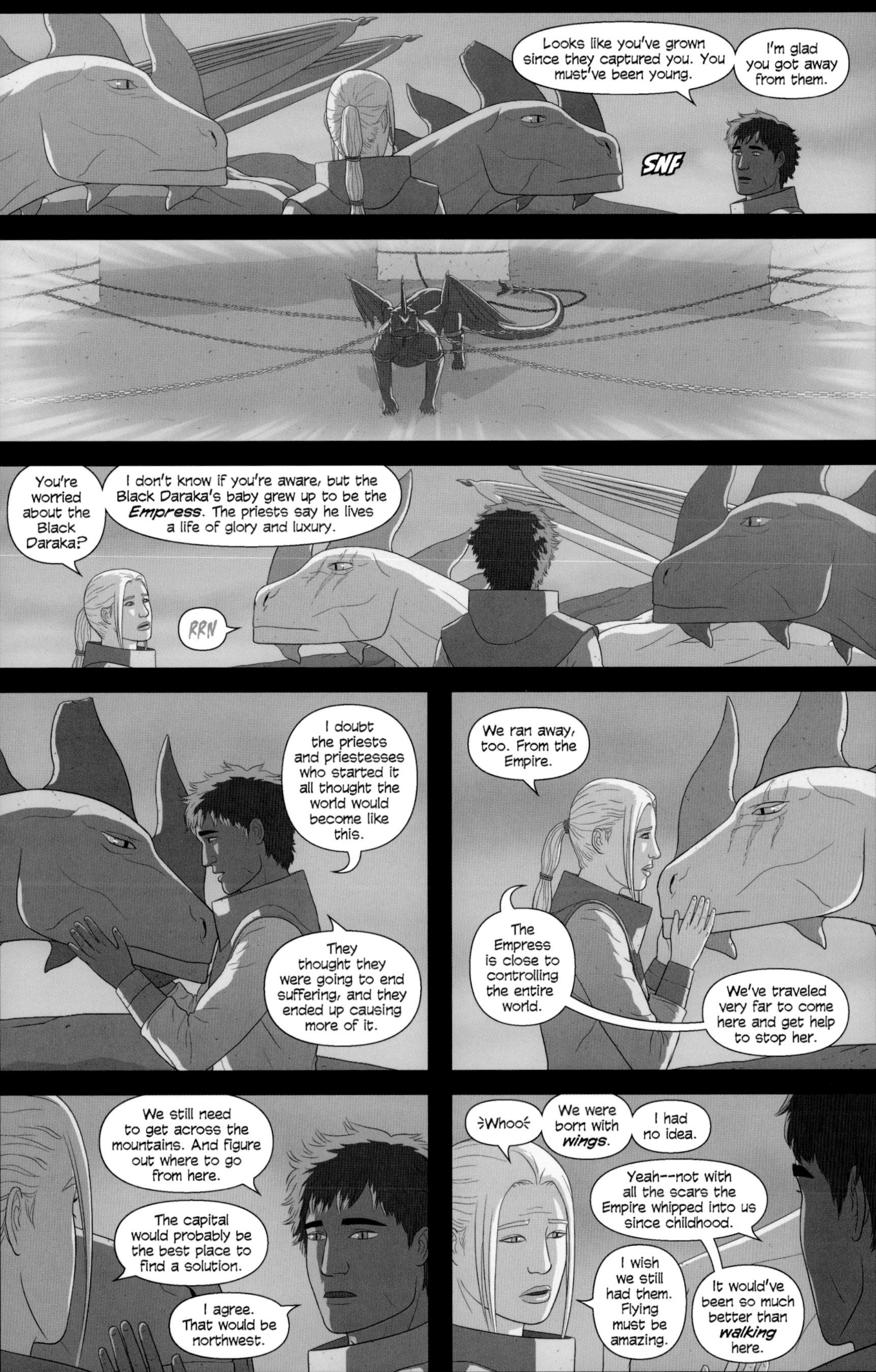
Looks like you've grown since they captured you. You must've been young.
I'm glad you got away from them.
SNF
You're worried about the Black Daraka?
I don't know if you're aware, but the Black Daraka's baby grew up to be the *Empress*. The priests say he lives a life of glory and luxury.
RRN
I doubt the priests and priestesses who started it all thought the world would become like this.
They thought they were going to end suffering, and they ended up causing more of it.
We ran away, too. From the Empire.
The Empress is close to controlling the entire world.
We've traveled very far to come here and get help to stop her.
We still need to get across the mountains. And figure out where to go from here.
The capital would probably be the best place to find a solution.
I agree. That would be northwest.
Whoo
We were born with *wings*.
I had no idea.
Yeah--not with all the scars the Empire whipped into us since childhood.
I wish we still had them. Flying must be amazing.
It would've been so much better than *walking* here.

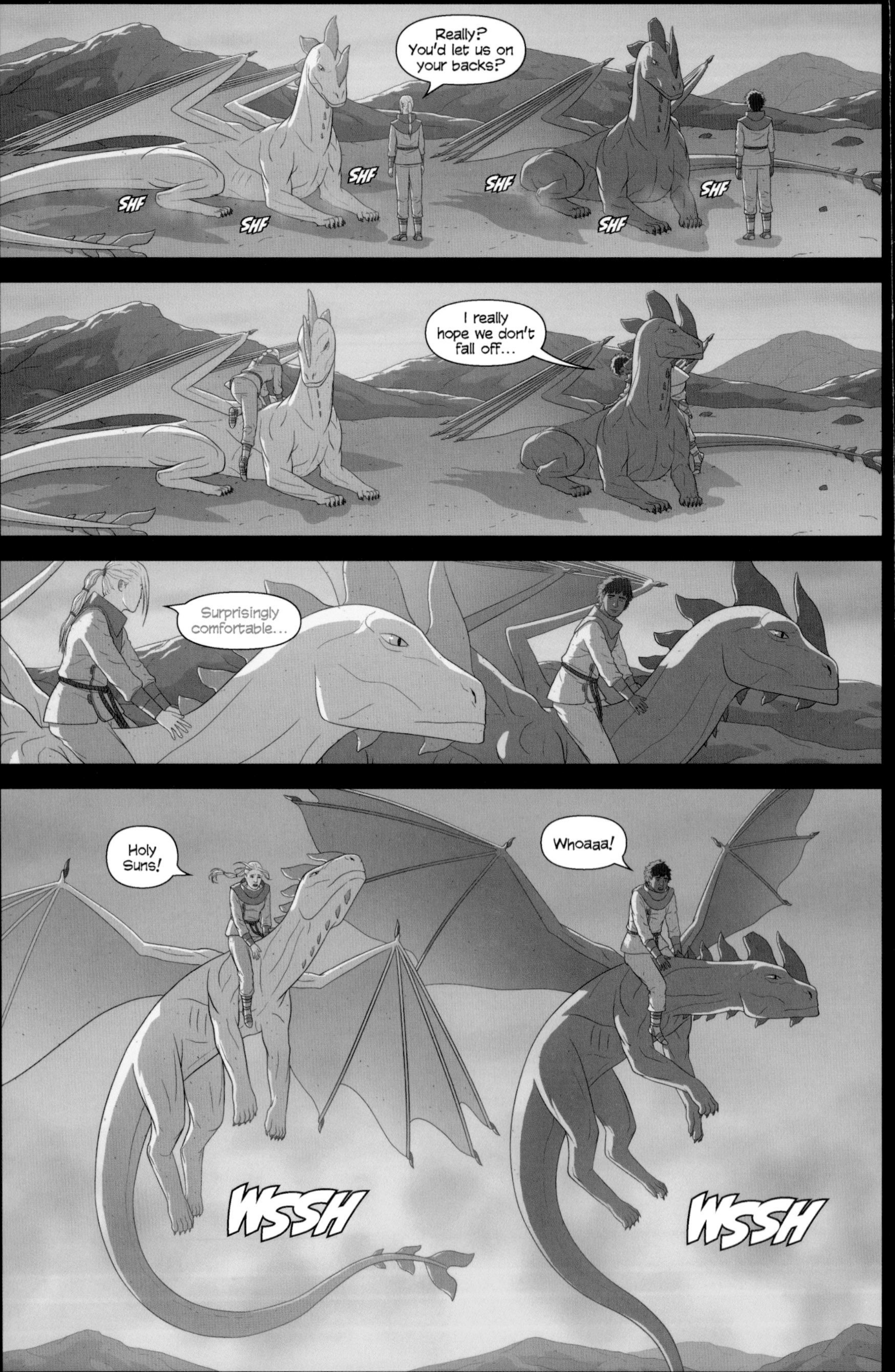
Really? You'd let us on your backs?
SHF
SHF
SHF
SHF
SHF
SHF
I really hope we don't fall off...
Surprisingly comfortable...
Holy Suns!
Whoaaa!
WSSH
WSSH

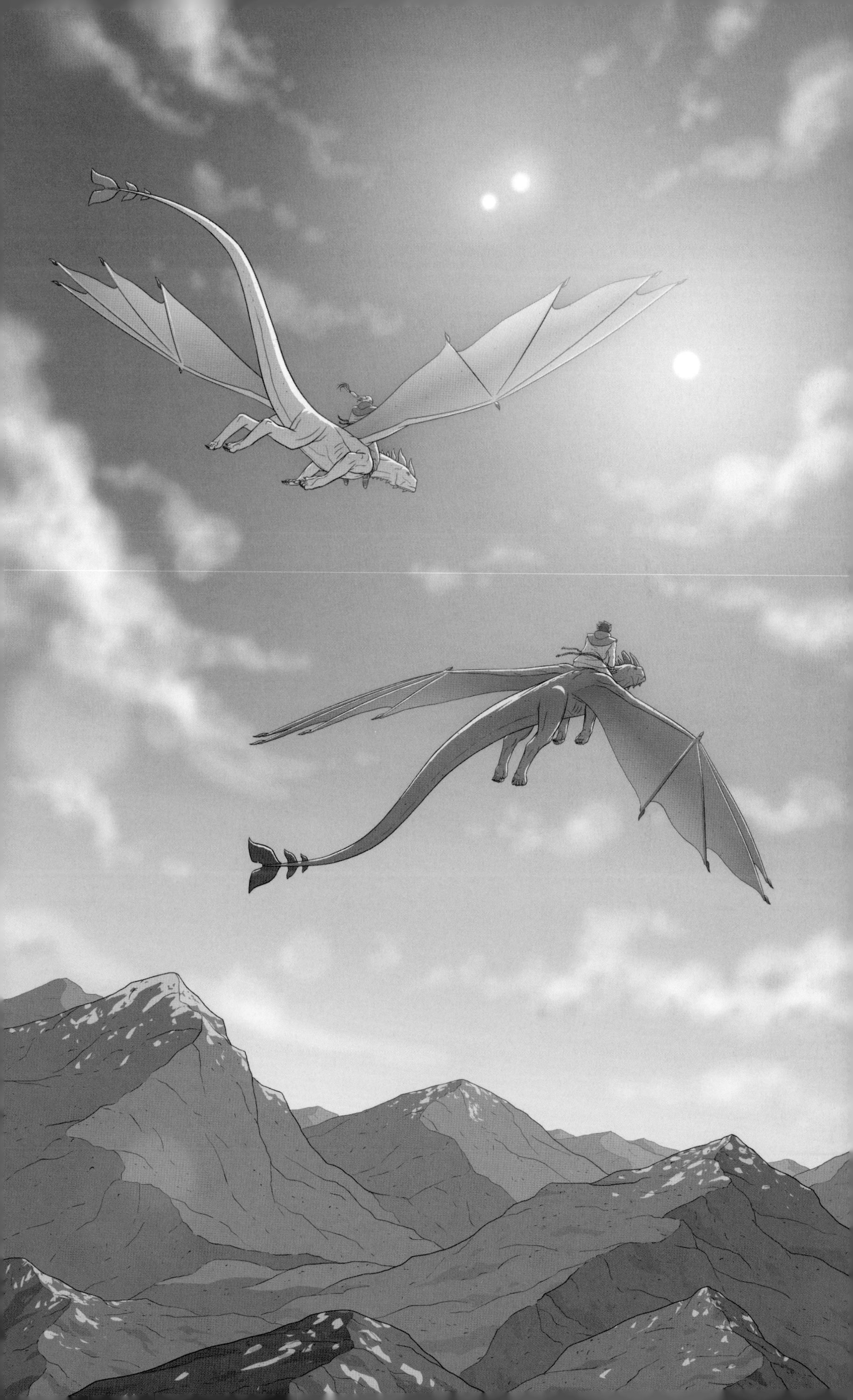

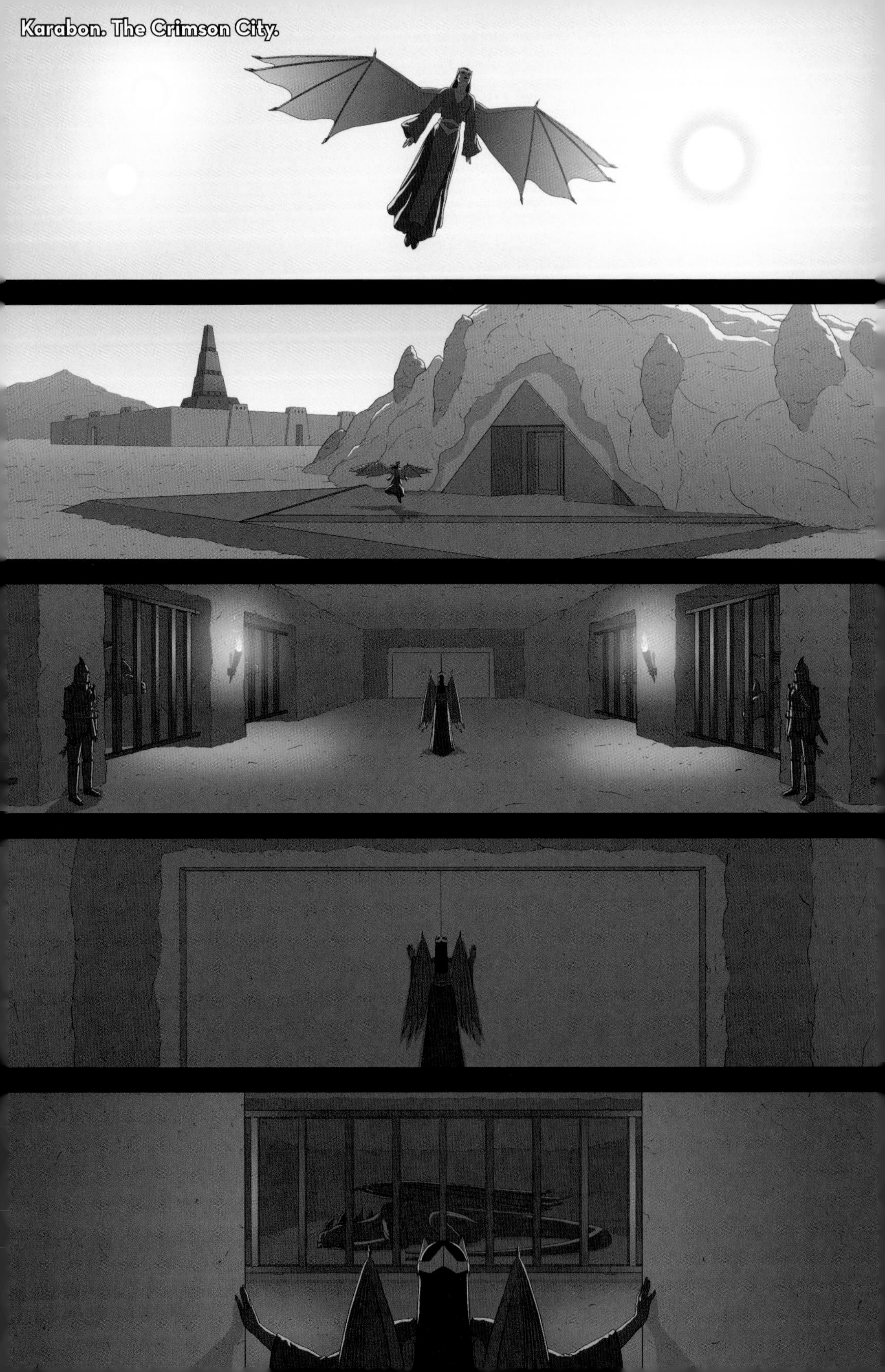
Karabon. The Crimson City.

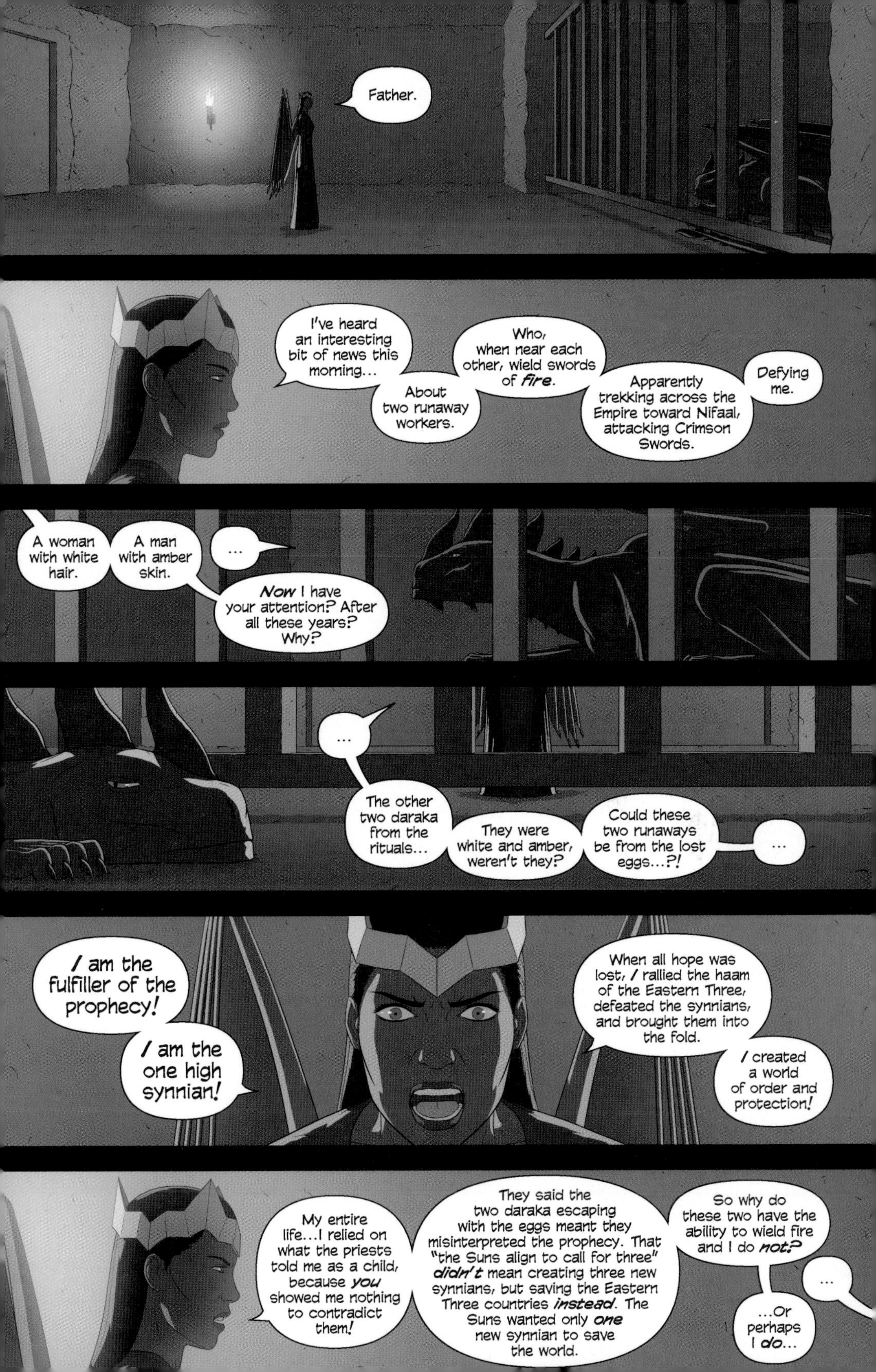
Father.
I've heard an interesting bit of news this morning...
About two runaway workers.
Who, when near each other, wield swords of *fire*.
Apparently trekking across the Empire toward Nifaal, attacking Crimson Swords.
Defying me.
A woman with white hair.
A man with amber skin.
...
Now I have your attention? After all these years? Why?
...
The other two daraka from the rituals...
They were white and amber, weren't they?
Could these two runaways be from the lost eggs...?!
...
I am the fulfiller of the prophecy!
I am the one high synnian!
When all hope was lost, *I* rallied the haam of the Eastern Three, defeated the synnians, and brought them into the fold.
I created a world of order and protection!
My entire life...I relied on what the priests told me as a child, because *you* showed me nothing to contradict them!
They said the two daraka escaping with the eggs meant they misinterpreted the prophecy. That "the Suns align to call for three" *didn't* mean creating three new synnians, but saving the Eastern Three countries *instead*. The Suns wanted only *one* new synnian to save the world.
So why do these two have the ability to wield fire and I do *not?*
...
...Or perhaps I *do*...

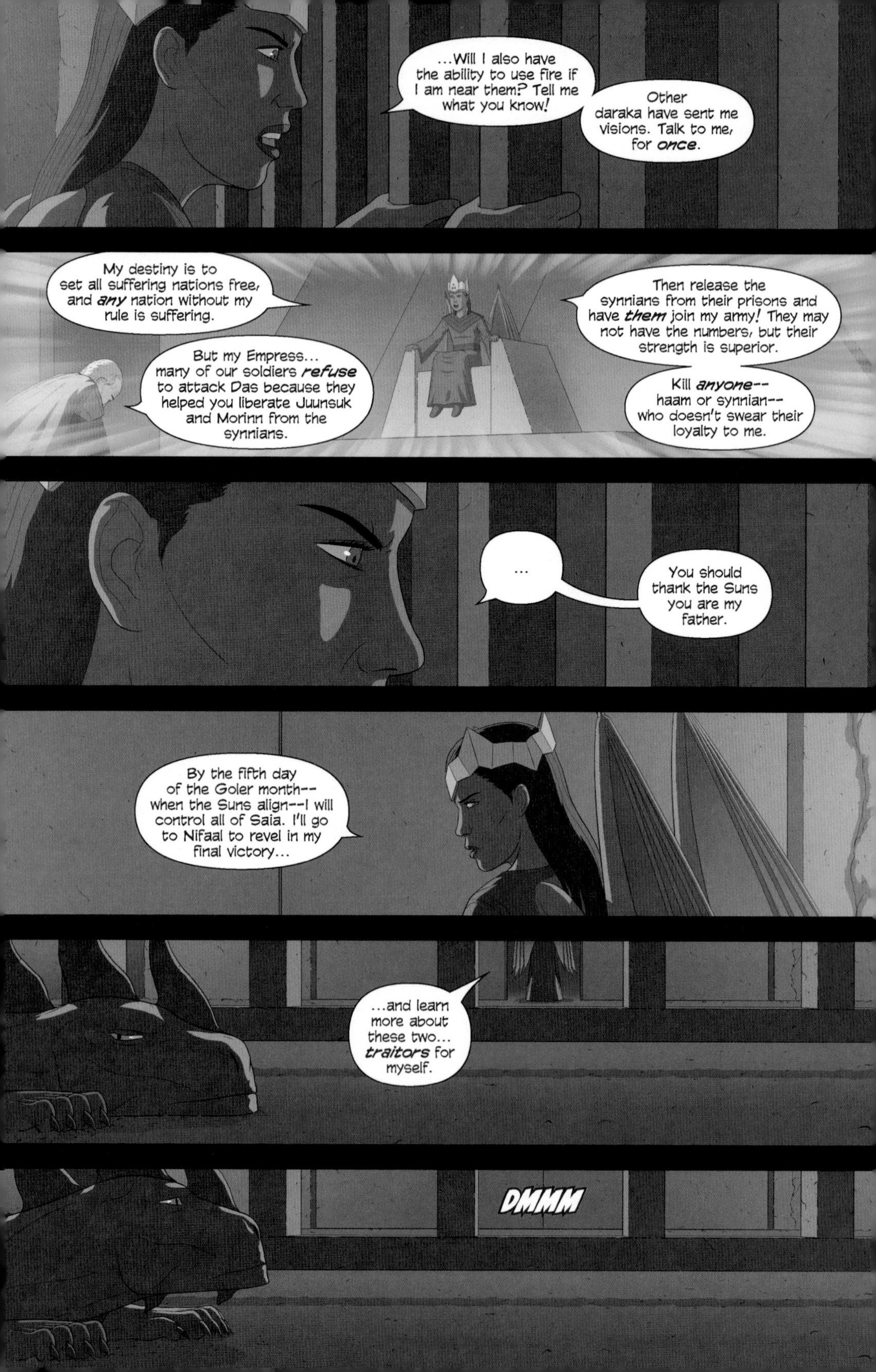
...Will I also have the ability to use fire if I am near them? Tell me what you know!
Other daraka have sent me visions. Talk to me, for *once*.
My destiny is to set all suffering nations free, and *any* nation without my rule is suffering.
But my Empress... many of our soldiers *refuse* to attack Das because they helped you liberate Juunsuk and Morinn from the synnians.
Then release the synnians from their prisons and have *them* join my army! They may not have the numbers, but their strength is superior.
Kill *anyone*-- haam or synnian-- who doesn't swear their loyalty to me.
...
You should thank the Suns you are my father.
By the fifth day of the Goler month-- when the Suns align--I will control all of Saia. I'll go to Nifaal to revel in my final victory...
...and learn more about these two... *traitors* for myself.
DMMM

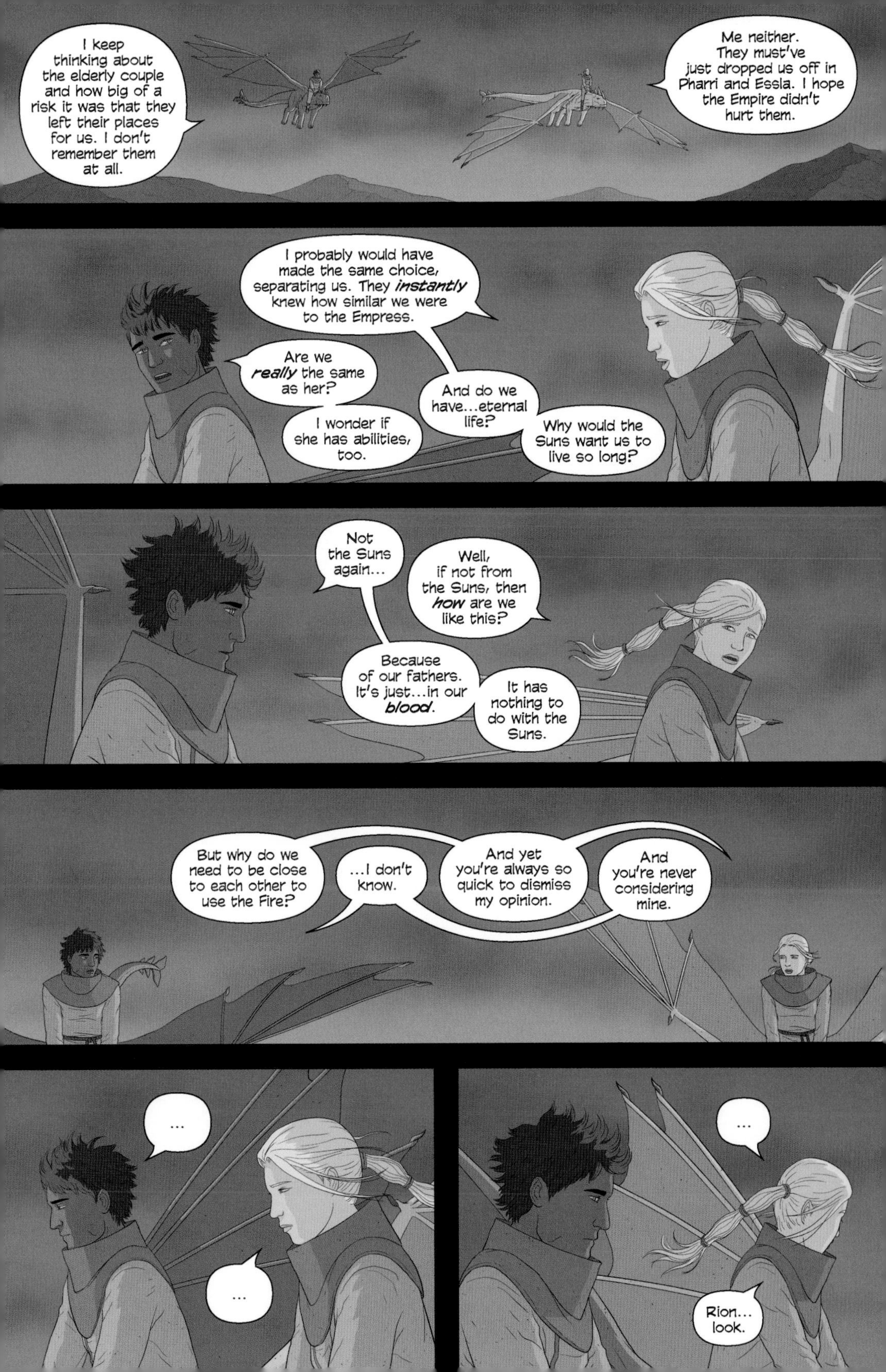

I keep thinking about the elderly couple and how big of a risk it was that they left their places for us. I don't remember them at all.
Me neither. They must've just dropped us off in Pharri and Essla. I hope the Empire didn't hurt them.
I probably would have made the same choice, separating us. They *instantly* knew how similar we were to the Empress.
Are we *really* the same as her?
I wonder if she has abilities, too.
And do we have...eternal life?
Why would the Suns want us to live so long?
Not the Suns again...
Well, if not from the Suns, then *how* are we like this?
Because of our fathers. It's just...in our *blood*.
It has nothing to do with the Suns.
But why do we need to be close to each other to use the Fire?
...I don't know.
And yet you're always so quick to dismiss my opinion.
And you're never considering mine.
...
...
...
Rion... look.

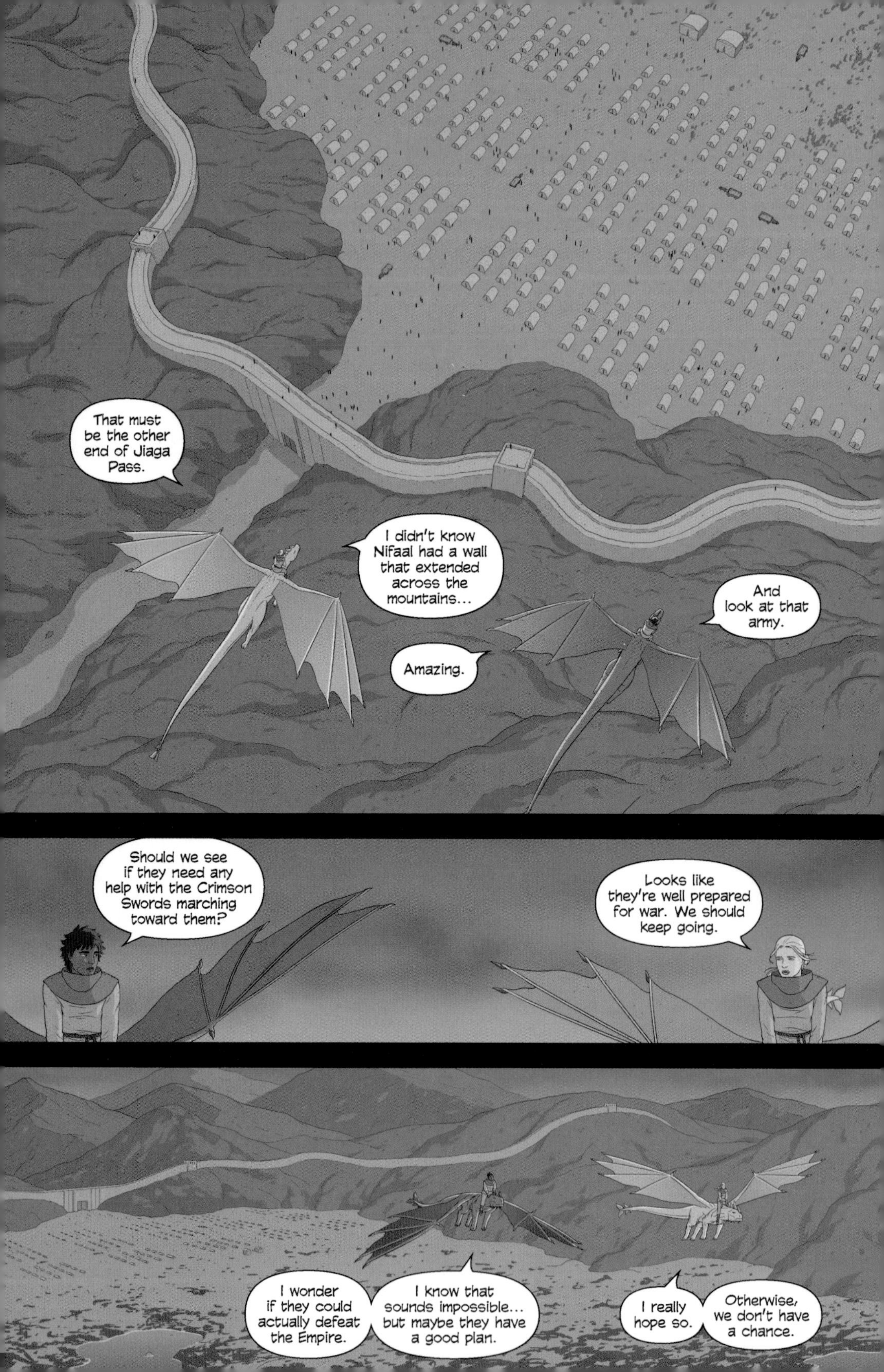
That must be the other end of Jiaga Pass.
I didn't know Nifaal had a wall that extended across the mountains...
Amazing.
And look at that army.
Should we see if they need any help with the Crimson Swords marching toward them?
Looks like they're well prepared for war. We should keep going.
I wonder if they could actually defeat the Empire.
I know that sounds impossible... but maybe they have a good plan.
I really hope so.
Otherwise, we don't have a chance.

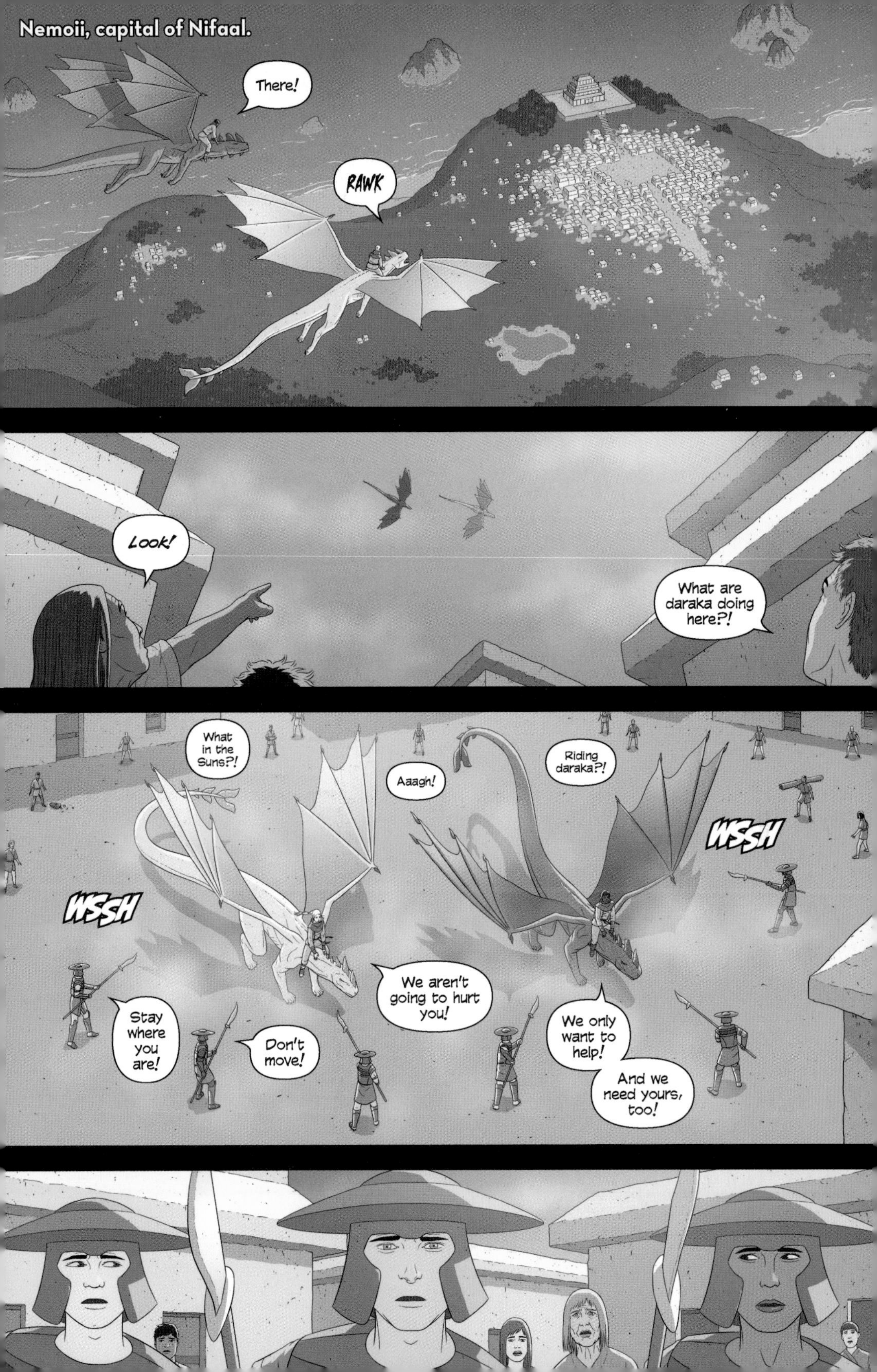

Nemoii, capital of Nifaal.
There!
RAWK
Look!
What are daraka doing here?!
What in the Suns?!
Aaagh!
Riding daraka?!
WSSH
WSSH
We aren't going to hurt you!
Stay where you are!
Don't move!
We only want to help!
And we need yours, too!

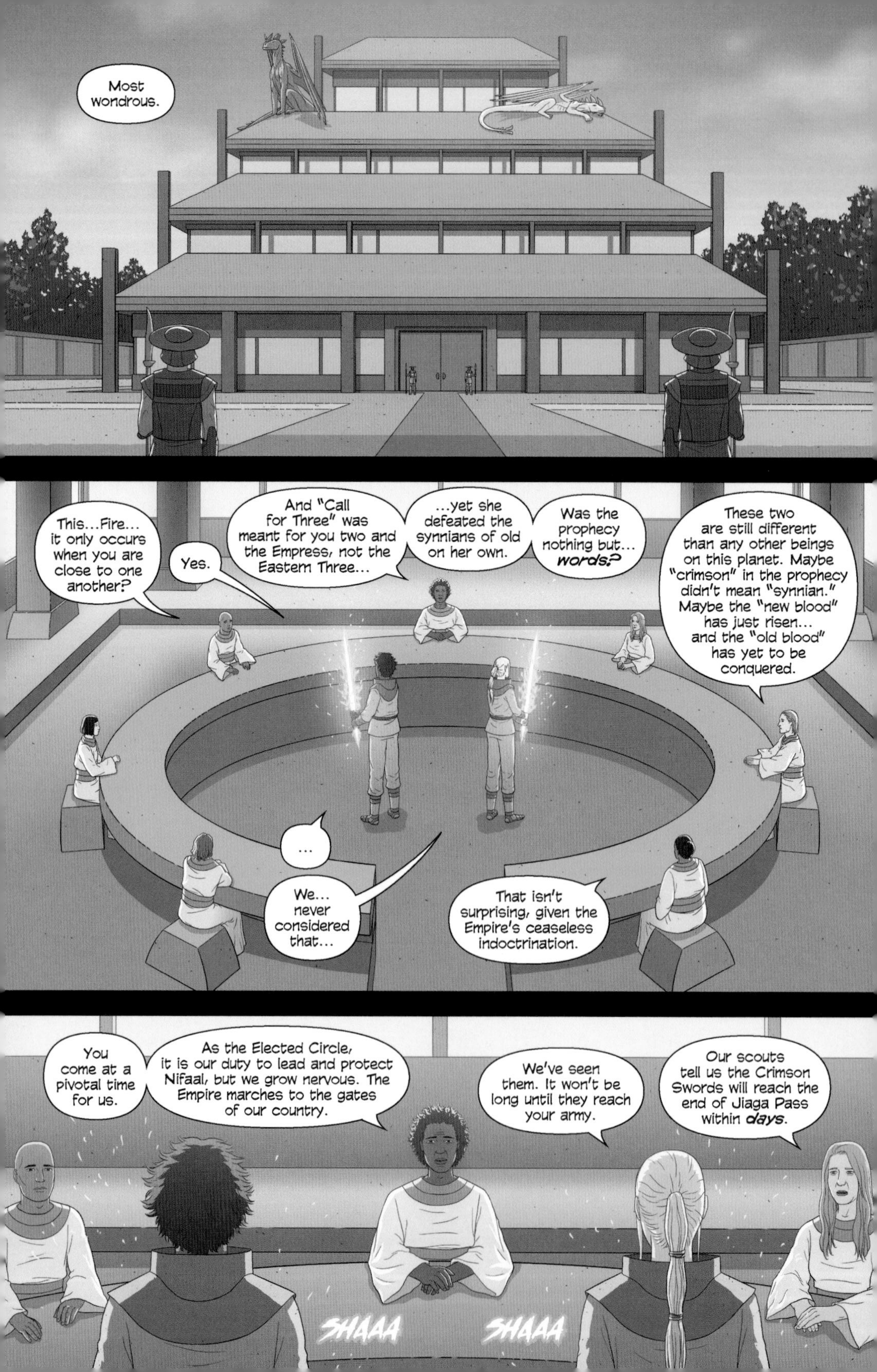

Most wondrous.
This...Fire... it only occurs when you are close to one another?
Yes.
And "Call for Three" was meant for you two and the Empress, not the Eastern Three...
...yet she defeated the synnians of old on her own.
Was the prophecy nothing but... *words?*
These two are still different than any other beings on this planet. Maybe "crimson" in the prophecy didn't mean "synnian." Maybe the "new blood" has just risen... and the "old blood" has yet to be conquered.
...
We... never considered that...
That isn't surprising, given the Empire's ceaseless indoctrination.
You come at a pivotal time for us.
As the Elected Circle, it is our duty to lead and protect Nifaal, but we grow nervous. The Empire marches to the gates of our country.
We've seen them. It won't be long until they reach your army.
Our scouts tell us the Crimson Swords will reach the end of Jiaga Pass within *days*.
SHAAA
SHAAA

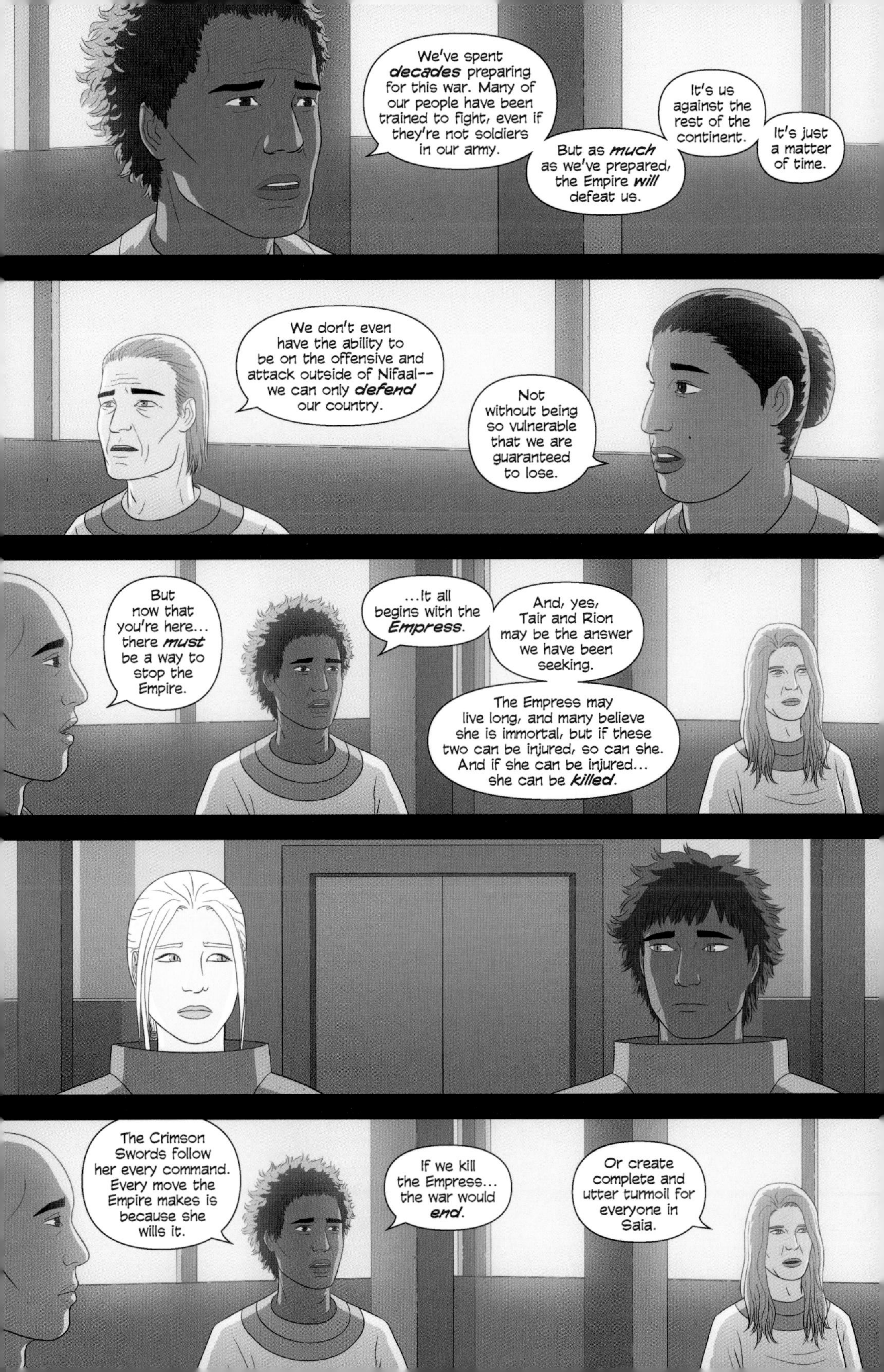
We've spent decades preparing for this war. Many of our people have been trained to fight, even if they're not soldiers in our army.
But as much as we've prepared, the Empire will defeat us.
It's us against the rest of the continent.
It's just a matter of time.
We don't even have the ability to be on the offensive and attack outside of Nifaal-- we can only defend our country.
Not without being so vulnerable that we are guaranteed to lose.
But now that you're here... there must be a way to stop the Empire.
...It all begins with the Empress.
And, yes, Tair and Rion may be the answer we have been seeking.
The Empress may live long, and many believe she is immortal, but if these two can be injured, so can she. And if she can be injured... she can be killed.
The Crimson Swords follow her every command. Every move the Empire makes is because she wills it.
If we kill the Empress... the war would end.
Or create complete and utter turmoil for everyone in Saia.

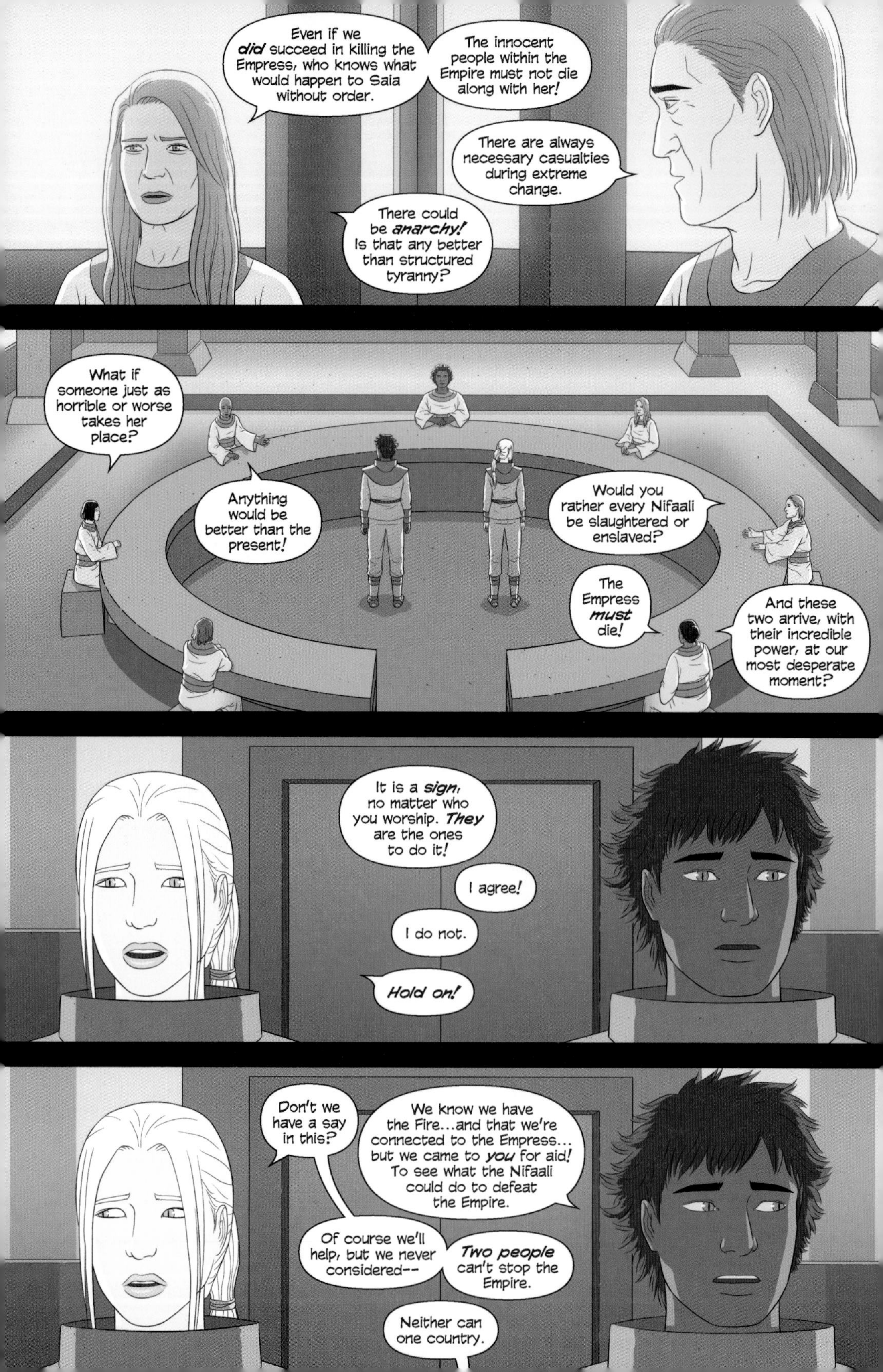
Even if we *did* succeed in killing the Empress, who knows what would happen to Saia without order.
The innocent people within the Empire must not die along with her!
There are always necessary casualties during extreme change.
There could be ***anarchy!*** Is that any better than structured tyranny?
What if someone just as horrible or worse takes her place?
Anything would be better than the present!
Would you rather every Nifaali be slaughtered or enslaved?
The Empress ***must*** die!
And these two arrive, with their incredible power, at our most desperate moment?
It is a ***sign***, no matter who you worship. ***They*** are the ones to do it!
I agree!
I do not.
Hold on!
Don't we have a say in this?
We know we have the Fire...and that we're connected to the Empress... but we came to ***you*** for aid! To see what the Nifaali could do to defeat the Empire.
Of course we'll help, but we never considered--
Two people can't stop the Empire.
Neither can one country.

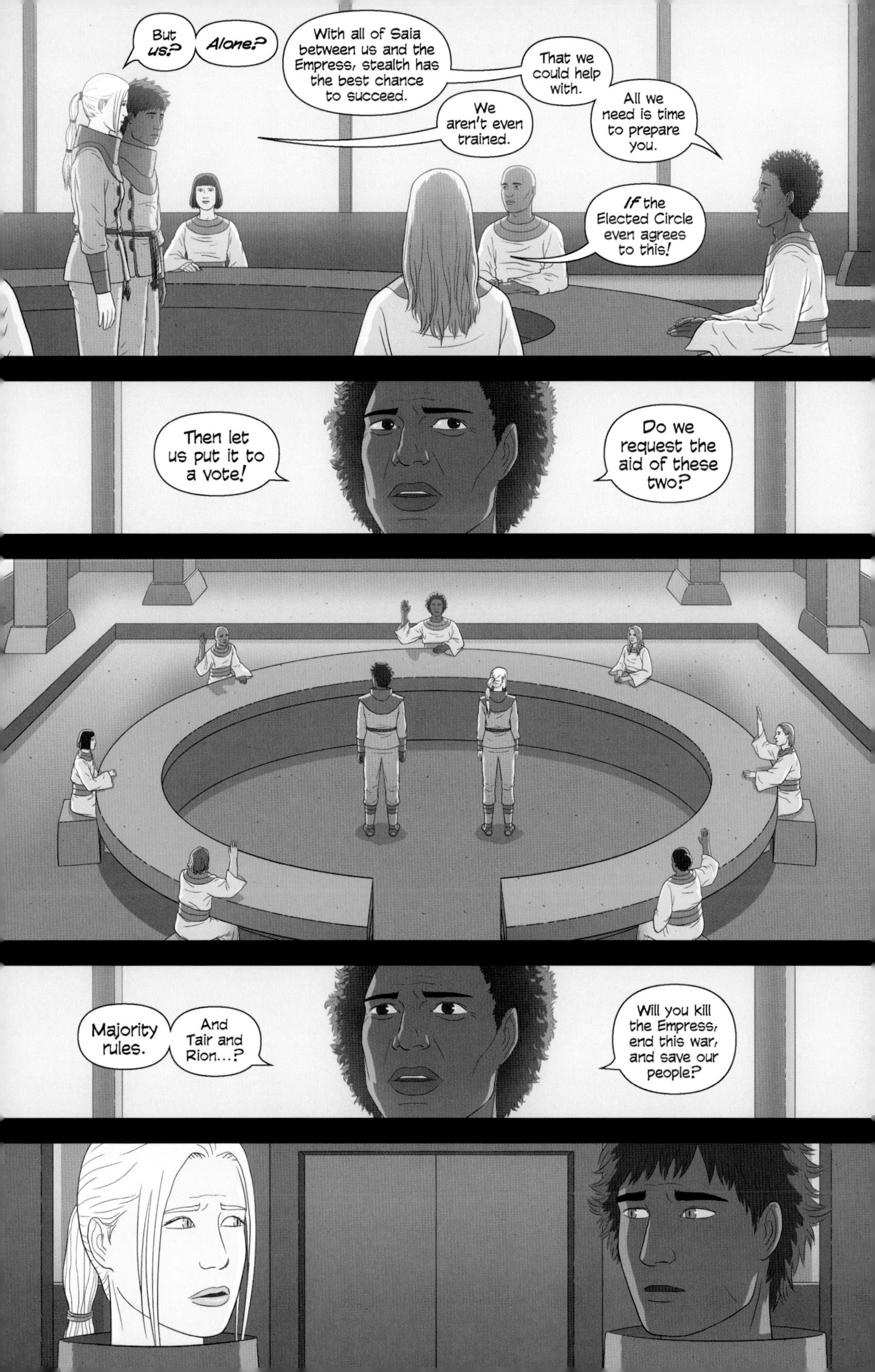
But us?
Alone?
With all of Saia between us and the Empress, stealth has the best chance to succeed.
That we could help with.
We aren't even trained.
All we need is time to prepare you.
If the Elected Circle even agrees to this!
Then let us put it to a vote!
Do we request the aid of these two?
Majority rules.
And Tair and Rion...?
Will you kill the Empress, end this war, and save our people?

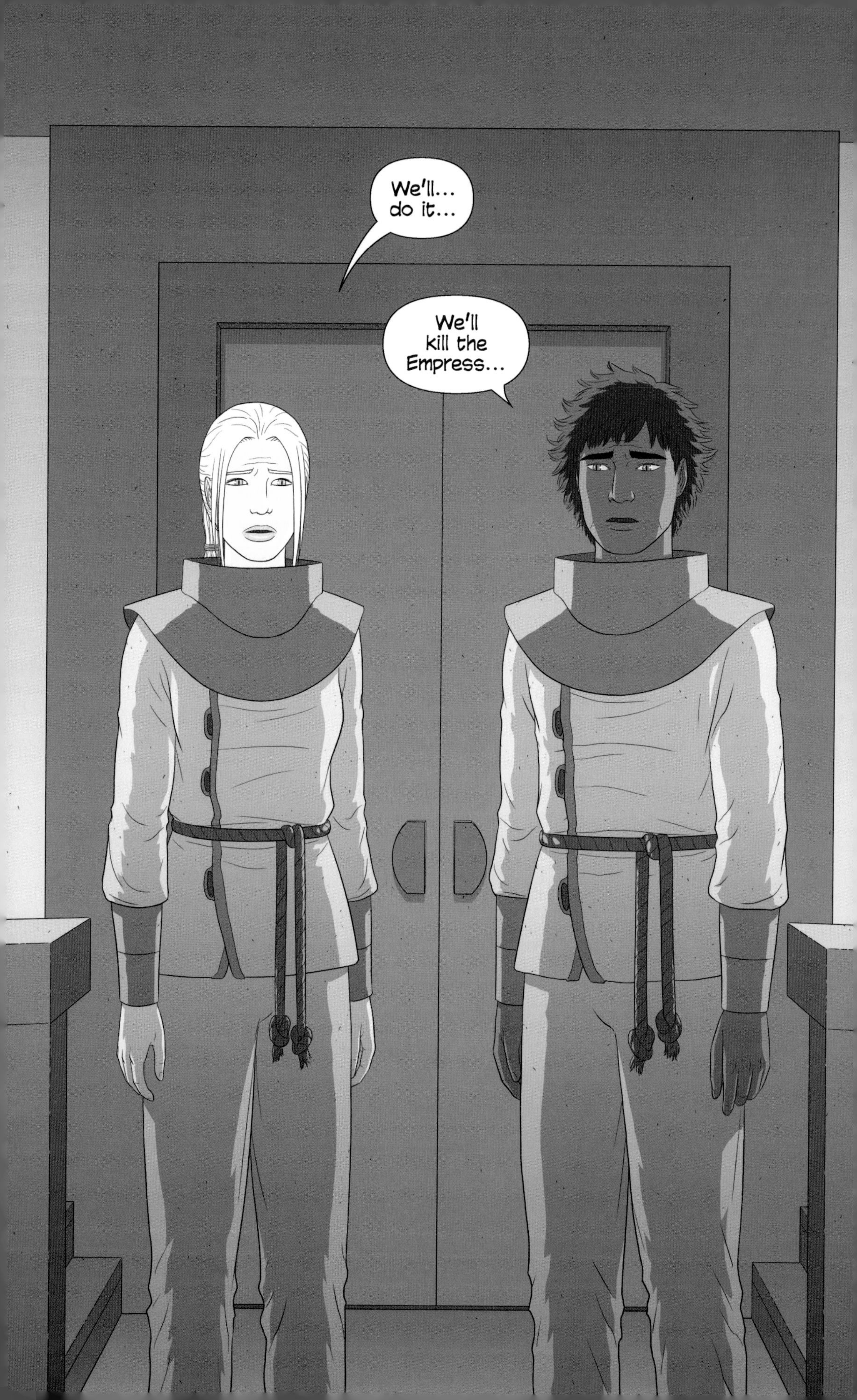
We'll... do it...
We'll kill the Empress...

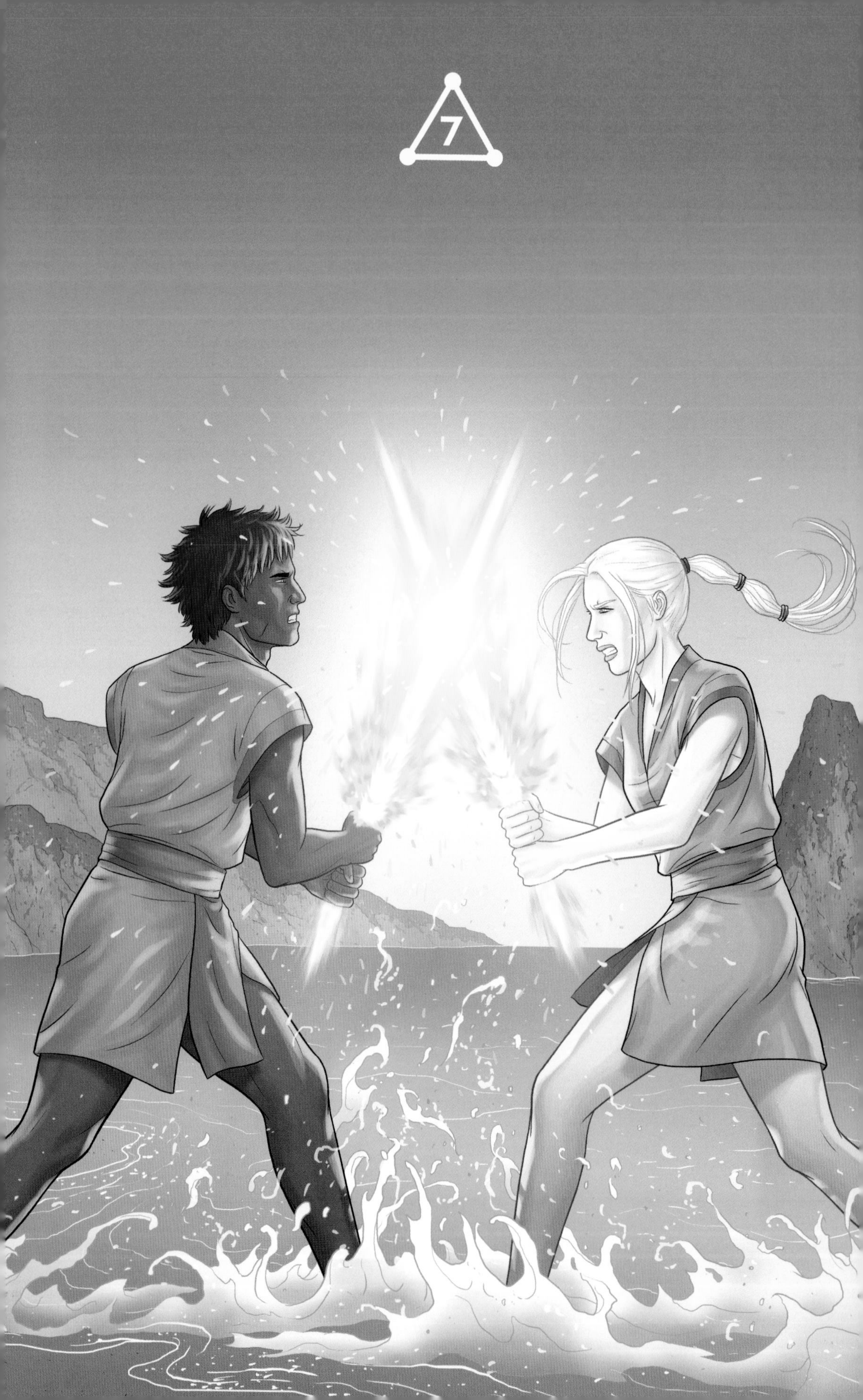
7

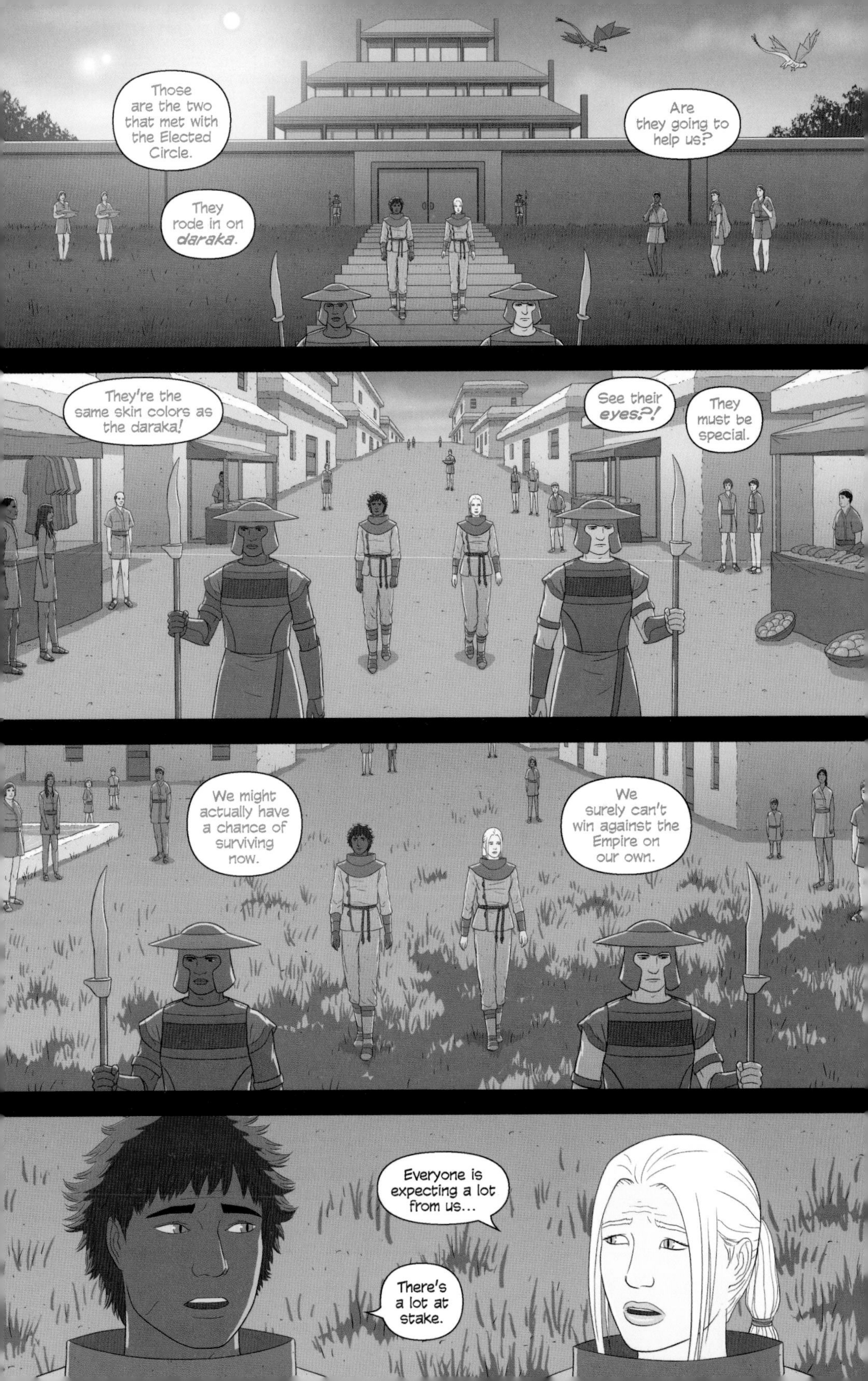
Those are the two that met with the Elected Circle.
They rode in on *daraka*.
Are they going to help us?
They're the same skin colors as the daraka!
See their *eyes?!*
They must be special.
We might actually have a chance of surviving now.
We surely can't win against the Empire on our own.
Everyone is expecting a lot from us...
There's a lot at stake.

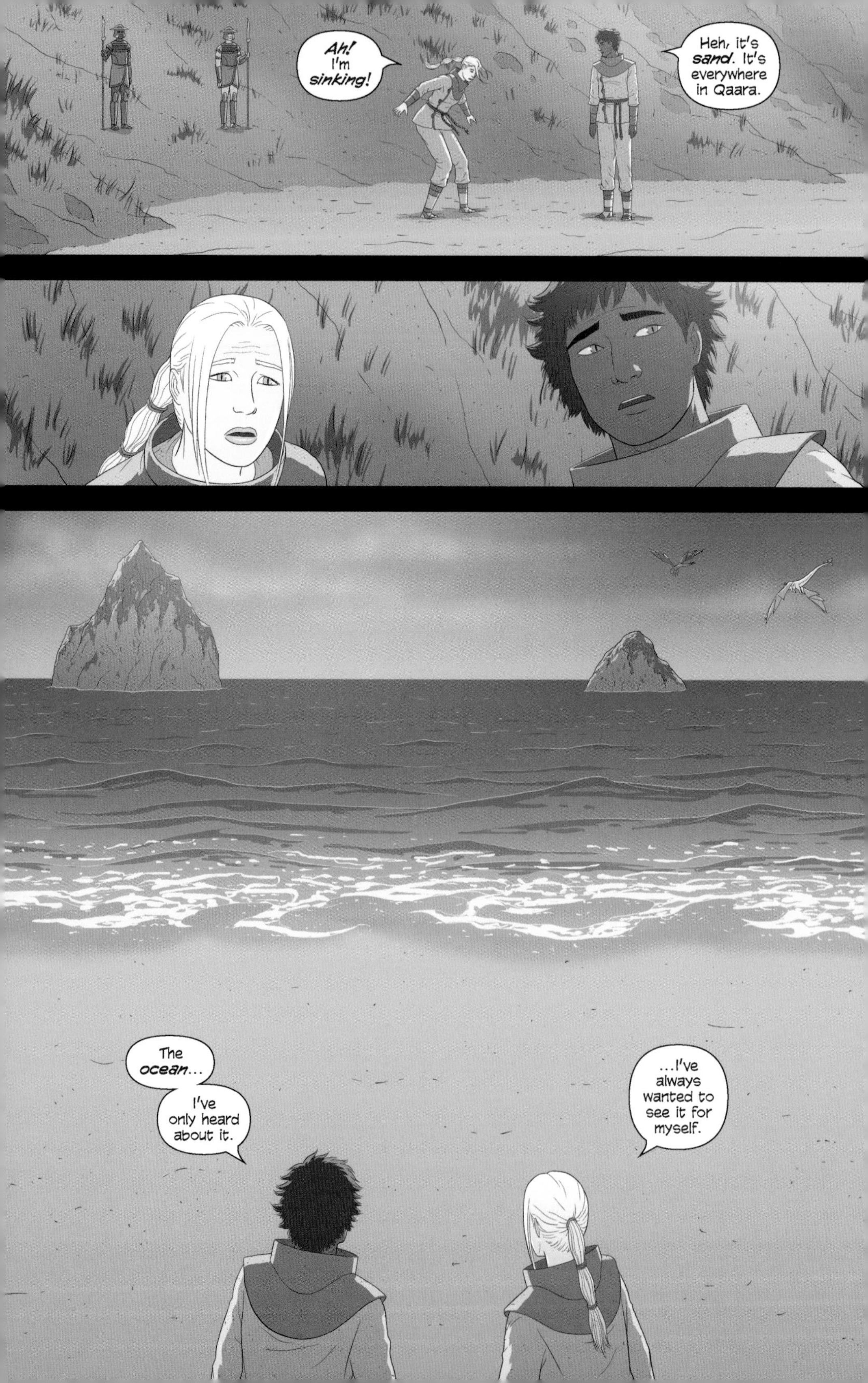
Ah! I'm sinking!
Heh, it's sand. It's everywhere in Qaara.
The ocean...
I've only heard about it.
...I've always wanted to see it for myself.

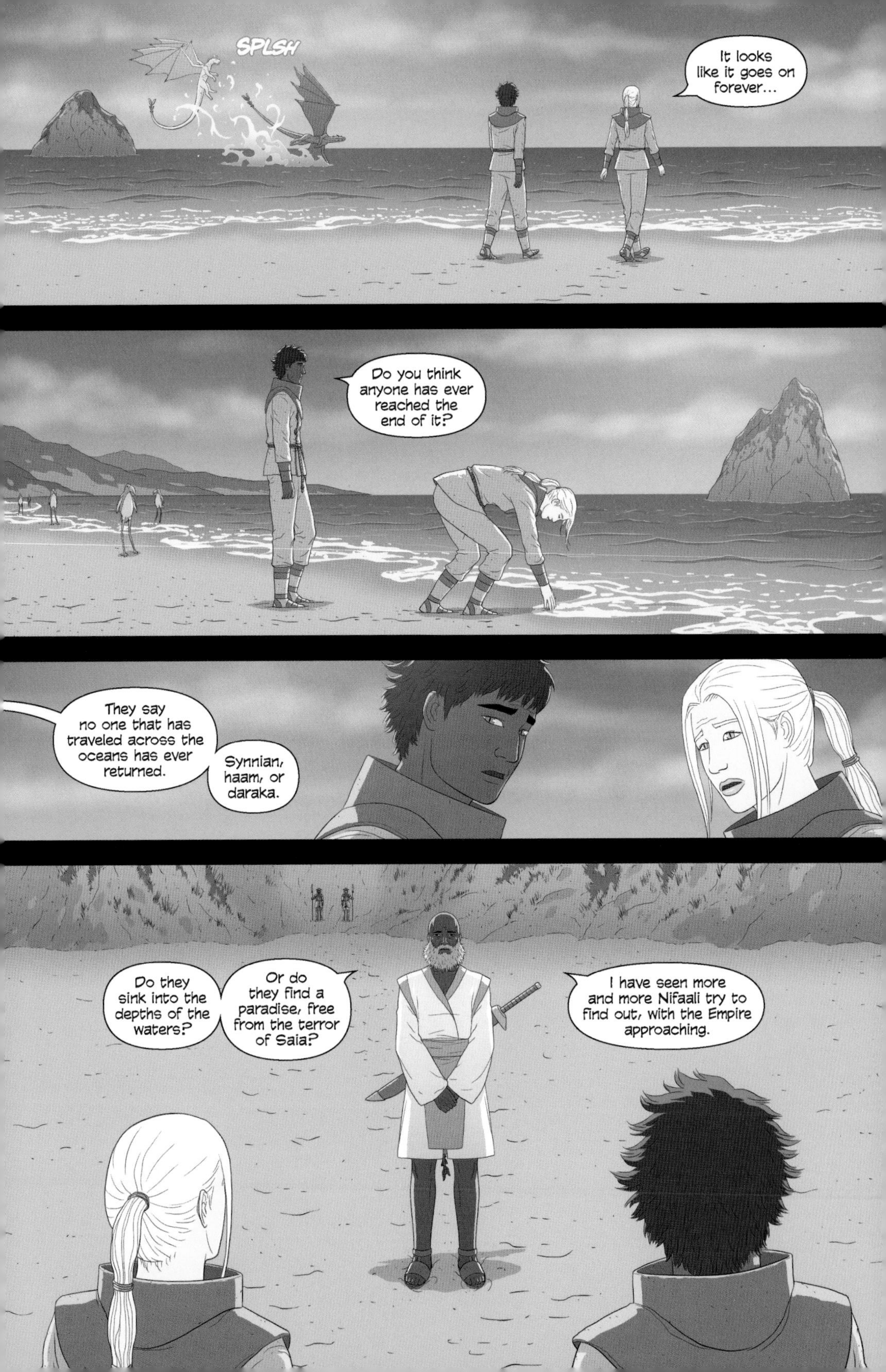
SPLSH
It looks like it goes on forever...
Do you think anyone has ever reached the end of it?
They say no one that has traveled across the oceans has ever returned.
Synnian, haam, or daraka.
Do they sink into the depths of the waters?
Or do they find a paradise, free from the terror of Saia?
I have seen more and more Nifaali try to find out, with the Empire approaching.

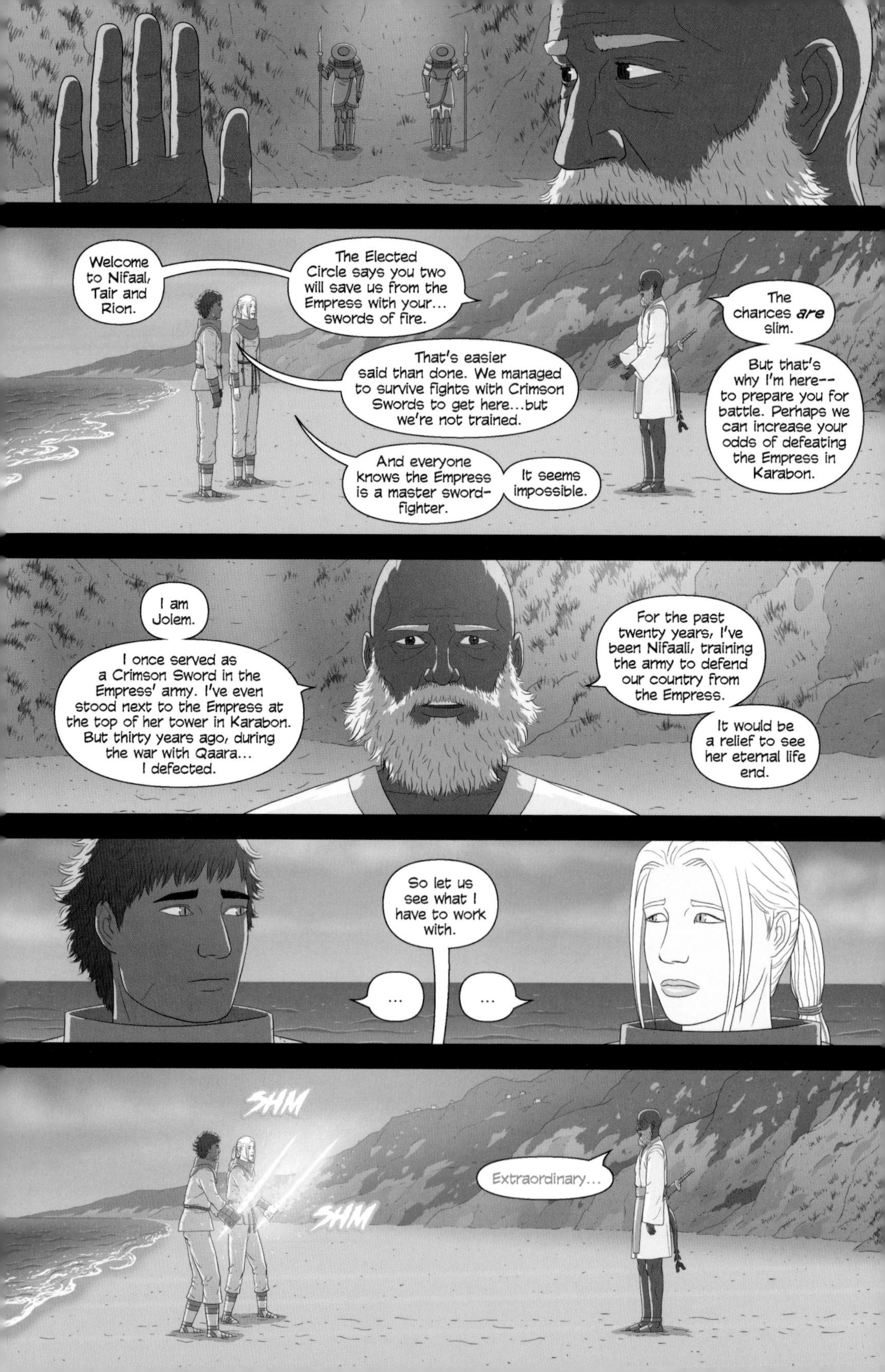
Welcome to Nifaal, Tair and Rion.
The Elected Circle says you two will save us from the Empress with your... swords of fire.
The chances *are* slim.
But that's why I'm here-- to prepare you for battle. Perhaps we can increase your odds of defeating the Empress in Karabon.
That's easier said than done. We managed to survive fights with Crimson Swords to get here...but we're not trained.
And everyone knows the Empress is a master sword-fighter.
It seems impossible.
I am Jolem.
I once served as a Crimson Sword in the Empress' army. I've even stood next to the Empress at the top of her tower in Karabon. But thirty years ago, during the war with Qaara... I defected.
For the past twenty years, I've been Nifaali, training the army to defend our country from the Empress.
It would be a relief to see her eternal life end.
So let us see what I have to work with.
...
...
SHM
SHM
Extraordinary...

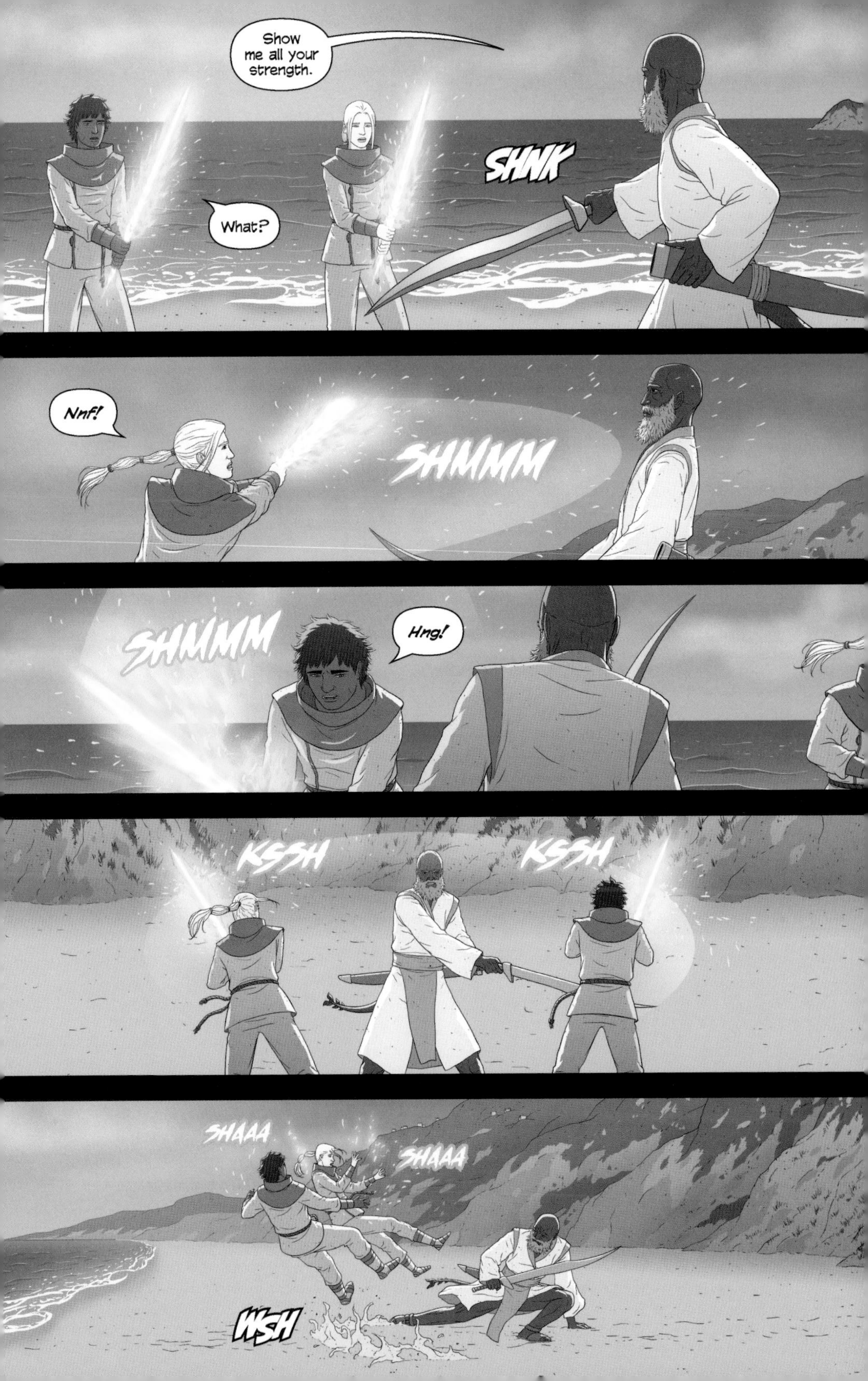
Show me all your strength.
What?
SHNK
Nnf!
SHMMM
SHMMM
Hng!
KSSH
KSSH
SHAAA
SHAAA
WSH

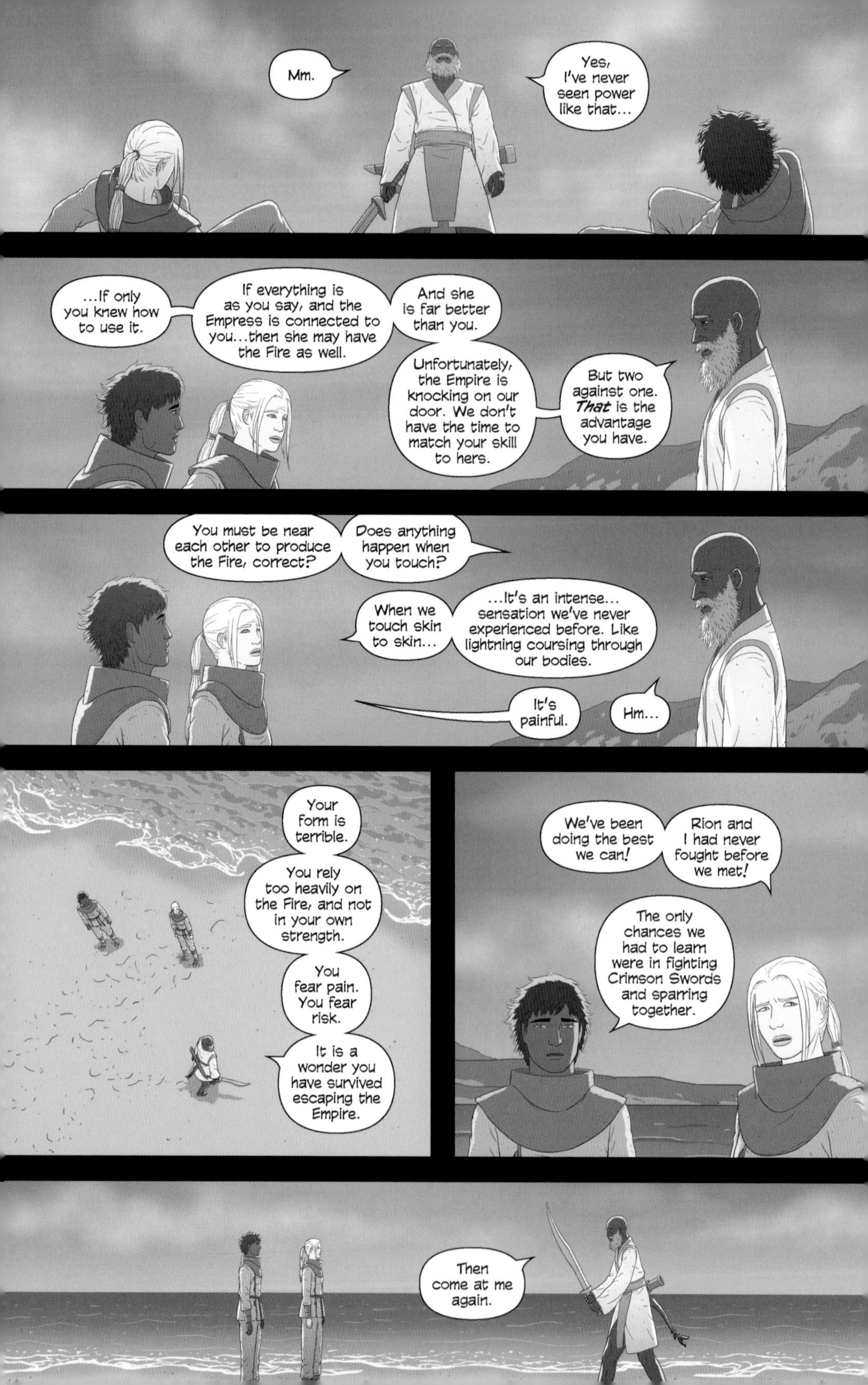
Mm.
Yes, I've never seen power like that...
...If only you knew how to use it.
If everything is as you say, and the Empress is connected to you...then she may have the Fire as well.
And she is far better than you.
Unfortunately, the Empire is knocking on our door. We don't have the time to match your skill to hers.
But two against one. *That* is the advantage you have.
You must be near each other to produce the Fire, correct?
Does anything happen when you touch?
When we touch skin to skin...
...It's an intense... sensation we've never experienced before. Like lightning coursing through our bodies.
It's painful.
Hm...
Your form is terrible.
You rely too heavily on the Fire, and not in your own strength.
You fear pain. You fear risk.
It is a wonder you have survived escaping the Empire.
We've been doing the best we can!
Rion and I had never fought before we met!
The only chances we had to learn were in fighting Crimson Swords and sparring together.
Then come at me again.

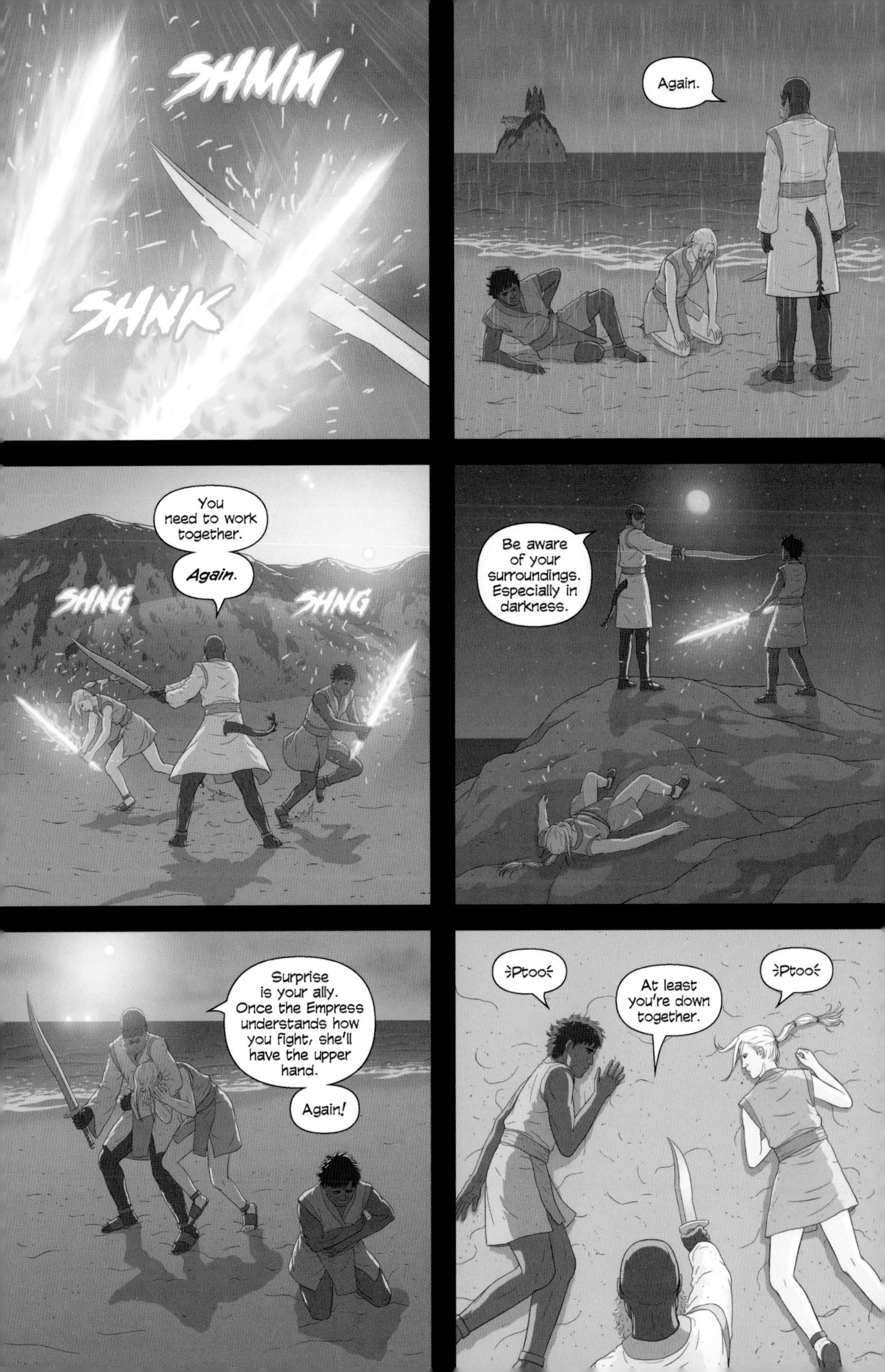
SHMM
SHNK
Again.
You need to work together.
Again.
SHNG
SHNG
Be aware of your surroundings. Especially in darkness.
Surprise is your ally. Once the Empress understands how you fight, she'll have the upper hand.
Again!
Ptoo
At least you're down together.
Ptoo

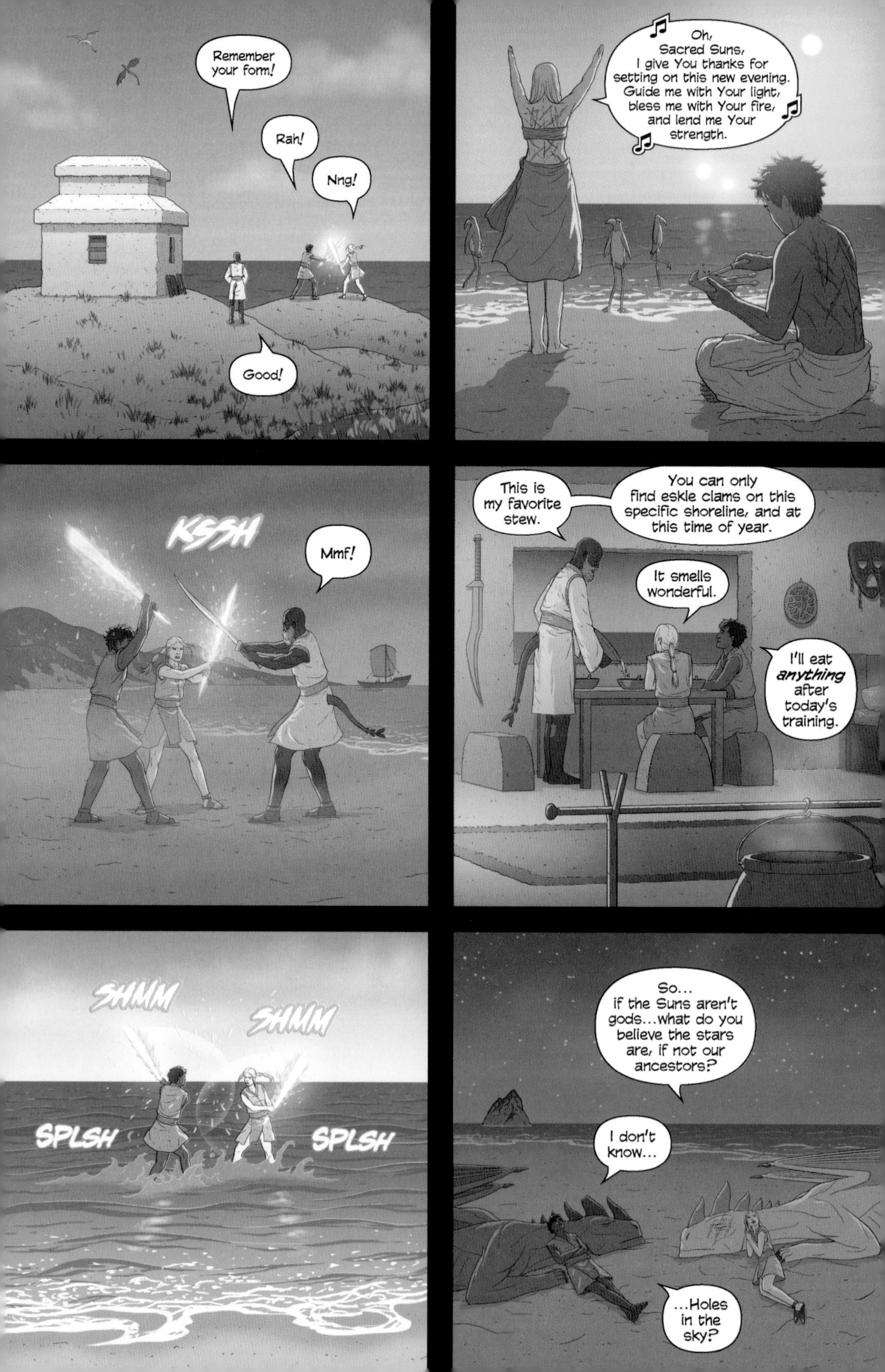
Remember your form!
Rah!
Nng!
Good!
Oh, Sacred Suns, I give You thanks for setting on this new evening. Guide me with Your light, bless me with Your fire, and lend me Your strength.
KSSH
Mmf!
This is my favorite stew.
You can only find eskle clams on this specific shoreline, and at this time of year.
It smells wonderful.
I'll eat *anything* after today's training.
SHMM
SHMM
SPLSH
SPLSH
So... if the Suns aren't gods...what do you believe the stars are, if not our ancestors?
I don't know...
...Holes in the sky?

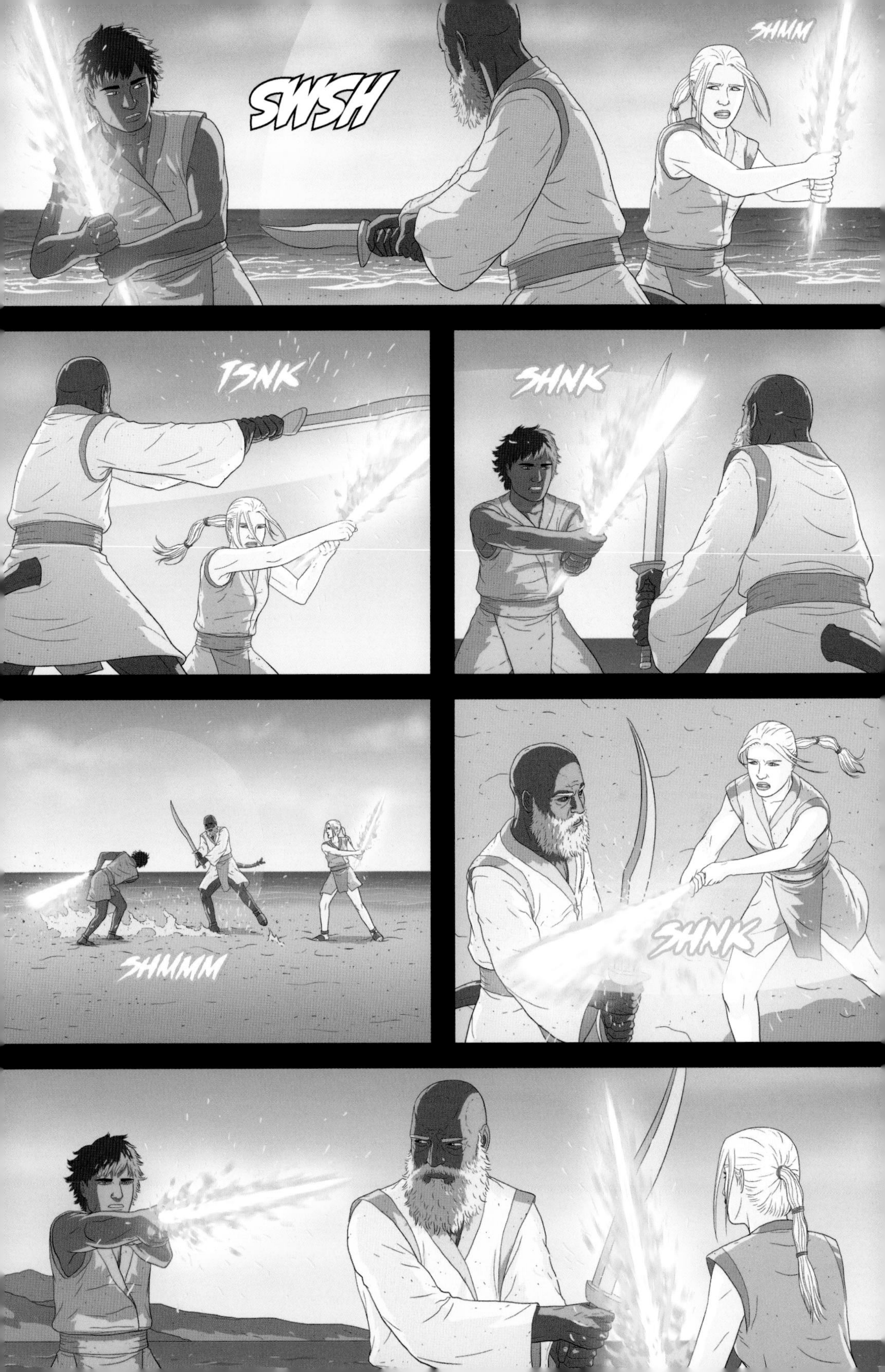
SWSH
SHMM
TSNK
SHNK
SHMMM
SHNK

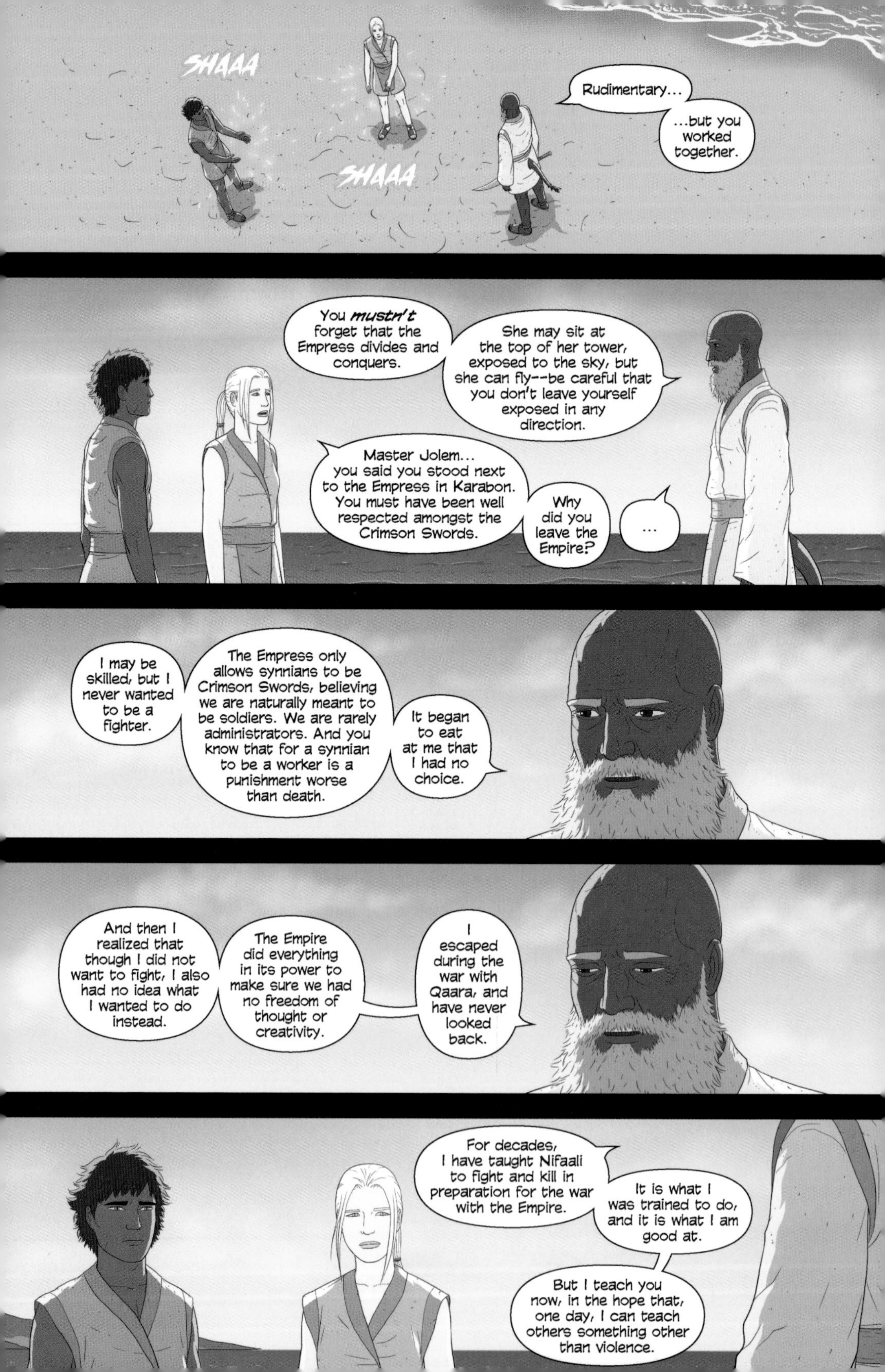
SHAAA
SHAAA
Rudimentary...
...but you worked together.
You *mustn't* forget that the Empress divides and conquers.
She may sit at the top of her tower, exposed to the sky, but she can fly--be careful that you don't leave yourself exposed in any direction.
Master Jolem... you said you stood next to the Empress in Karabon. You must have been well respected amongst the Crimson Swords.
Why did you leave the Empire?
...
I may be skilled, but I never wanted to be a fighter.
The Empress only allows synnians to be Crimson Swords, believing we are naturally meant to be soldiers. We are rarely administrators. And you know that for a synnian to be a worker is a punishment worse than death.
It began to eat at me that I had no choice.
And then I realized that though I did not want to fight, I also had no idea what I wanted to do instead.
The Empire did everything in its power to make sure we had no freedom of thought or creativity.
I escaped during the war with Qaara, and have never looked back.
For decades, I have taught Nifaali to fight and kill in preparation for the war with the Empire.
It is what I was trained to do, and it is what I am good at.
But I teach you now, in the hope that, one day, I can teach others something other than violence.

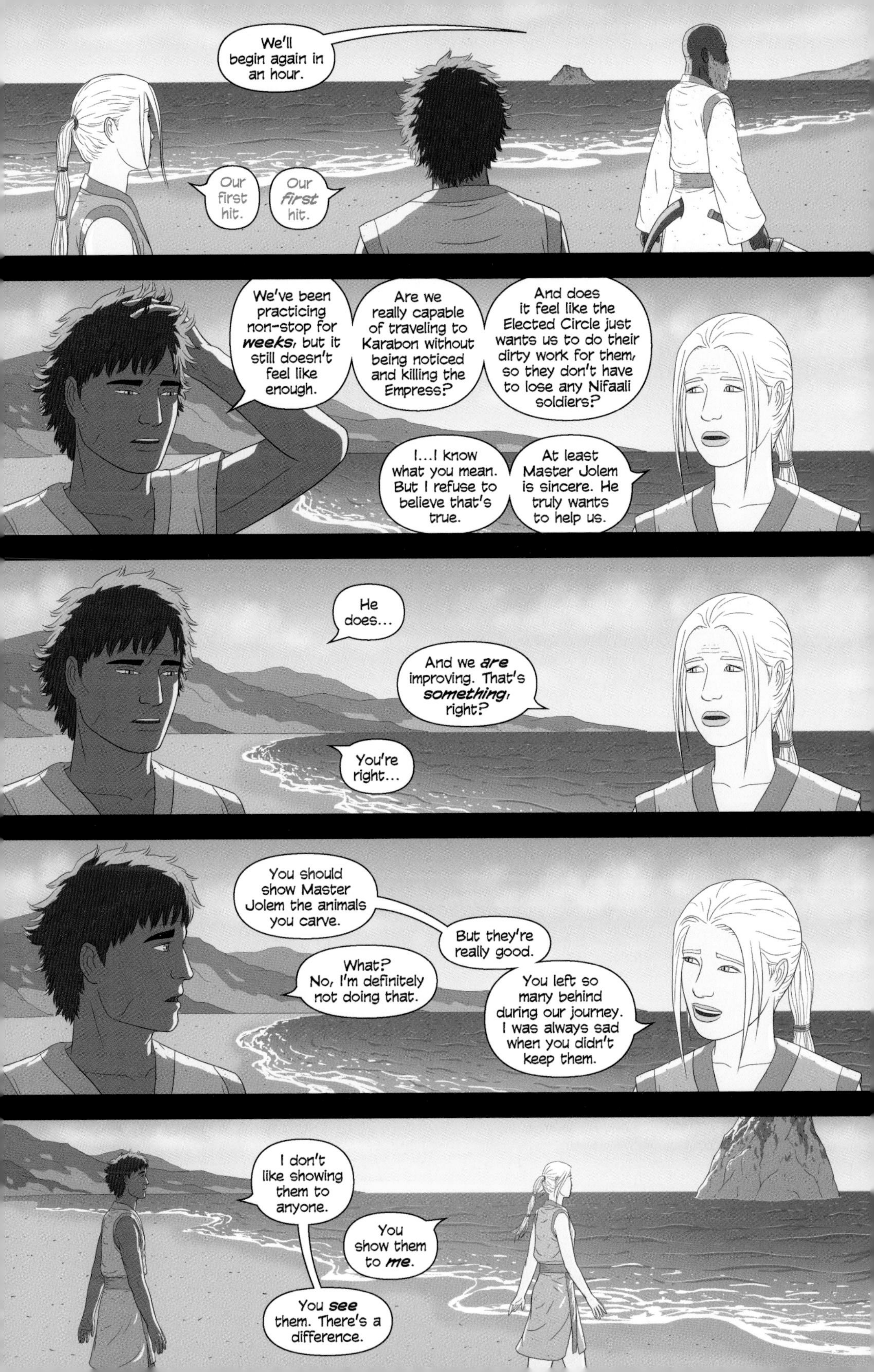
We'll begin again in an hour.
Our first hit.
Our *first* hit.
We've been practicing non-stop for *weeks*, but it still doesn't feel like enough.
Are we really capable of traveling to Karabon without being noticed and killing the Empress?
And does it feel like the Elected Circle just wants us to do their dirty work for them, so they don't have to lose any Nifaali soldiers?
I...I know what you mean. But I refuse to believe that's true.
At least Master Jolem is sincere. He truly wants to help us.
He does...
And we *are* improving. That's *something*, right?
You're right...
You should show Master Jolem the animals you carve.
But they're really good.
What? No, I'm definitely not doing that.
You left so many behind during our journey. I was always sad when you didn't keep them.
I don't like showing them to anyone.
You show them to *me*.
You *see* them. There's a difference.

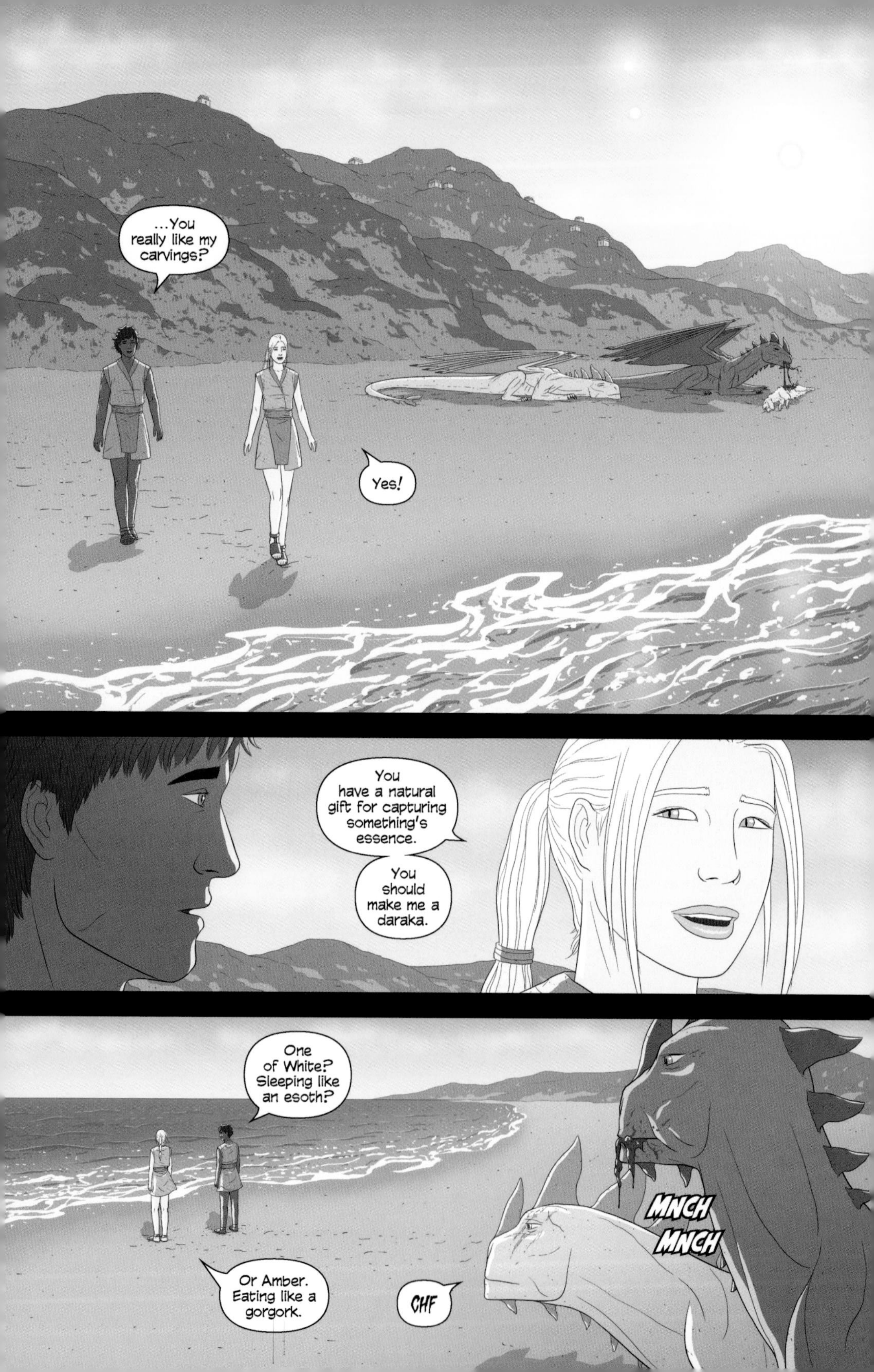

...You really like my carvings?
Yes!
You have a natural gift for capturing something's essence.
You should make me a daraka.
One of White? Sleeping like an esoth?
Or Amber. Eating like a gorgork.
CHF
MNCH MNCH

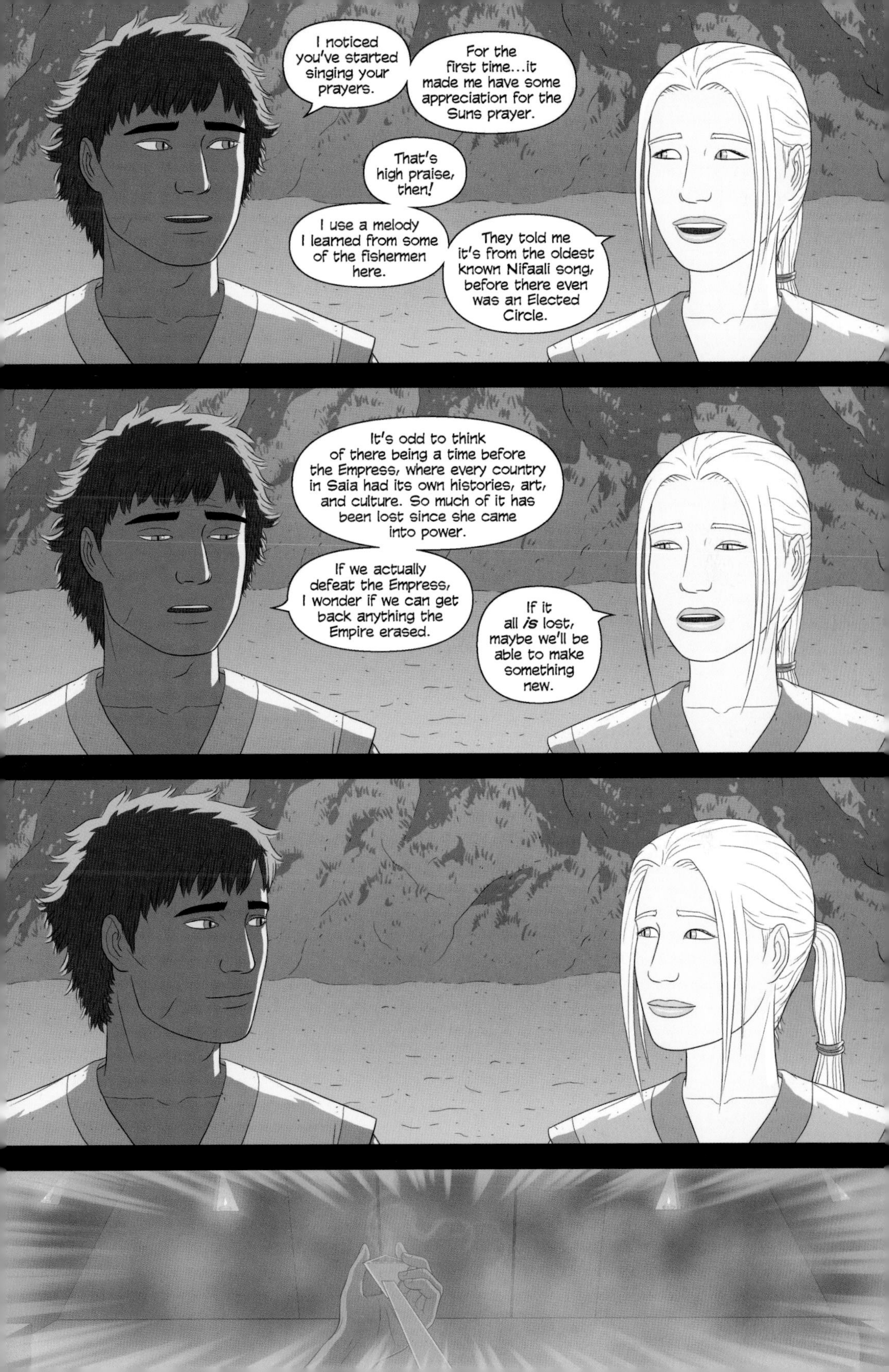
I noticed you've started singing your prayers.
For the first time...it made me have some appreciation for the Suns prayer.
That's high praise, then!
I use a melody I learned from some of the fishermen here.
They told me it's from the oldest known Nifaali song, before there even was an Elected Circle.
It's odd to think of there being a time before the Empress, where every country in Saia had its own histories, art, and culture. So much of it has been lost since she came into power.
If we actually defeat the Empress, I wonder if we can get back anything the Empire erased.
If it all *is* lost, maybe we'll be able to make something new.

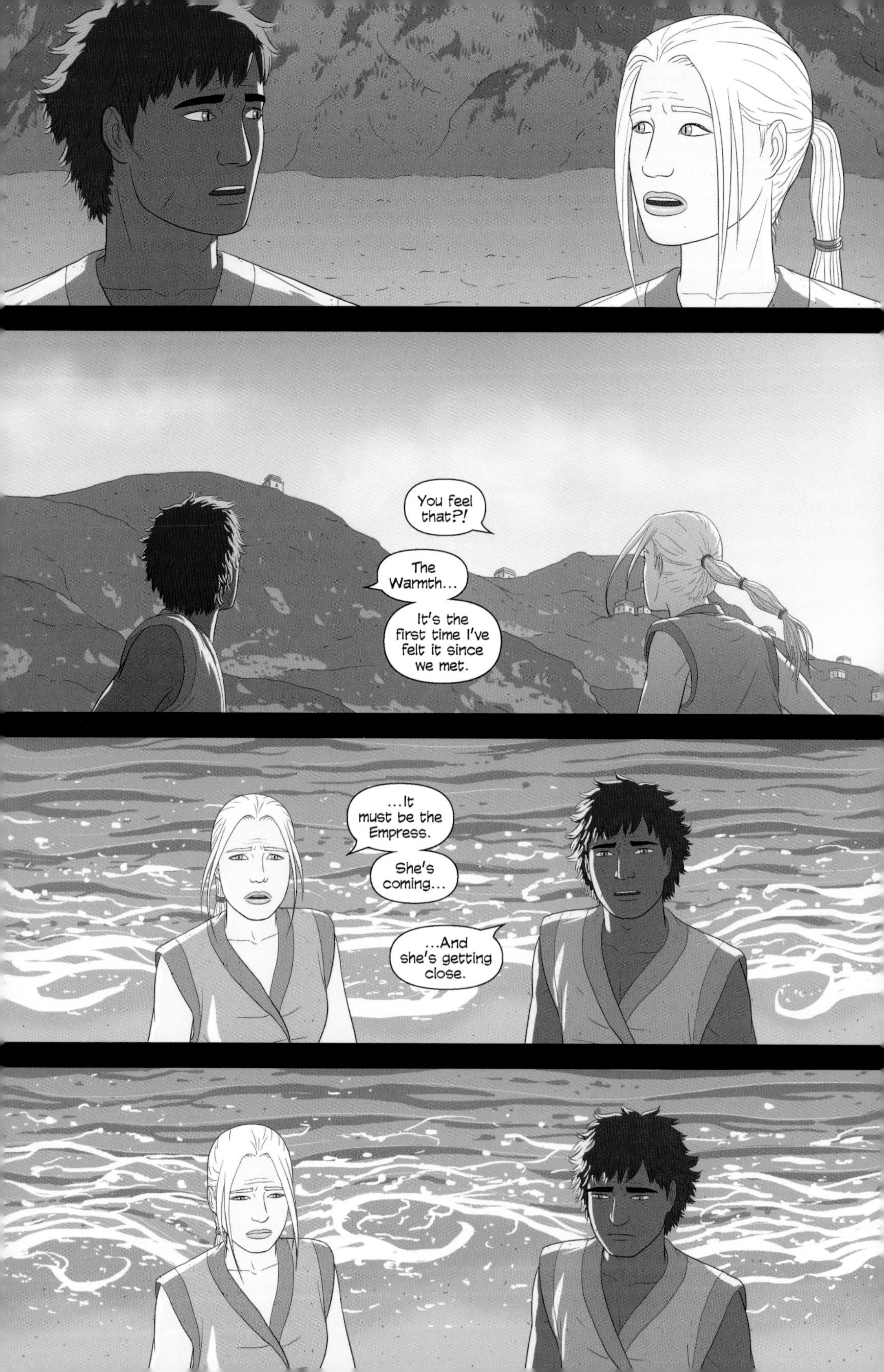
You feel that?!
The Warmth...
It's the first time I've felt it since we met.
...It must be the Empress.
She's coming...
...And she's getting close.

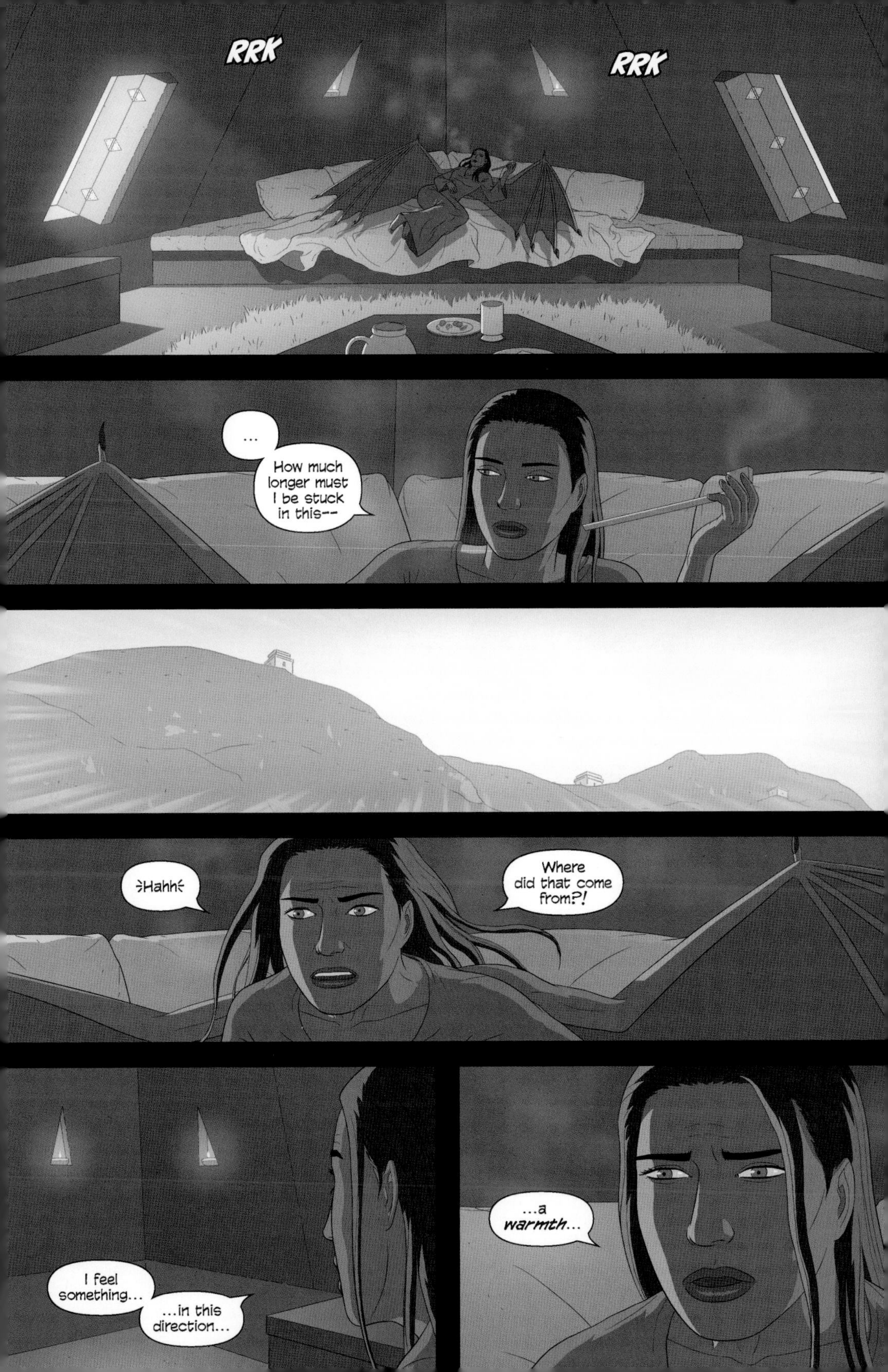
RRK
RRK
...
How much longer must I be stuck in this--
Hahh
Where did that come from?!
I feel something...
...in this direction...
...a *warmth*...

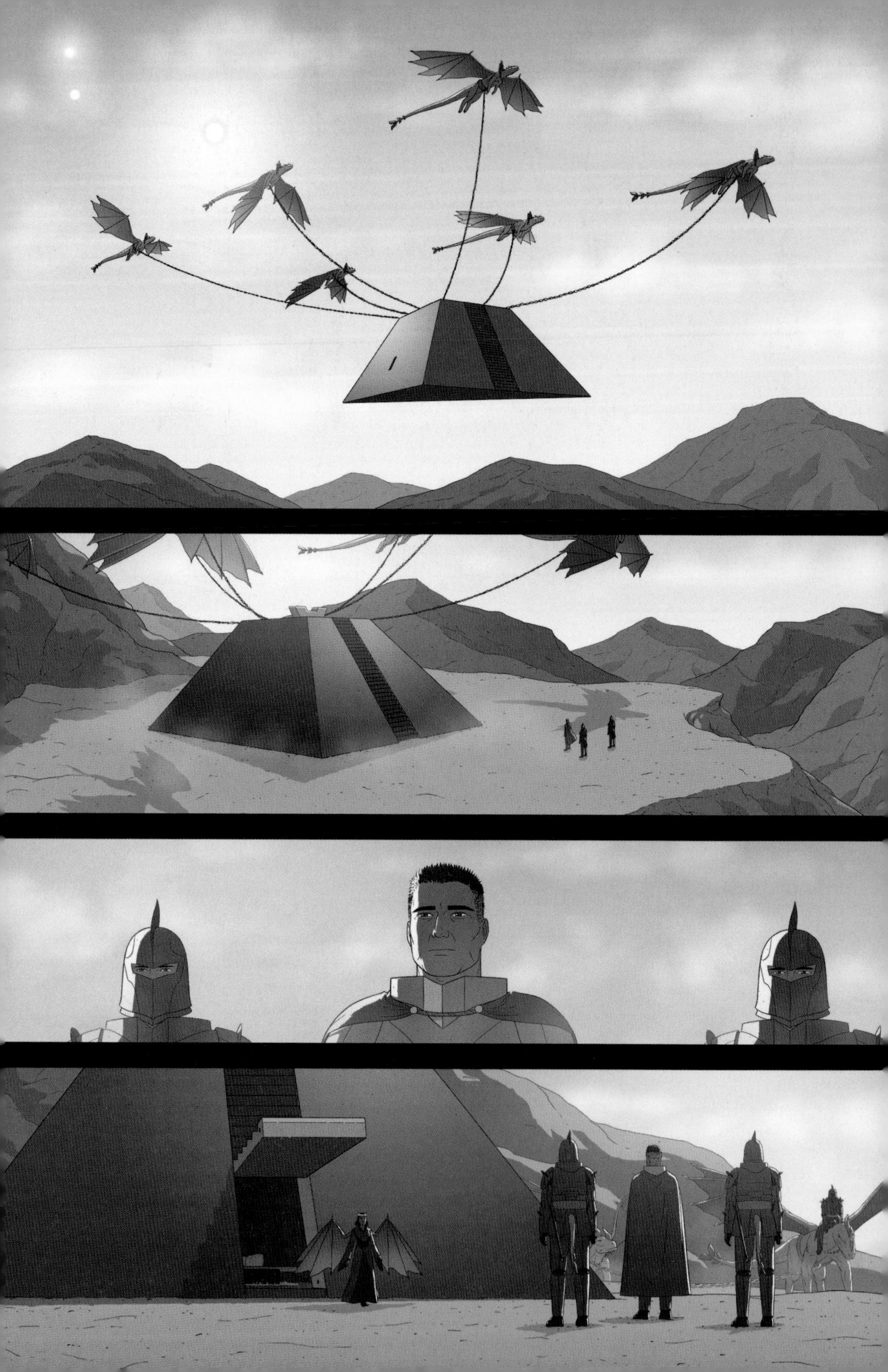

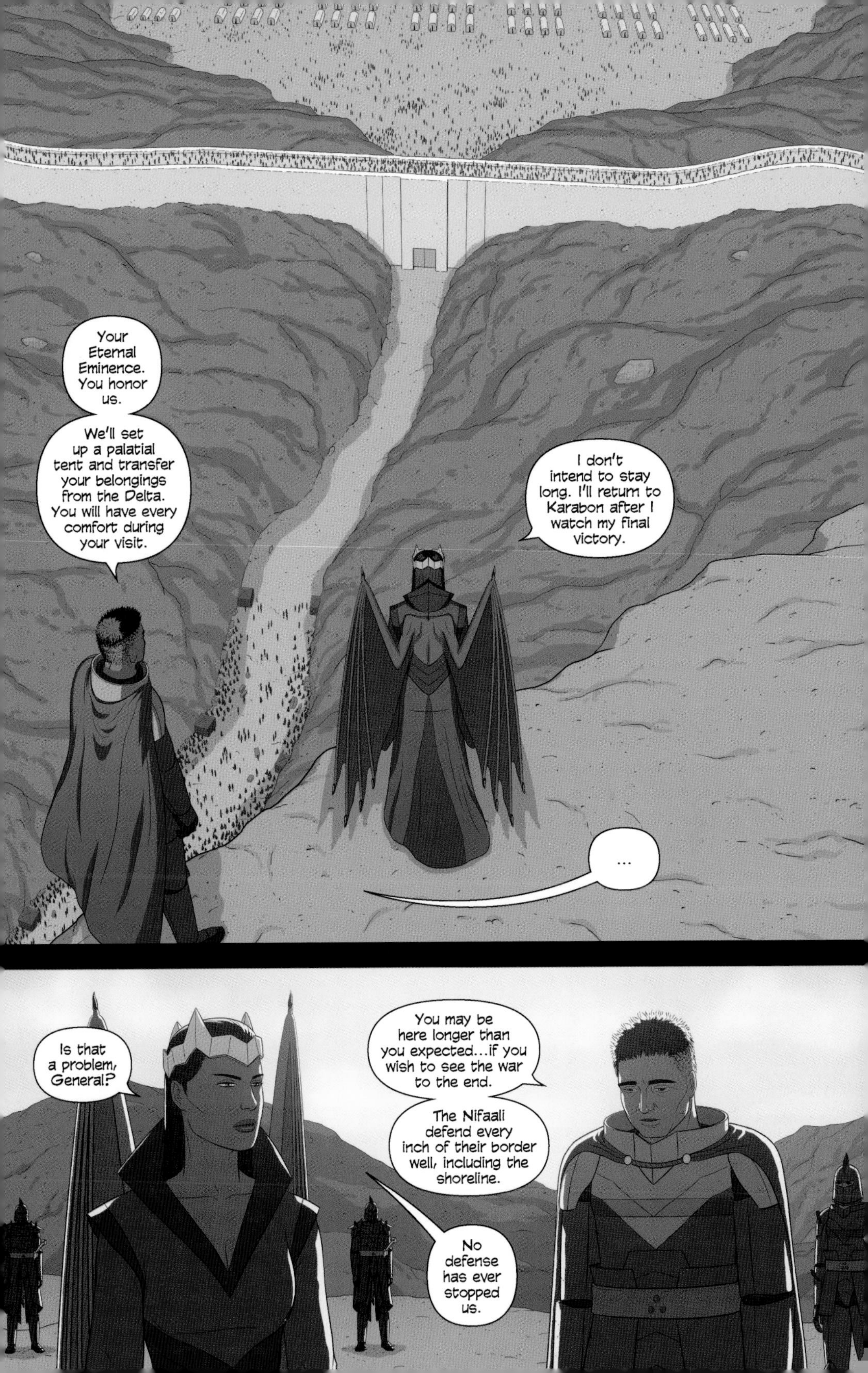
Your Eternal Eminence. You honor us.
We'll set up a palatial tent and transfer your belongings from the Delta. You will have every comfort during your visit.
I don't intend to stay long. I'll return to Karabon after I watch my final victory.
...
Is that a problem, General?
You may be here longer than you expected...if you wish to see the war to the end.
The Nifaali defend every inch of their border well, including the shoreline.
No defense has ever stopped us.

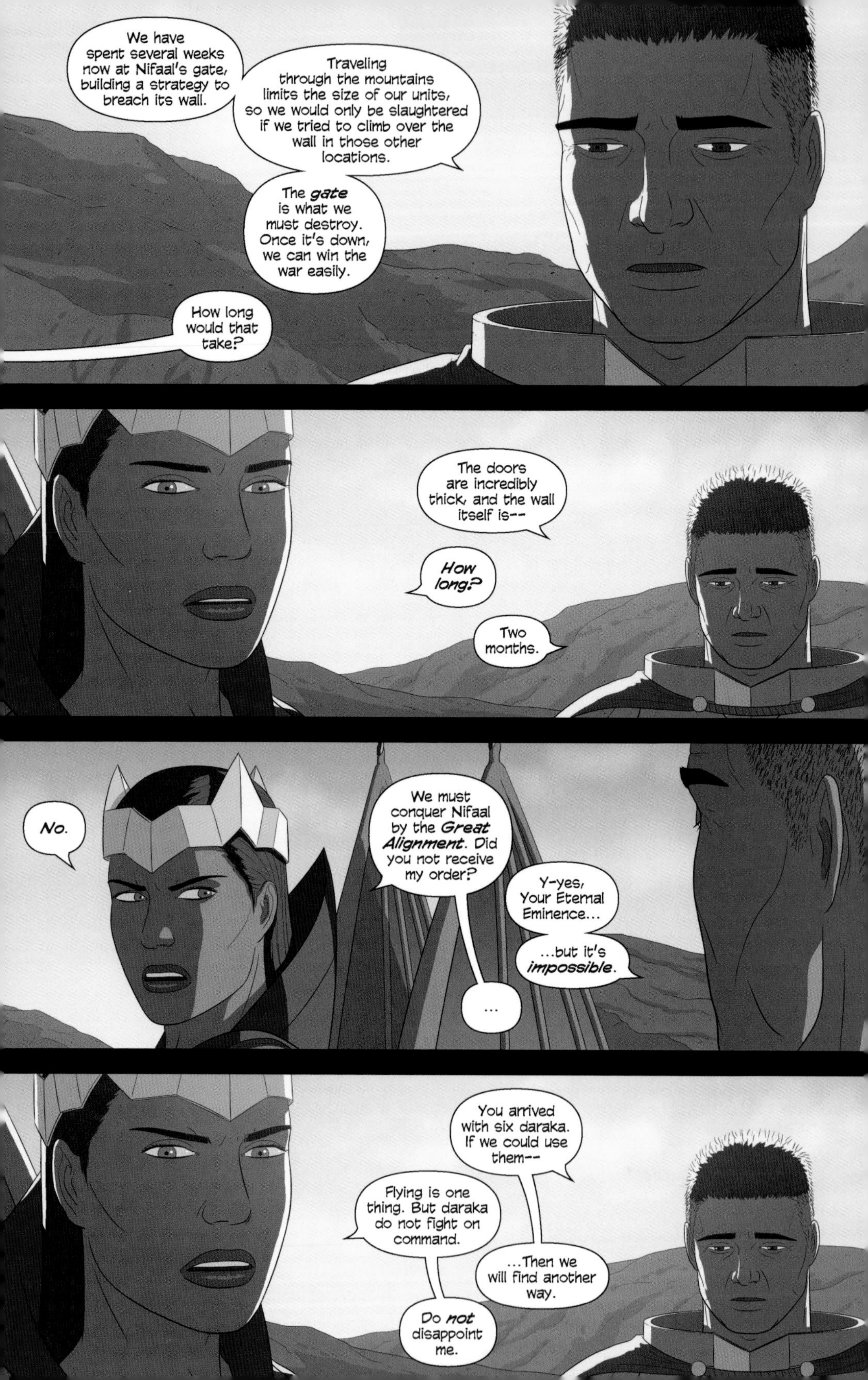
We have spent several weeks now at Nifaal's gate, building a strategy to breach its wall.
Traveling through the mountains limits the size of our units, so we would only be slaughtered if we tried to climb over the wall in those other locations.
The *gate* is what we must destroy. Once it's down, we can win the war easily.
How long would that take?
The doors are incredibly thick, and the wall itself is--
How long?
Two months.
No.
We must conquer Nifaal by the *Great Alignment*. Did you not receive my order?
Y-yes, Your Eternal Eminence...
...but it's *impossible*.
...
You arrived with six daraka. If we could use them--
Flying is one thing. But daraka do not fight on command.
...Then we will find another way.
Do *not* disappoint me.

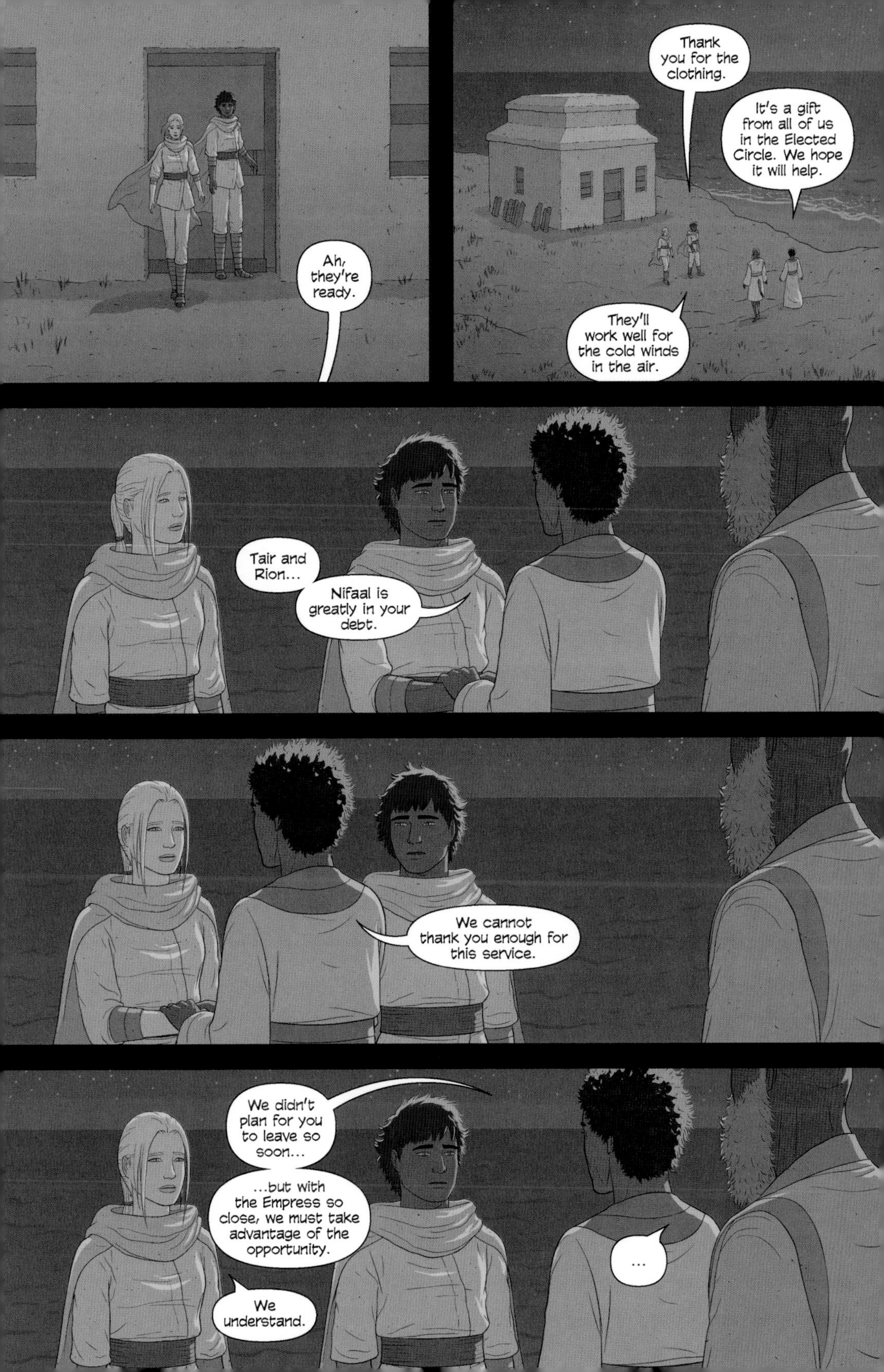

Ah, they're ready.
Thank you for the clothing.
It's a gift from all of us in the Elected Circle. We hope it will help.
They'll work well for the cold winds in the air.
Tair and Rion...
Nifaal is greatly in your debt.
We cannot thank you enough for this service.
We didn't plan for you to leave so soon...
...but with the Empress so close, we must take advantage of the opportunity.
We understand.
...

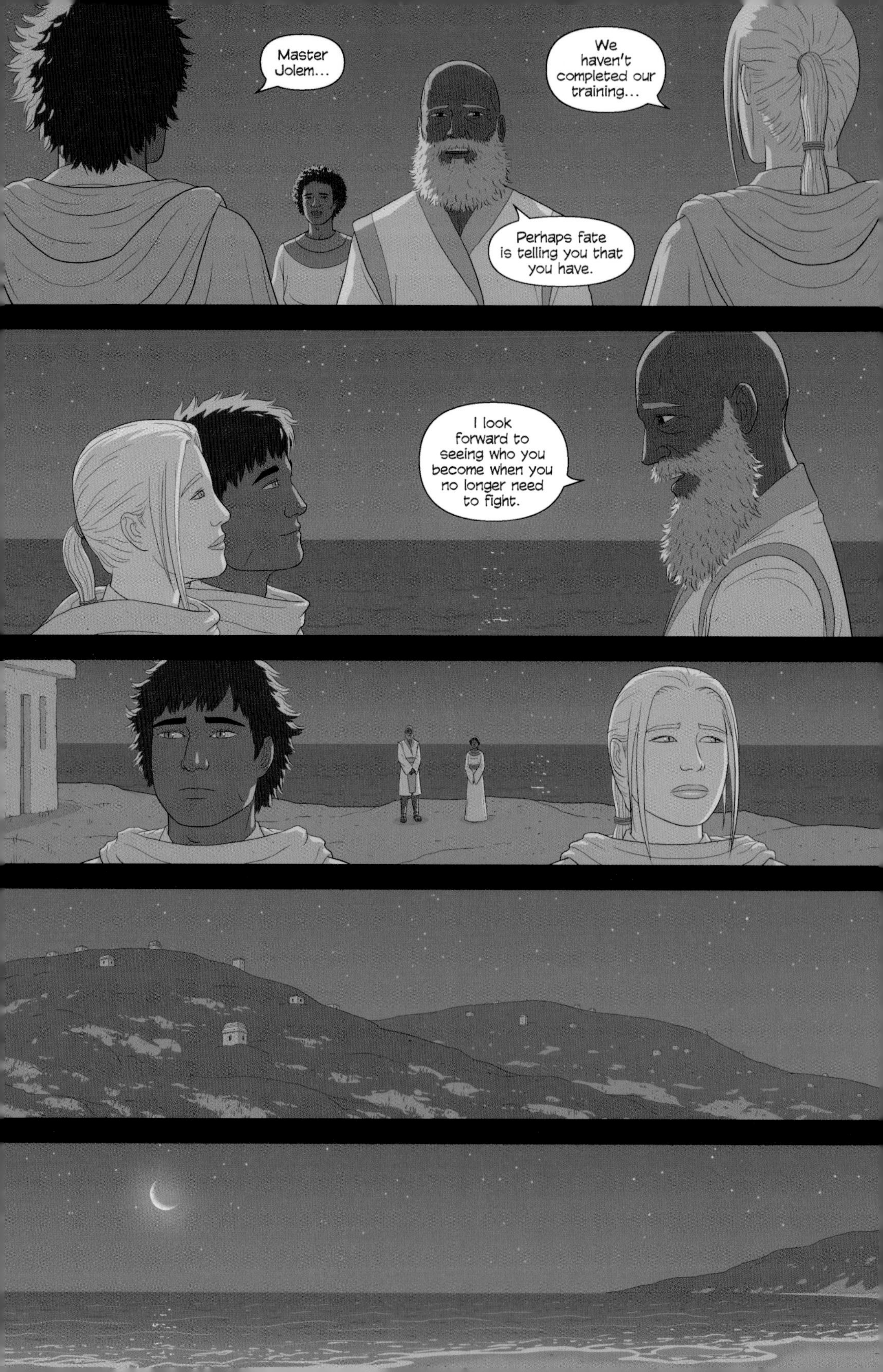
Master Jolem...
We haven't completed our training...
Perhaps fate is telling you that you have.
I look forward to seeing who you become when you no longer need to fight.

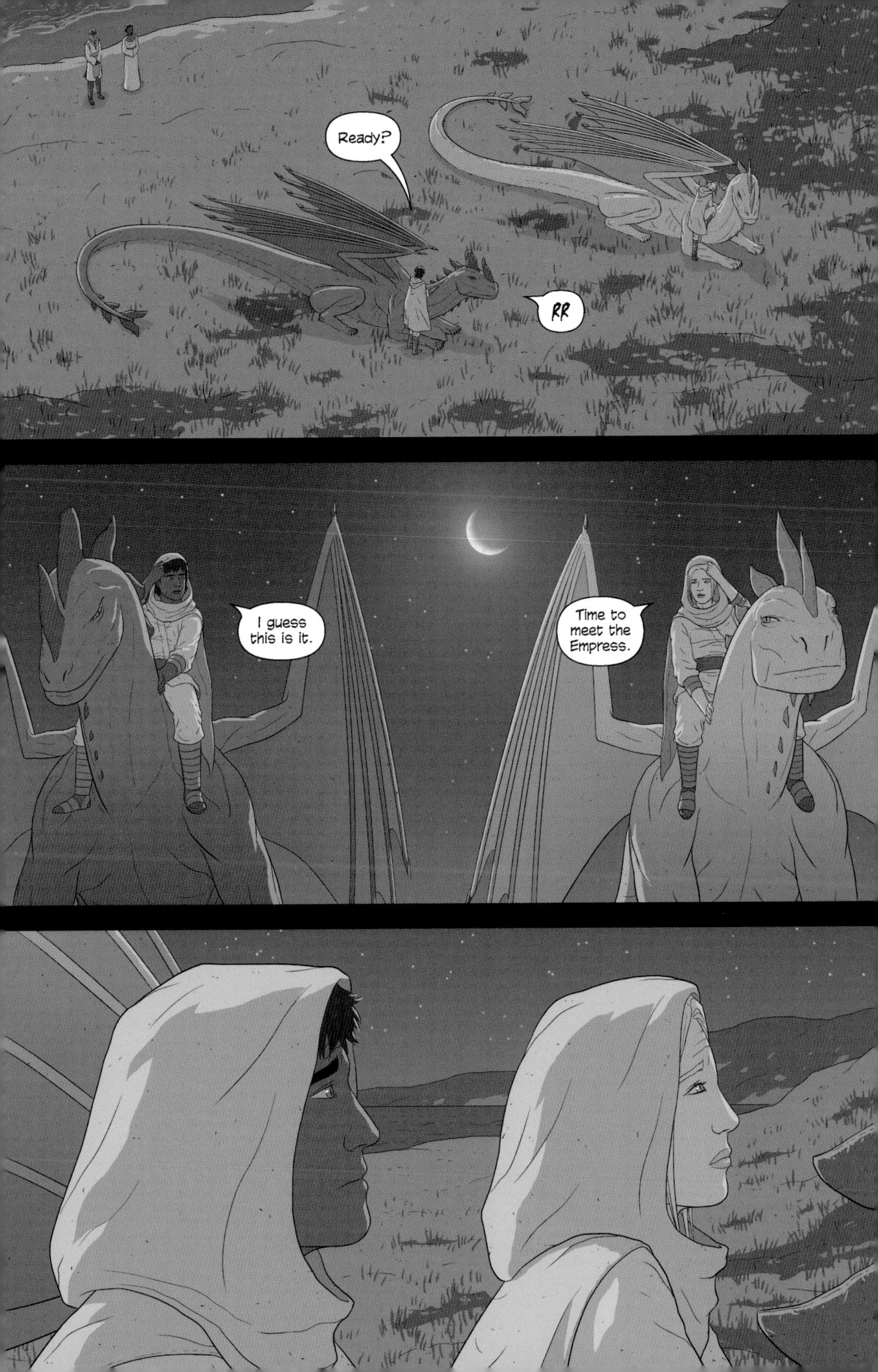
Ready?
RR
I guess this is it.
Time to meet the Empress.

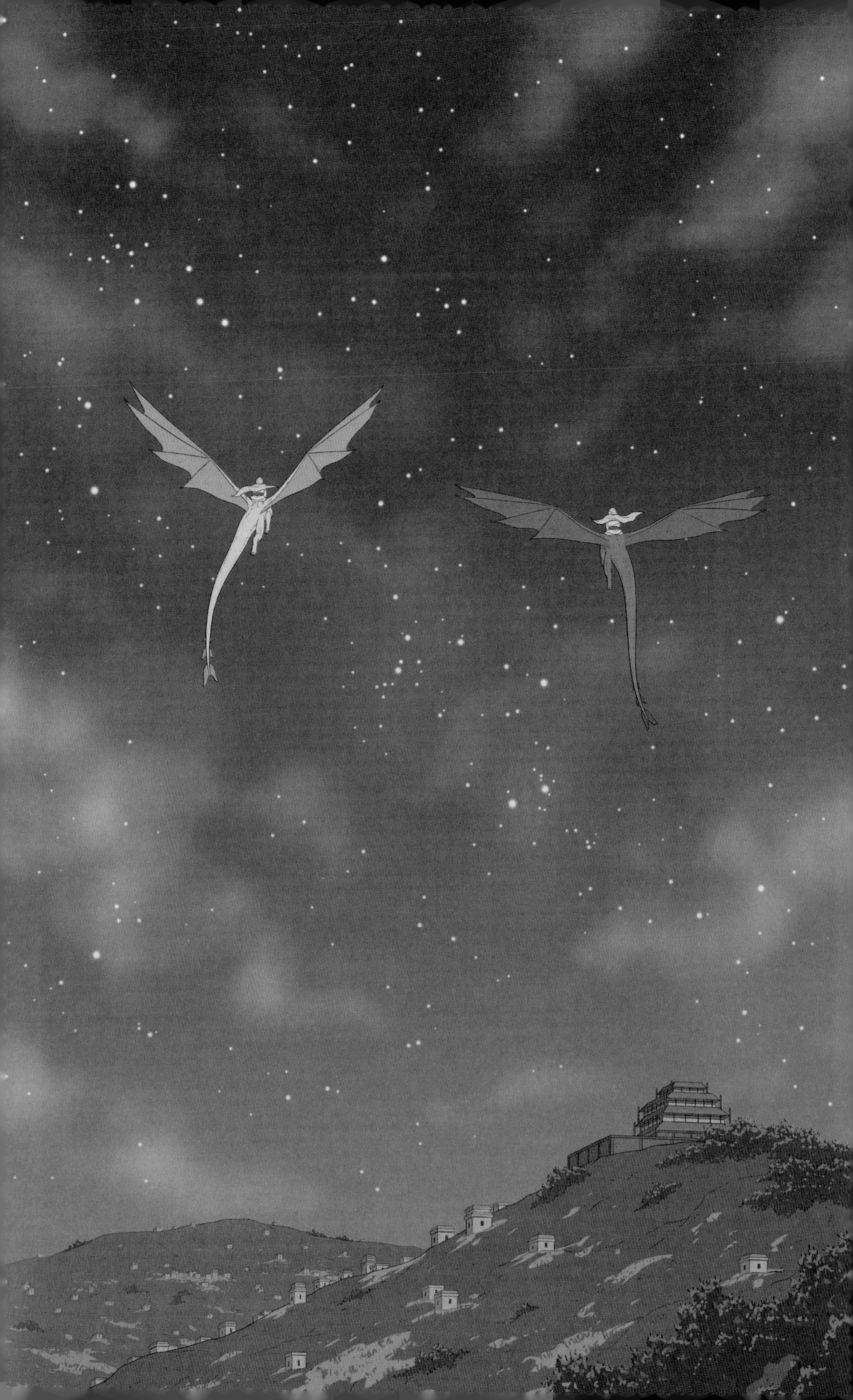

8

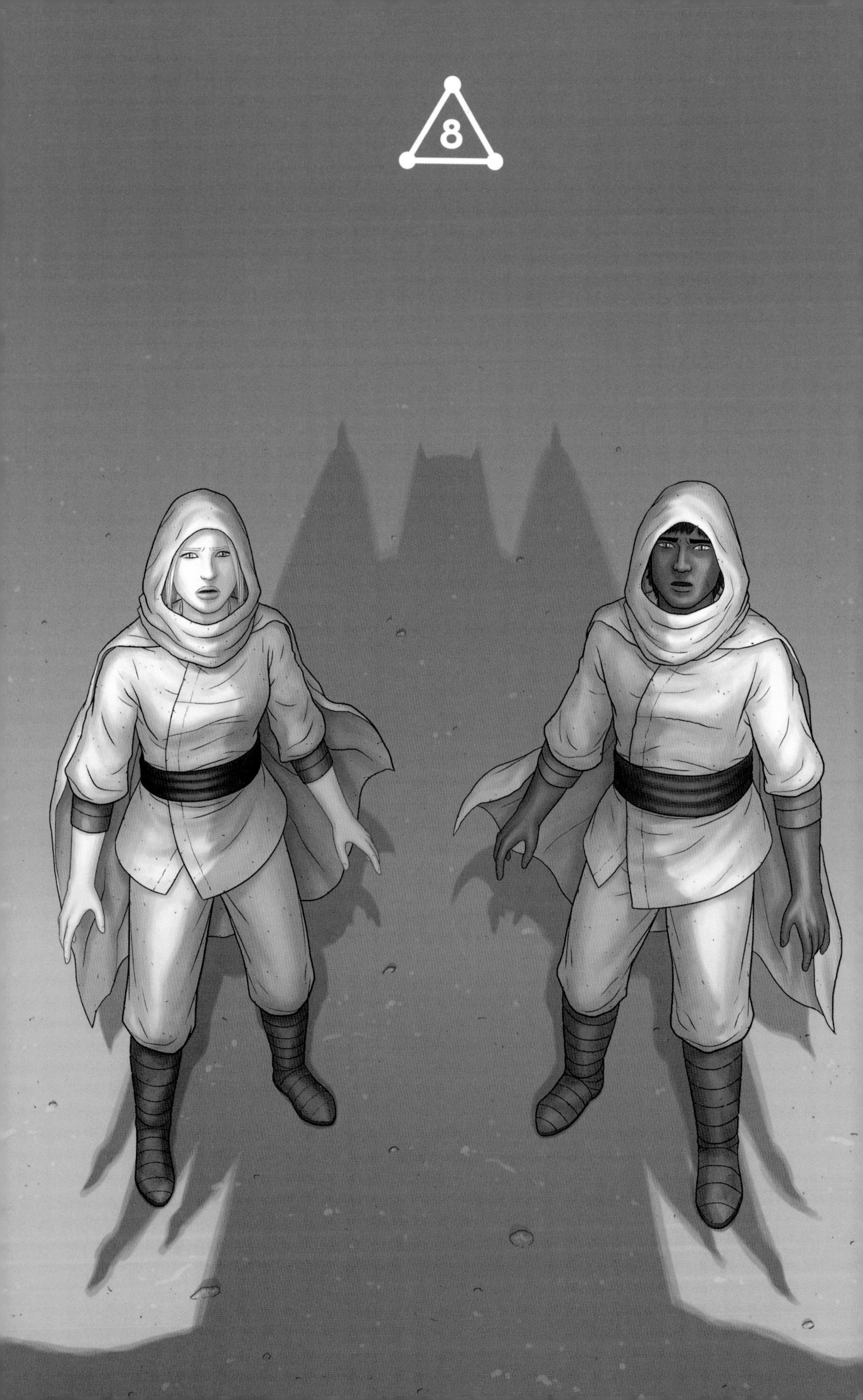

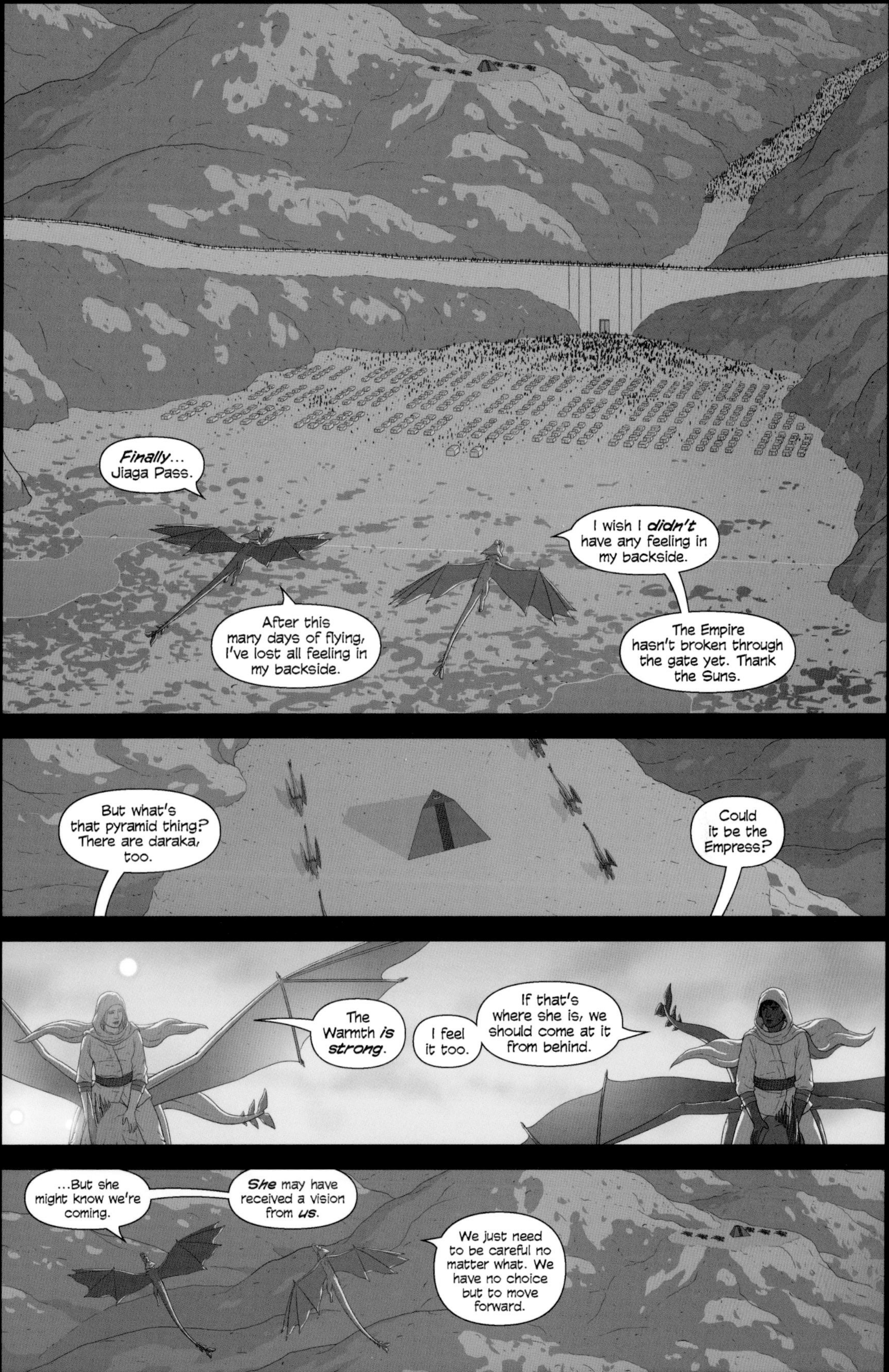
Finally... Jiaga Pass.
After this many days of flying, I've lost all feeling in my backside.
I wish I ***didn't*** have any feeling in my backside.
The Empire hasn't broken through the gate yet. Thank the Suns.
But what's that pyramid thing? There are daraka, too.
Could it be the Empress?
The Warmth ***is strong***.
I feel it too.
If that's where she is, we should come at it from behind.
...But she might know we're coming.
She may have received a vision from ***us***.
We just need to be careful no matter what. We have no choice but to move forward.

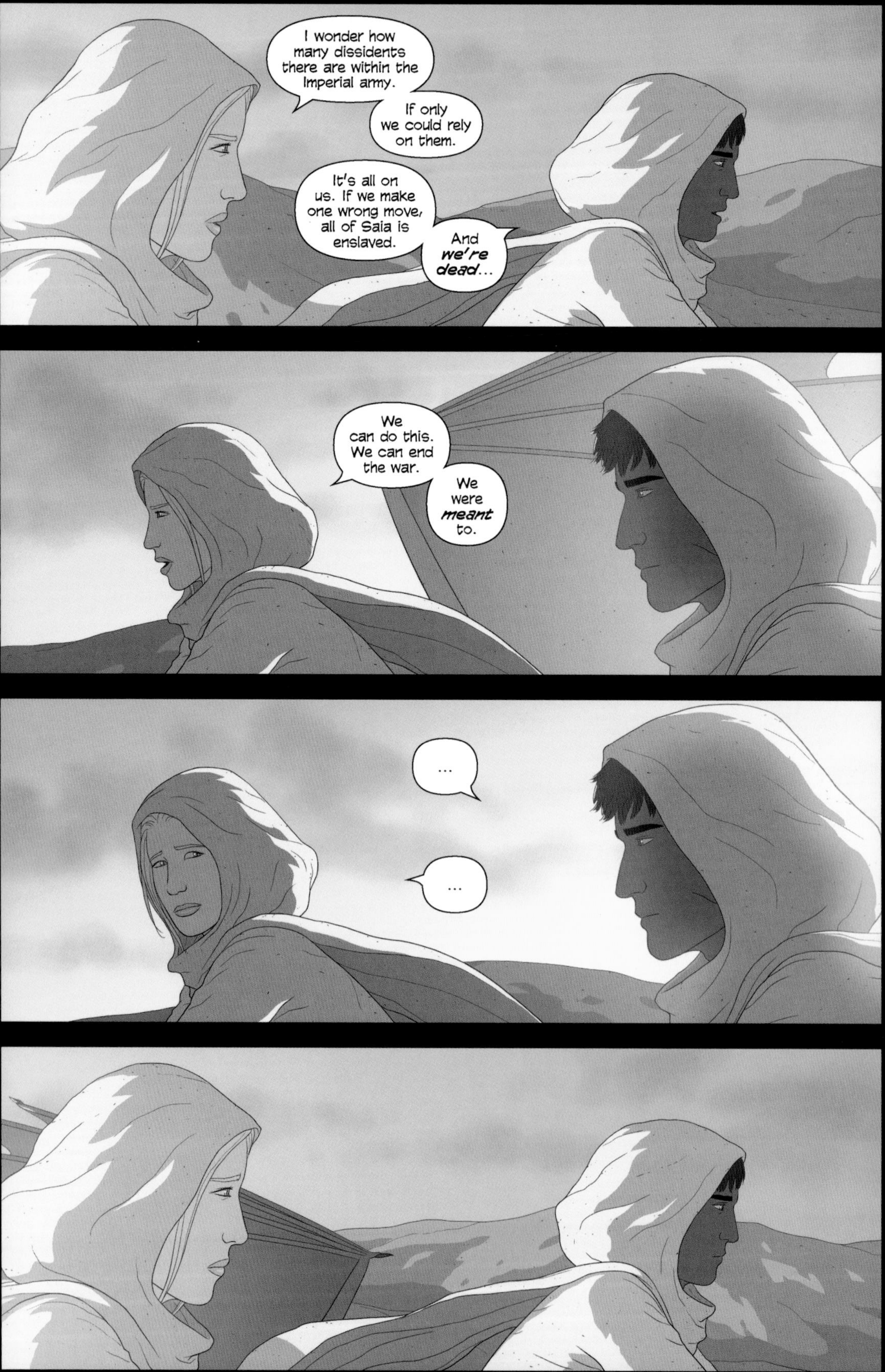
I wonder how many dissidents there are within the Imperial army.
If only we could rely on them.
It's all on us. If we make one wrong move, all of Saia is enslaved.
And *we're dead*...
We can do this. We can end the war.
We were *meant* to.
...
...

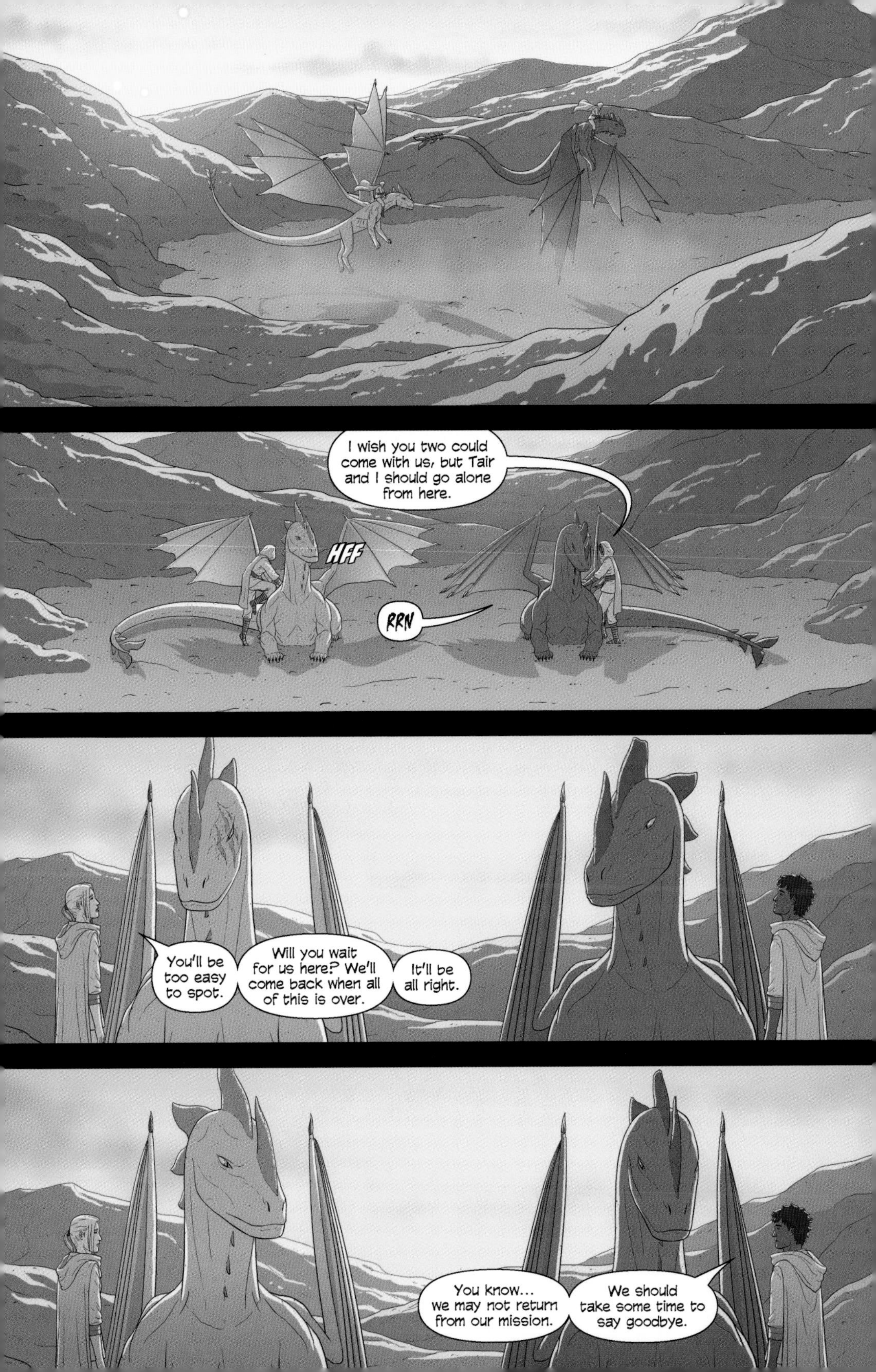
I wish you two could come with us, but Tair and I should go alone from here.
HFF
RRN
You'll be too easy to spot.
Will you wait for us here? We'll come back when all of this is over.
It'll be all right.
You know... we may not return from our mission.
We should take some time to say goodbye.

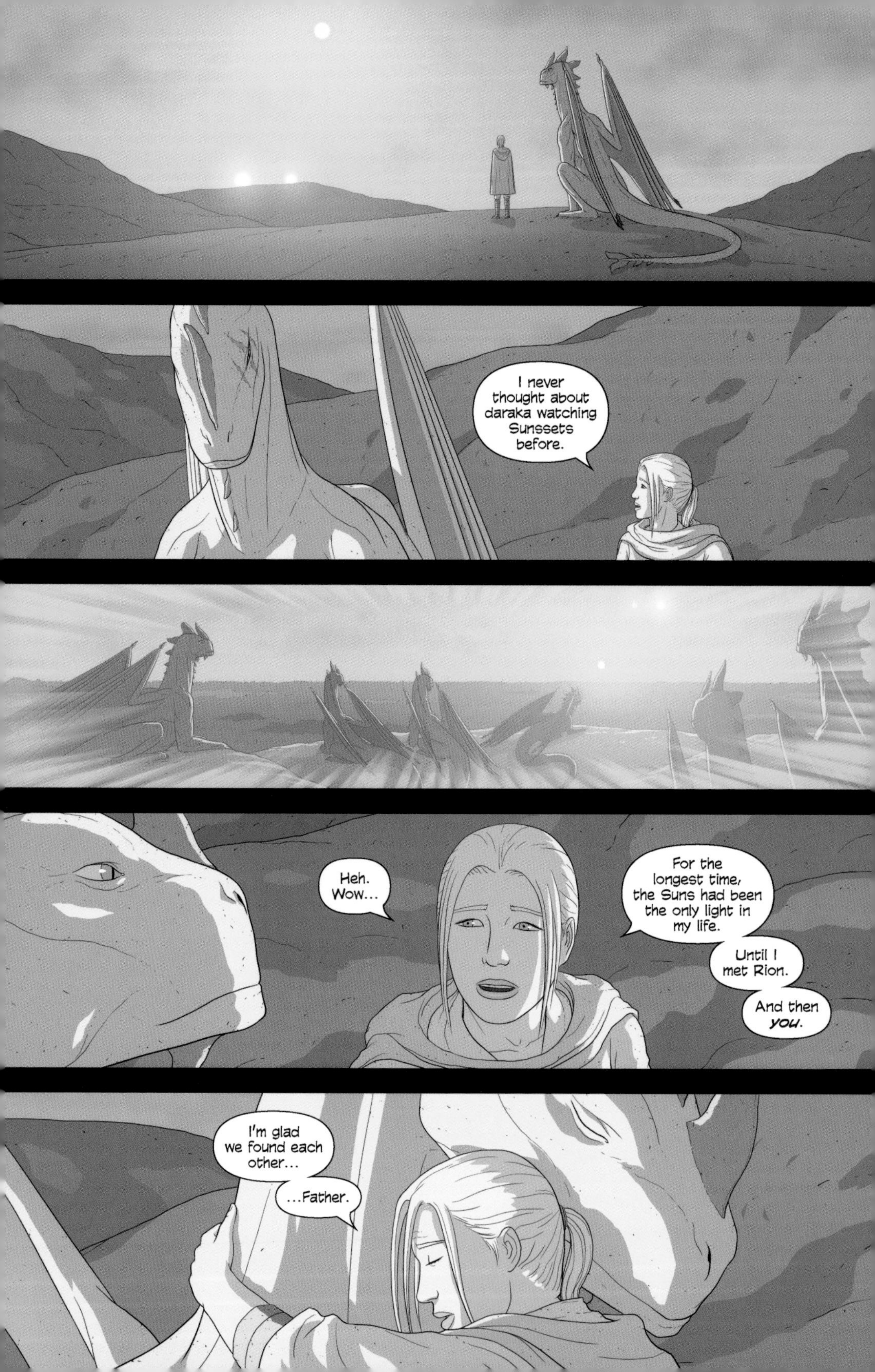
I never thought about daraka watching Sunssets before.
Heh. Wow...
For the longest time, the Suns had been the only light in my life.
Until I met Rion.
And then *you*.
I'm glad we found each other...
...Father.

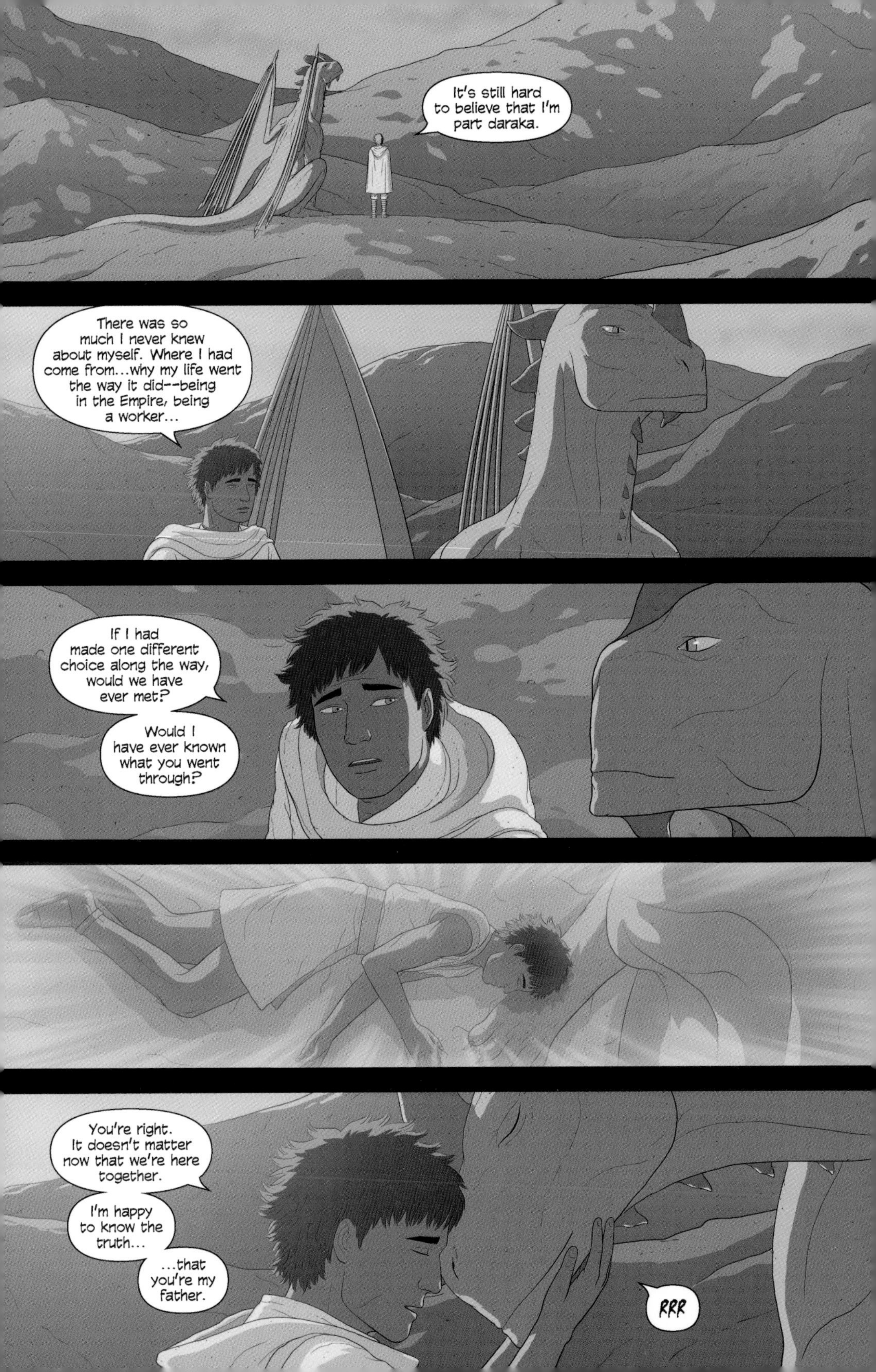
It's still hard to believe that I'm part daraka.
There was so much I never knew about myself. Where I had come from...why my life went the way it did--being in the Empire, being a worker...
If I had made one different choice along the way, would we have ever met?
Would I have ever known what you went through?
You're right. It doesn't matter now that we're here together.
I'm happy to know the truth...
...that you're my father.
RRR

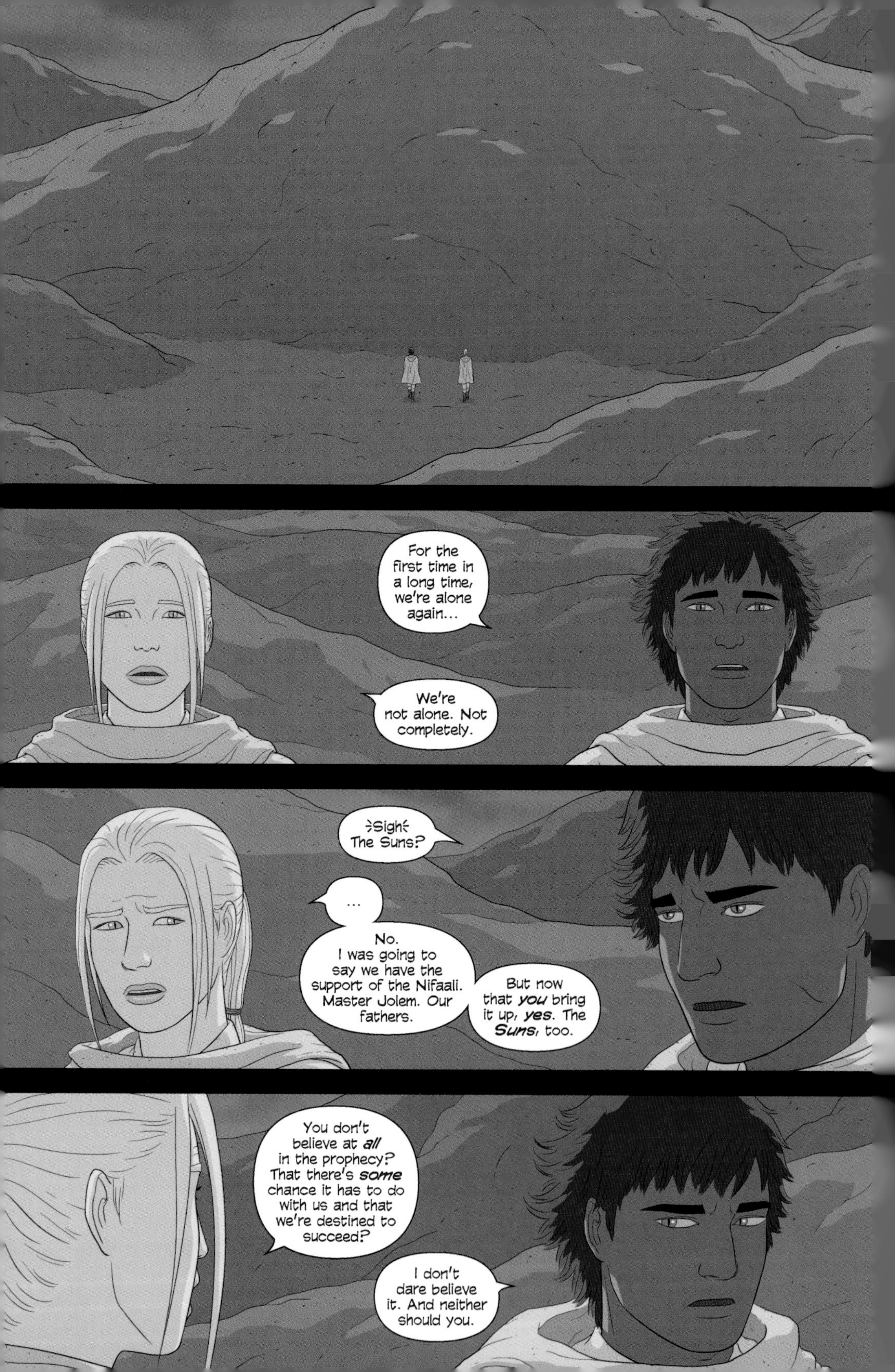
For the first time in a long time, we're alone again...
We're not alone. Not completely.
⊰Sigh⊱ The Suns?
...
No. I was going to say we have the support of the Nifaali. Master Jolem. Our fathers.
But now that *you* bring it up, ***yes***. The ***Suns***, too.
You don't believe at ***all*** in the prophecy? That there's ***some*** chance it has to do with us and that we're destined to succeed?
I don't dare believe it. And neither should you.

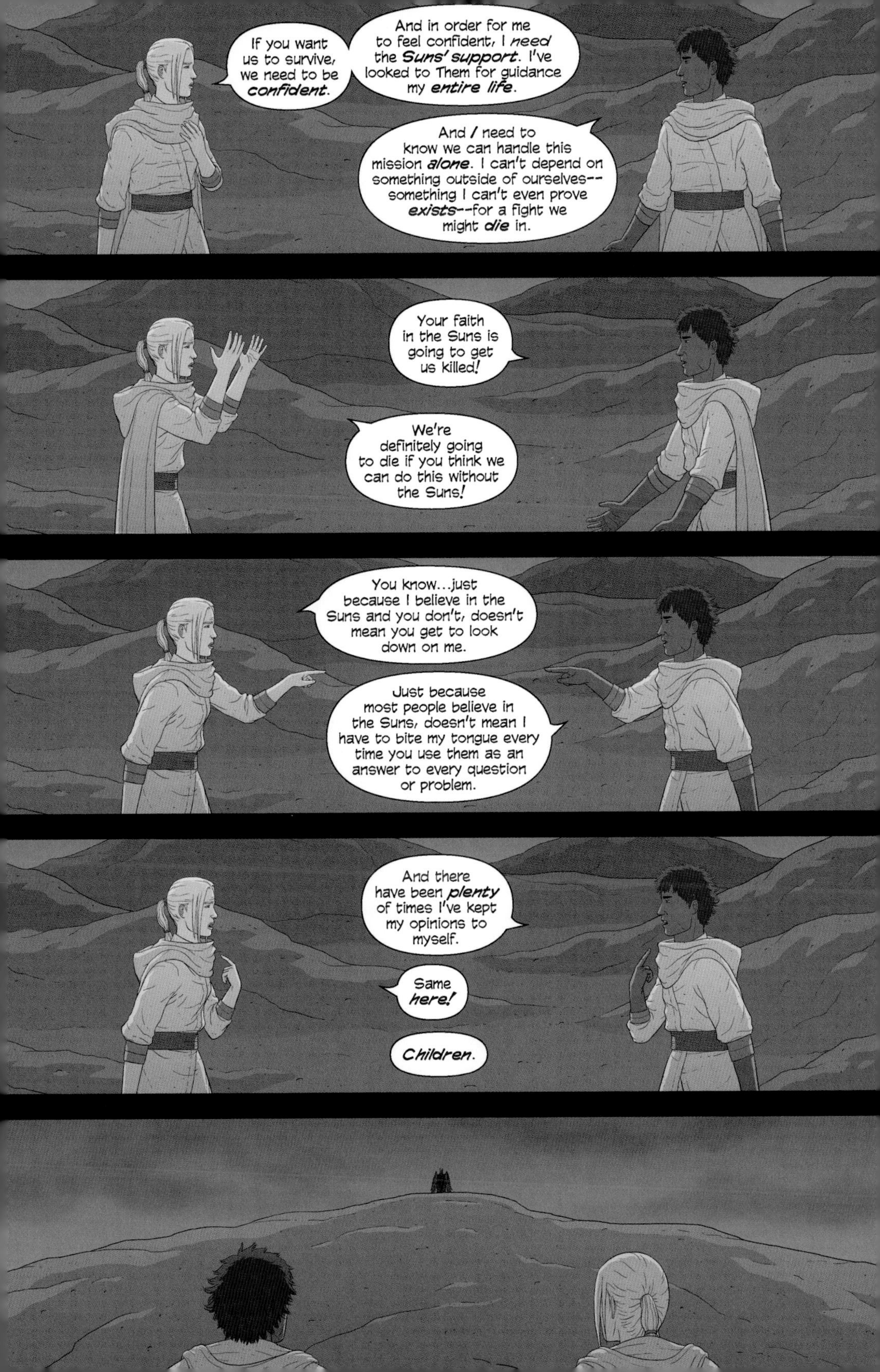
If you want us to survive, we need to be *confident*.
And in order for me to feel confident, I *need* the *Suns' support*. I've looked to Them for guidance my *entire life*.
And *I* need to know we can handle this mission *alone*. I can't depend on something outside of ourselves--something I can't even prove *exists*--for a fight we might *die* in.
Your faith in the Suns is going to get us killed!
We're definitely going to die if you think we can do this without the Suns!
You know...just because I believe in the Suns and you don't, doesn't mean you get to look down on me.
Just because most people believe in the Suns, doesn't mean I have to bite my tongue every time you use them as an answer to every question or problem.
And there have been *plenty* of times I've kept my opinions to myself.
Same *here!*
Children.

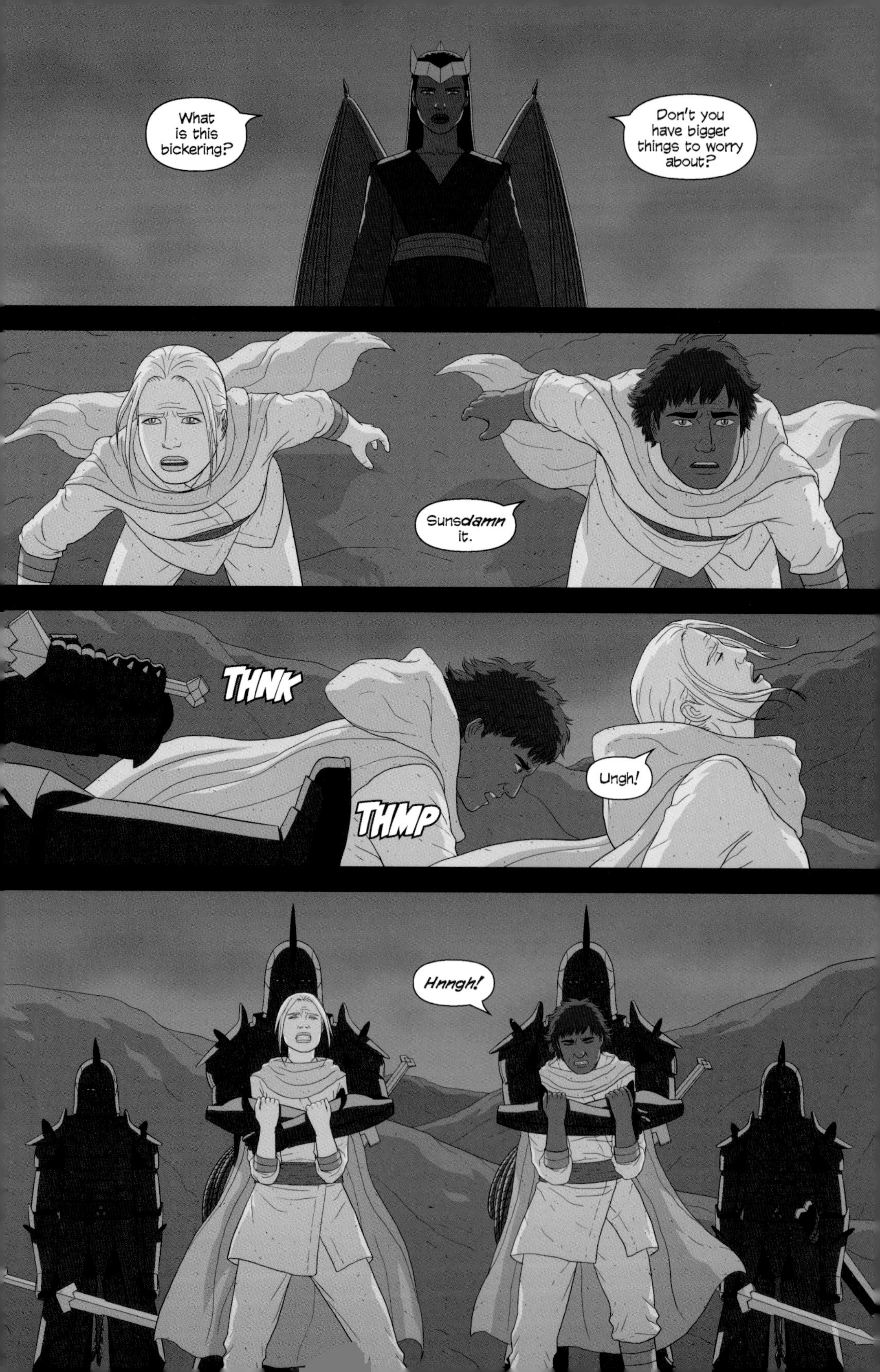
What is this bickering?
Don't you have bigger things to worry about?
Sunsdamn it.
THNK
THMP
Ungh!
Hnngh!

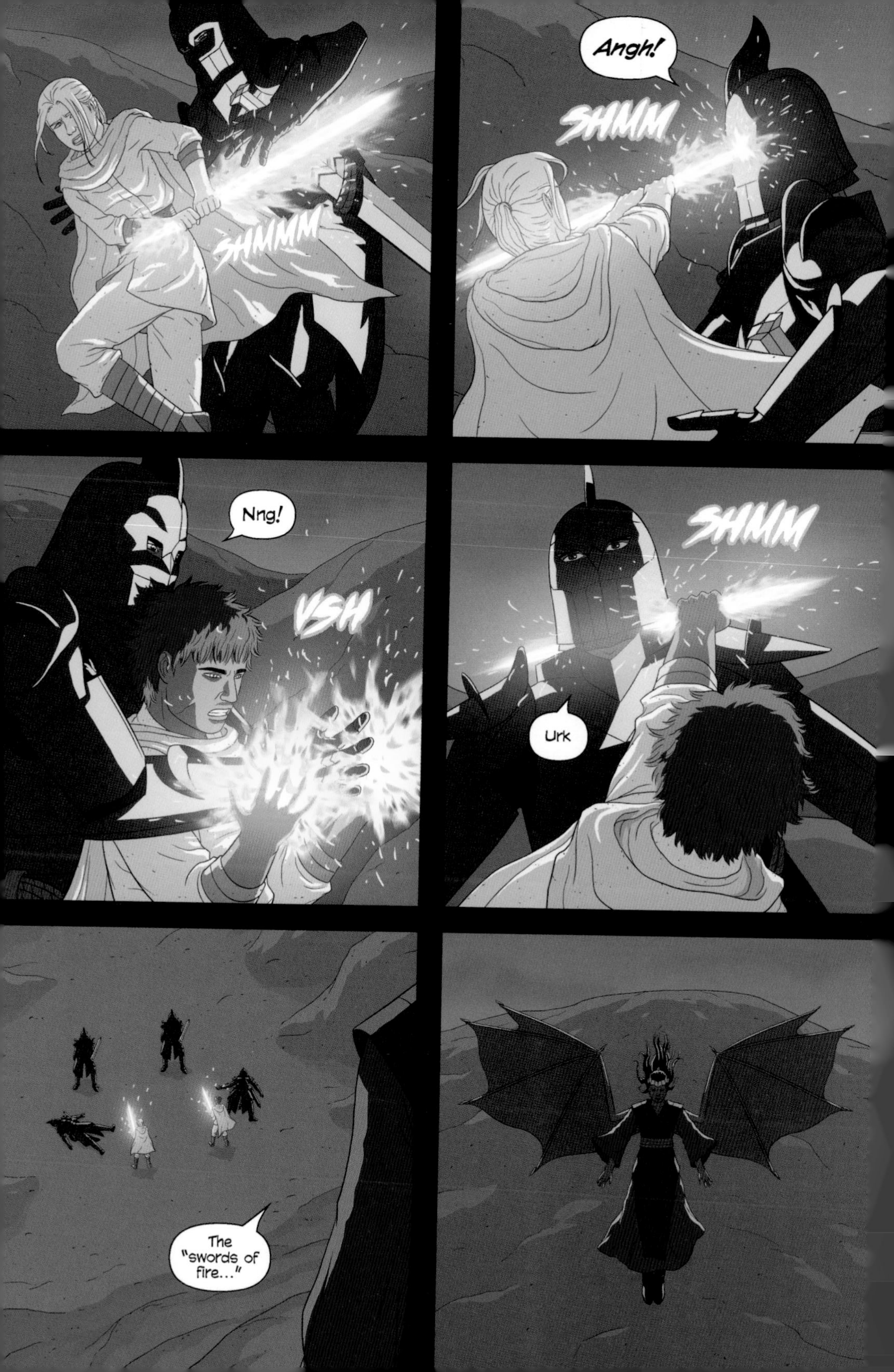
SHMMM
Angh!
SHMM
Nng!
VSH
SHMM
Urk
The "swords of fire..."

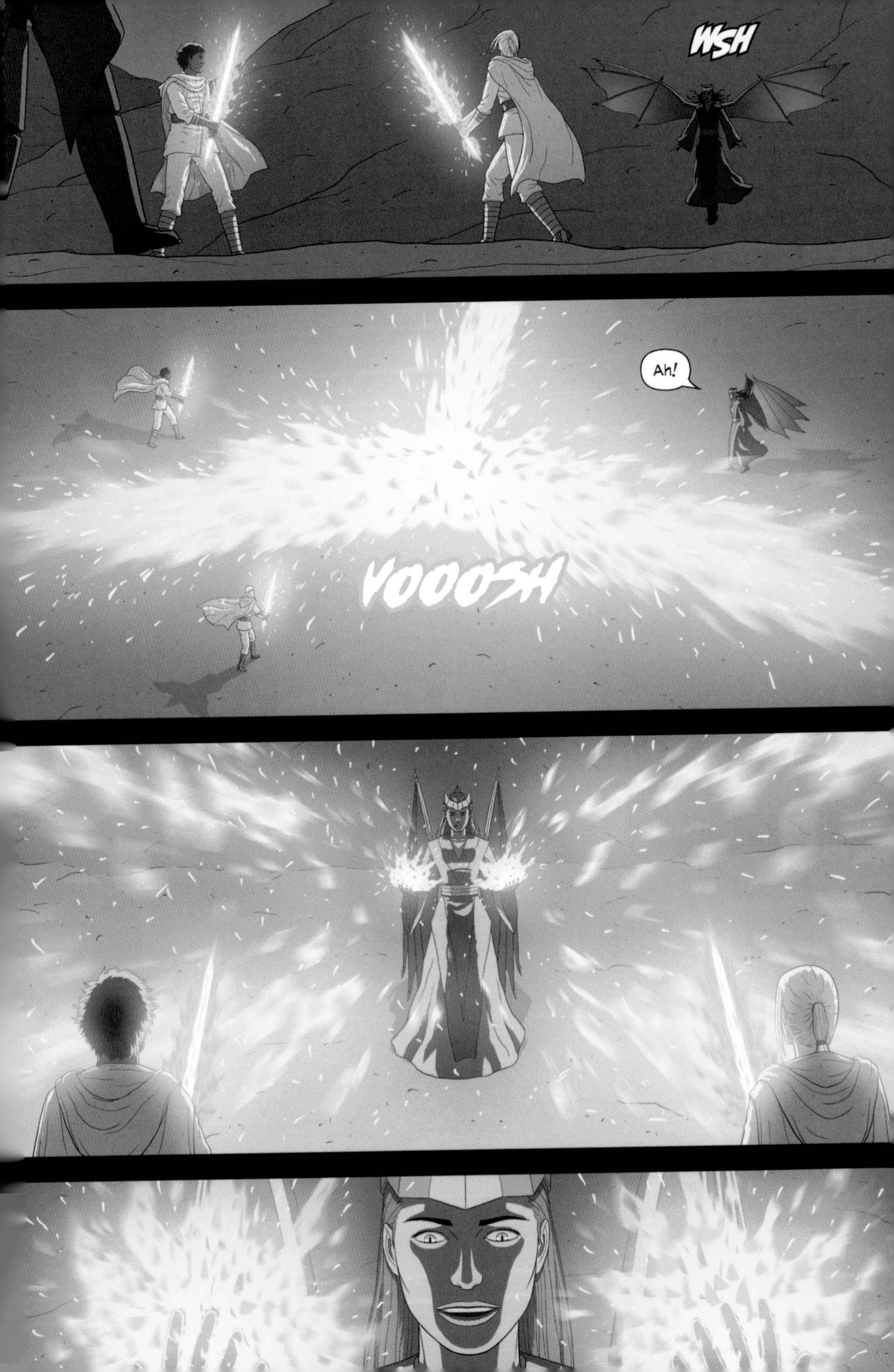
WSH
Ah!
VOOOSH

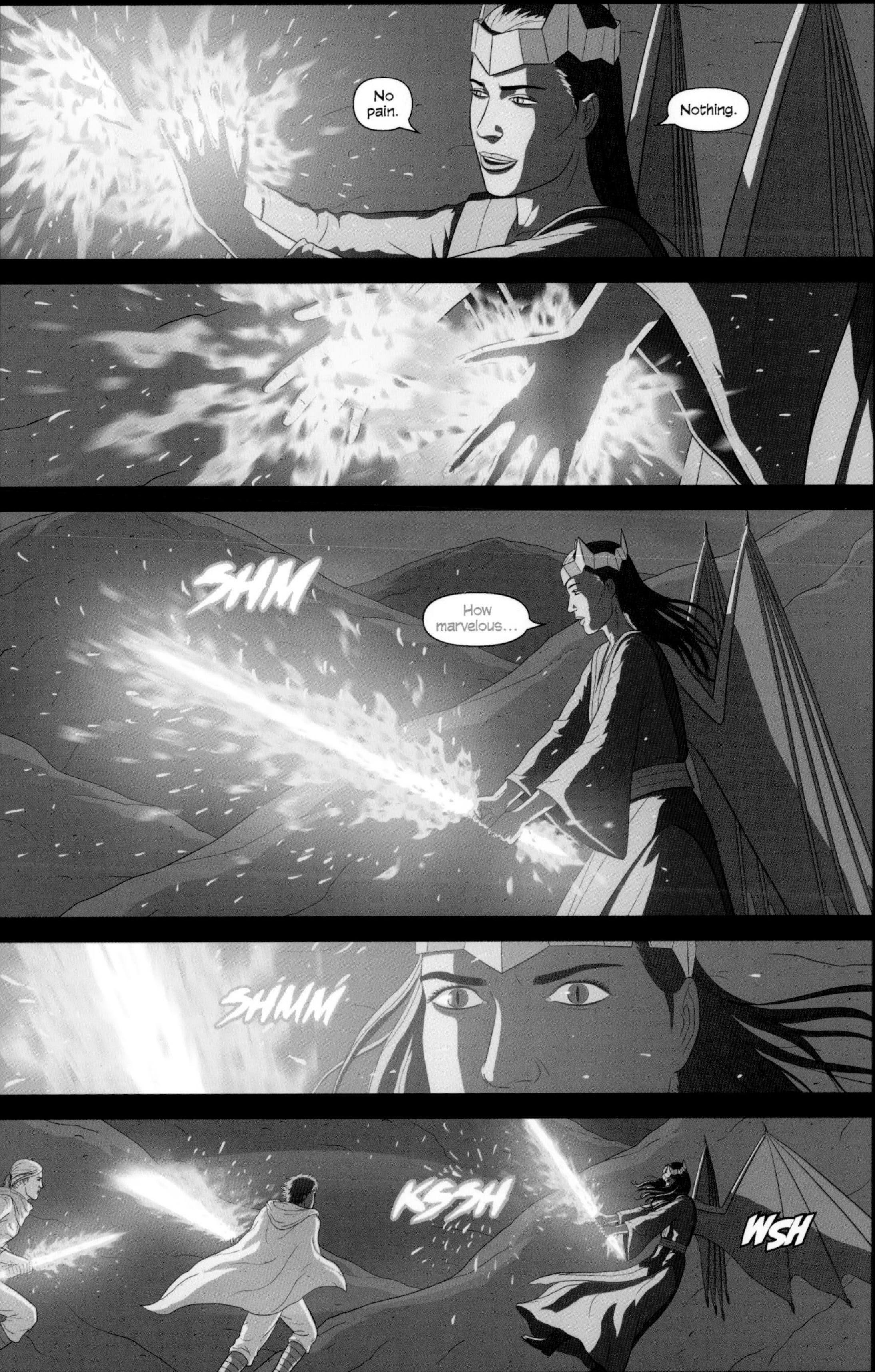
No pain.
Nothing.
SHM
How marvelous...
SHMM
KSSH
WSH

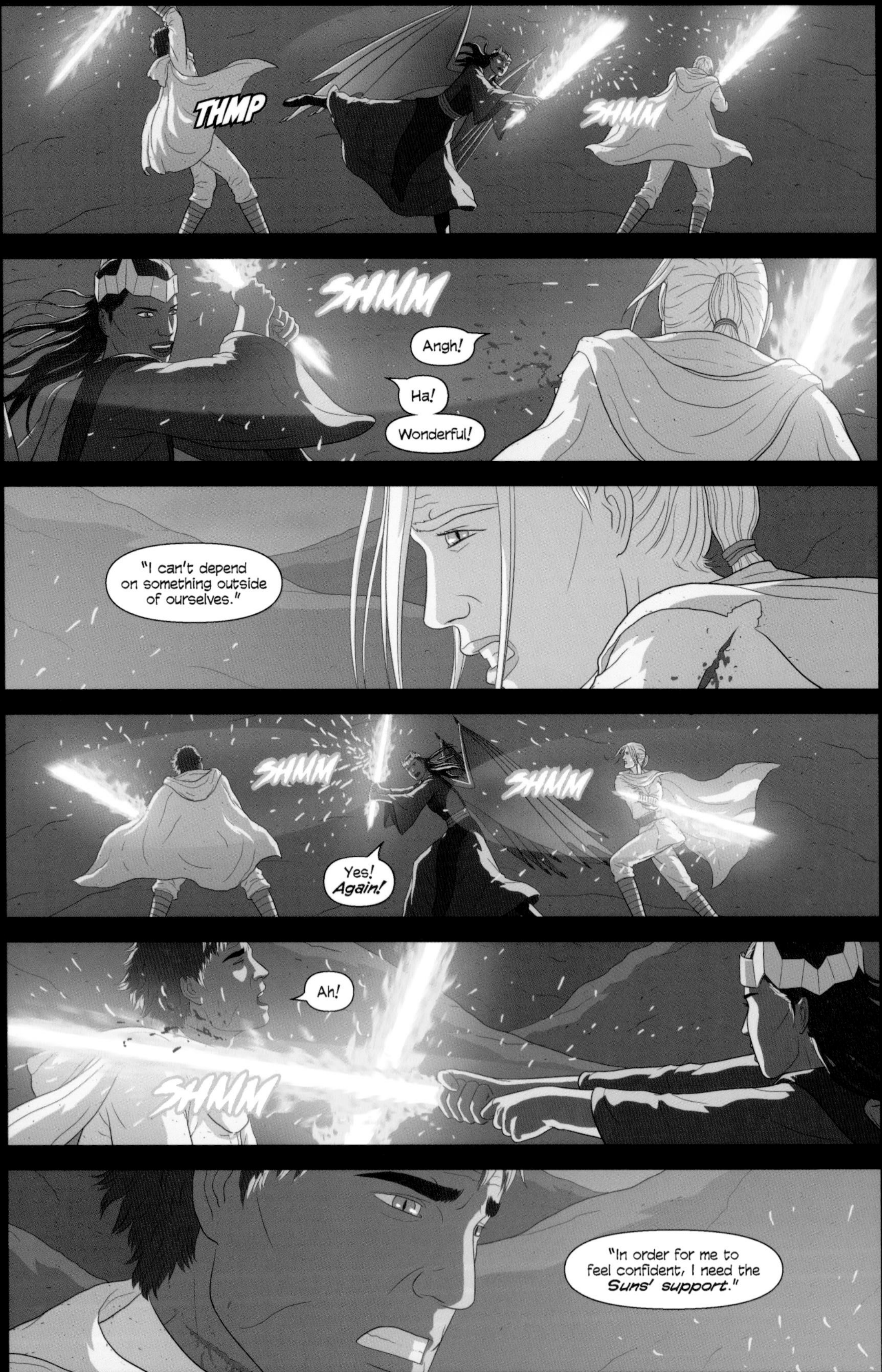
THMP
SHMM
SHMM
Angh!
Ha!
Wonderful!
"I can't depend on something outside of ourselves."
SHMM
SHMM
Yes! Again!
Ah!
SHMM
"In order for me to feel confident, I need the Suns' support."

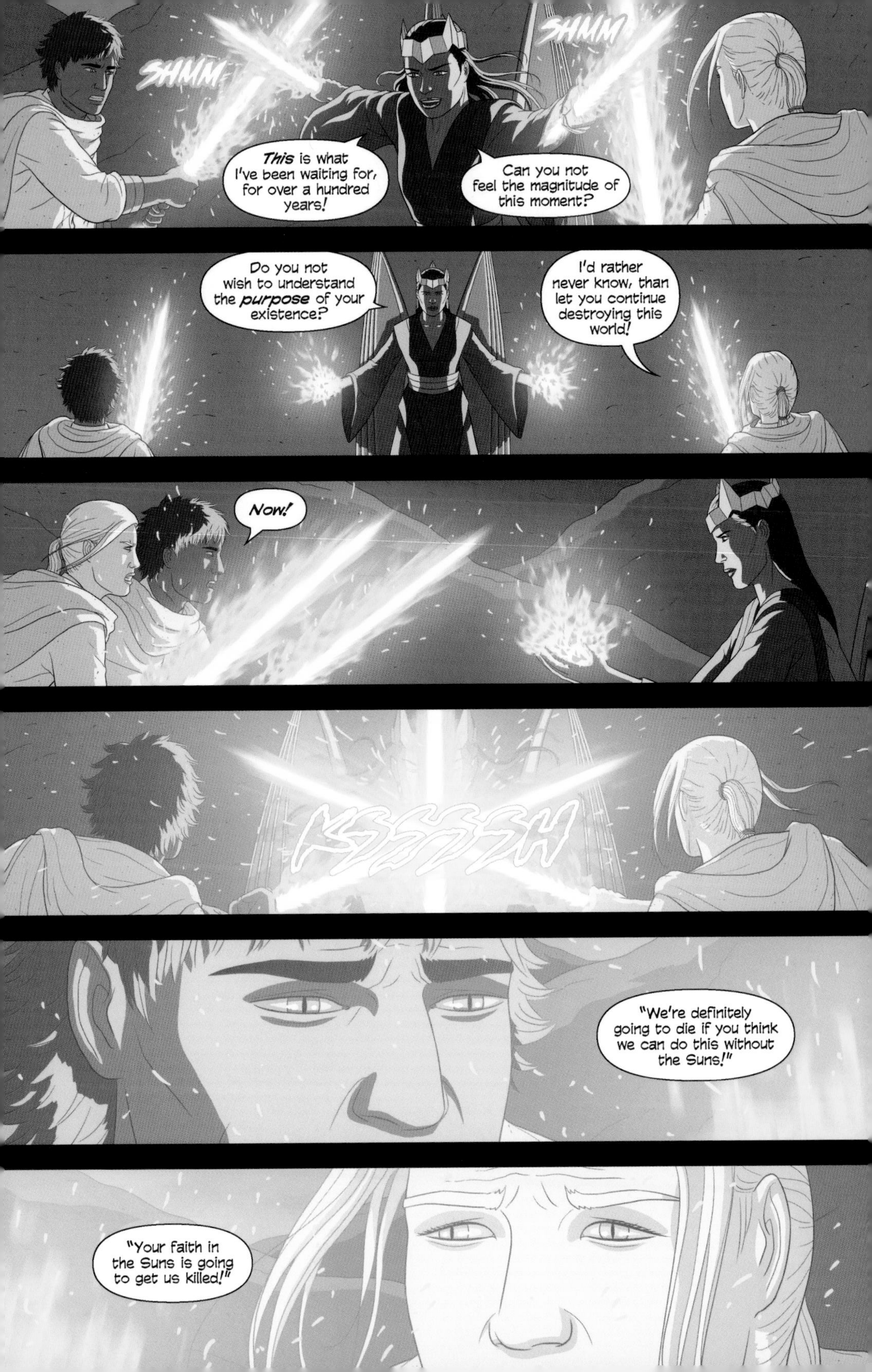
SHMM
SHMM
This is what I've been waiting for, for over a hundred years!
Can you not feel the magnitude of this moment?
Do you not wish to understand the *purpose* of your existence?
I'd rather never know, than let you continue destroying this world!
Now!
KSSSSH
"We're definitely going to die if you think we can do this without the Suns!"
"Your faith in the Suns is going to get us killed!"

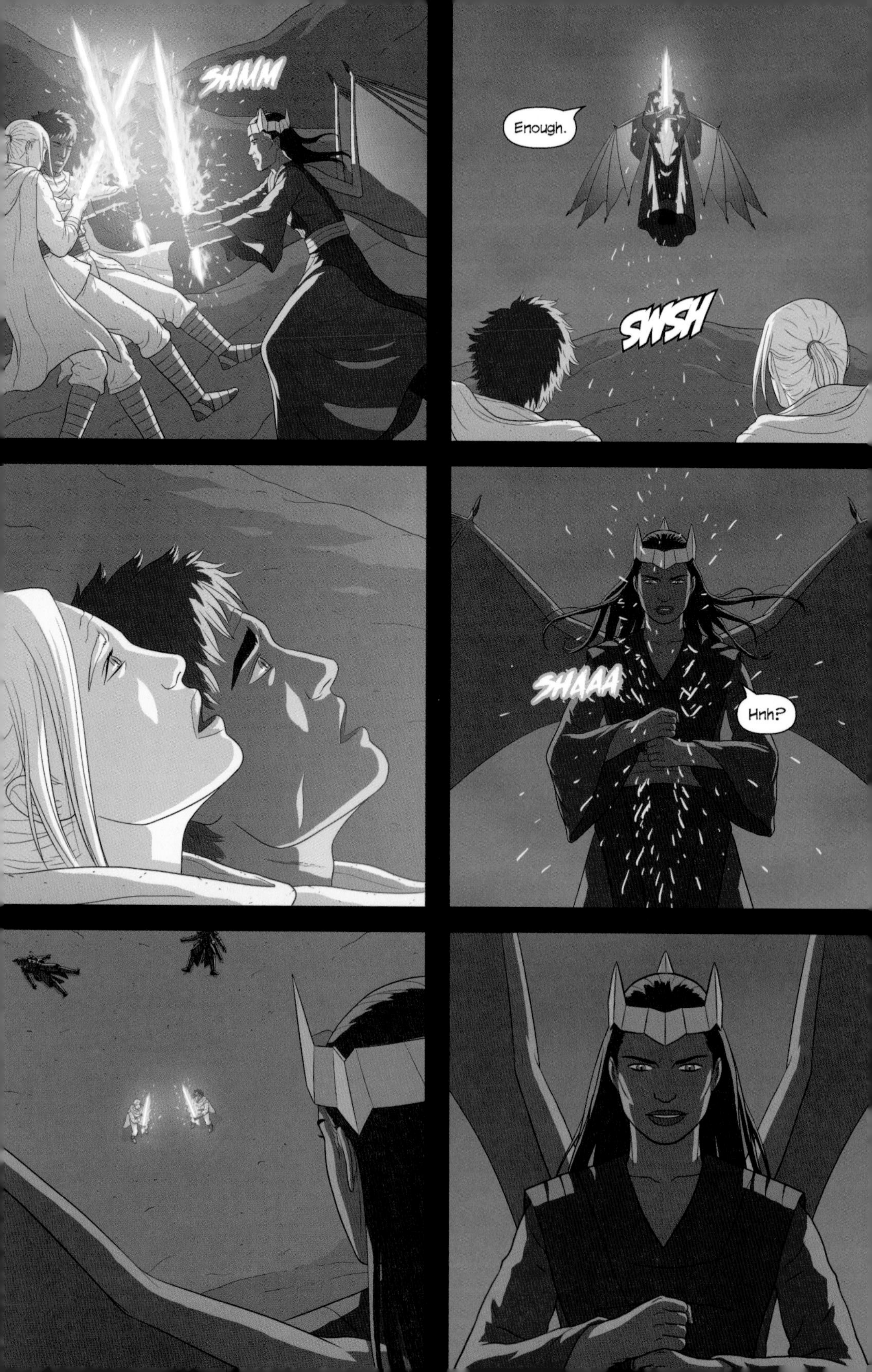
SHMM
Enough.
SWSH
SHAAA
Hnh?

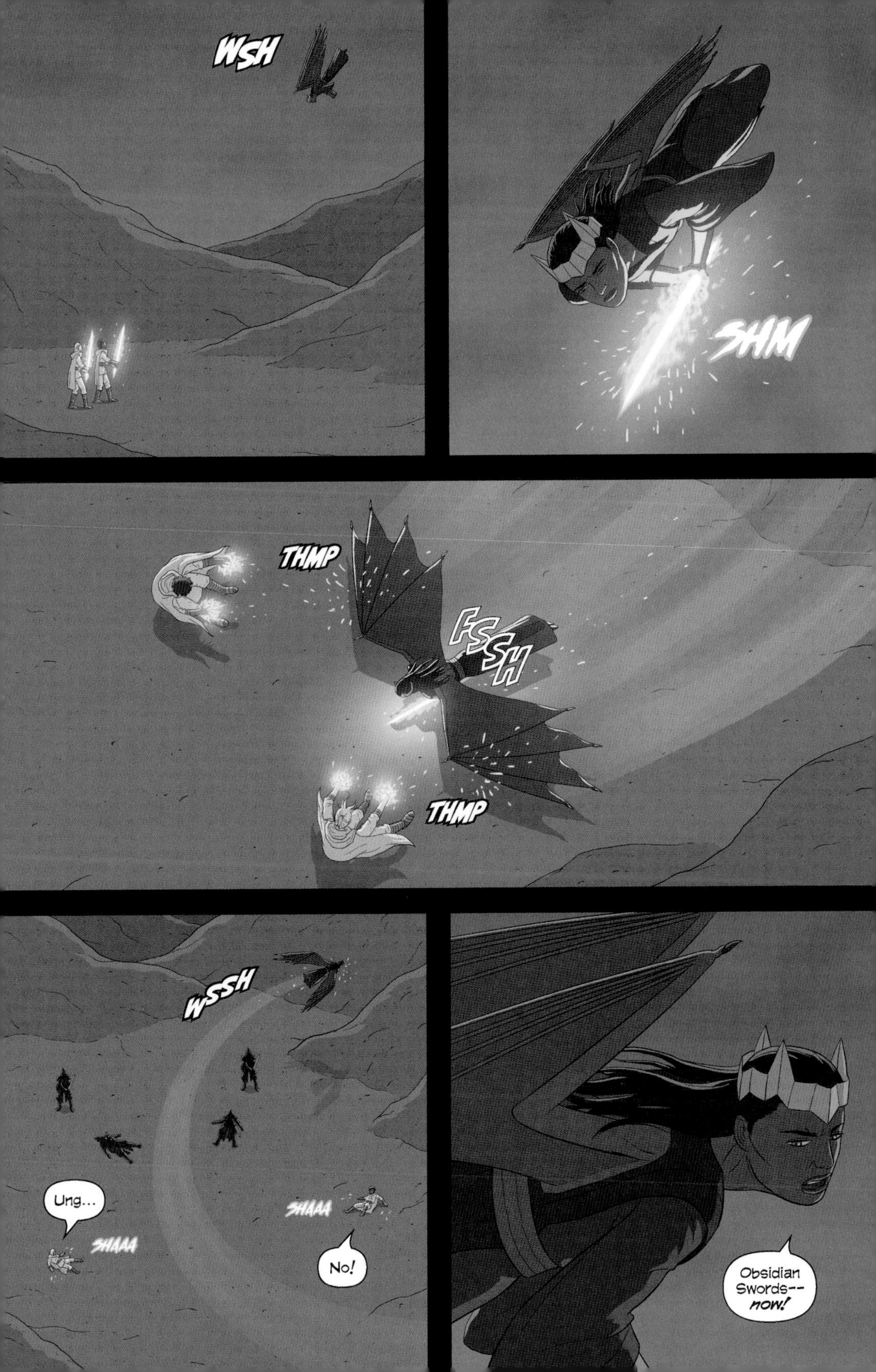
WSH
SHM
THMP
FSSH
THMP
WSSH
Ung...
SHAAA
SHAAA
No!
Obsidian Swords--now!

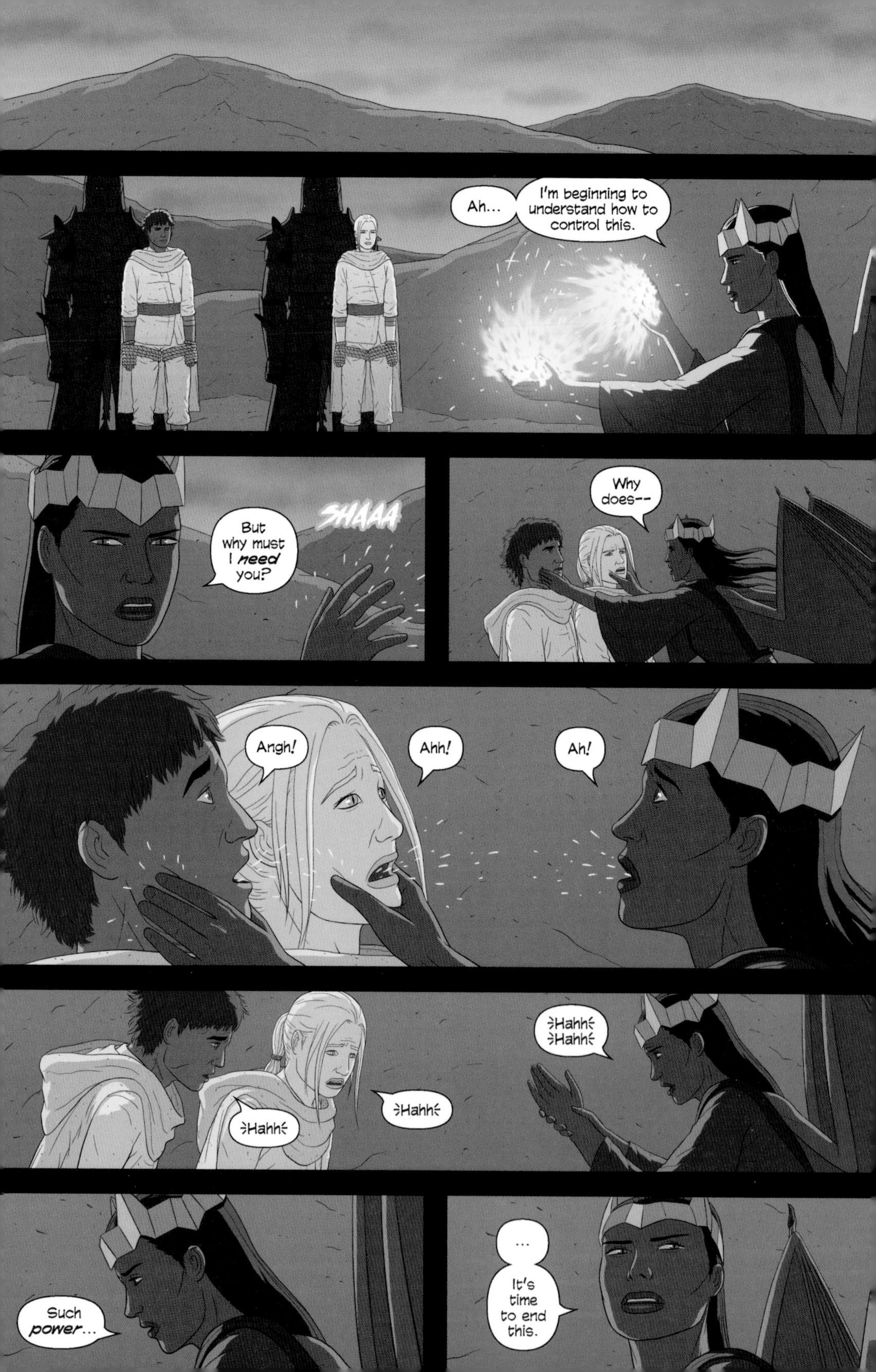
Ah...
I'm beginning to understand how to control this.
SHAAA
But why must I need you?
Why does--
Angh!
Ahh!
Ah!
Hahh Hahh
Hahh
Hahh
Such power...
...
It's time to end this.

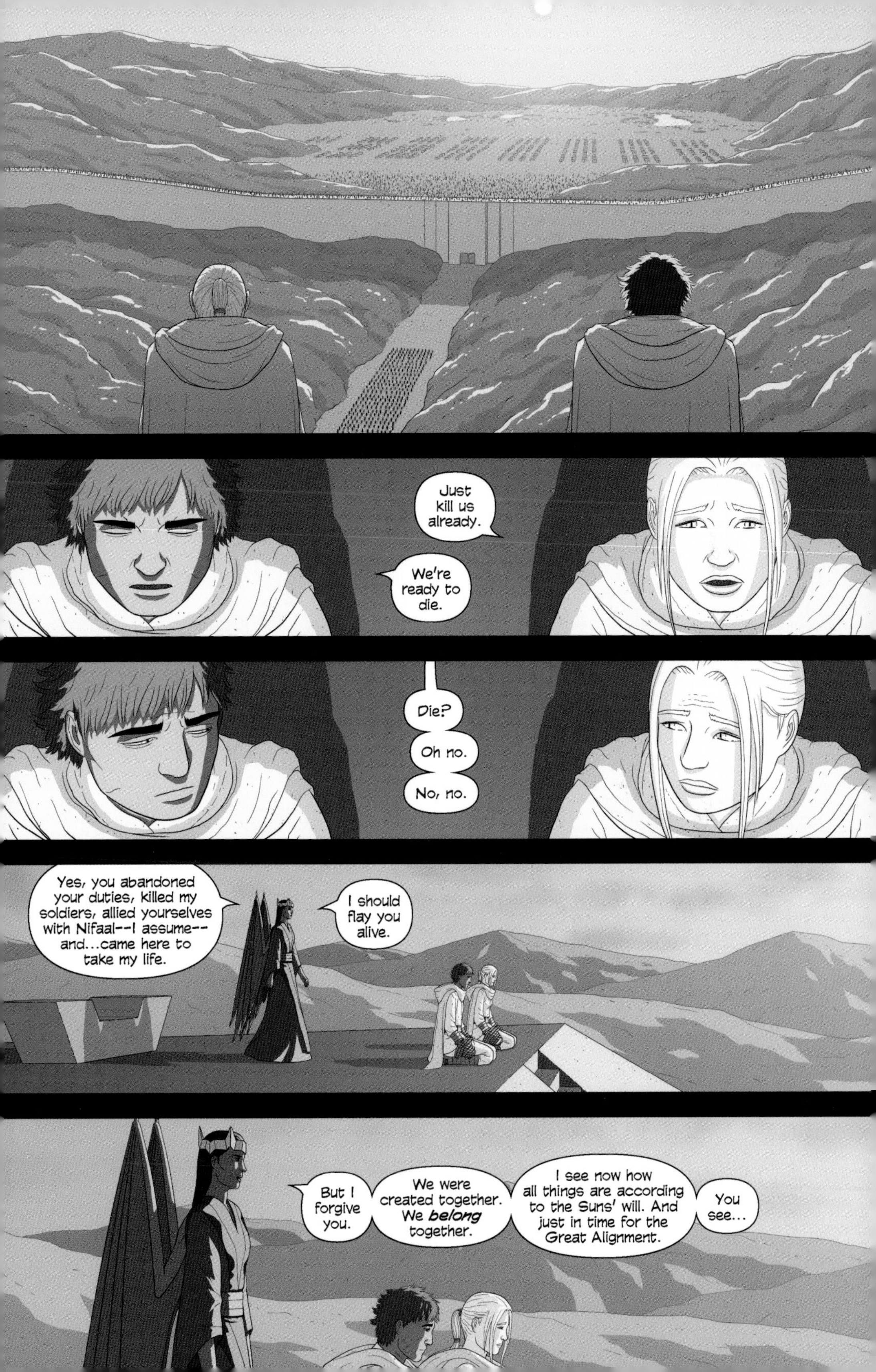
Just kill us already.
We're ready to die.
Die?
Oh no.
No, no.
Yes, you abandoned your duties, killed my soldiers, allied yourselves with Nifaal--I assume--and...came here to take my life.
I should flay you alive.
But I forgive you.
We were created together. We *belong* together.
I see now how all things are according to the Suns' will. And just in time for the Great Alignment.
You see...

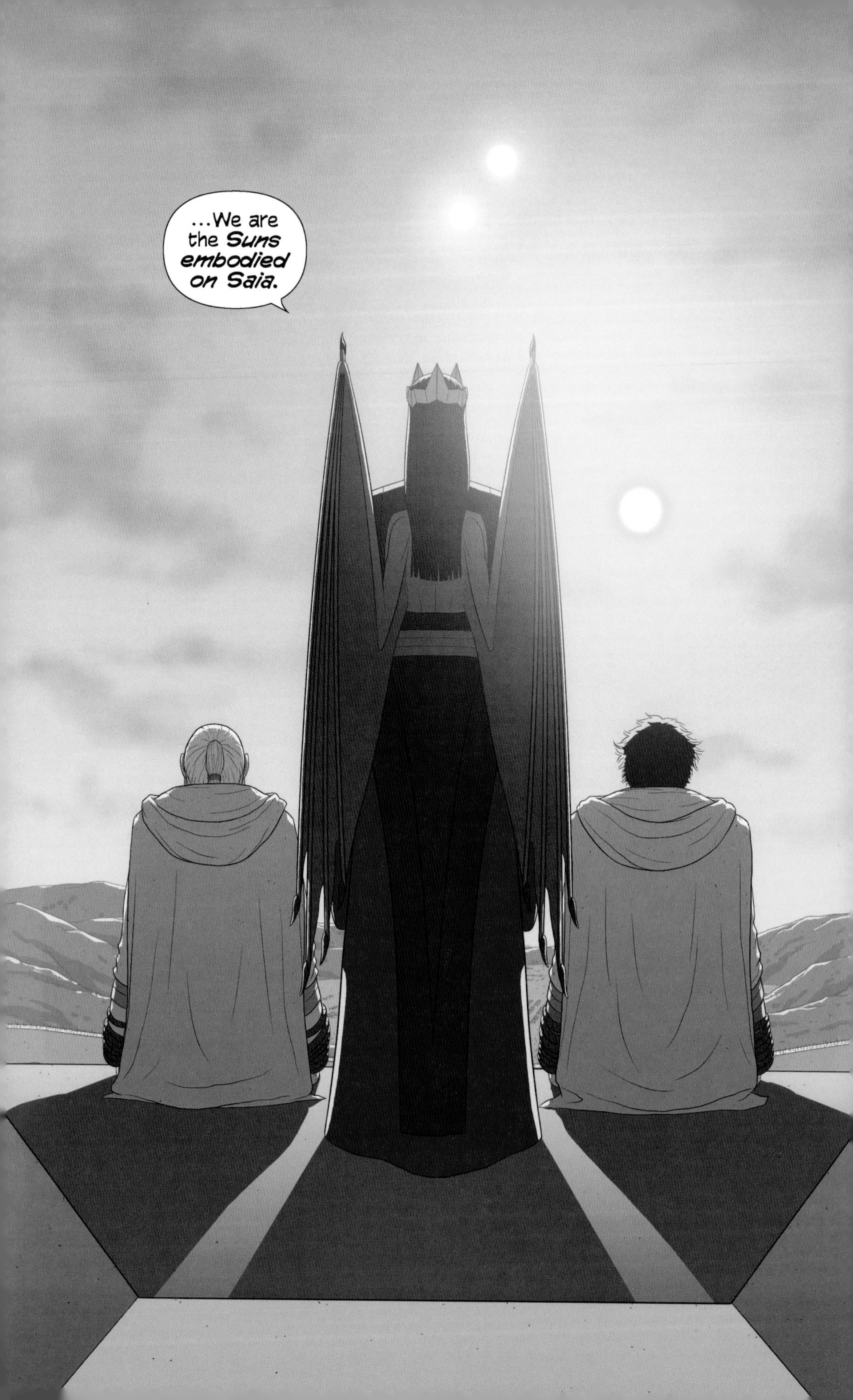
...We are the *Suns* *embodied* *on Saia*.

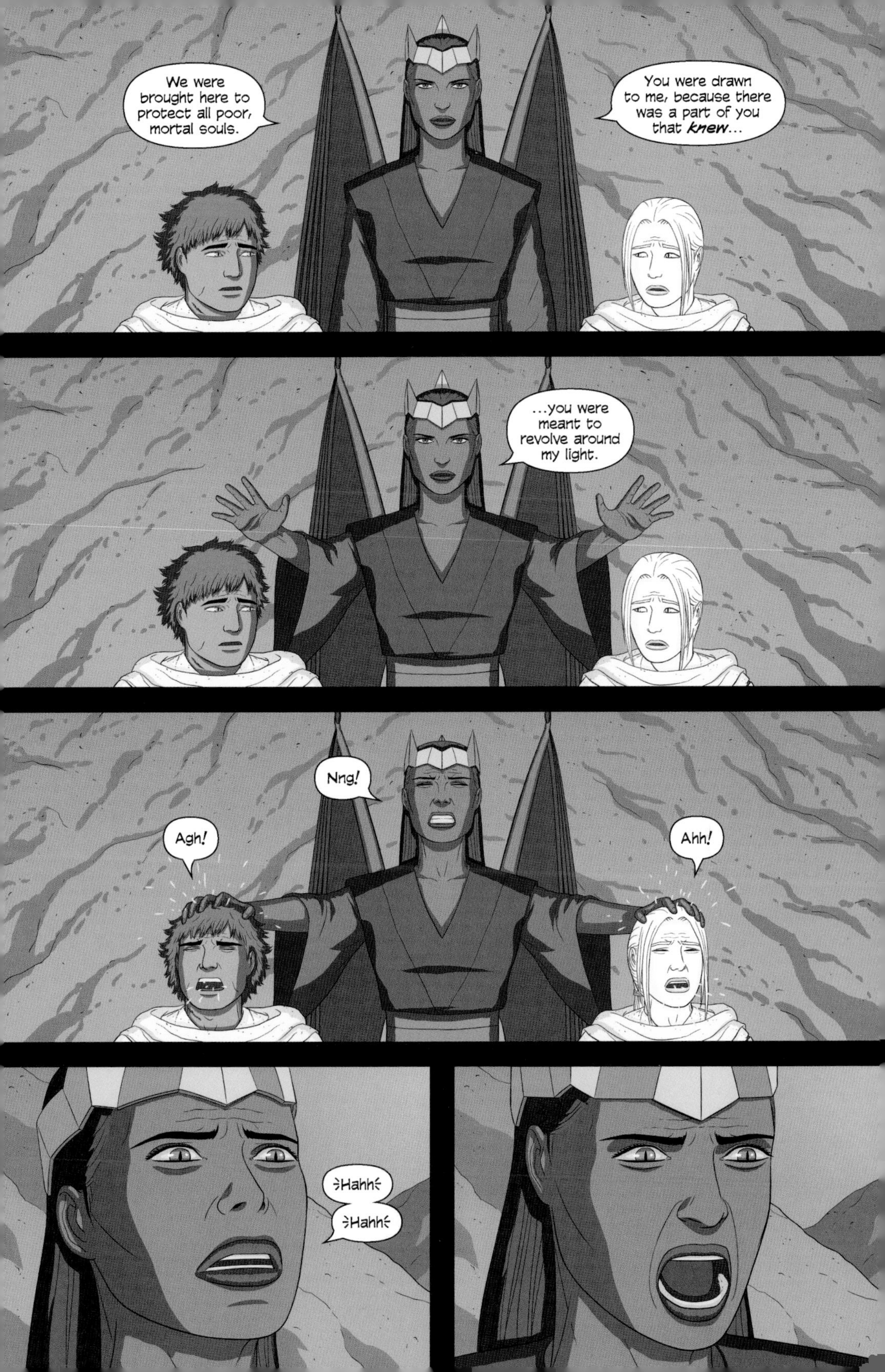
We were brought here to protect all poor, mortal souls.
You were drawn to me, because there was a part of you that *knew*...
...you were meant to revolve around my light.
Nng!
Agh!
Ahh!
Hahh
Hahh

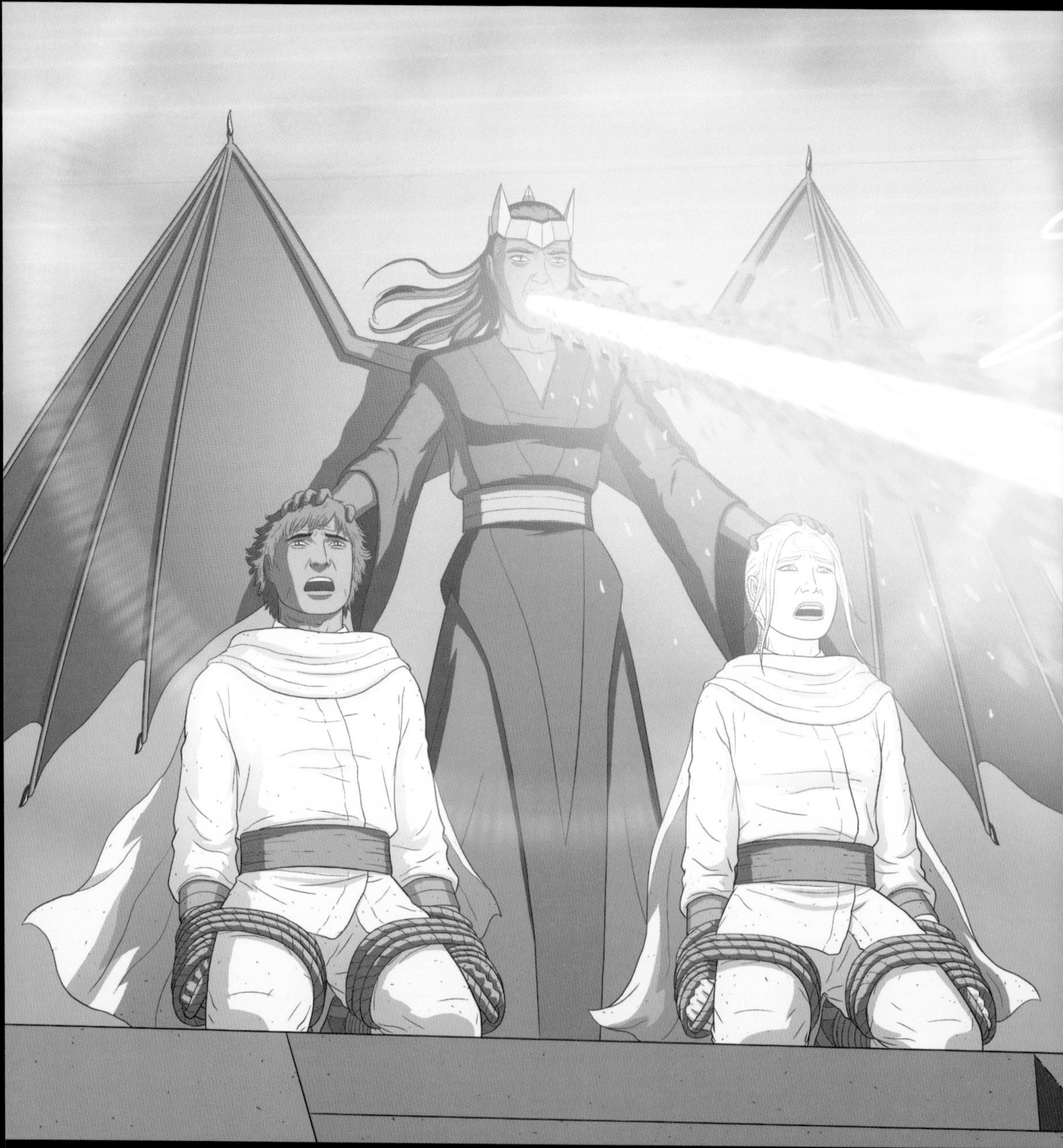

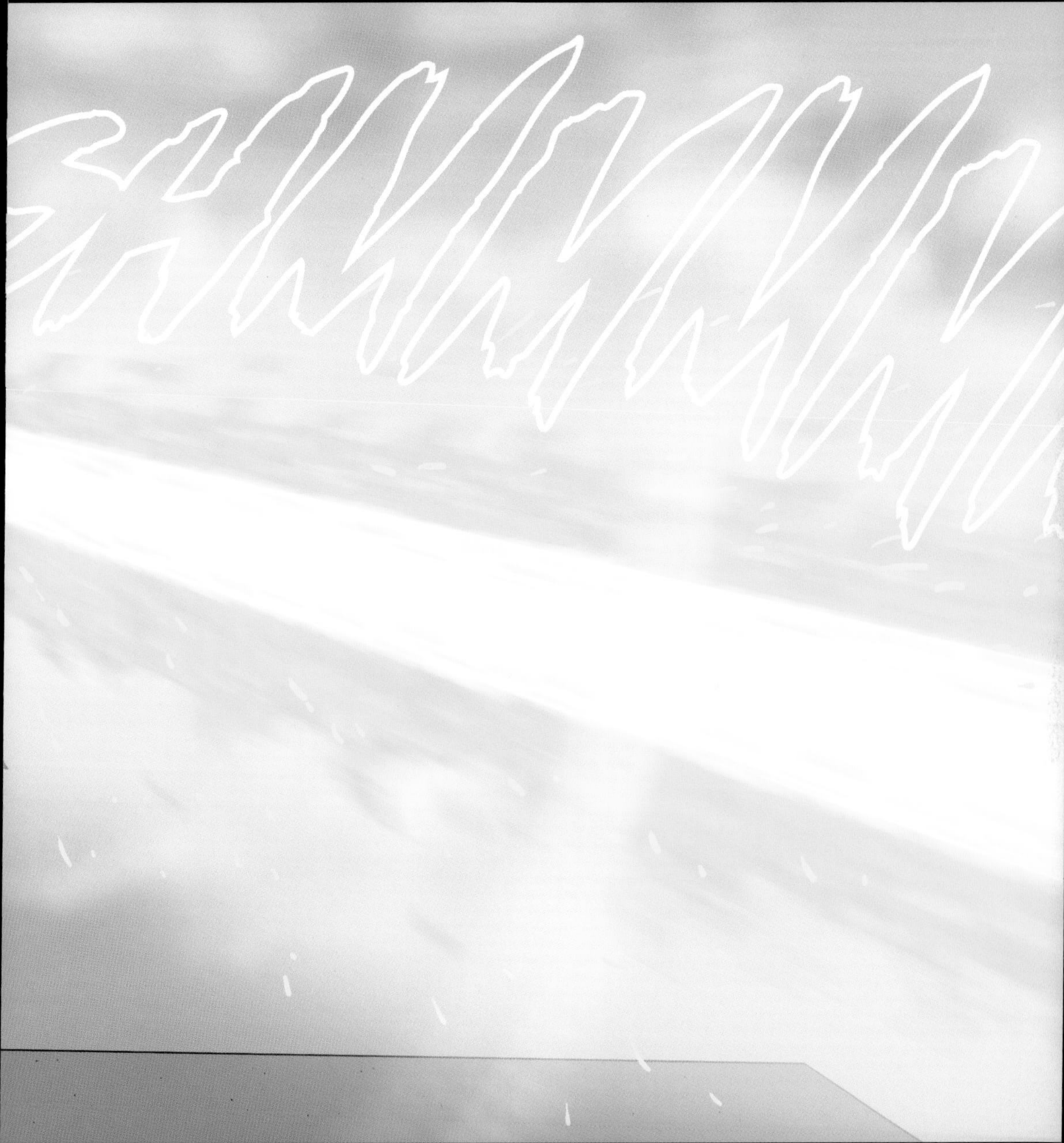

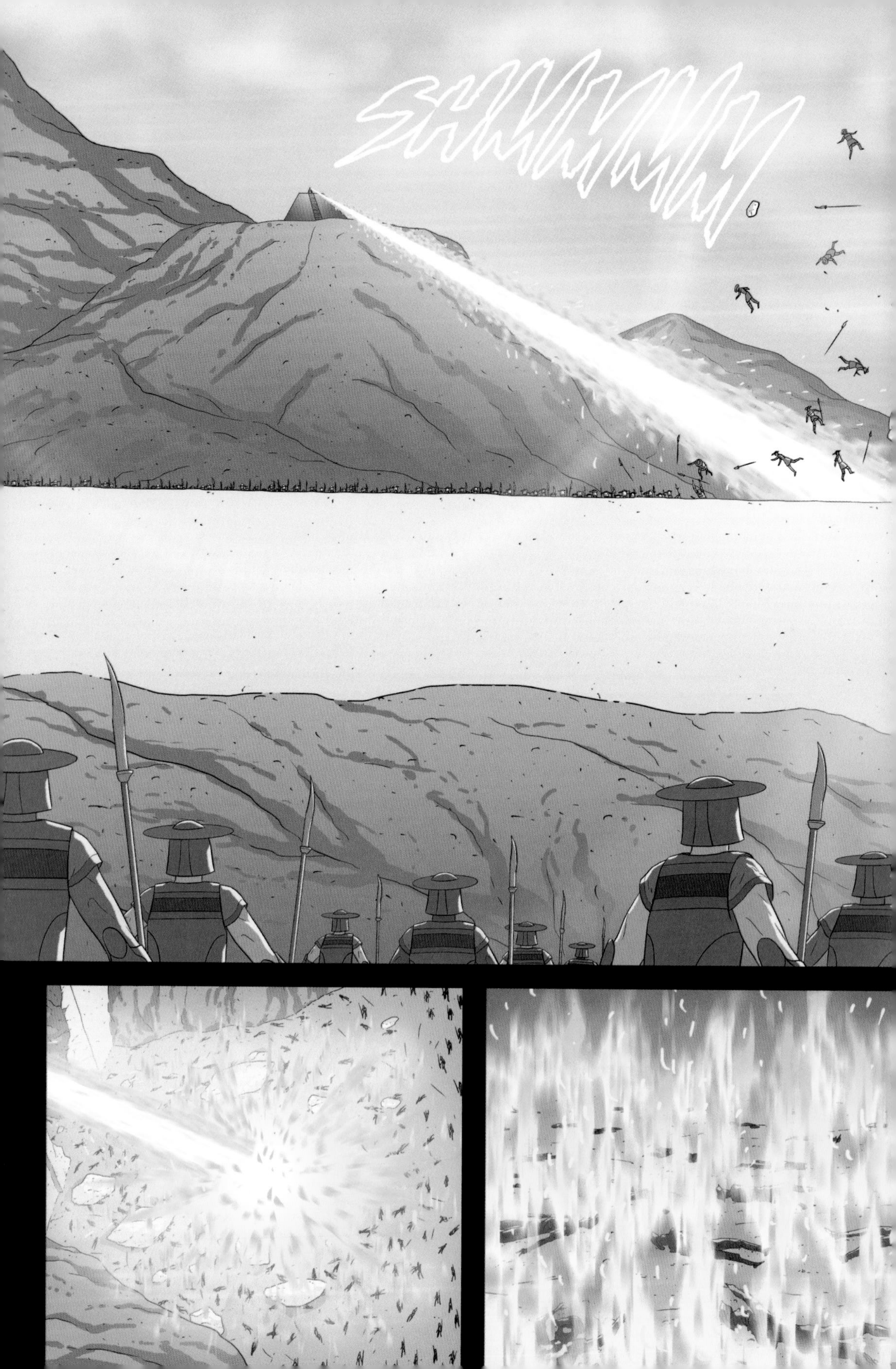

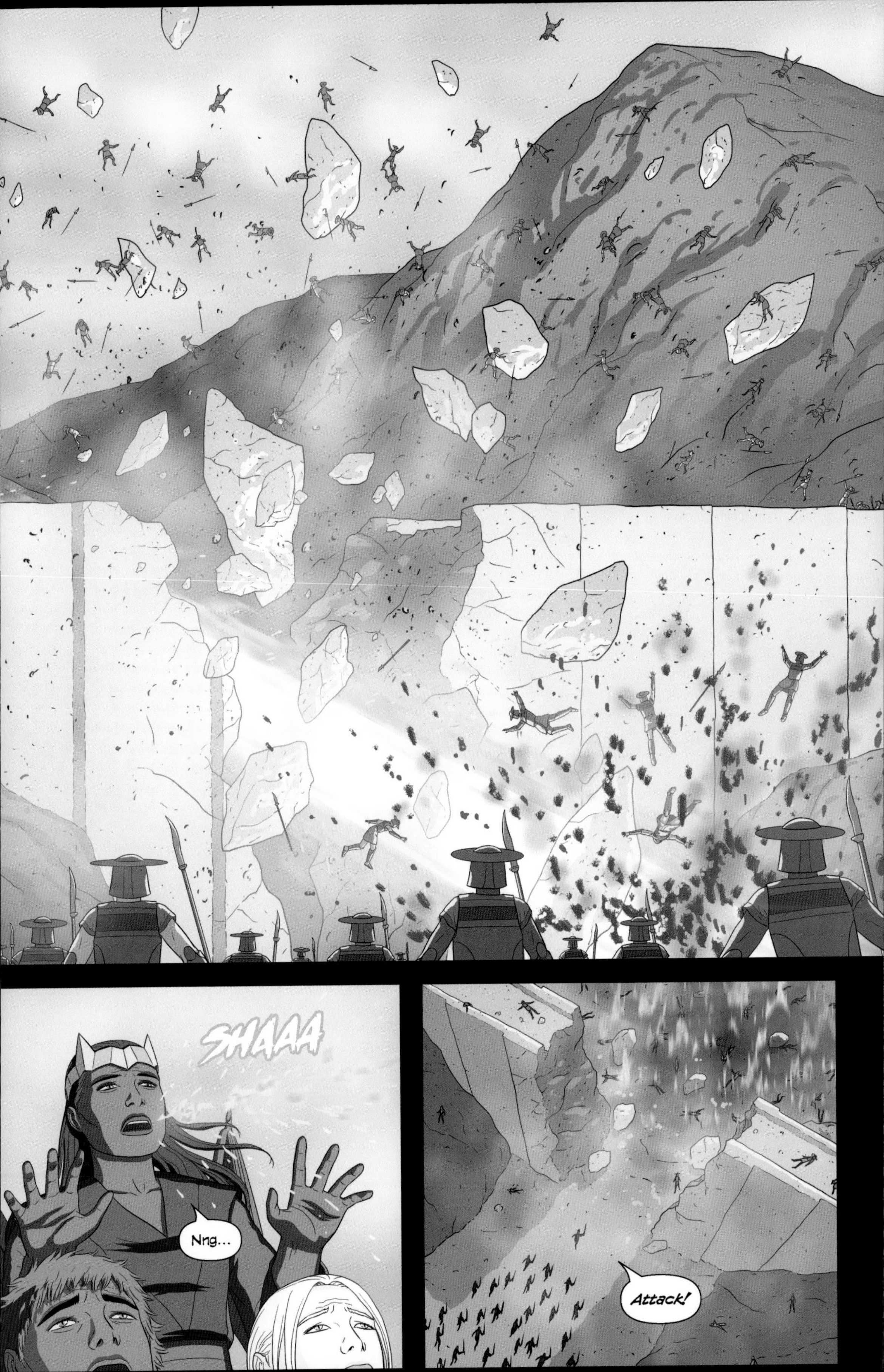
SHAAA
Nng...
Attack!

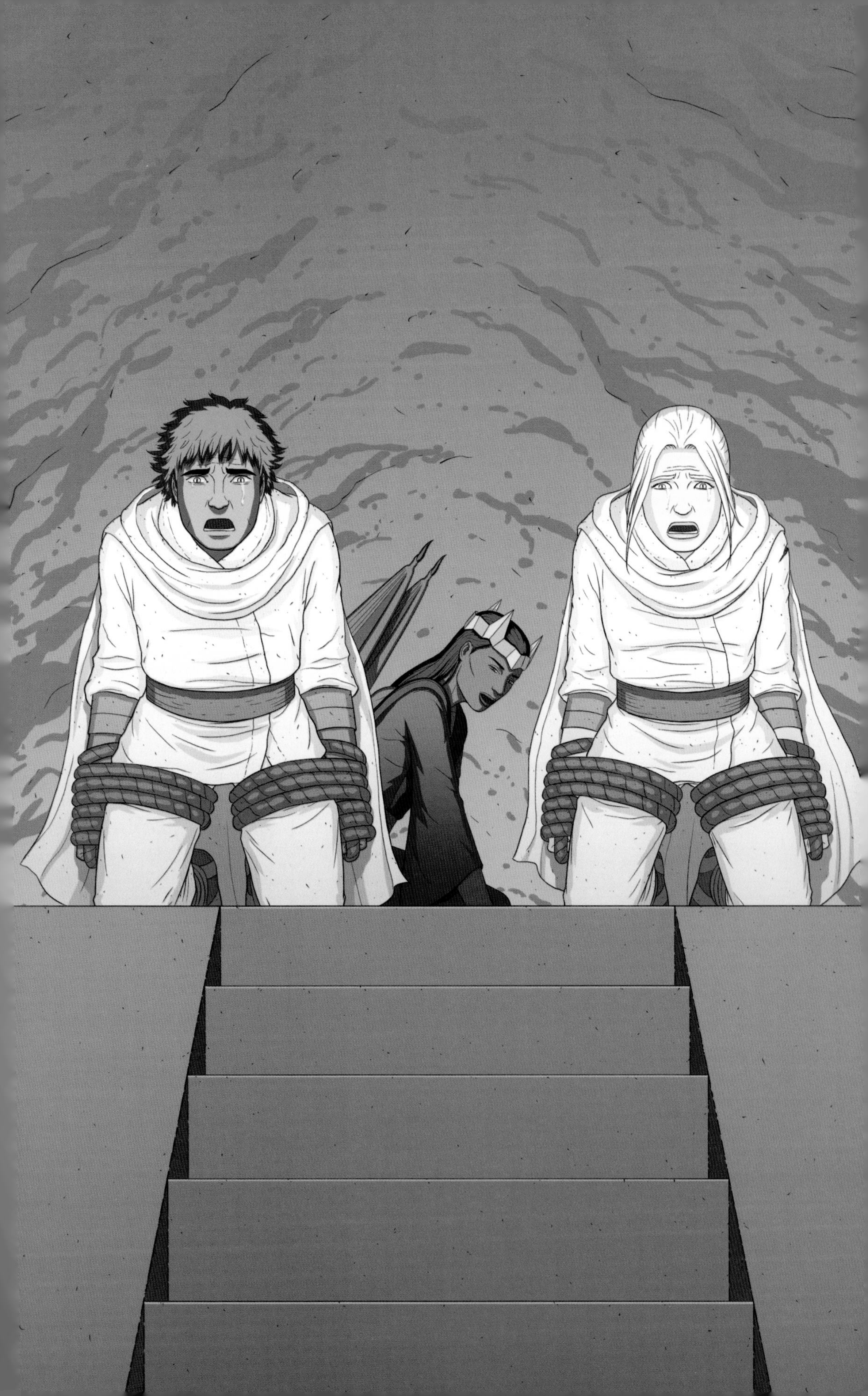

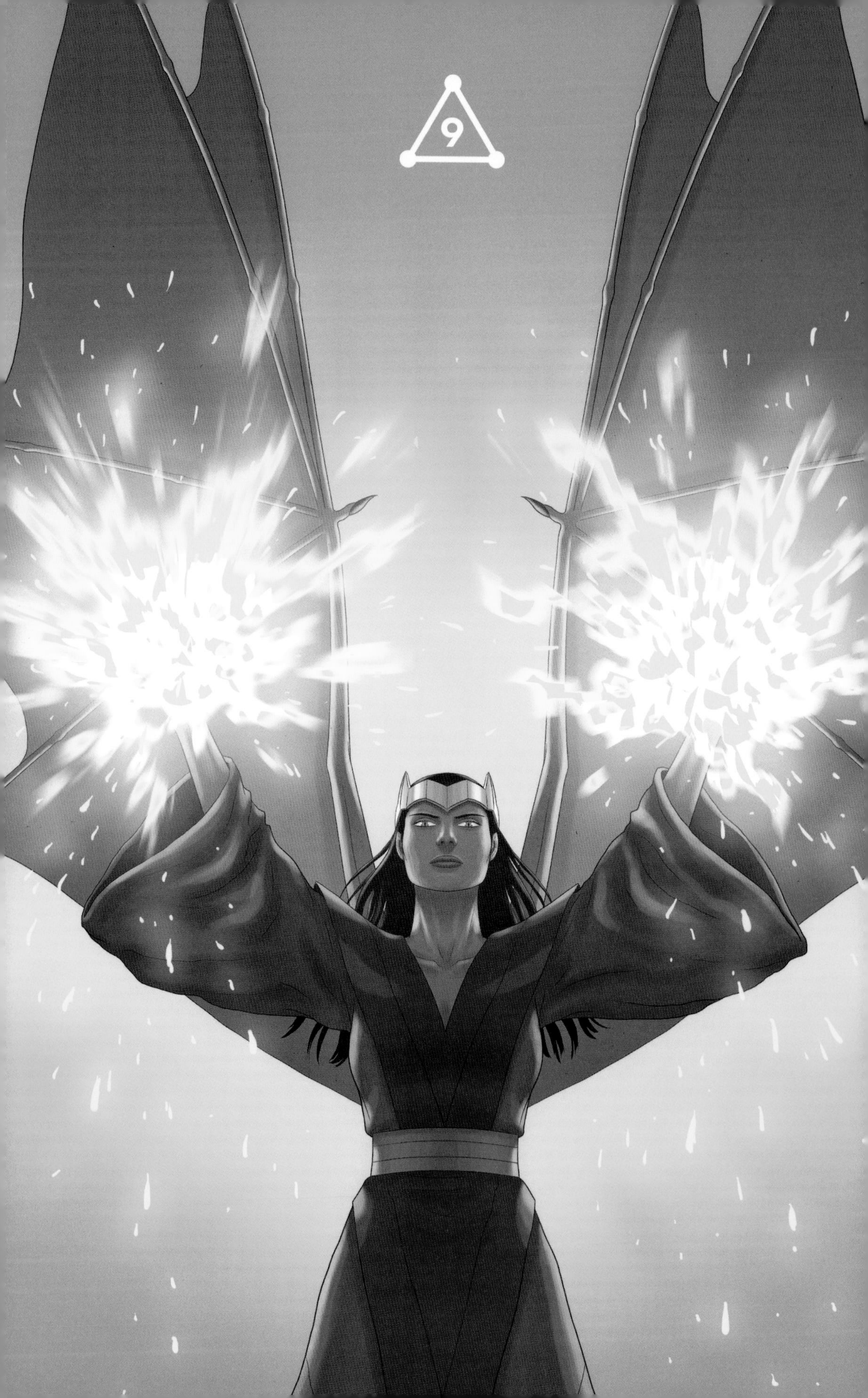
9

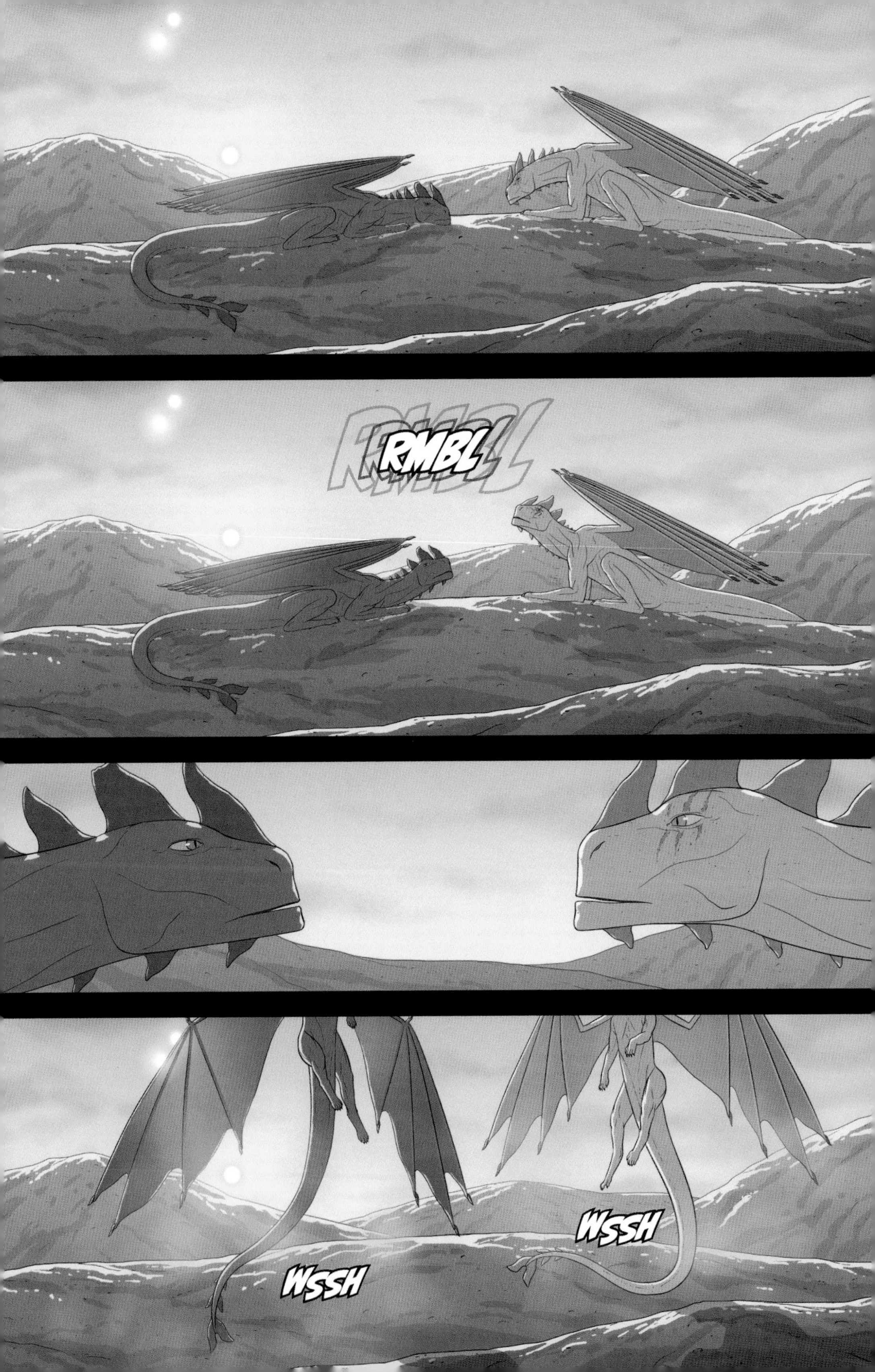
RMBL
RMBL
WSSH
WSSH

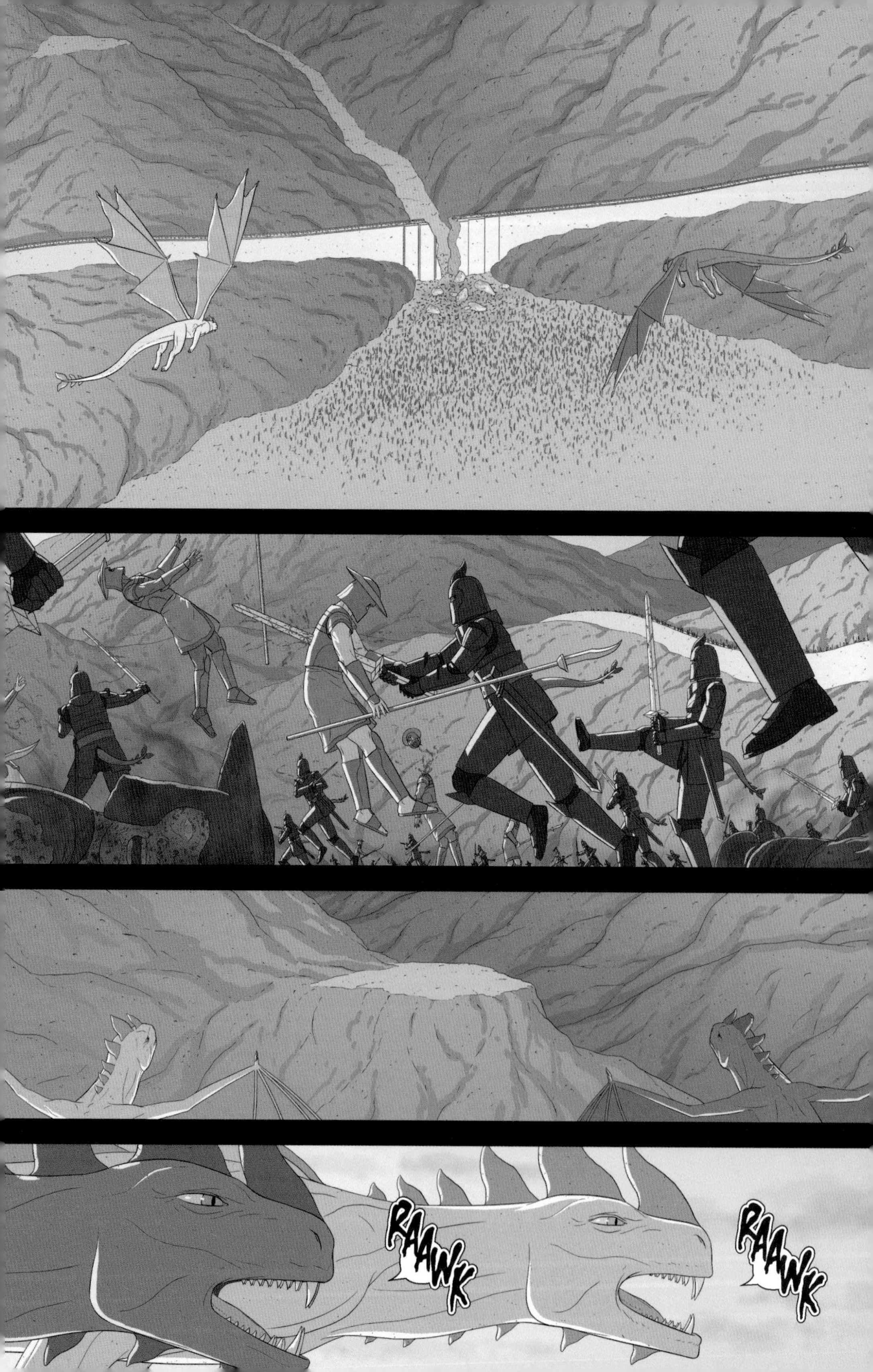
RAAWK
RAAWK

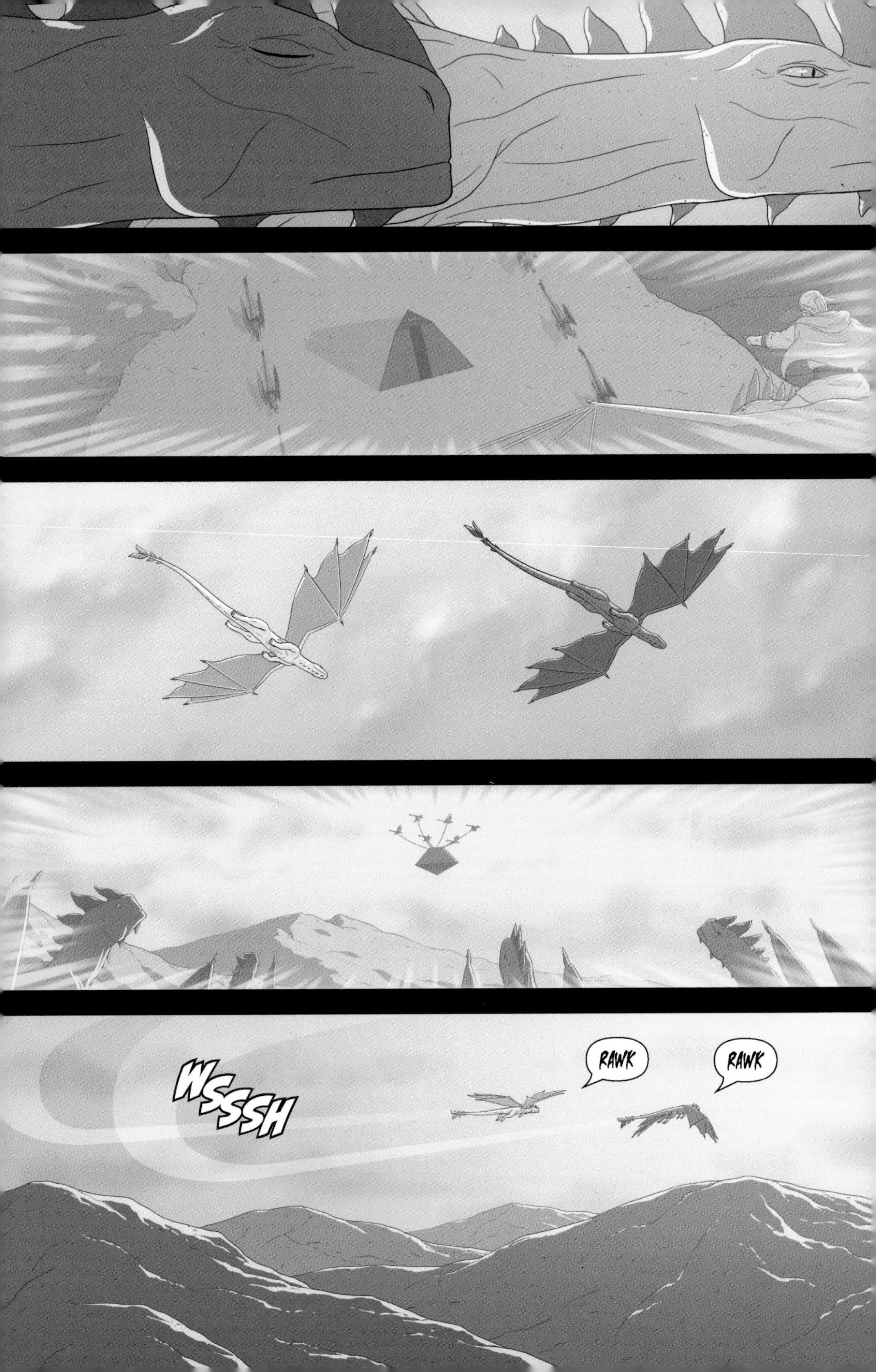
WSSSH
RAWK
RAWK

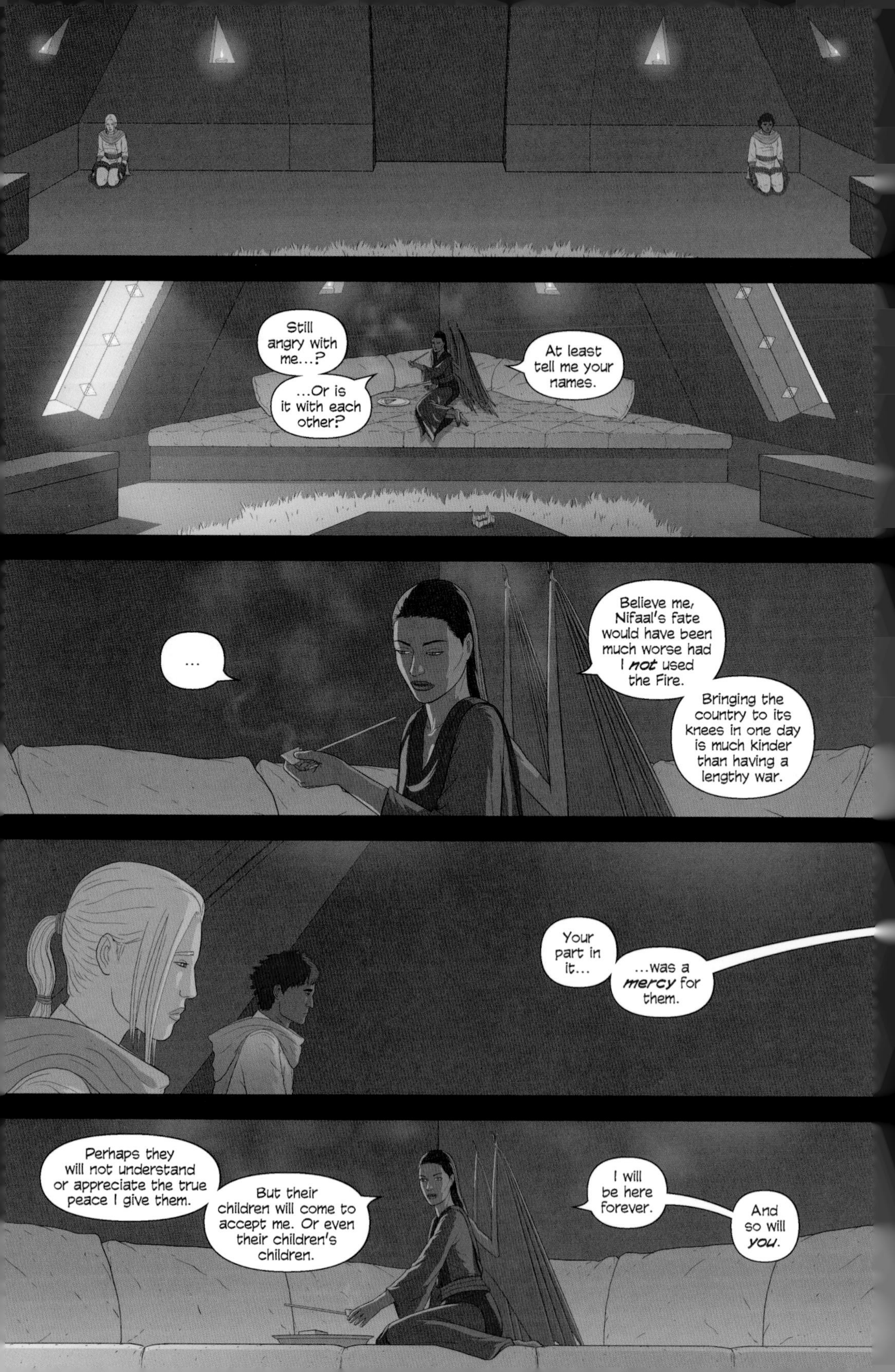
Still angry with me...?
...Or is it with each other?
At least tell me your names.
...
Believe me, Nifaal's fate would have been much worse had I *not* used the Fire.
Bringing the country to its knees in one day is much kinder than having a lengthy war.
Your part in it...
...was a *mercy* for them.
Perhaps they will not understand or appreciate the true peace I give them.
But their children will come to accept me. Or even their children's children.
I will be here forever.
And so will *you*.

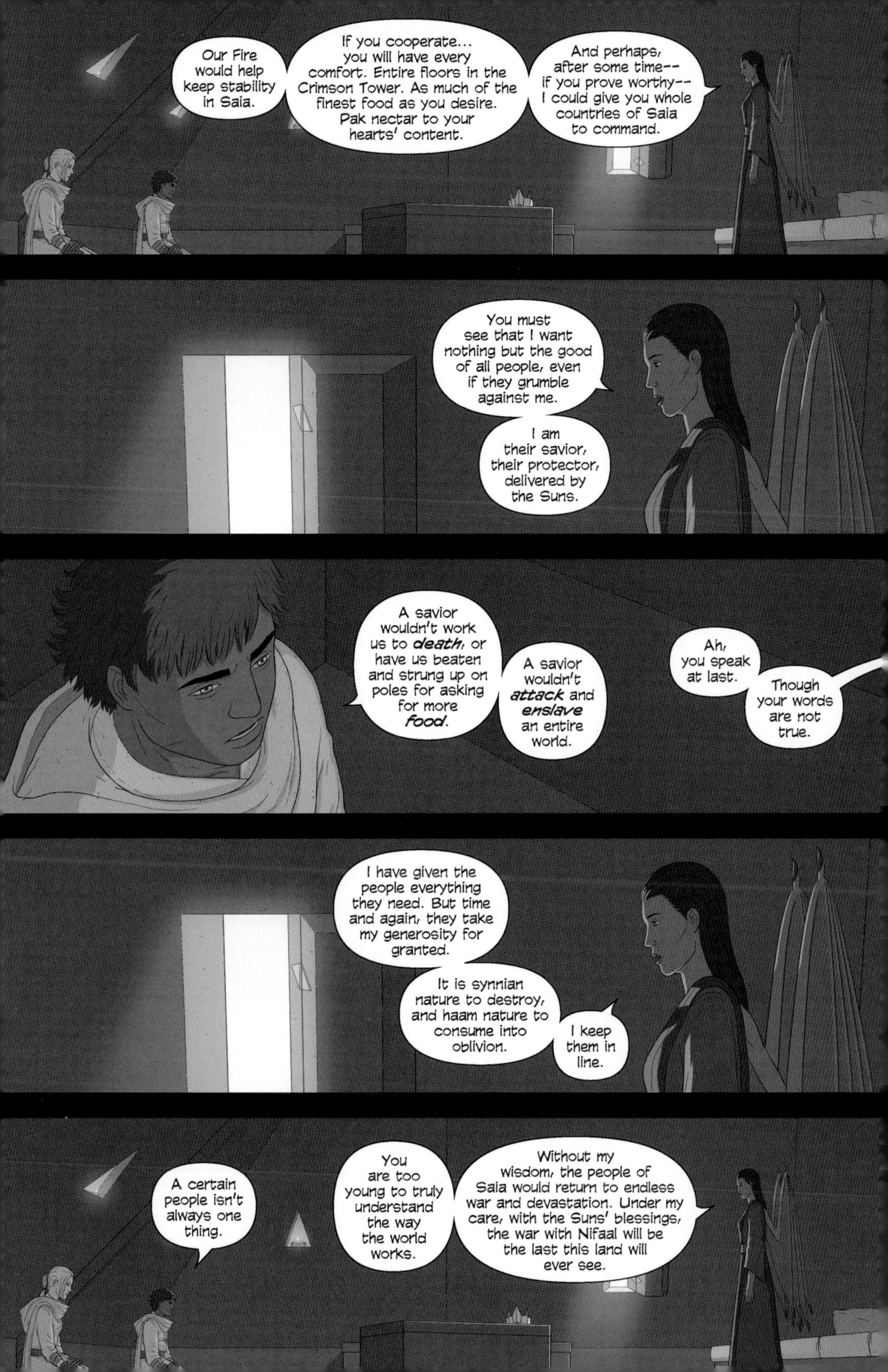
Our Fire would help keep stability in Saia.
If you cooperate... you will have every comfort. Entire floors in the Crimson Tower. As much of the finest food as you desire. Pak nectar to your hearts' content.
And perhaps, after some time-- if you prove worthy-- I could give you whole countries of Saia to command.
You must see that I want nothing but the good of all people, even if they grumble against me.
I am their savior, their protector, delivered by the Suns.
A savior wouldn't work us to *death*, or have us beaten and strung up on poles for asking for more *food*.
A savior wouldn't *attack* and *enslave* an entire world.
Ah, you speak at last.
Though your words are not true.
I have given the people everything they need. But time and again, they take my generosity for granted.
It is synnian nature to destroy, and haam nature to consume into oblivion.
I keep them in line.
A certain people isn't always one thing.
You are too young to truly understand the way the world works.
Without my wisdom, the people of Saia would return to endless war and devastation. Under my care, with the Suns' blessings, the war with Nifaal will be the last this land will ever see.

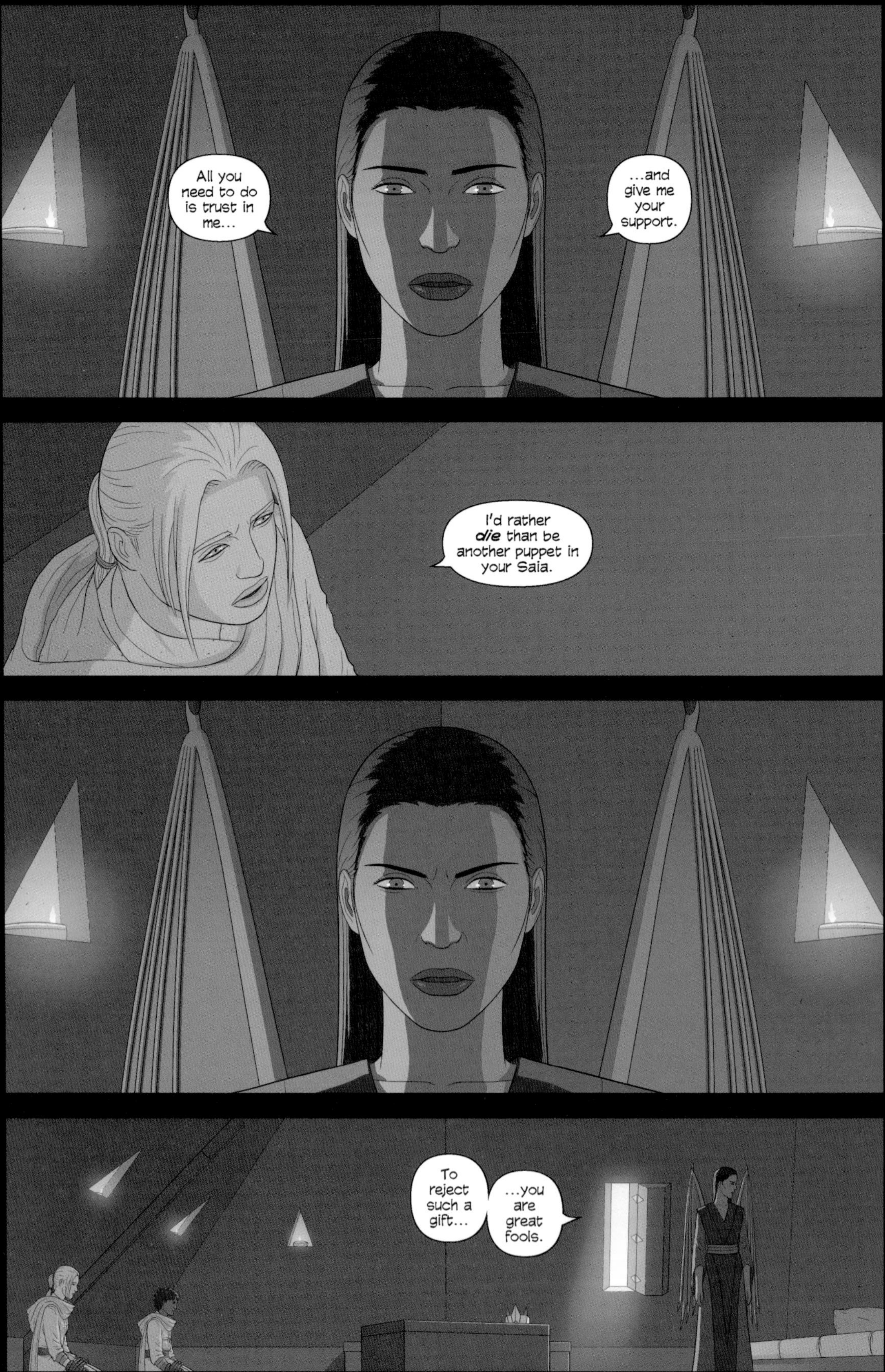
All you need to do is trust in me...
...and give me your support.
I'd rather *die* than be another puppet in your Saia.
To reject such a gift...
...you are great fools.

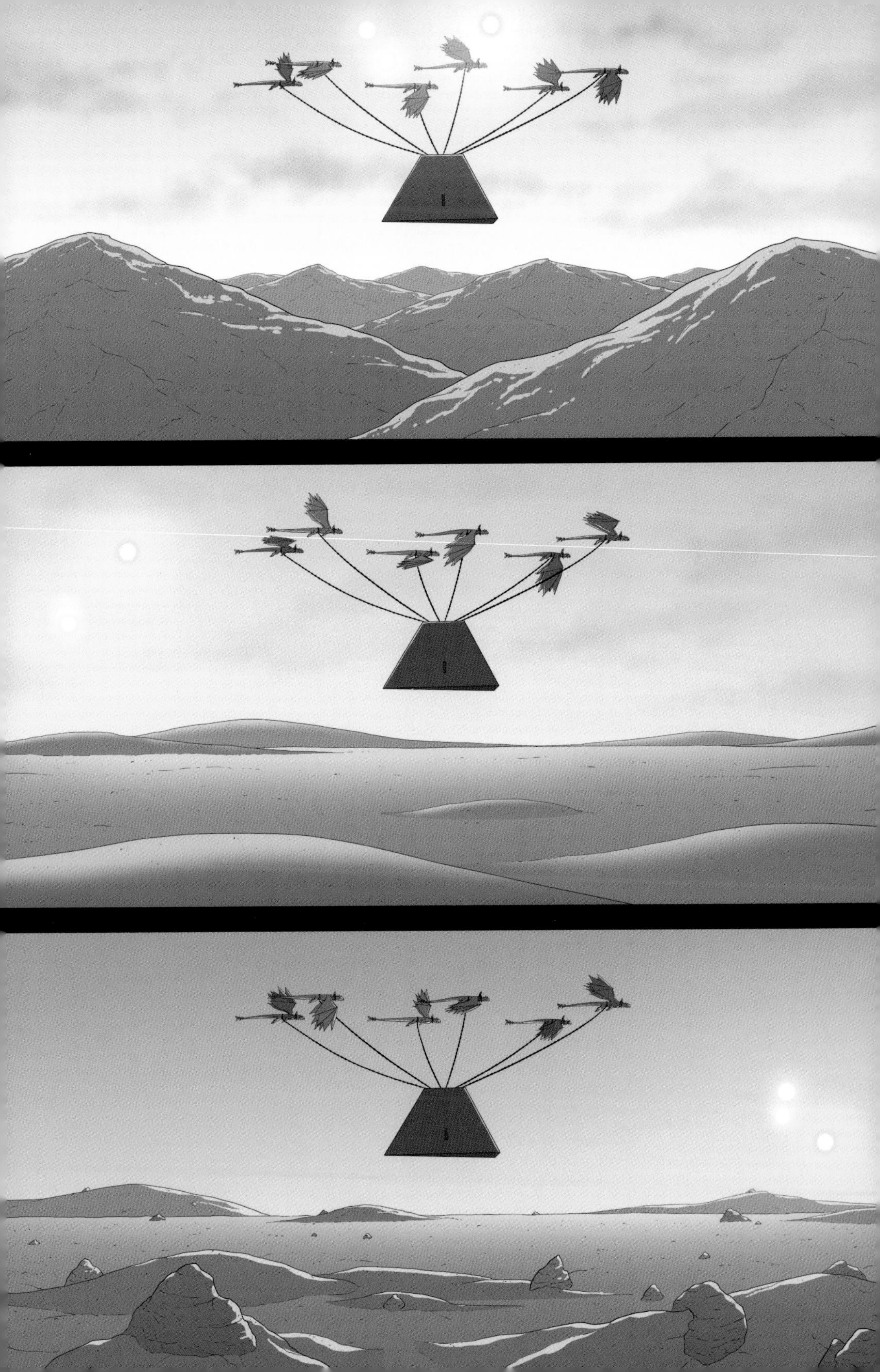

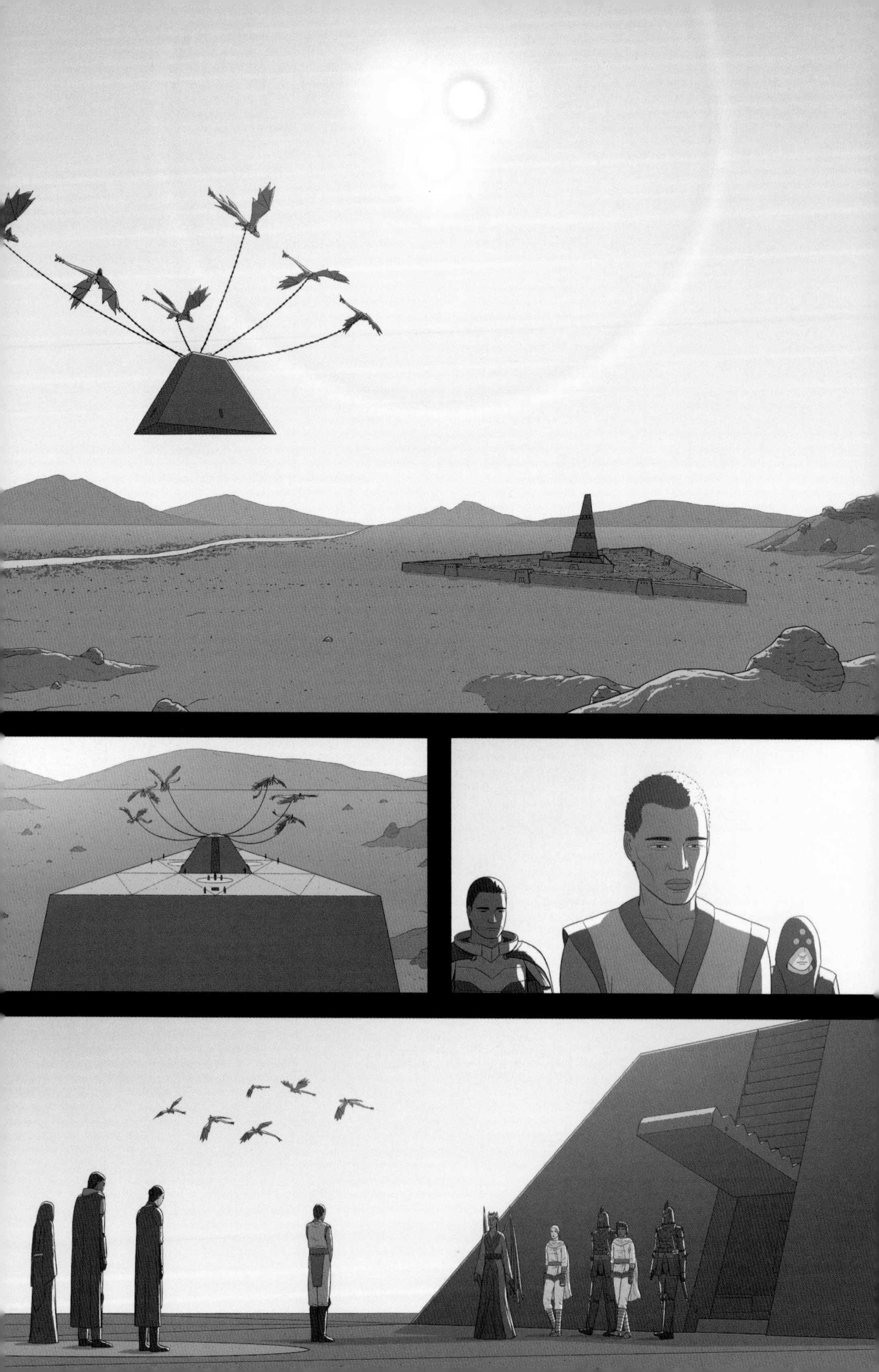

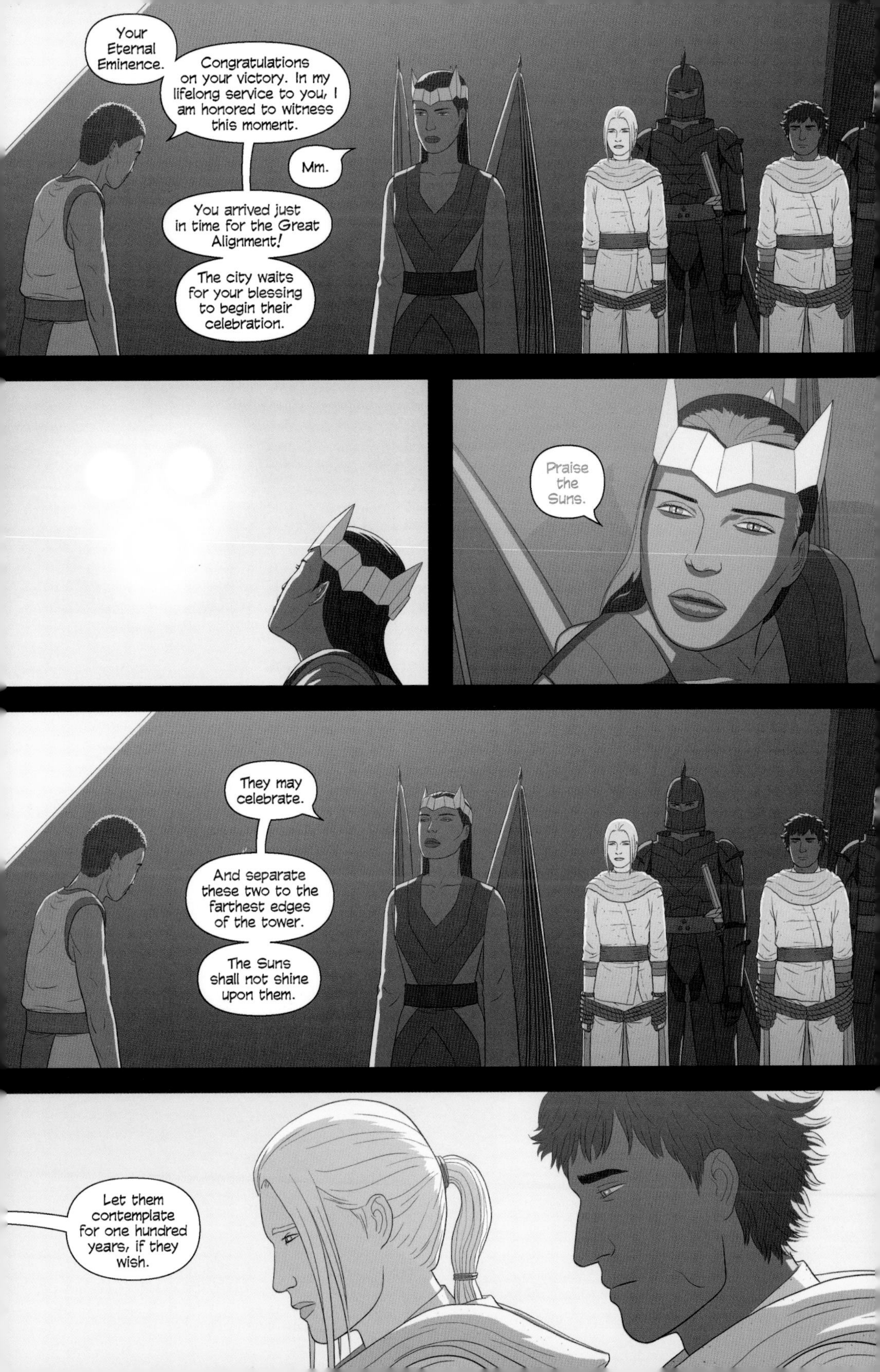
Your Eternal Eminence.
Congratulations on your victory. In my lifelong service to you, I am honored to witness this moment.
Mm.
You arrived just in time for the Great Alignment!
The city waits for your blessing to begin their celebration.
Praise the Suns.
They may celebrate.
And separate these two to the farthest edges of the tower.
The Suns shall not shine upon them.
Let them contemplate for one hundred years, if they wish.

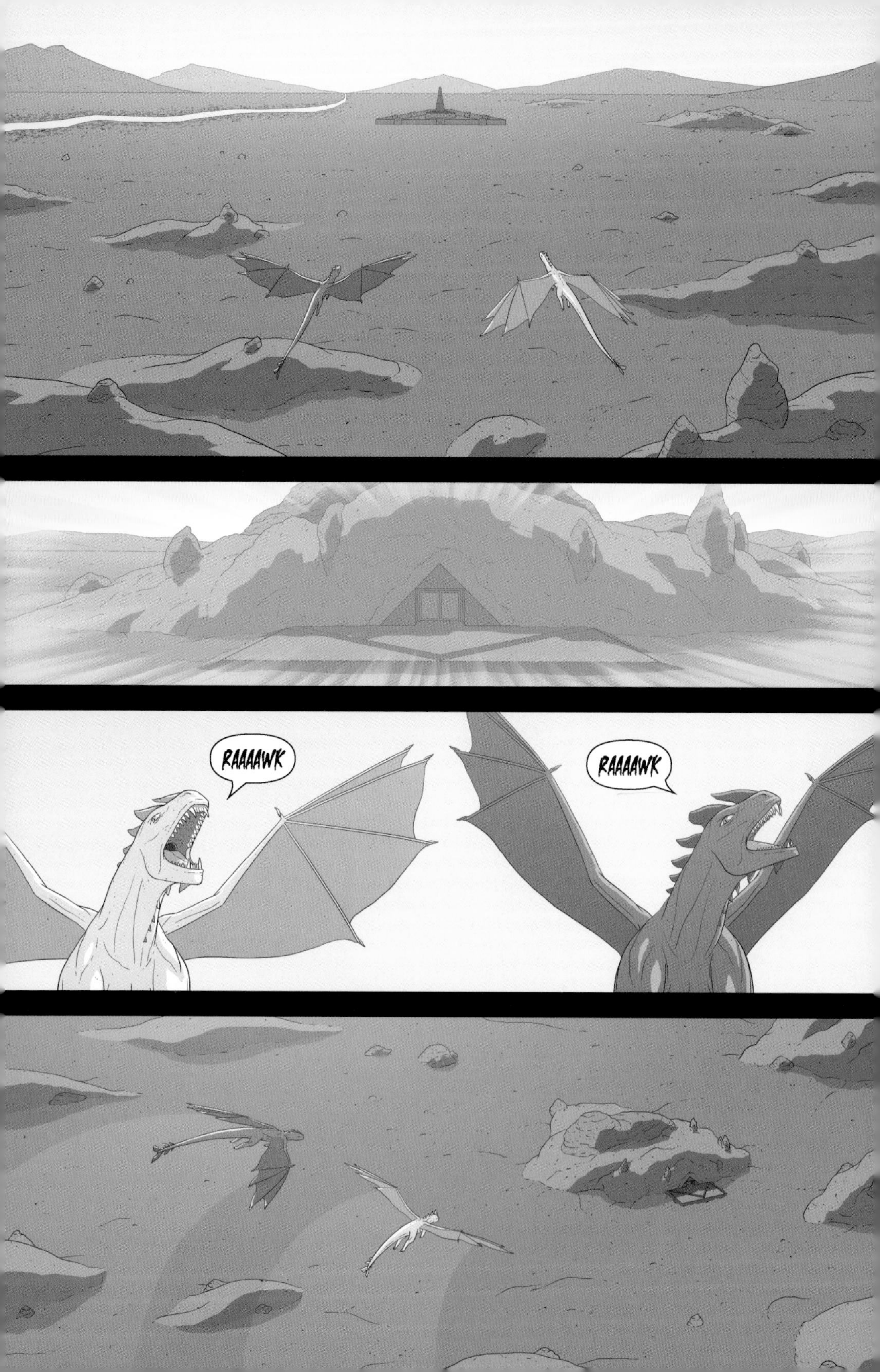
RAAAAWK
RAAAAWK

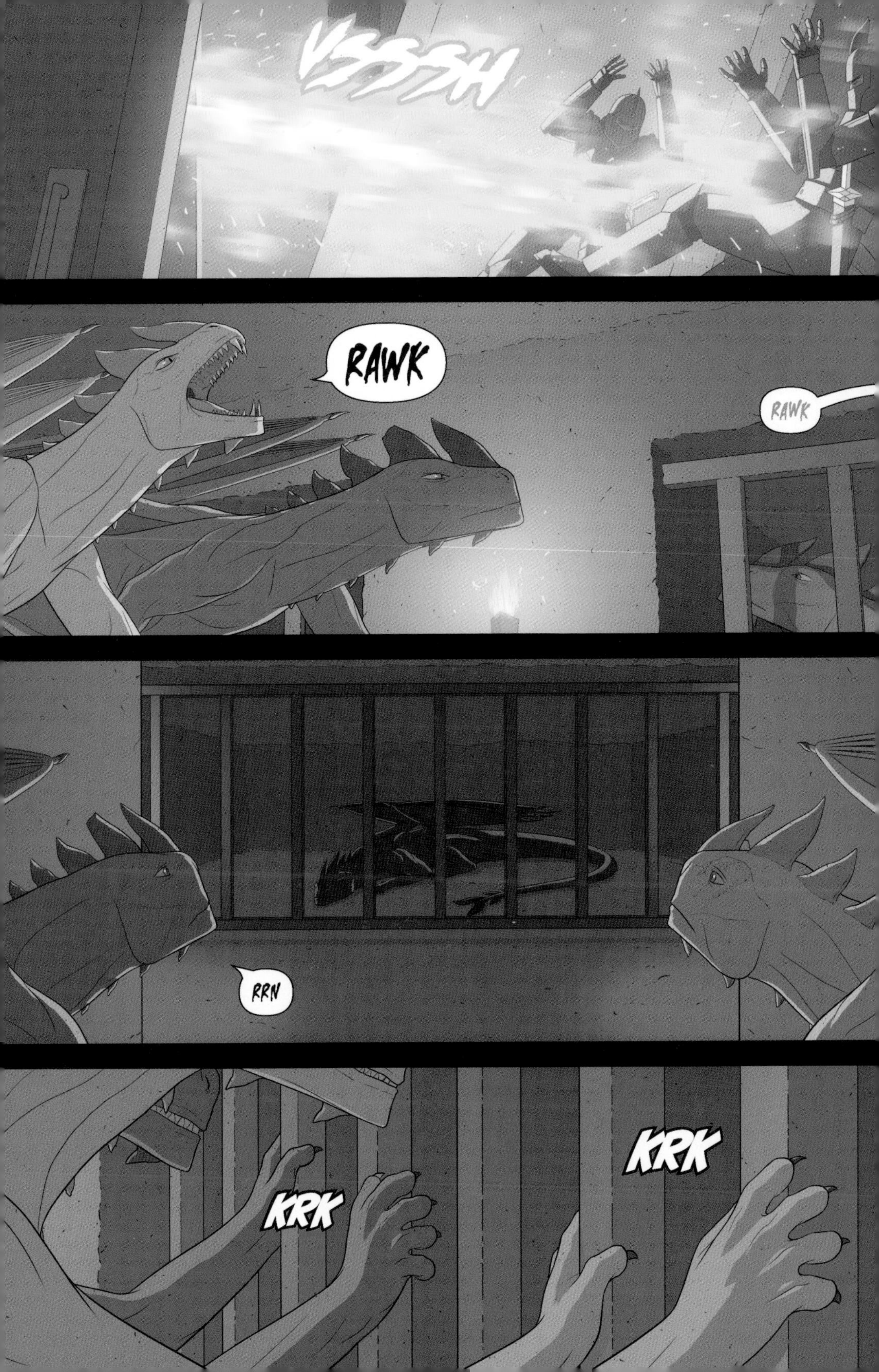
VSSSH
RAWK
RAWK
RRN
KRK
KRK

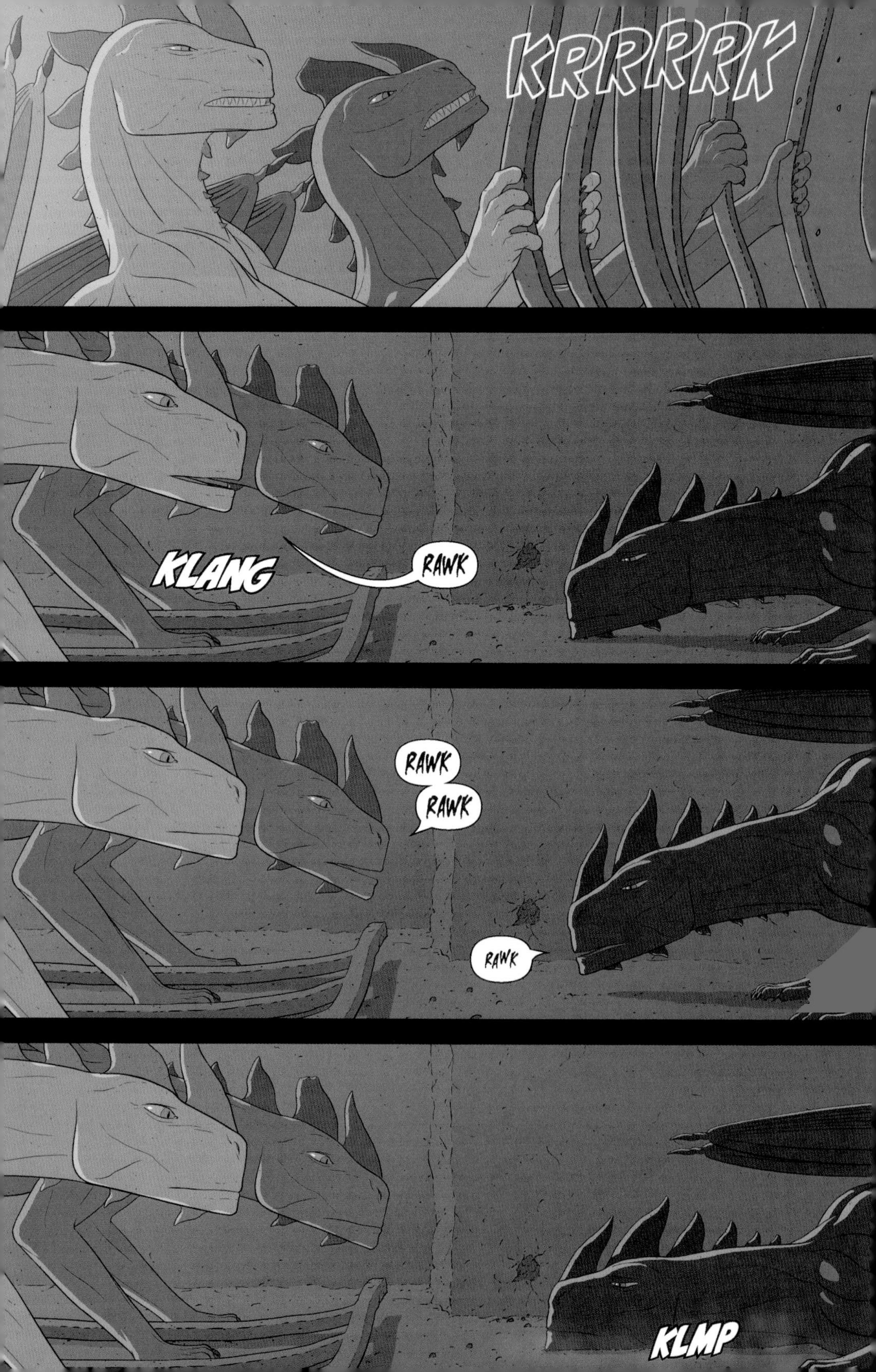
KRRRRK
KLANG
RAWK
RAWK
RAWK
RAWK
KLMP

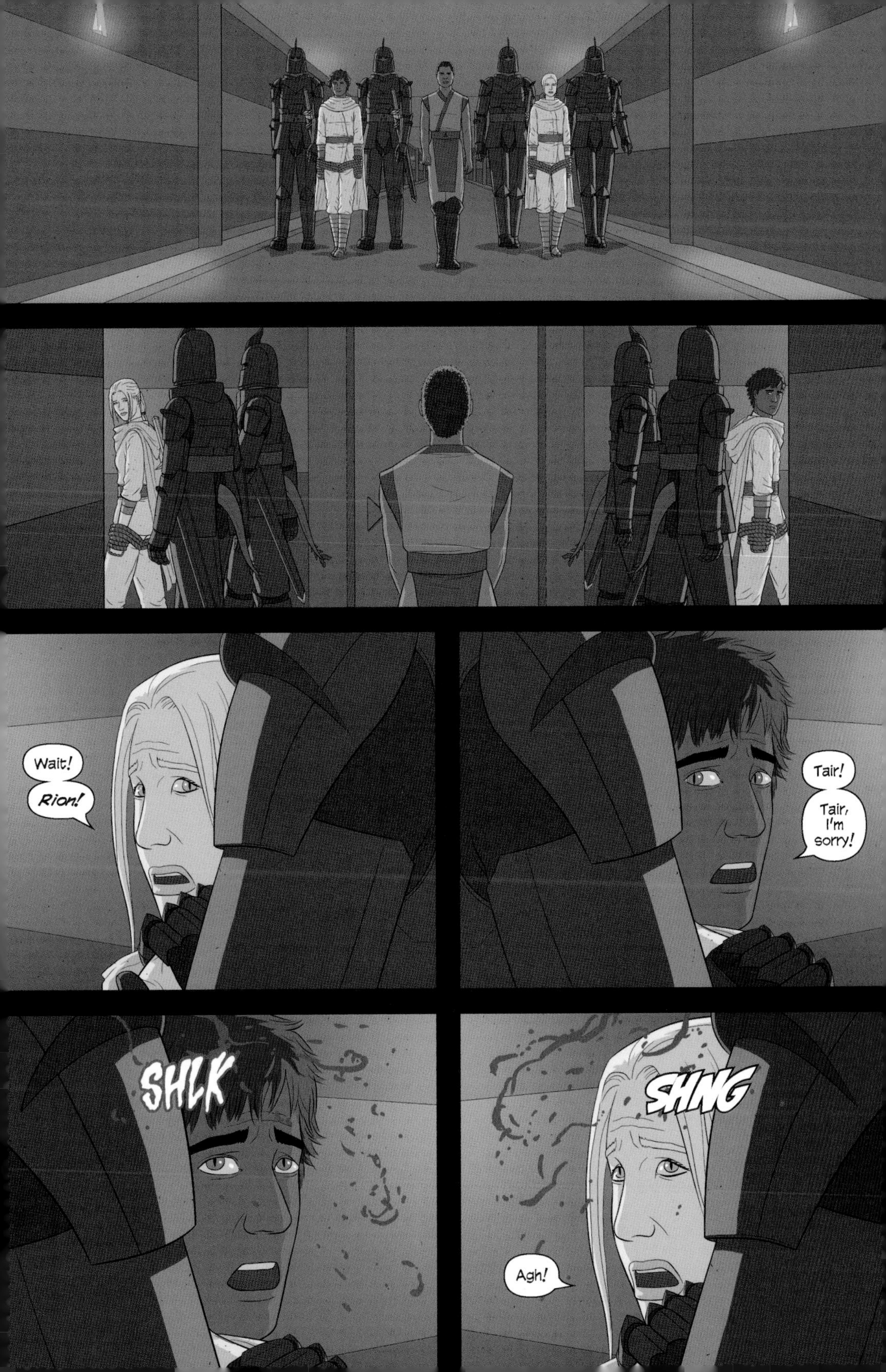
Wait!
Rion!
Tair!
Tair, I'm sorry!
SHLK
SHNG
Agh!

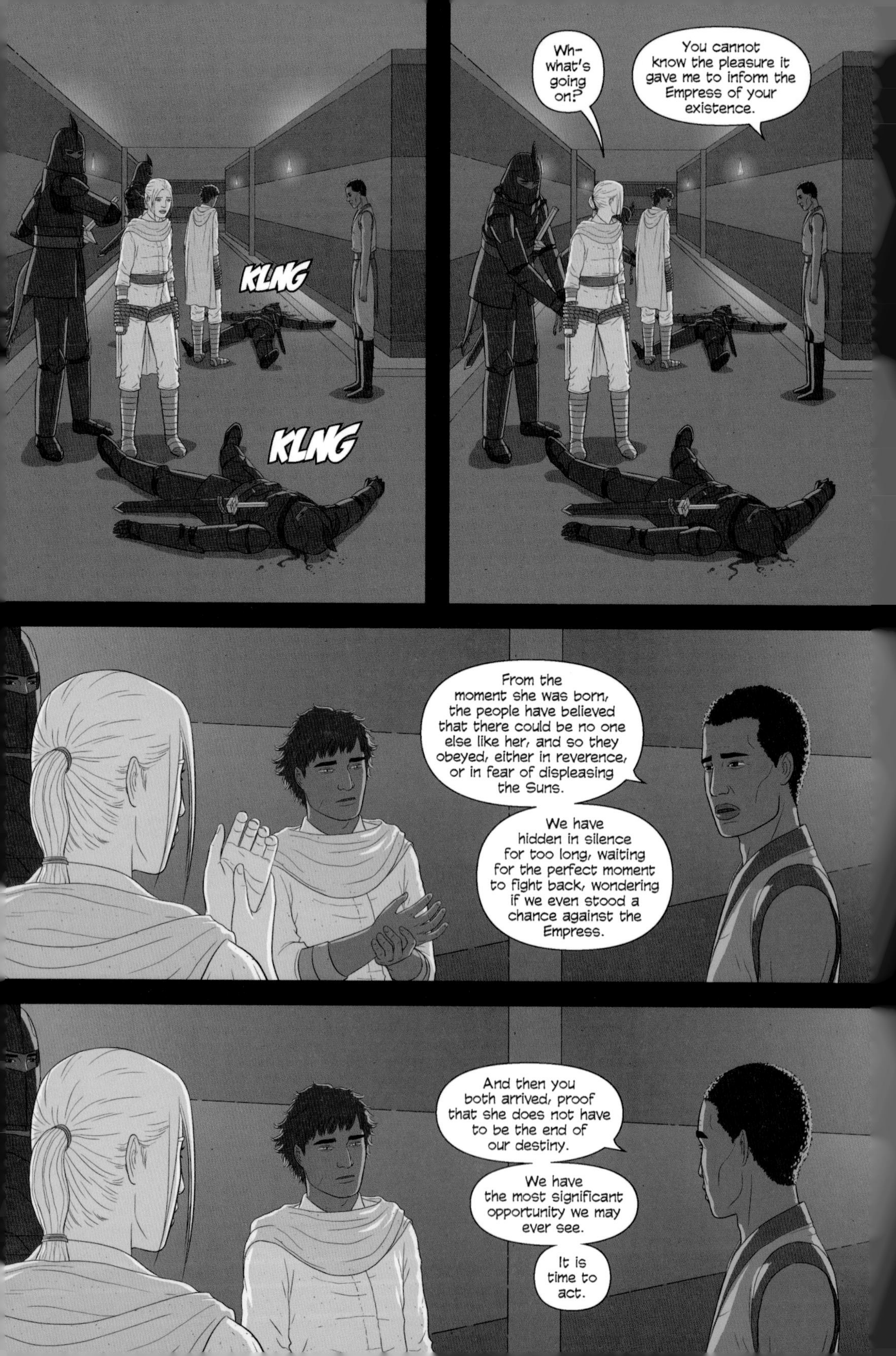
KLNG
KLNG
Wh-what's going on?
You cannot know the pleasure it gave me to inform the Empress of your existence.
From the moment she was born, the people have believed that there could be no one else like her, and so they obeyed, either in reverence, or in fear of displeasing the Suns.
We have hidden in silence for too long, waiting for the perfect moment to fight back, wondering if we even stood a chance against the Empress.
And then you both arrived, proof that she does not have to be the end of our destiny.
We have the most significant opportunity we may ever see.
It is time to act.

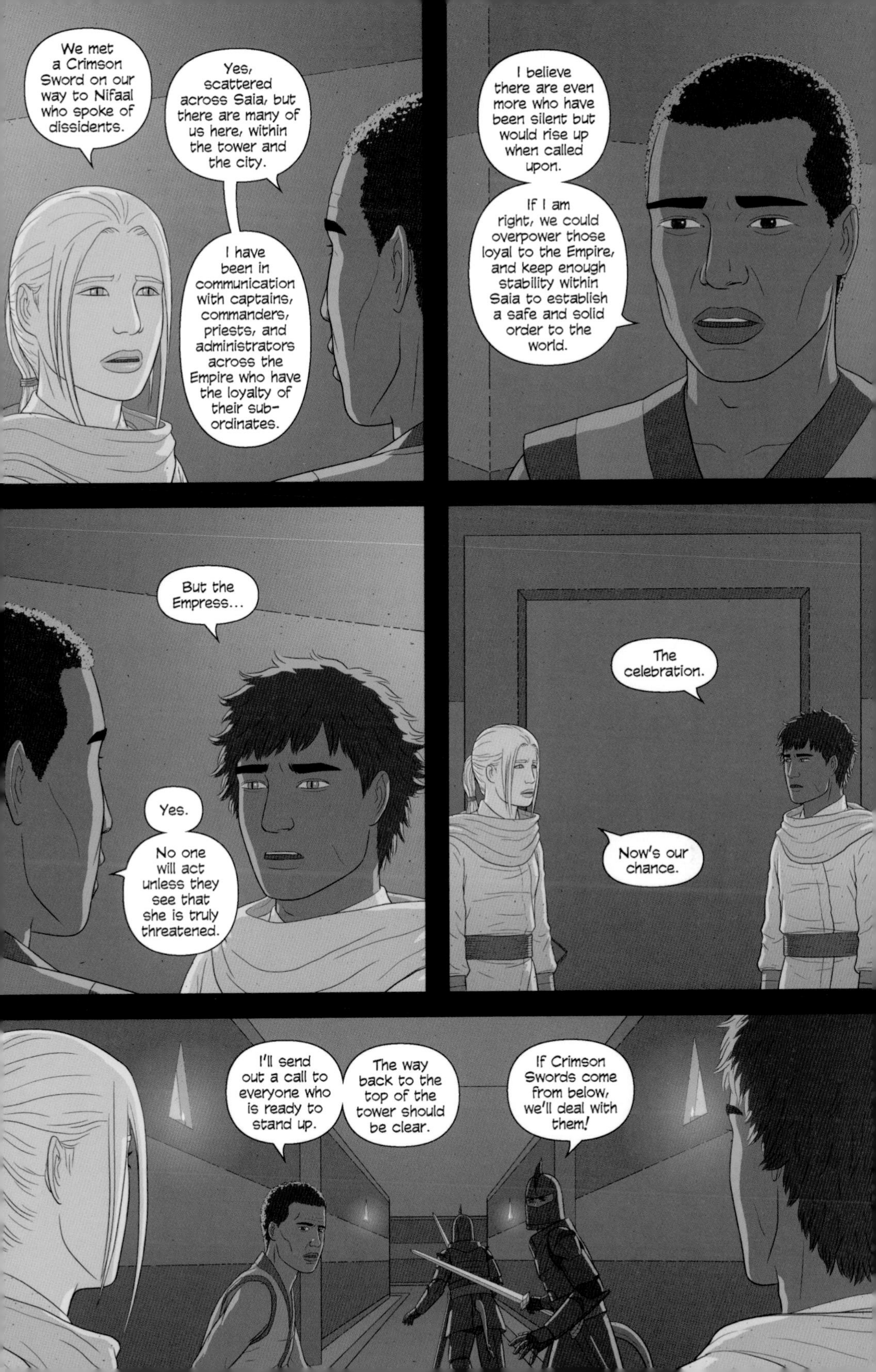
We met a Crimson Sword on our way to Nifaal who spoke of dissidents.
Yes, scattered across Saia, but there are many of us here, within the tower and the city.
I have been in communication with captains, commanders, priests, and administrators across the Empire who have the loyalty of their sub-ordinates.
I believe there are even more who have been silent but would rise up when called upon.
If I am right, we could overpower those loyal to the Empire, and keep enough stability within Saia to establish a safe and solid order to the world.
But the Empress...
Yes.
No one will act unless they see that she is truly threatened.
The celebration.
Now's our chance.
I'll send out a call to everyone who is ready to stand up.
The way back to the top of the tower should be clear.
If Crimson Swords come from below, we'll deal with them!

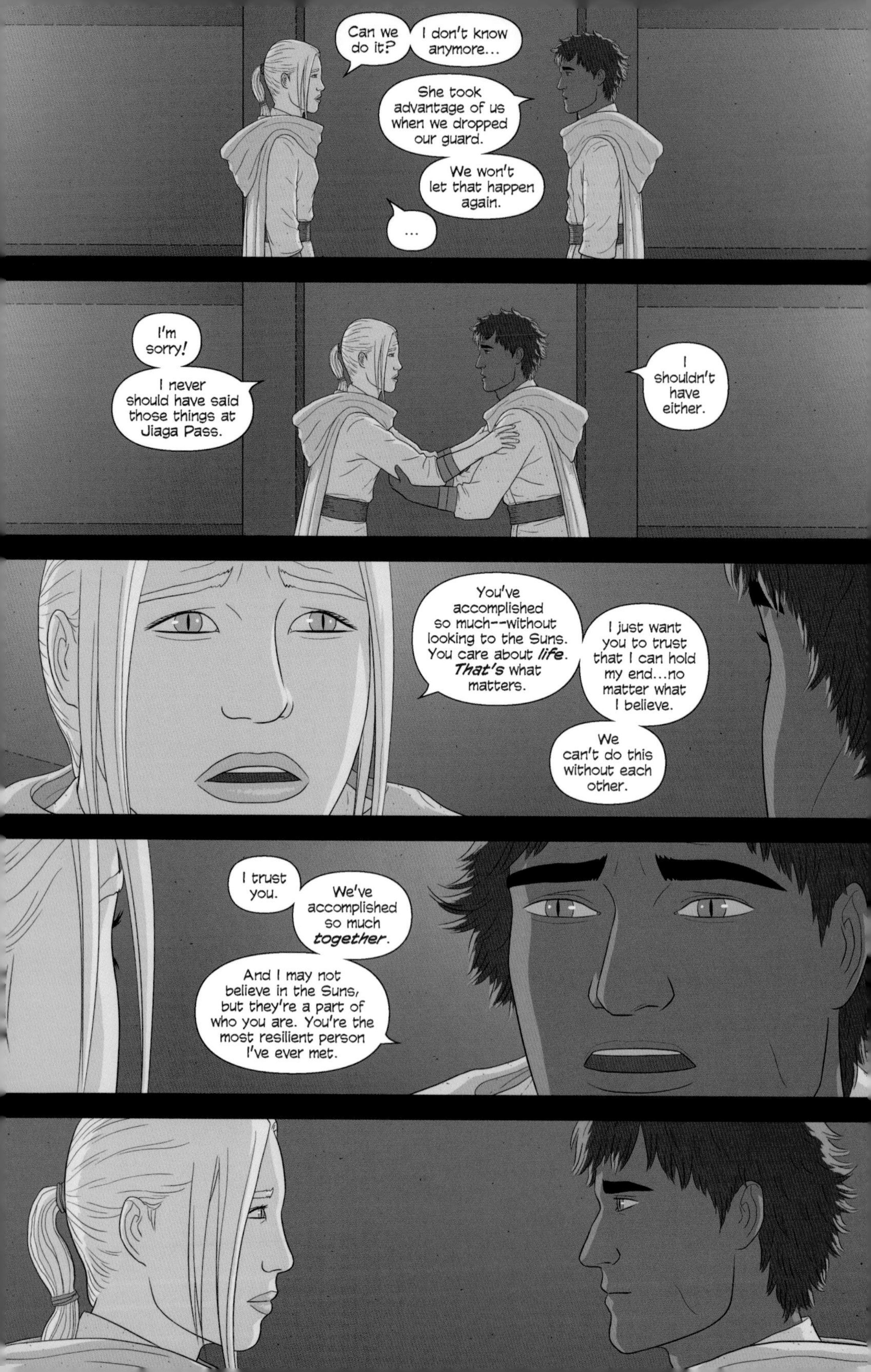

Can we do it?
I don't know anymore...
She took advantage of us when we dropped our guard.
We won't let that happen again.
...
I'm sorry!
I never should have said those things at Jiaga Pass.
I shouldn't have either.
You've accomplished so much--without looking to the Suns. You care about *life*. ***That's*** what matters.
I just want you to trust that I can hold my end...no matter what I believe.
We can't do this without each other.
I trust you.
We've accomplished so much ***together***.
And I may not believe in the Suns, but they're a part of who you are. You're the most resilient person I've ever met.

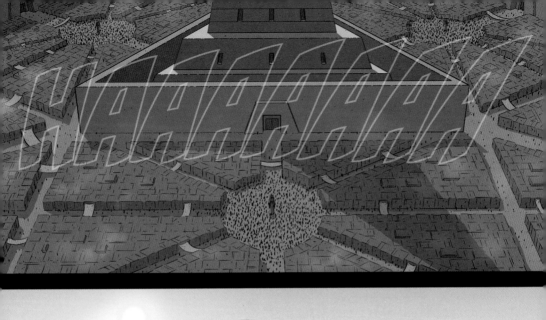

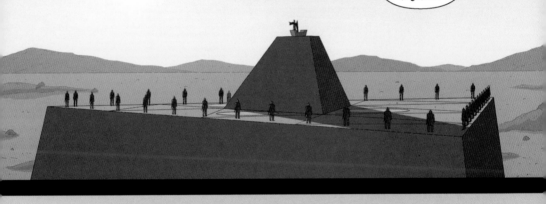

Behold!

The first Great Alignment *any* of us living have witnessed!

And so today begins a new age *all* of Saia will join in together.

But now that we have achieved our goal of unification, we must look ever onward to *prosperity*.

Harder work, greater achievements in innovation and understanding.

More glory for the world *you* desire!

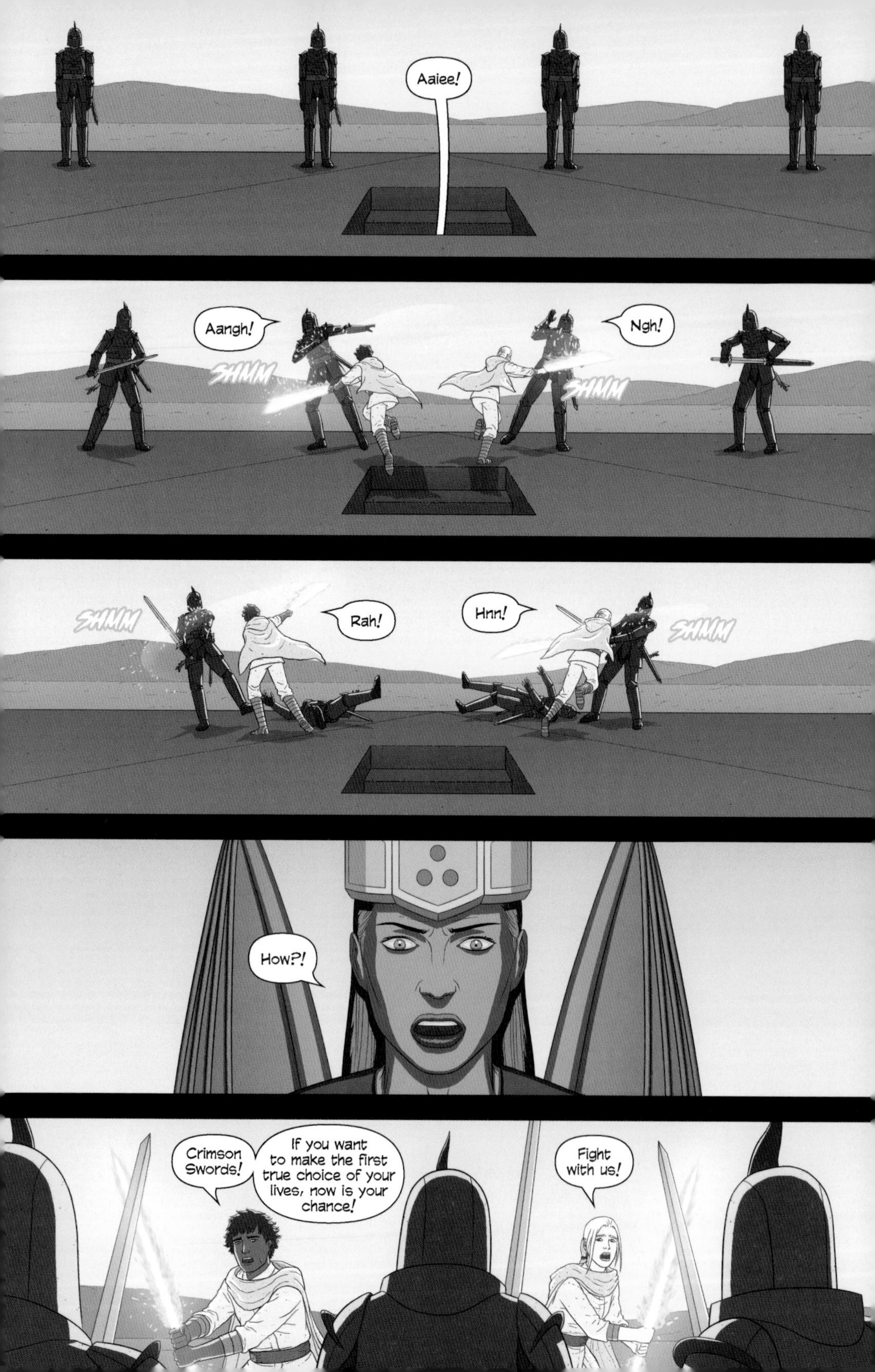
Aaiee!
Aangh!
SHMM
Ngh!
SHMM
SHMM
Rah!
Hnn!
SHMM
How?!
Crimson Swords!
If you want to make the first true choice of your lives, now is your chance!
Fight with us!

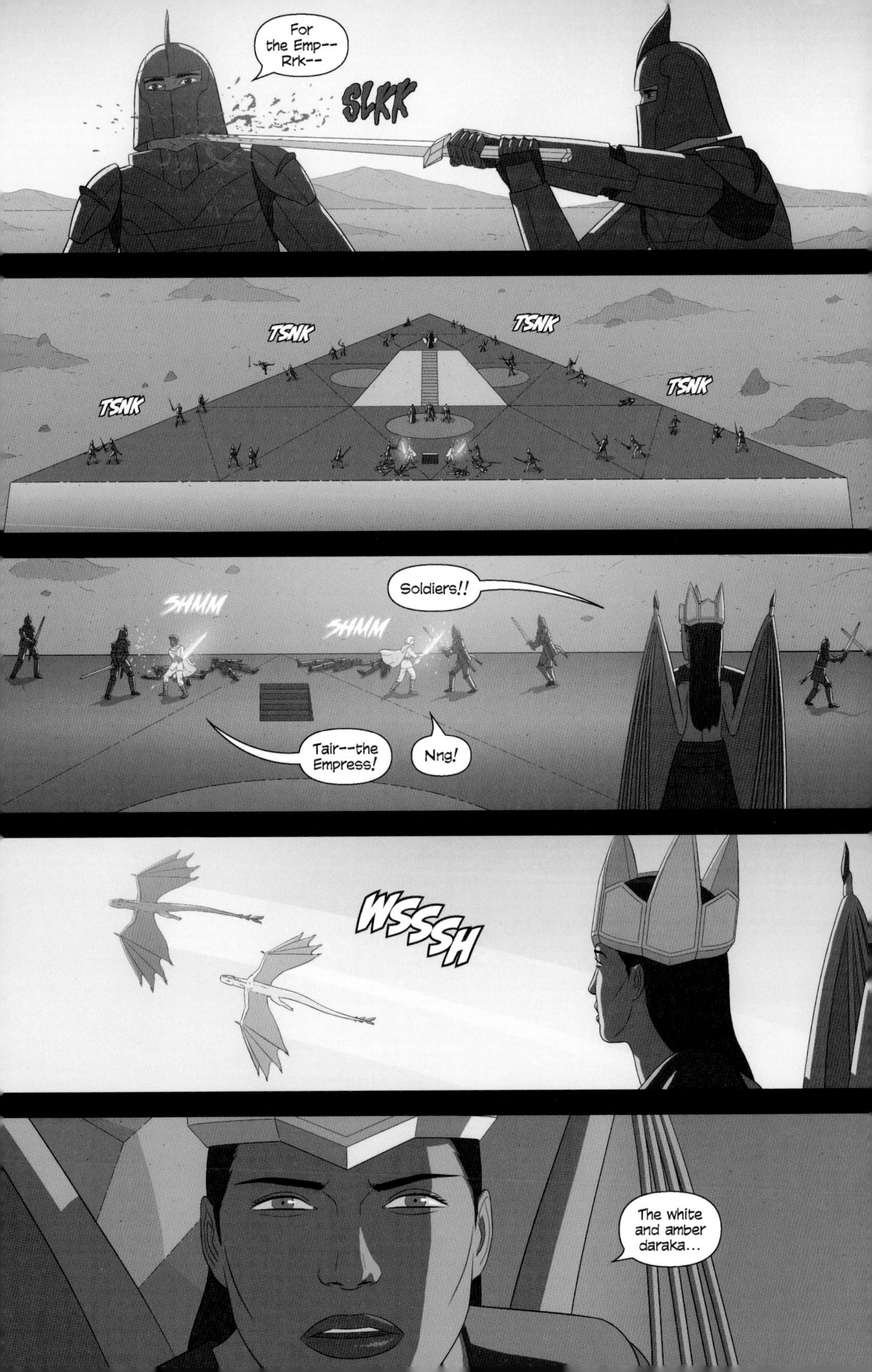

For the Emp-- Rrk--
SLKK
TSNK
TSNK
TSNK
TSNK
SHMM
SHMM
Soldiers!!
Tair--the Empress!
Nng!
WSSSH
The white and amber daraka...

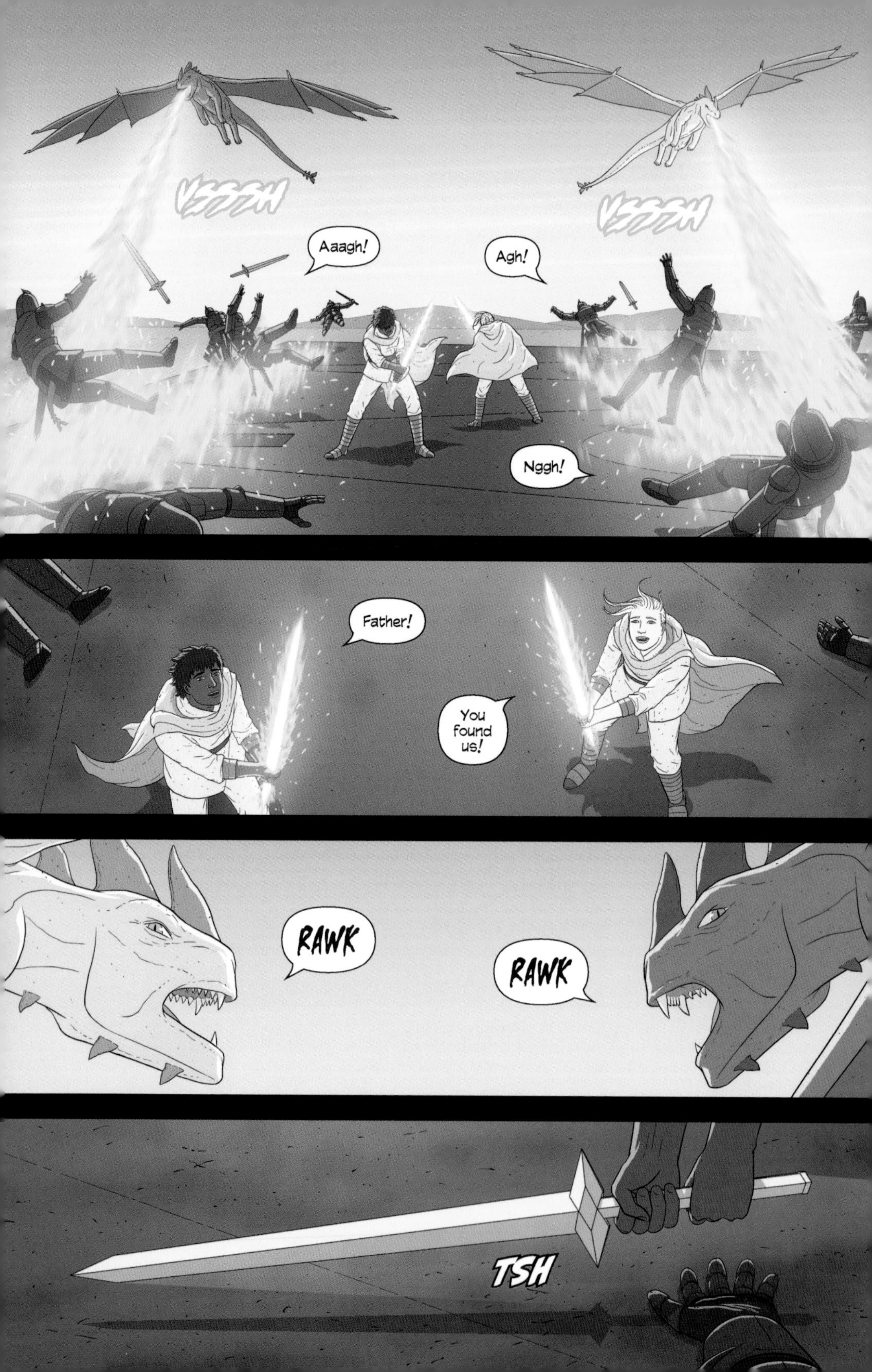
VSSSH
VSSSH
Aaaagh!
Agh!
Nggh!
Father!
You found us!
RAWK
RAWK
TSH

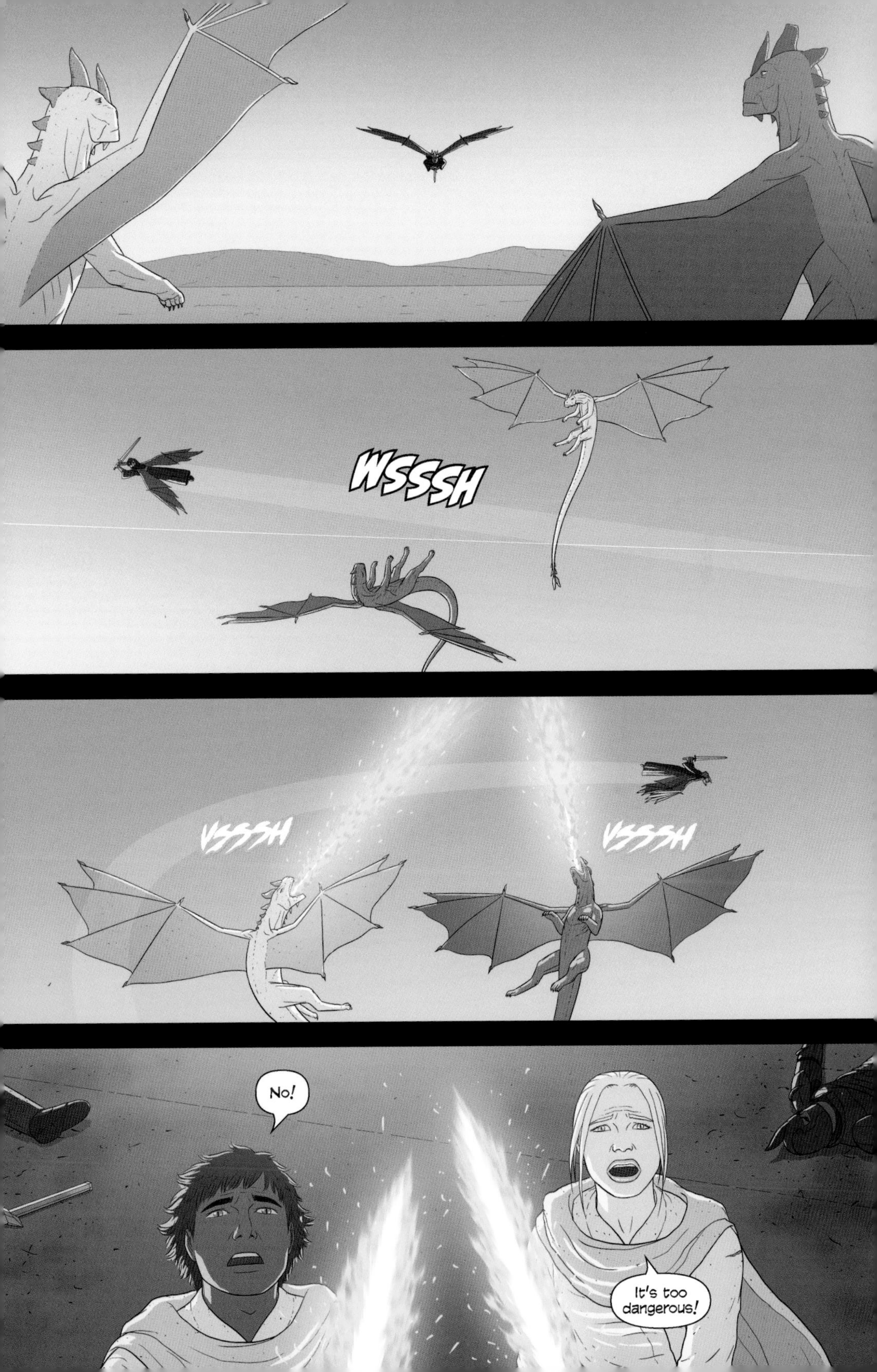
WSSSH
VSSSH
VSSSH
No!
It's too dangerous!

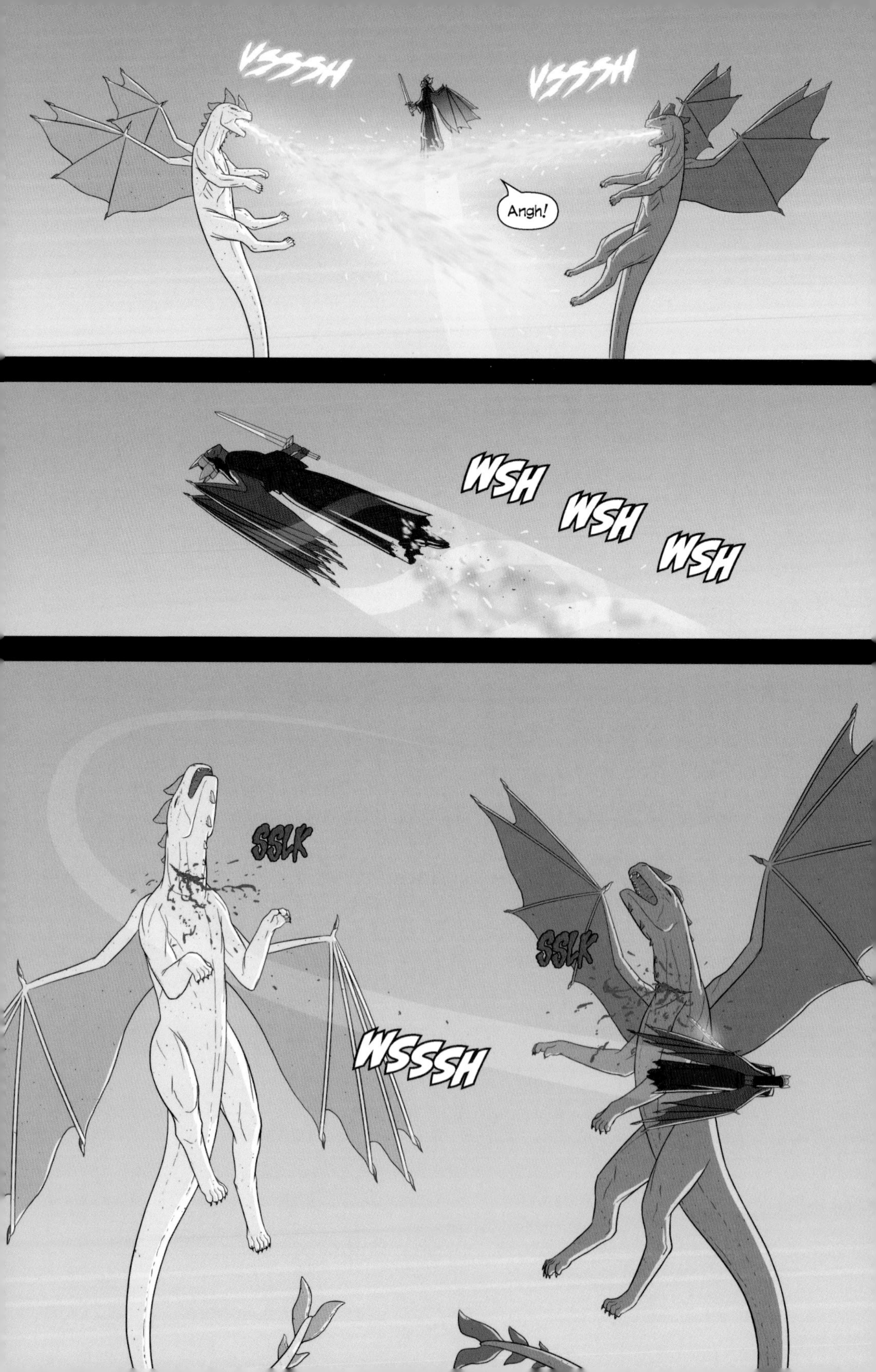
VSSSSH
VSSSSH
Angh!
WSH
WSH
WSH
SSLK
SSLK
WSSSH

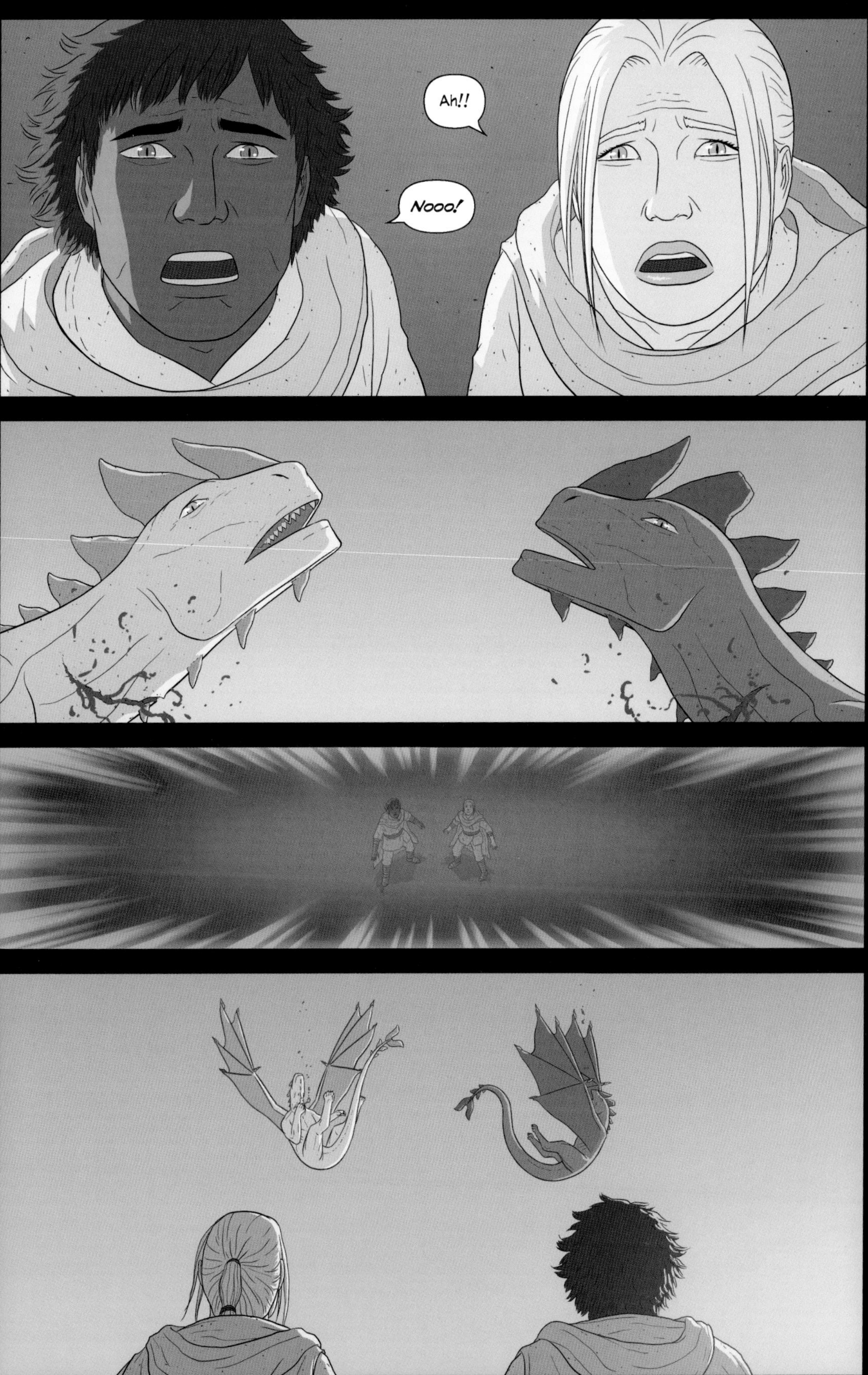
Ah!!
Nooo!

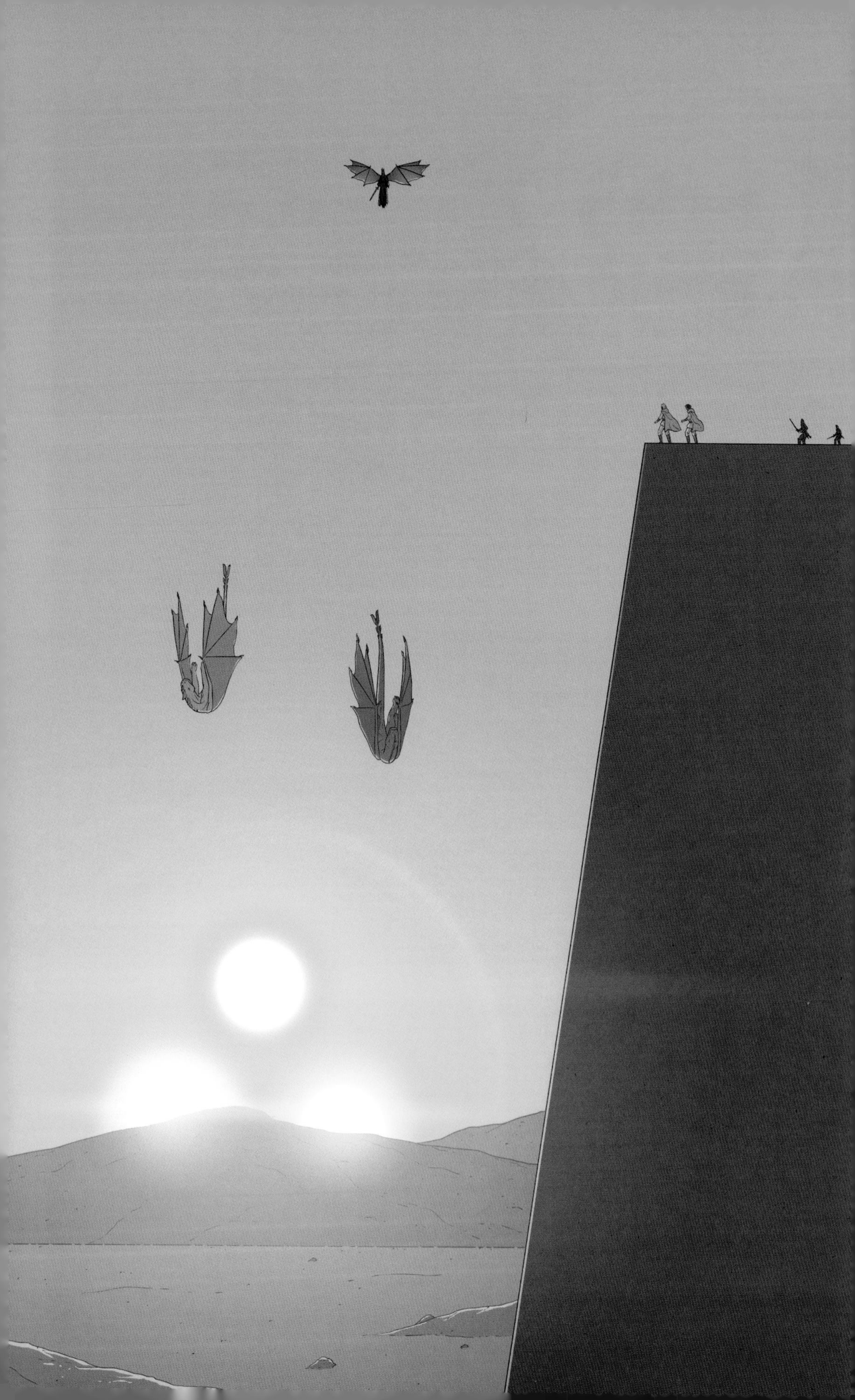

10

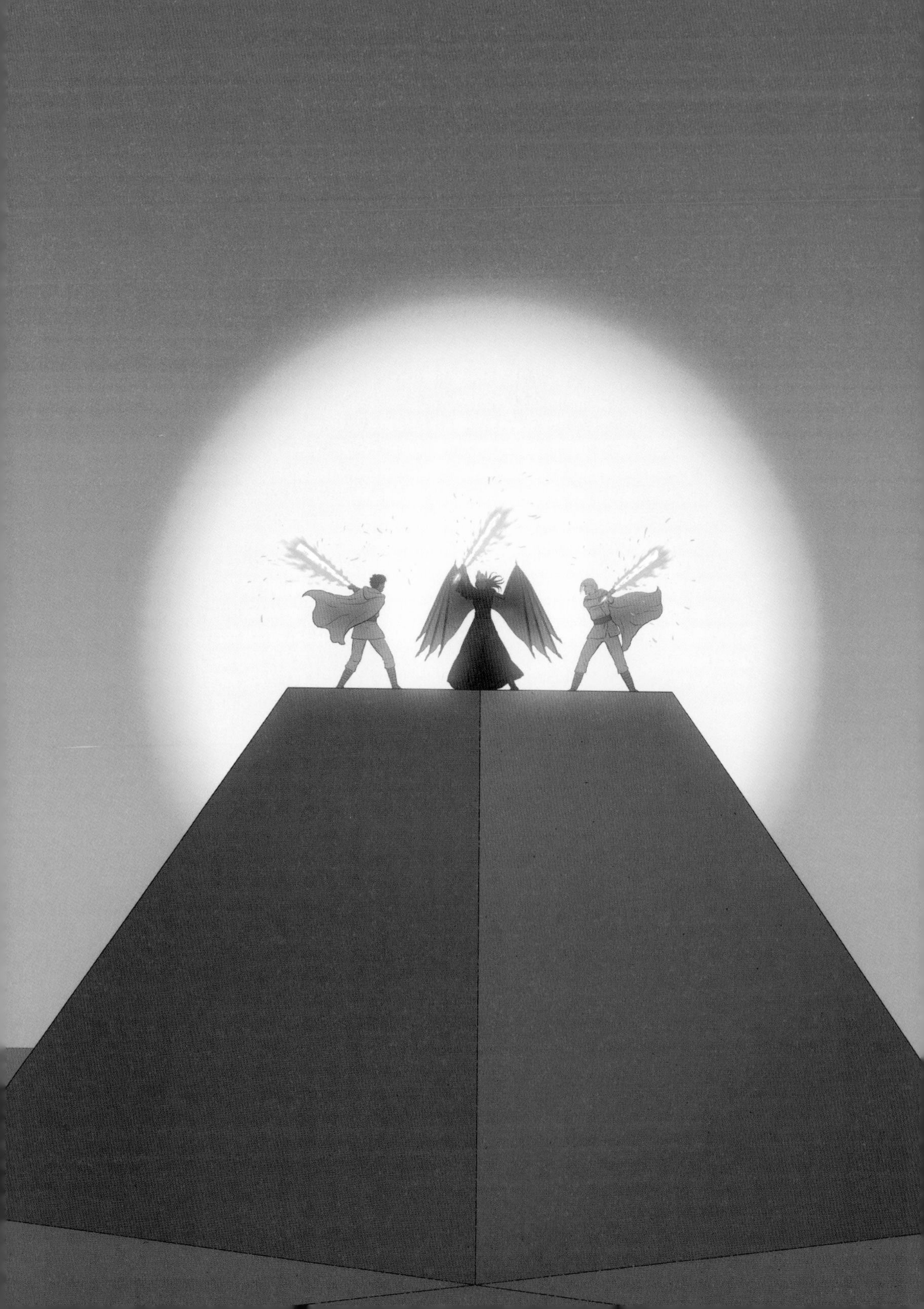

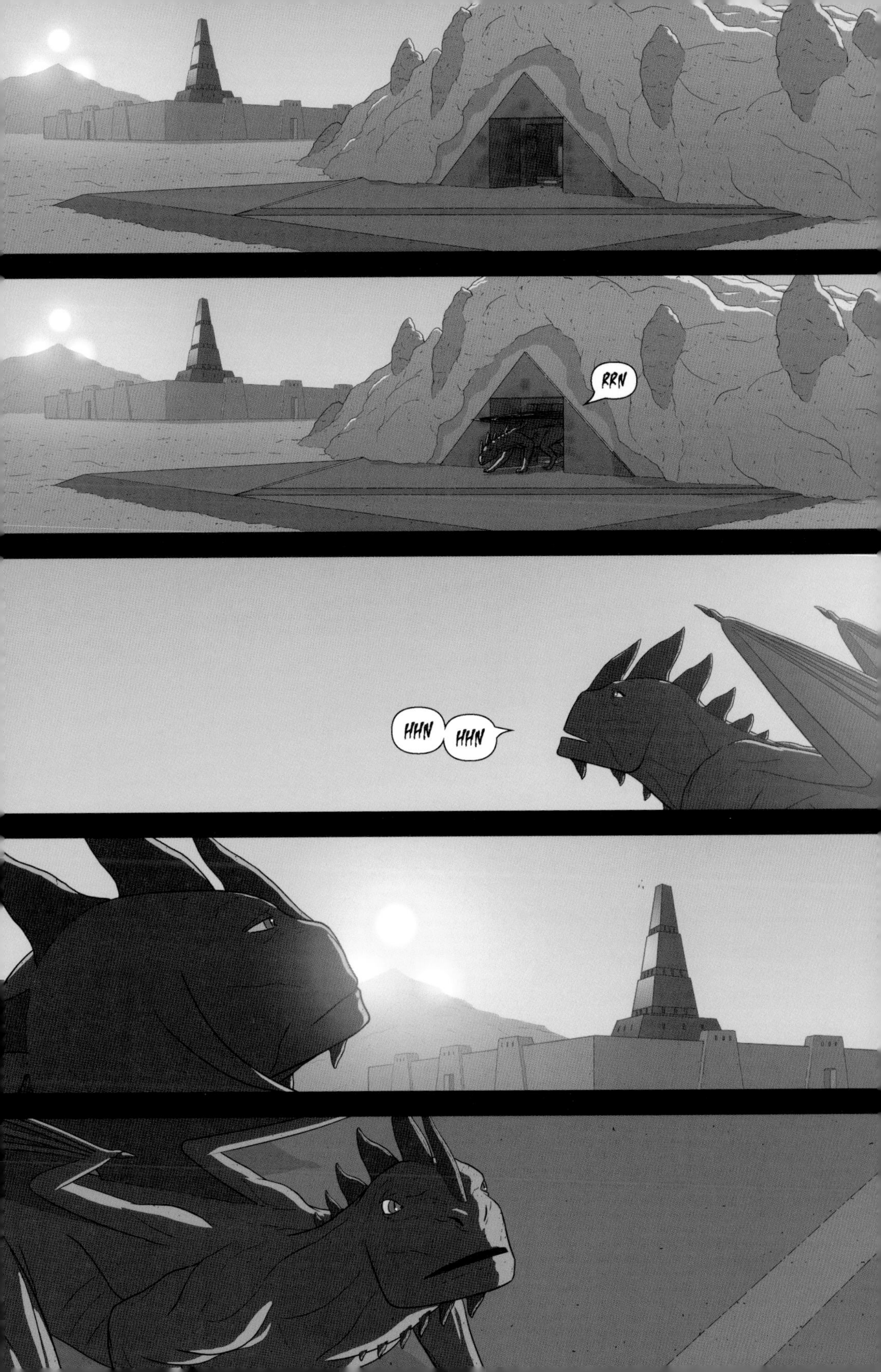
RRN
HHN
HHN

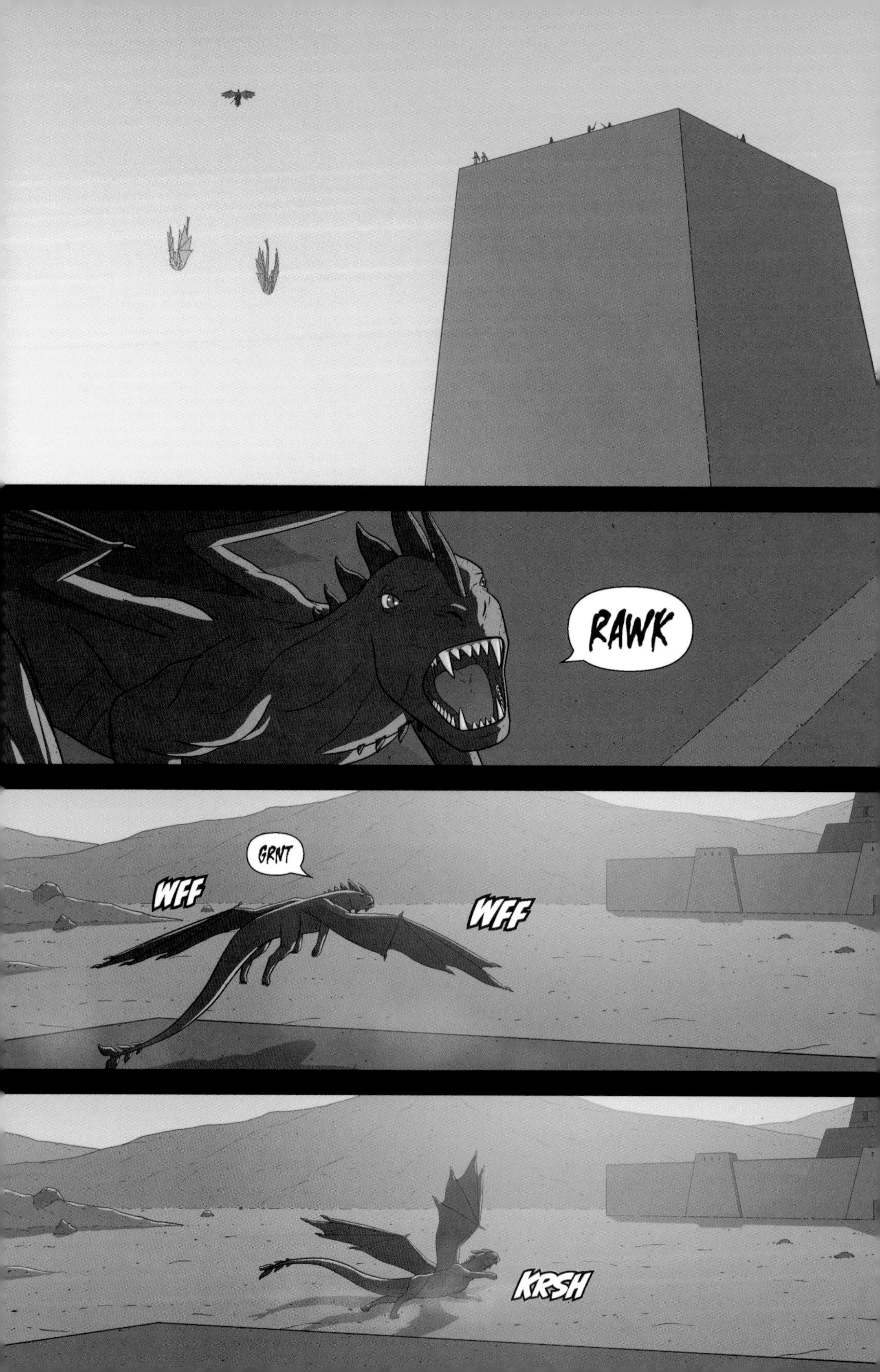
RAWK
GRNT
WFF
WFF
KRSH

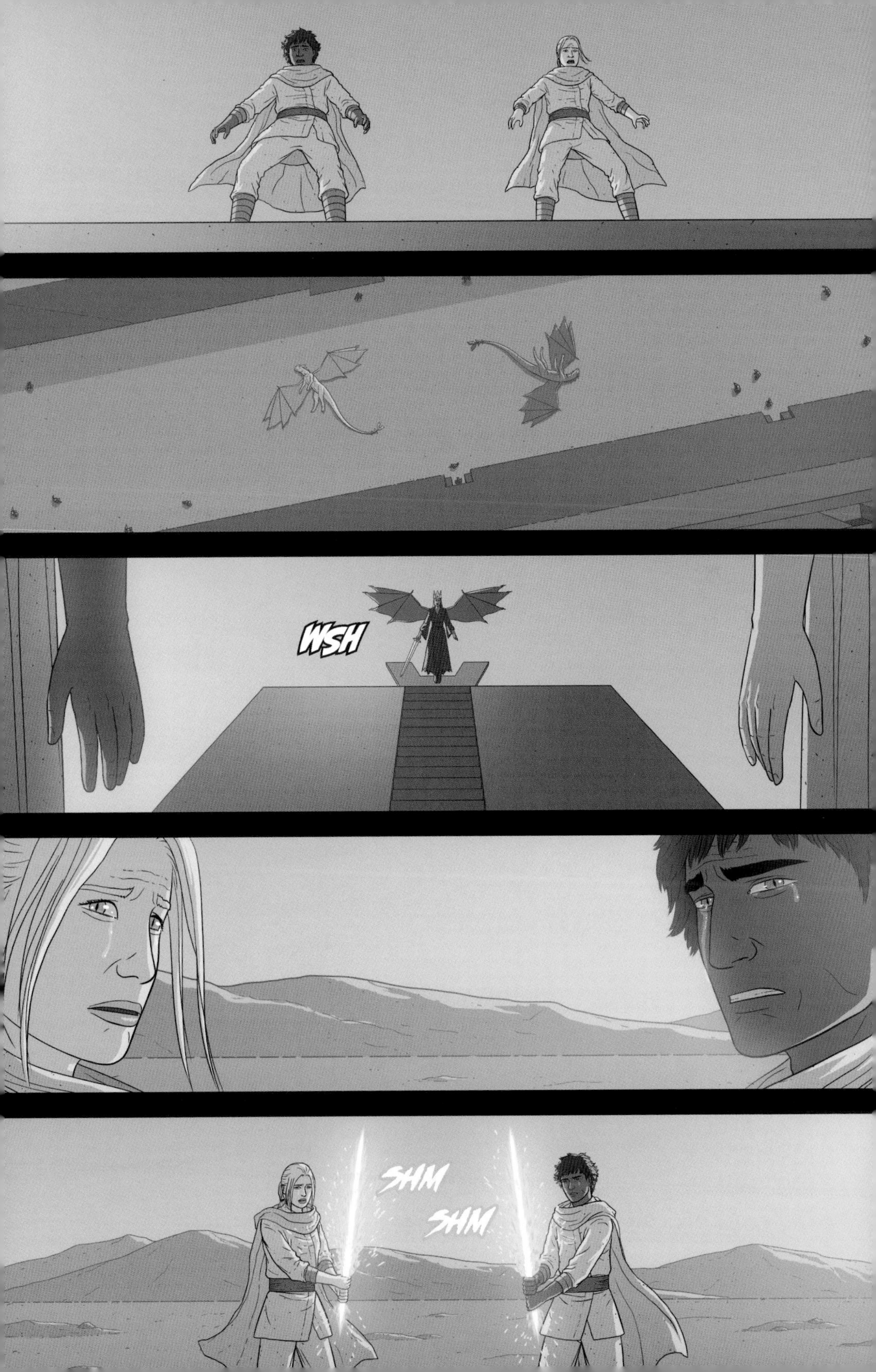
WSH
SHM
SHM

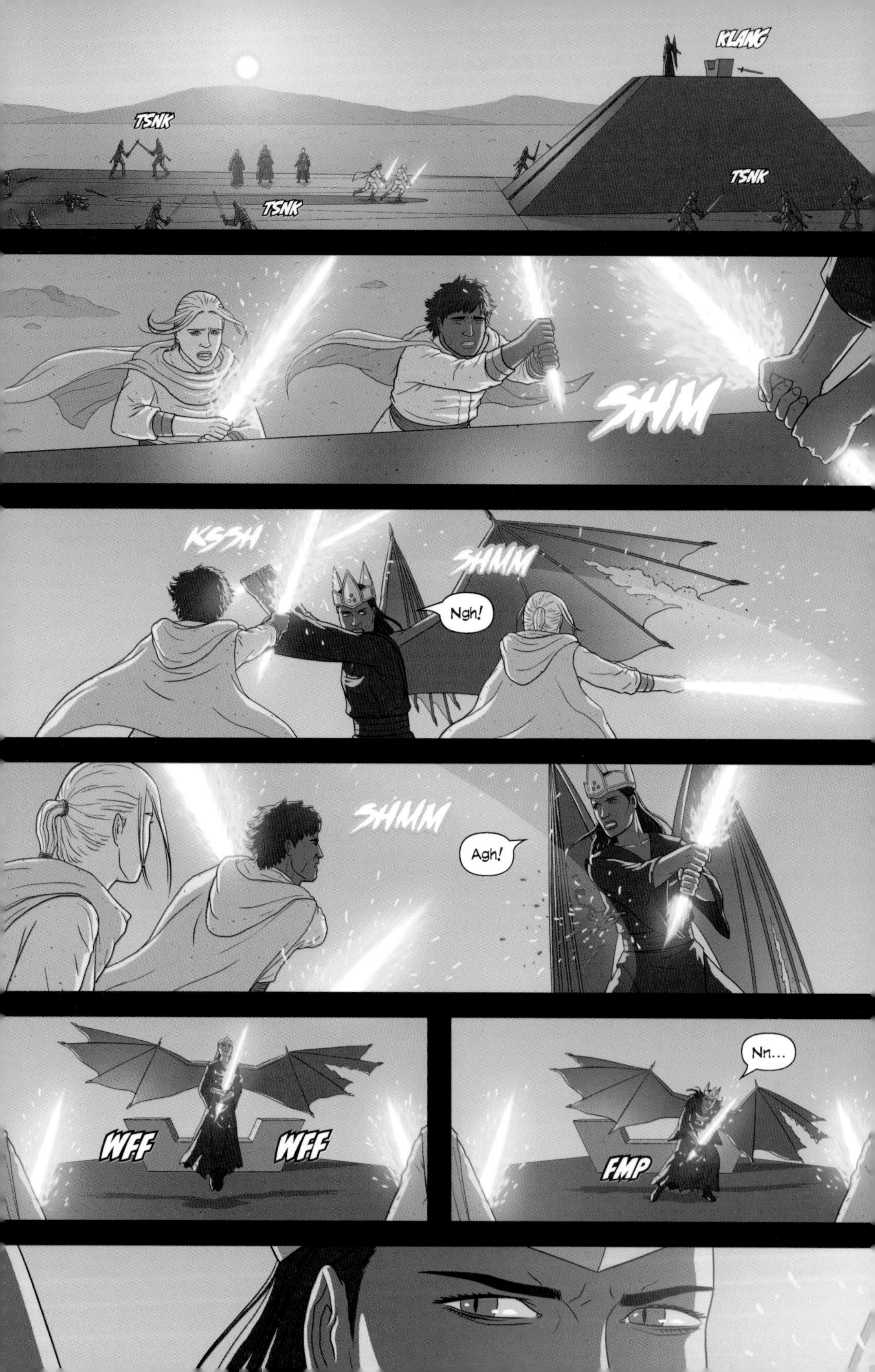
KLANG
TSNK
TSNK
TSNK
SHM
KSSH
SHMM
Ngh!
SHMM
Agh!
WFF
WFF
Nn...
FMP

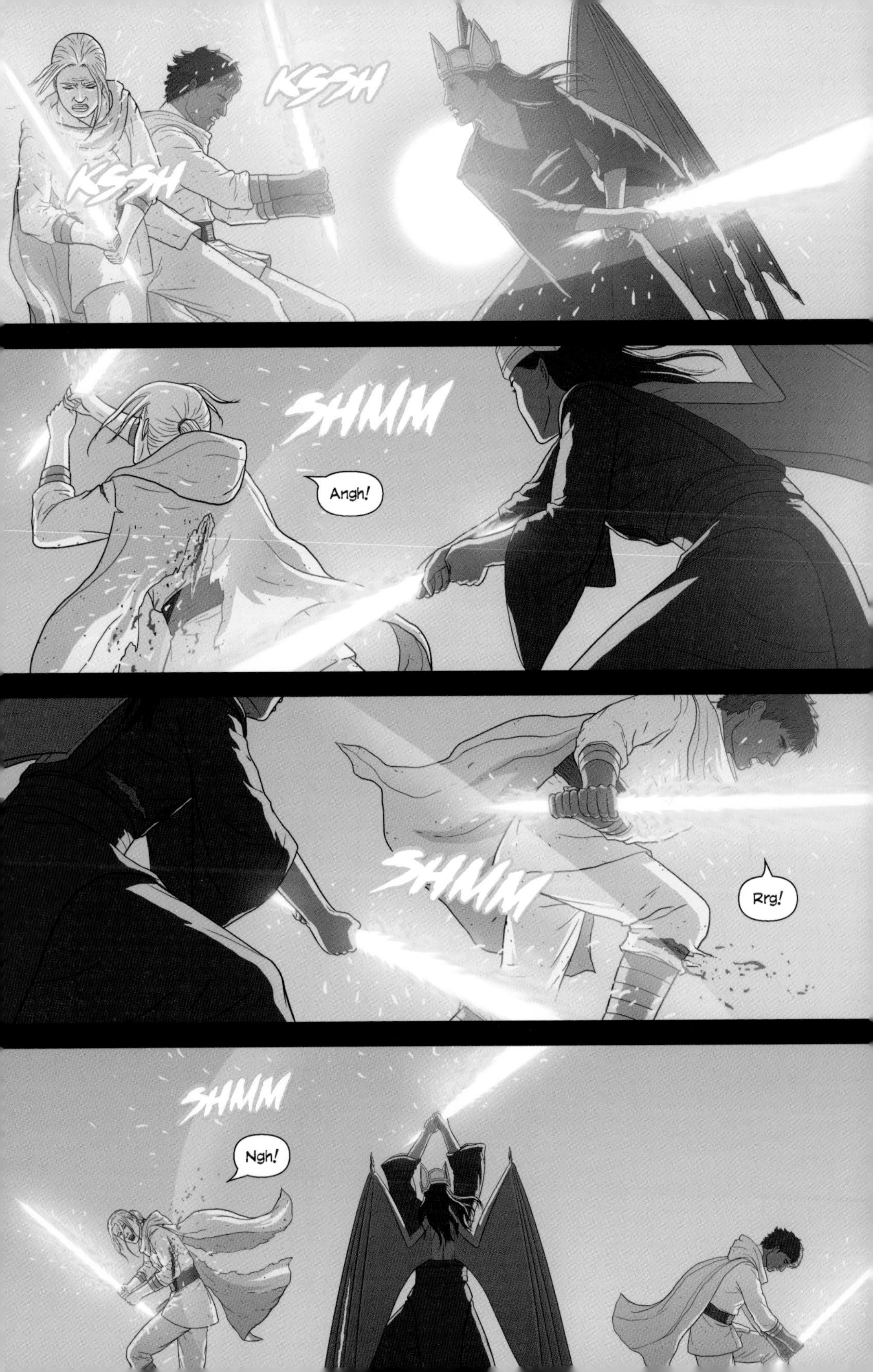
KSSH
KSSH
SHMM
Angh!
SHMM
Rrg!
SHMM
Ngh!

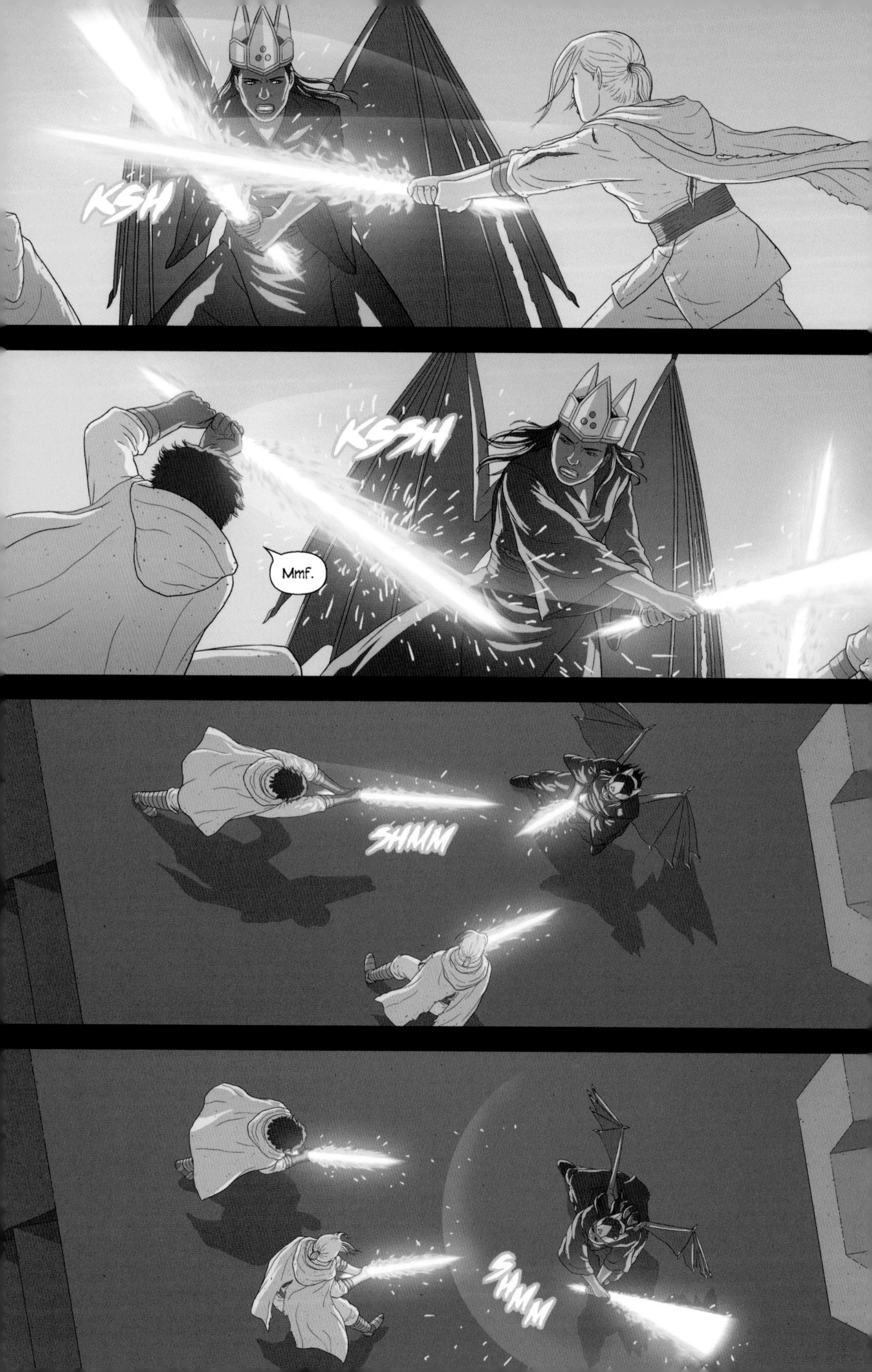
KSH
KSSH
Mmf.
SHMM
SHMM

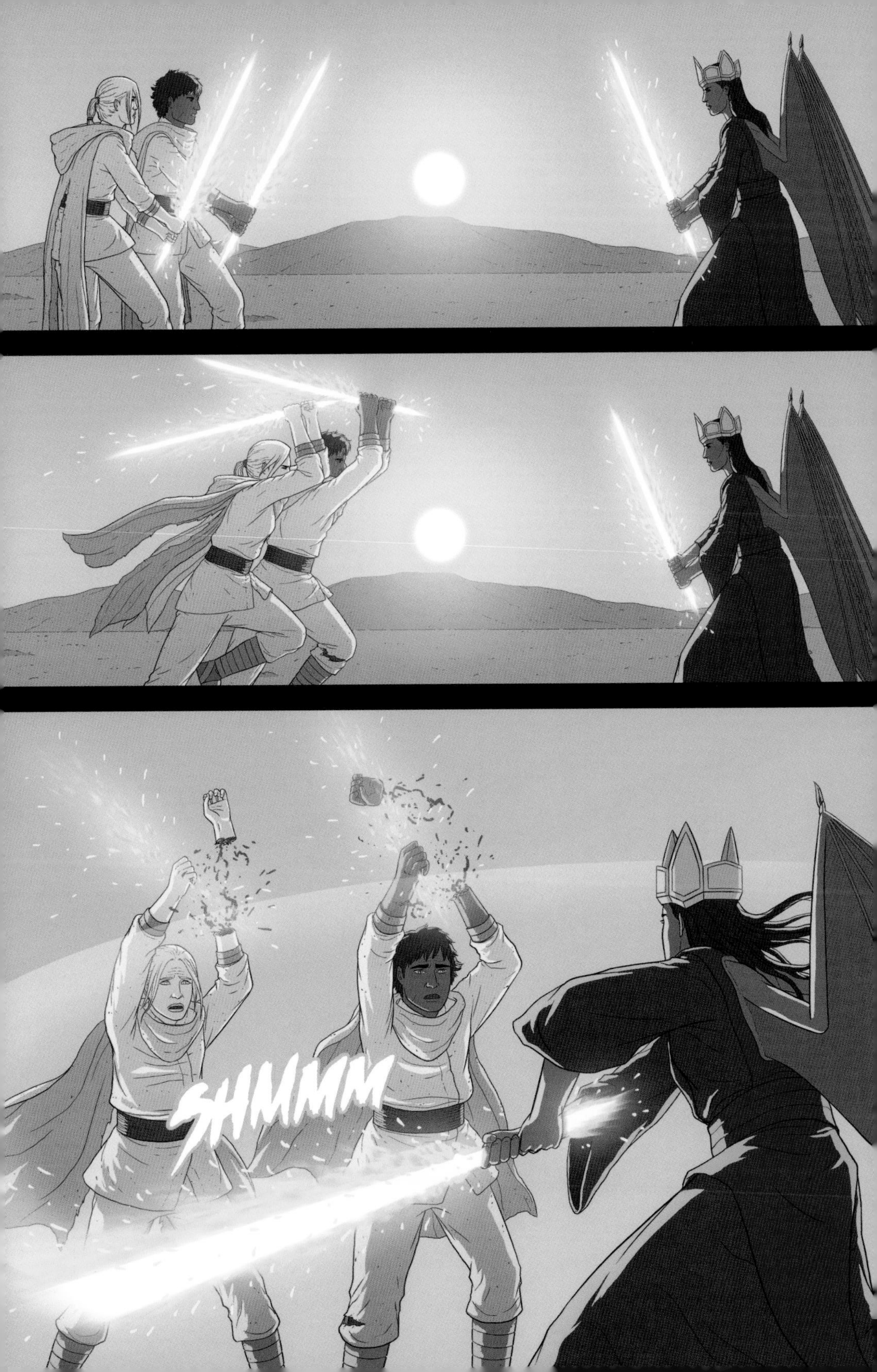
SHMMM

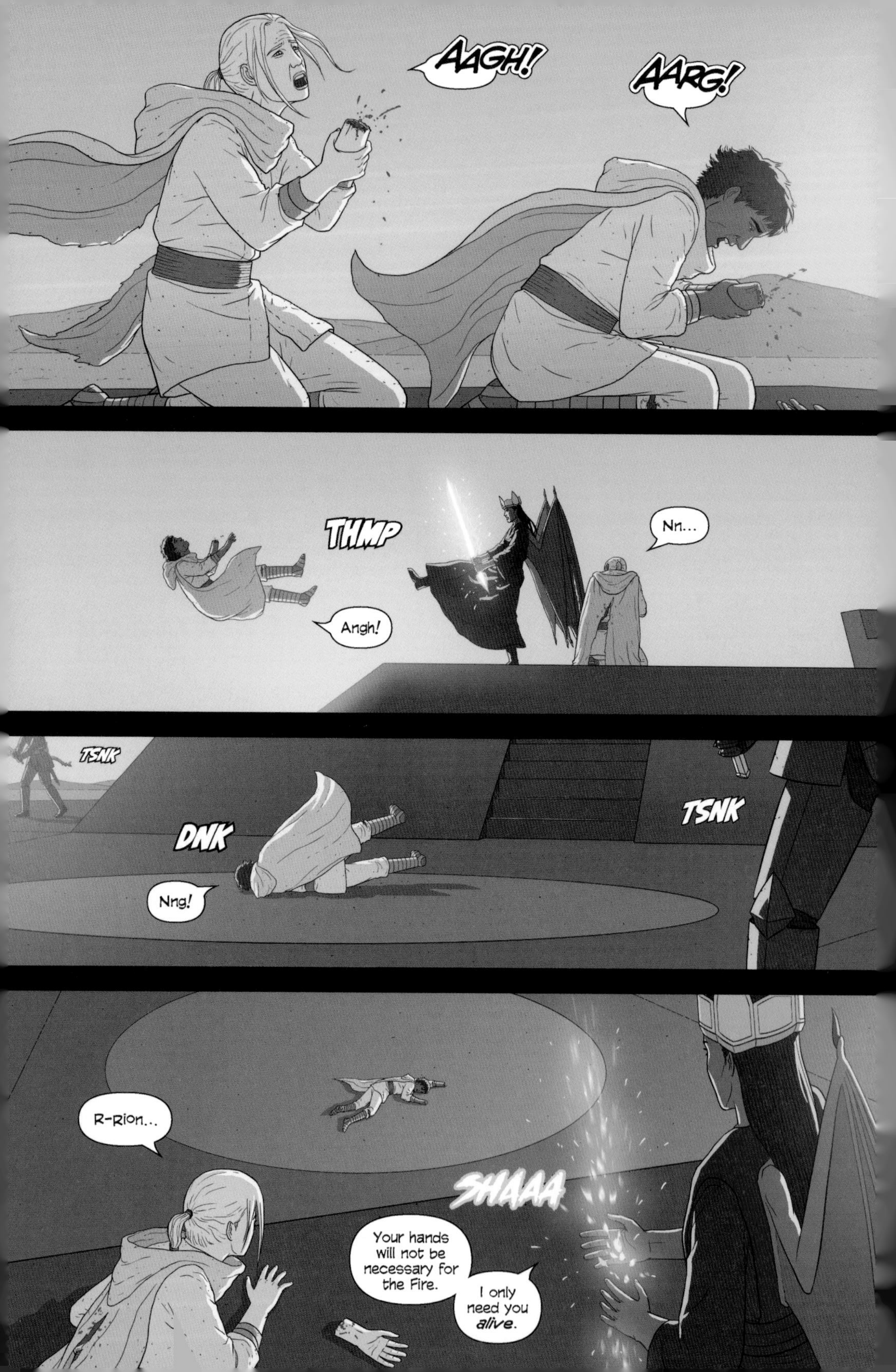
AAGH!
AARG!
THMP
Nn...
Angh!
TSNK
TSNK
DNK
Nng!
R-Rion...
SHAAA
Your hands will not be necessary for the Fire.
I only need you *alive*.

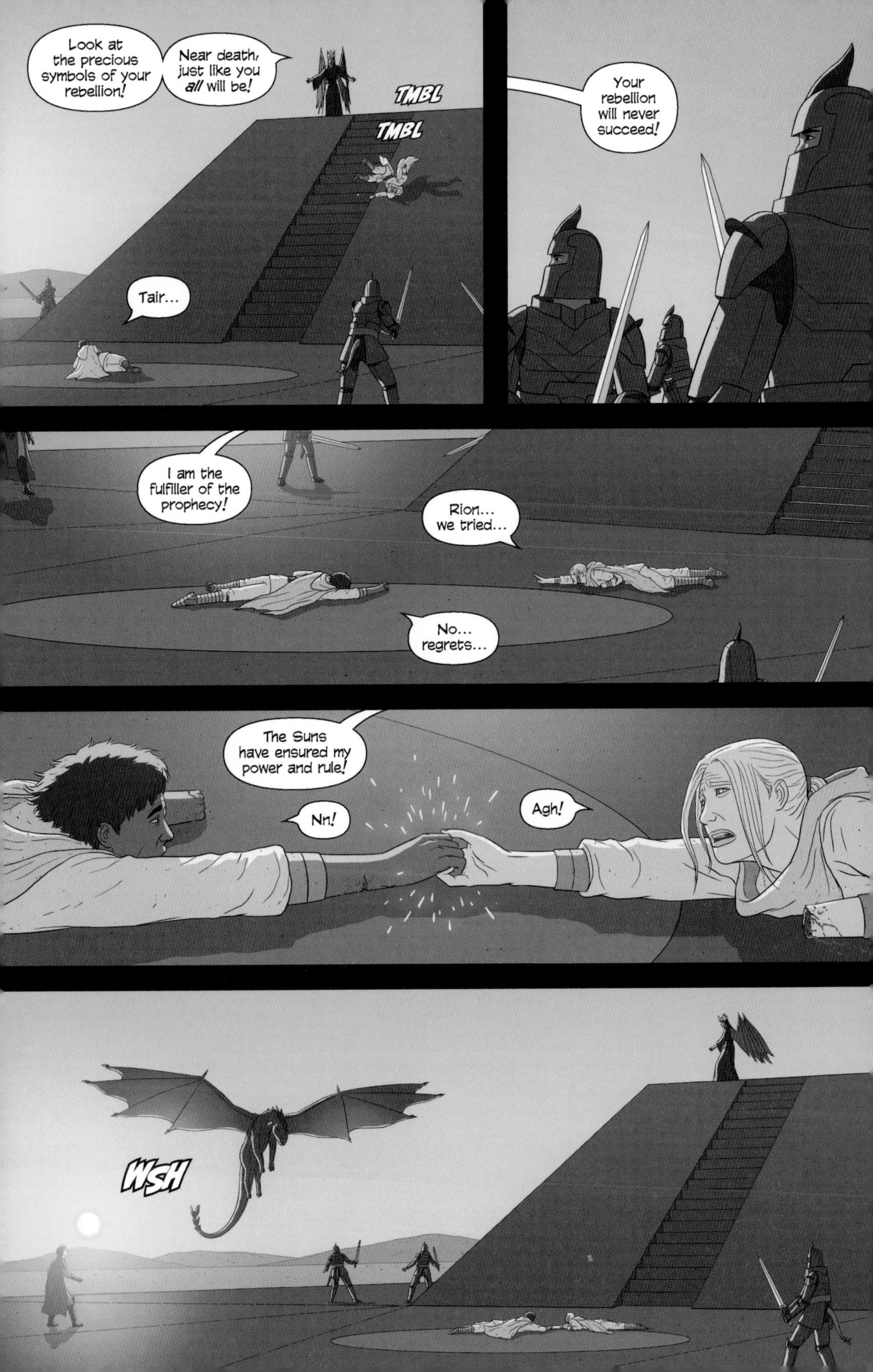
Look at the precious symbols of your rebellion!
Near death, just like you all will be!
TMBL
TMBL
Tair...
Your rebellion will never succeed!
I am the fulfiller of the prophecy!
Rion... we tried...
No... regrets...
The Suns have ensured my power and rule!
Nn!
Agh!
WSH

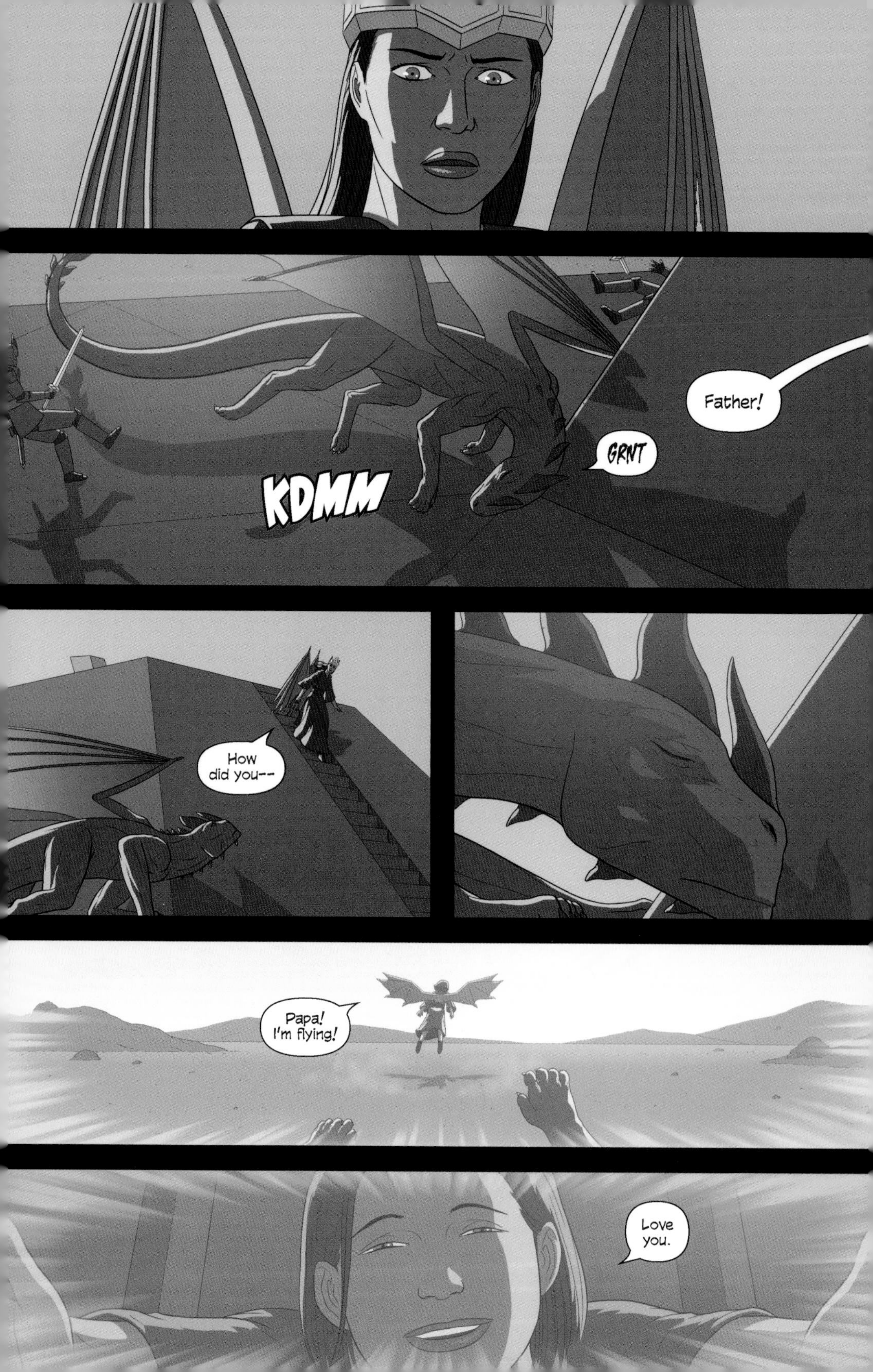
Father!
GRNT
KDMM
How did you--
Papa! I'm flying!
Love you.

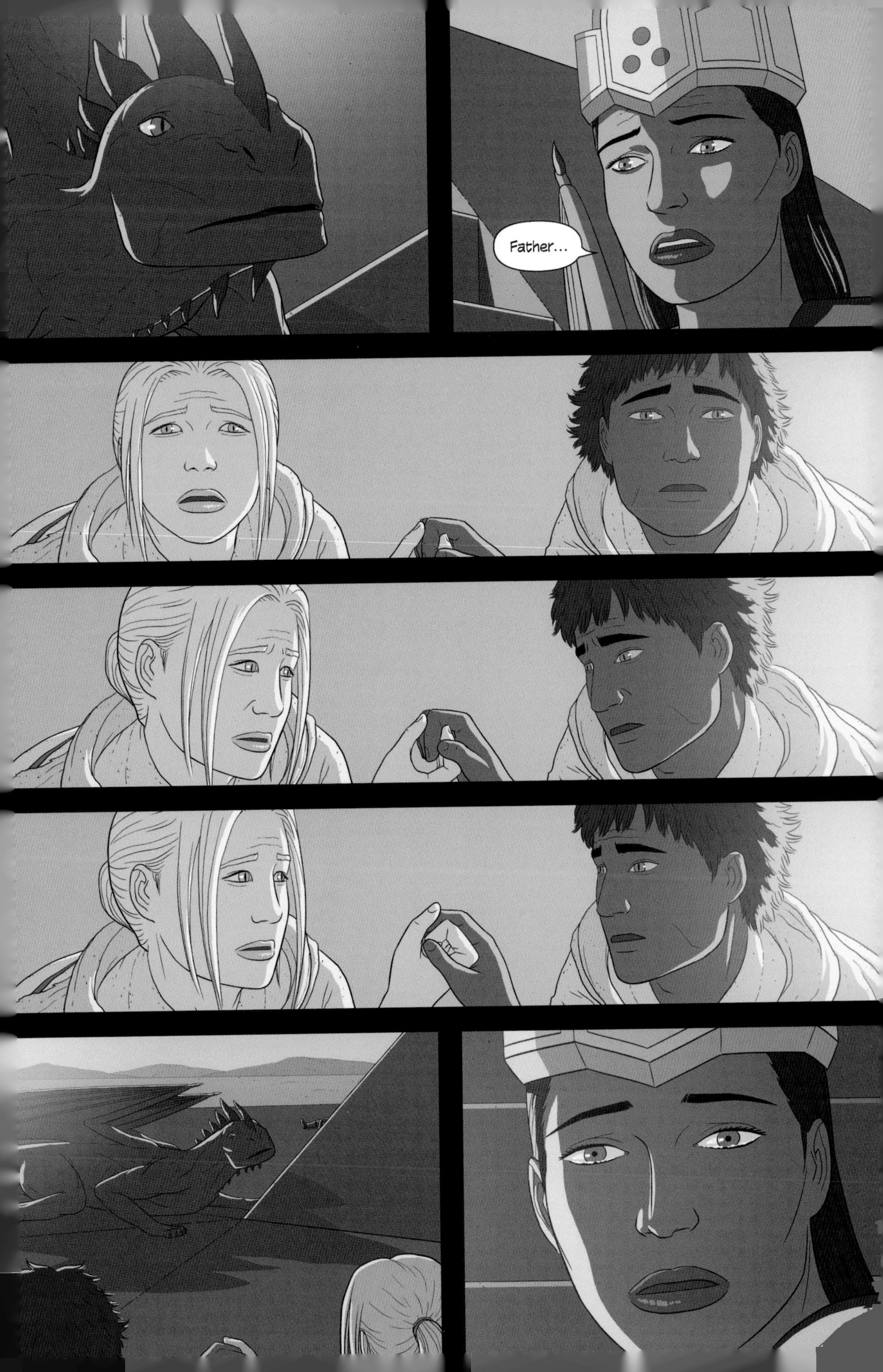
Father...

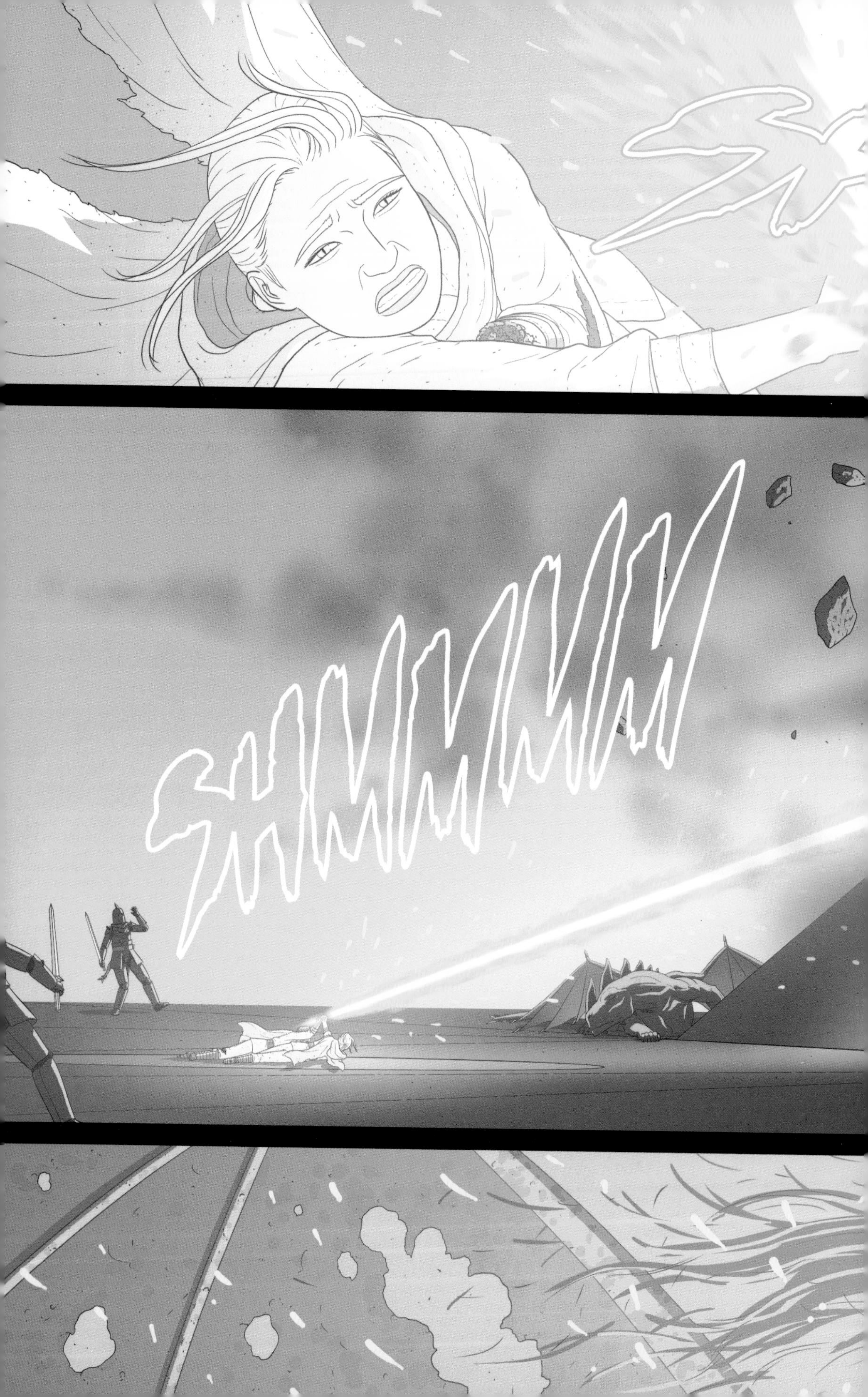
SHMMMMM

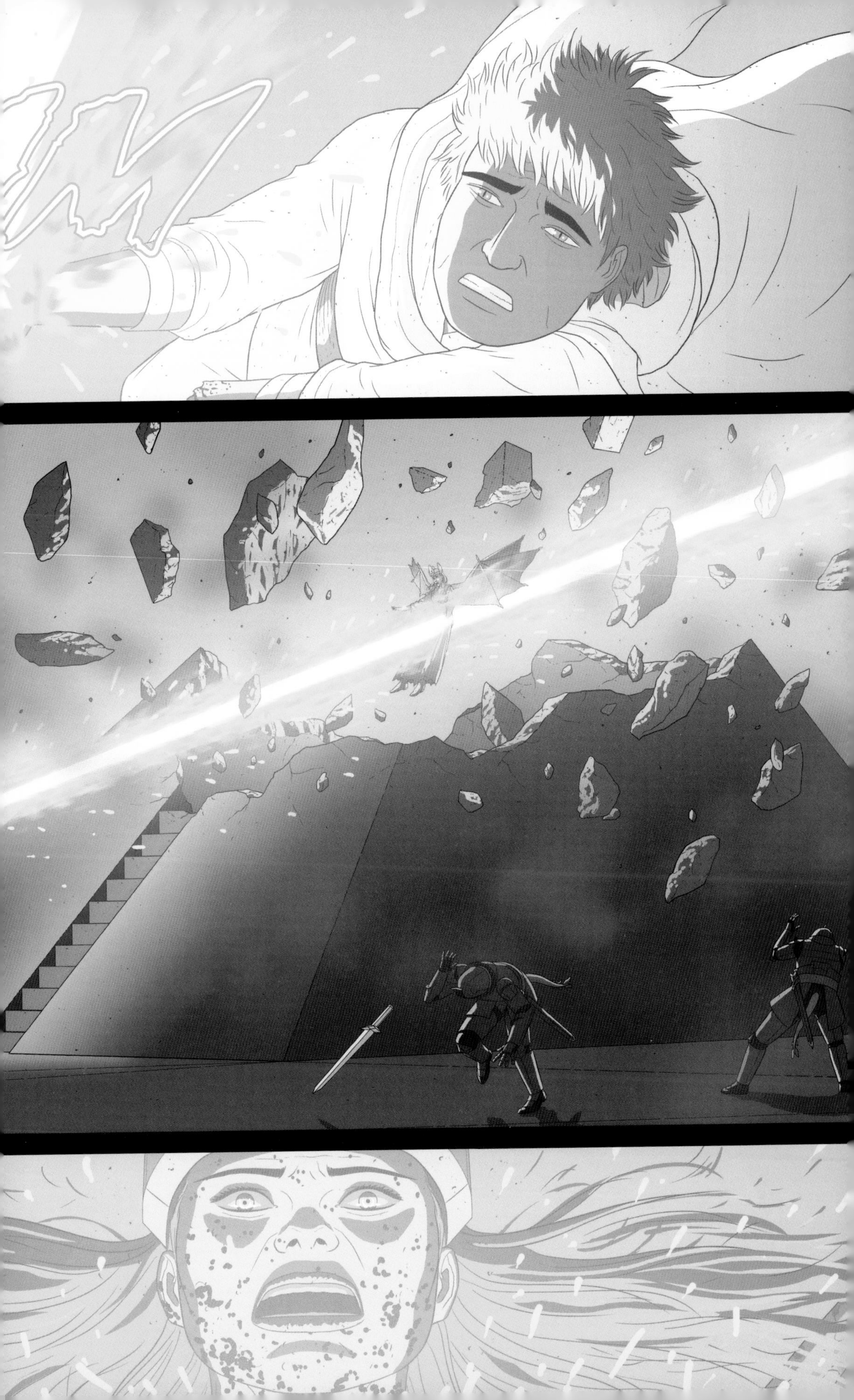

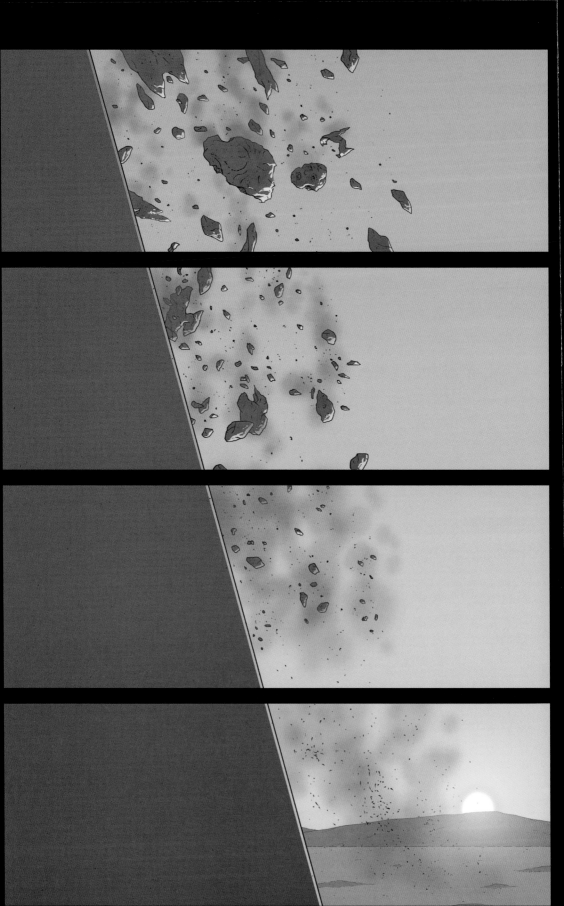

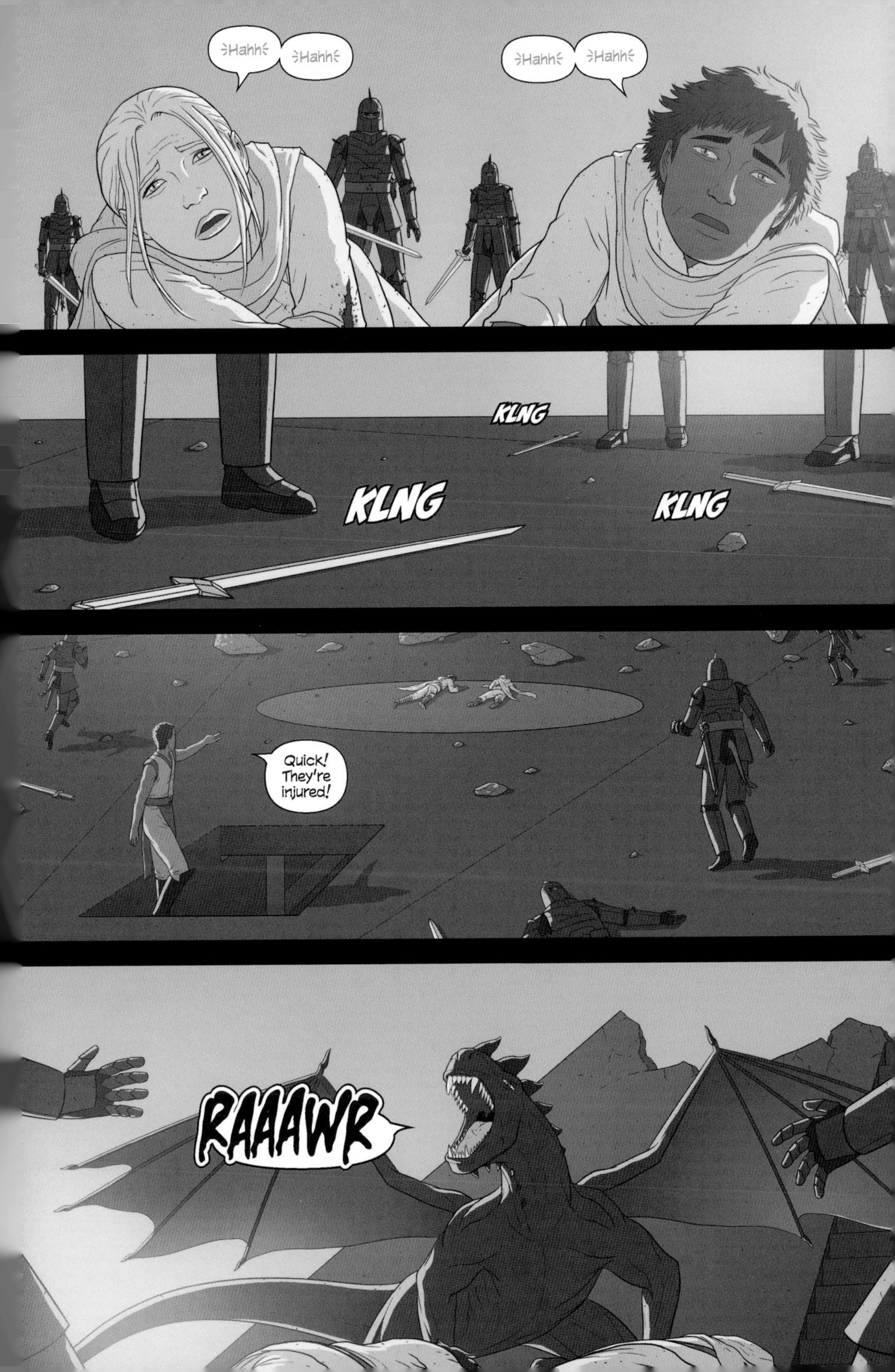
Hahh
Hahh
Hahh
Hahh
KLNG
KLNG
KLNG
Quick! They're injured!
RAAAWR

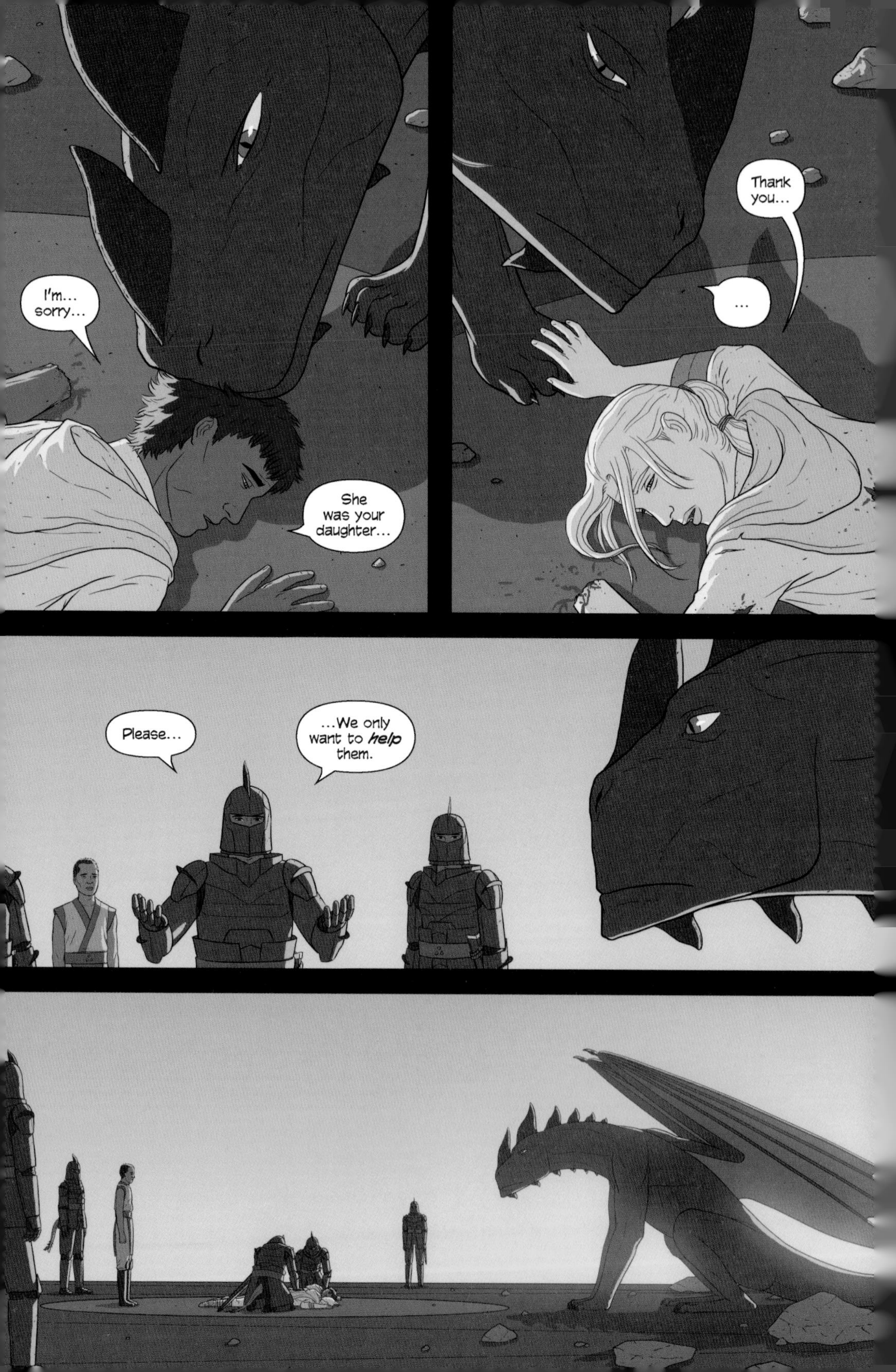
I'm... sorry...
She was your daughter...
Thank you...
...
Please...
...We only want to *help* them.

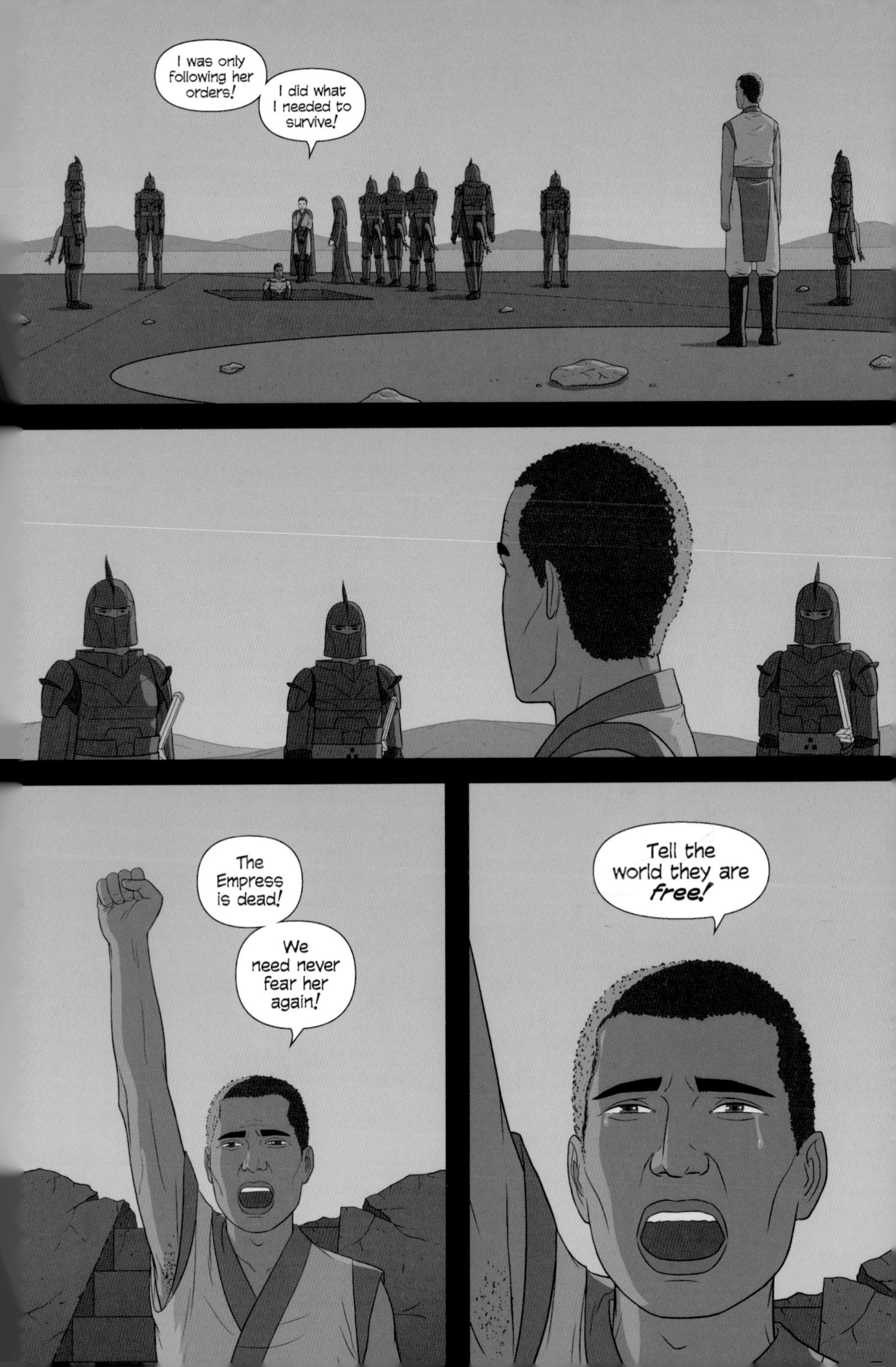
I was only following her orders!
I did what I needed to survive!
The Empress is dead!
We need never fear her again!
Tell the world they are *free!*

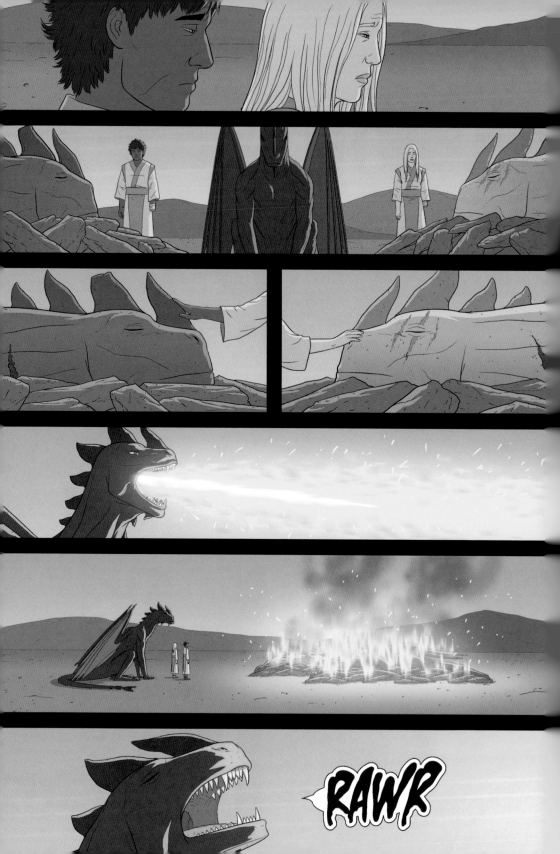

RAWR

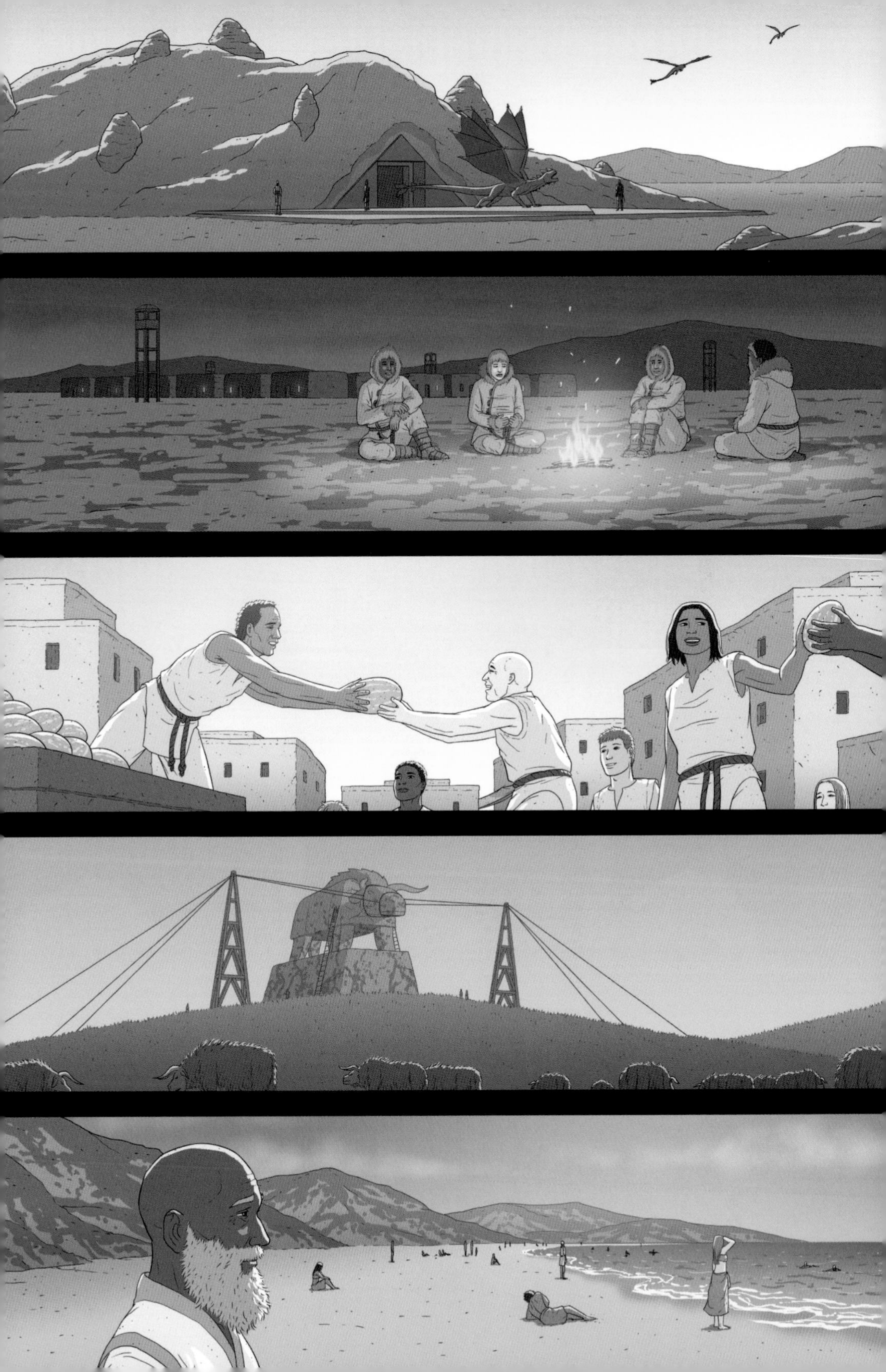

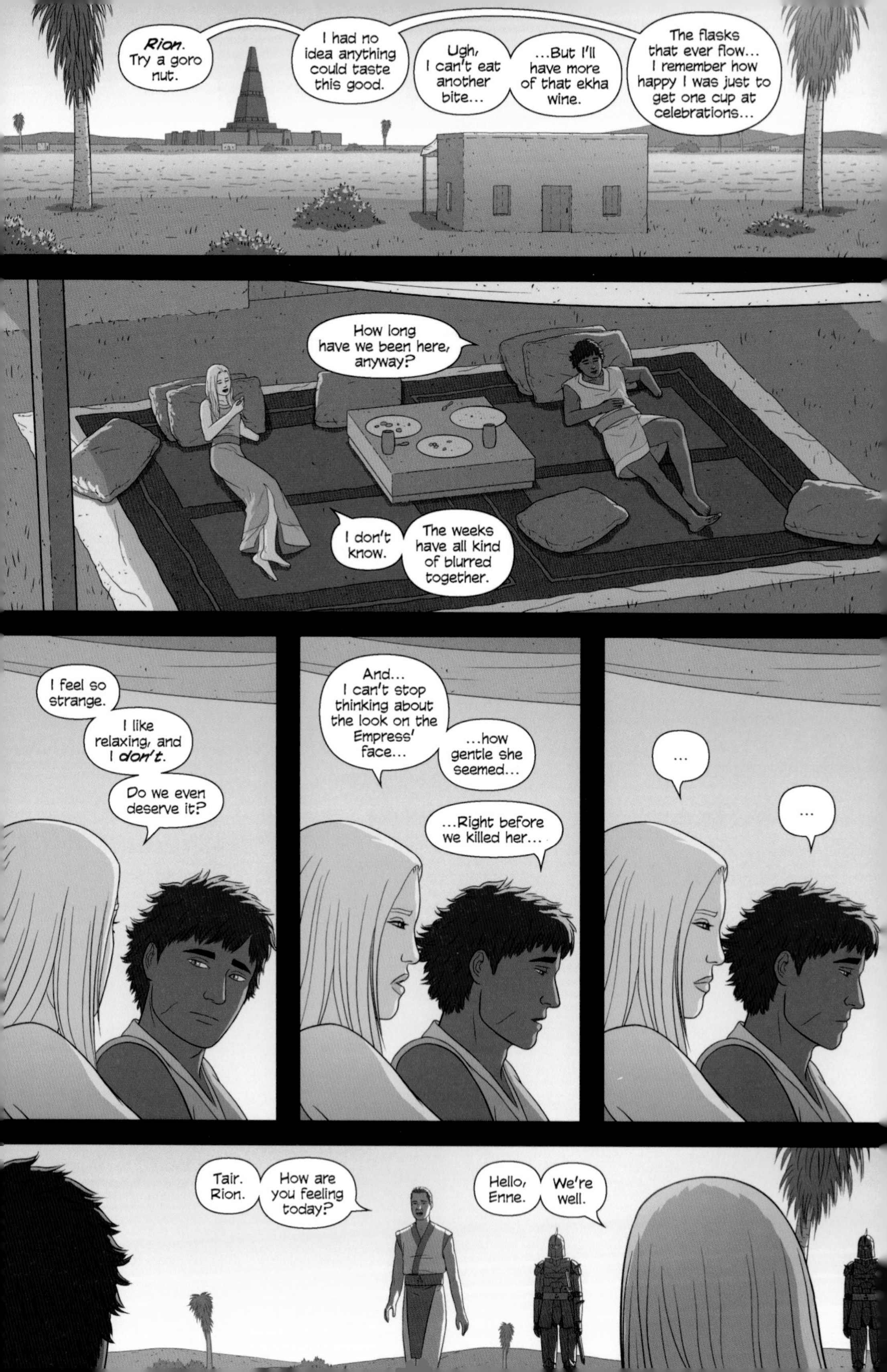
Rion. Try a goro nut.
I had no idea anything could taste this good.
Ugh, I can't eat another bite...
...But I'll have more of that ekha wine.
The flasks that ever flow... I remember how happy I was just to get one cup at celebrations...
How long have we been here, anyway?
I don't know.
The weeks have all kind of blurred together.
I feel so strange.
I like relaxing, and I don't.
Do we even deserve it?
And... I can't stop thinking about the look on the Empress' face...
...how gentle she seemed...
...Right before we killed her...
...
...
Tair. Rion.
How are you feeling today?
Hello, Enne.
We're well.

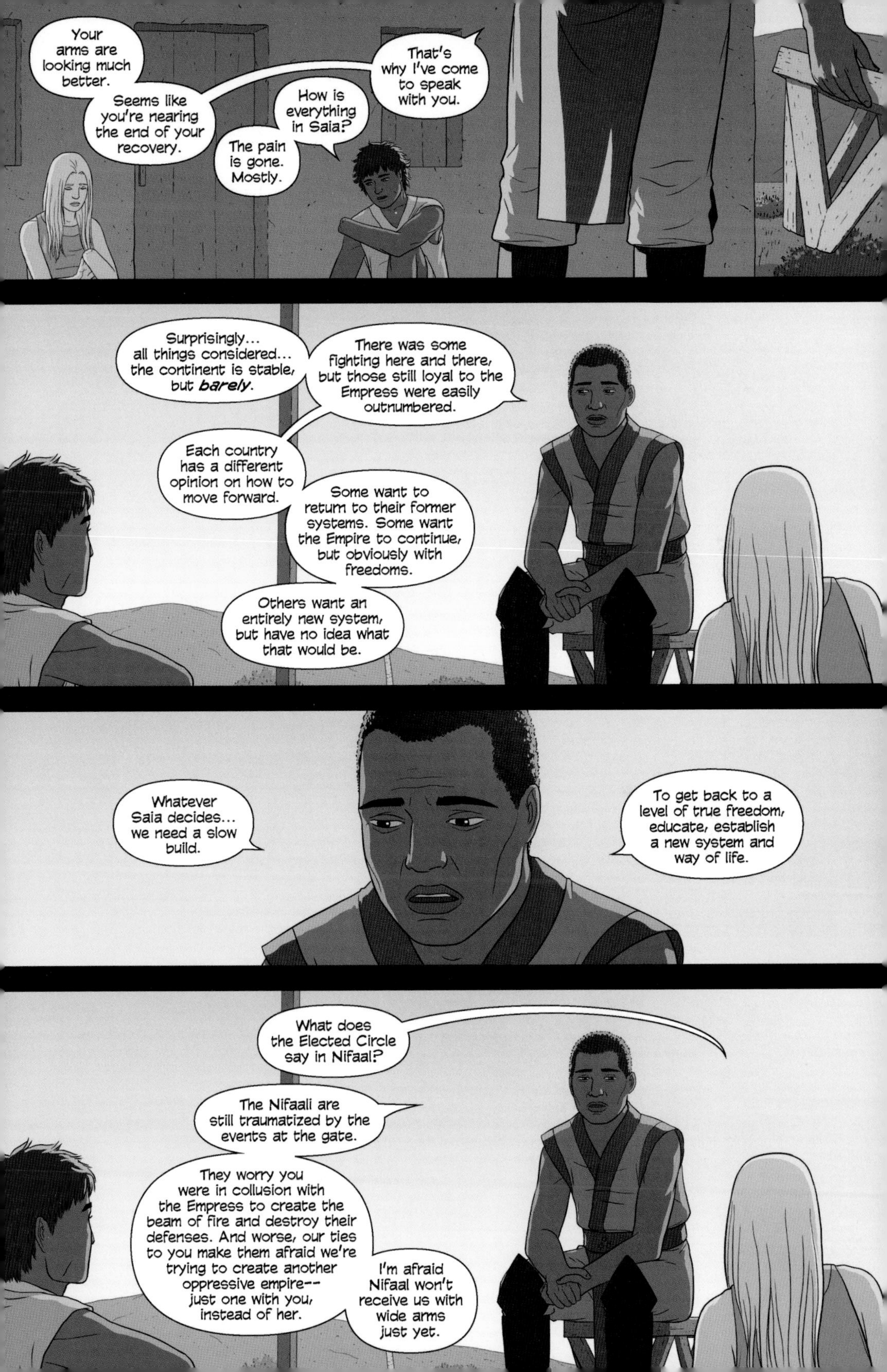
Your arms are looking much better.
Seems like you're nearing the end of your recovery.
The pain is gone. Mostly.
How is everything in Saia?
That's why I've come to speak with you.
Surprisingly... all things considered... the continent is stable, but *barely*.
There was some fighting here and there, but those still loyal to the Empress were easily outnumbered.
Each country has a different opinion on how to move forward.
Some want to return to their former systems. Some want the Empire to continue, but obviously with freedoms.
Others want an entirely new system, but have no idea what that would be.
Whatever Saia decides... we need a slow build.
To get back to a level of true freedom, educate, establish a new system and way of life.
What does the Elected Circle say in Nifaal?
The Nifaali are still traumatized by the events at the gate.
They worry you were in collusion with the Empress to create the beam of fire and destroy their defenses. And worse, our ties to you make them afraid we're trying to create another oppressive empire-- just one with you, instead of her.
I'm afraid Nifaal won't receive us with wide arms just yet.

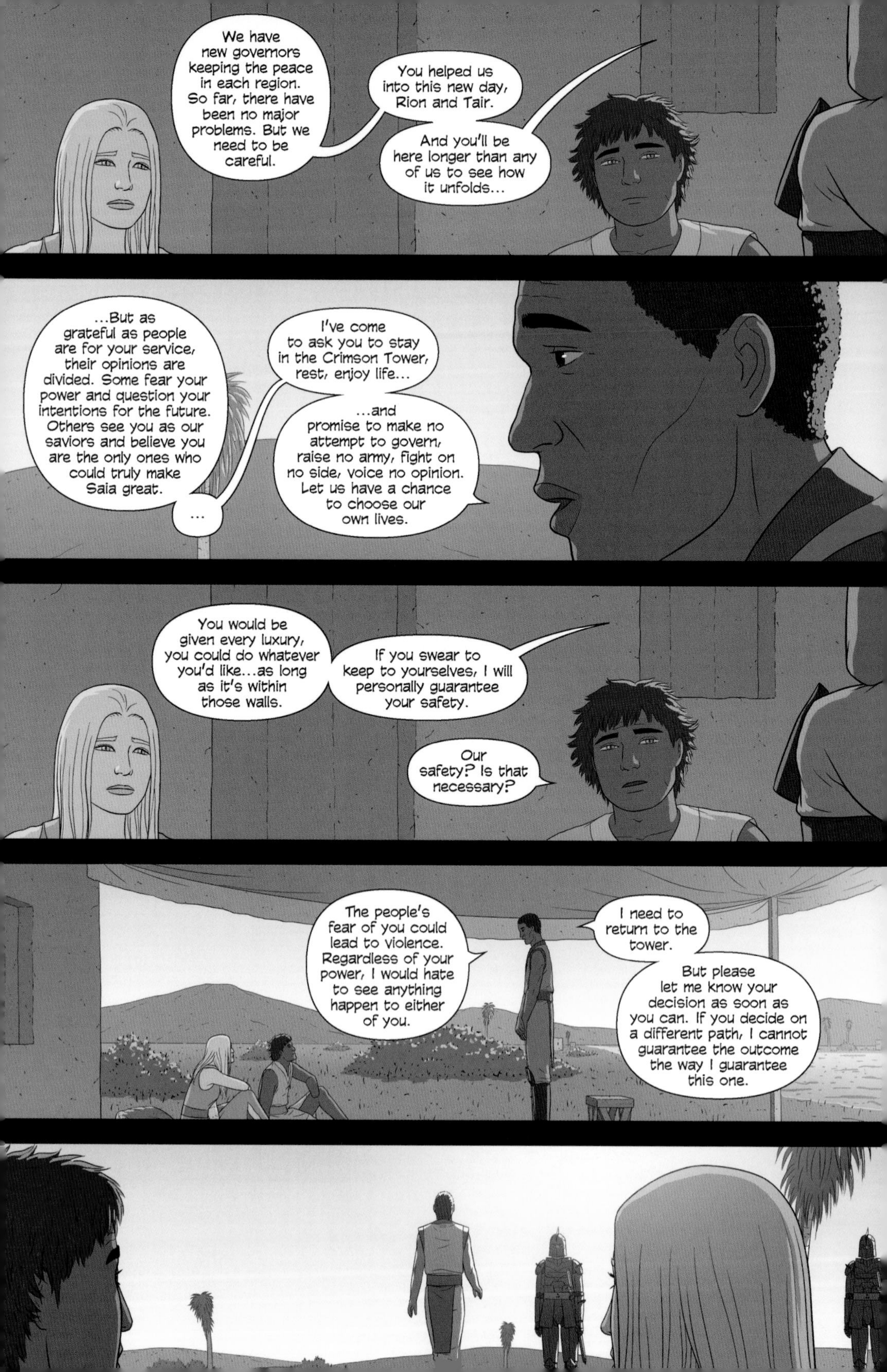
We have new governors keeping the peace in each region. So far, there have been no major problems. But we need to be careful.
You helped us into this new day, Rion and Tair.
And you'll be here longer than any of us to see how it unfolds...
...But as grateful as people are for your service, their opinions are divided. Some fear your power and question your intentions for the future. Others see you as our saviors and believe you are the only ones who could truly make Saia great.
...
I've come to ask you to stay in the Crimson Tower, rest, enjoy life...
...and promise to make no attempt to govern, raise no army, fight on no side, voice no opinion. Let us have a chance to choose our own lives.
You would be given every luxury, you could do whatever you'd like...as long as it's within those walls.
If you swear to keep to yourselves, I will personally guarantee your safety.
Our safety? Is that necessary?
The people's fear of you could lead to violence. Regardless of your power, I would hate to see anything happen to either of you.
I need to return to the tower.
But please let me know your decision as soon as you can. If you decide on a different path, I cannot guarantee the outcome the way I guarantee this one.

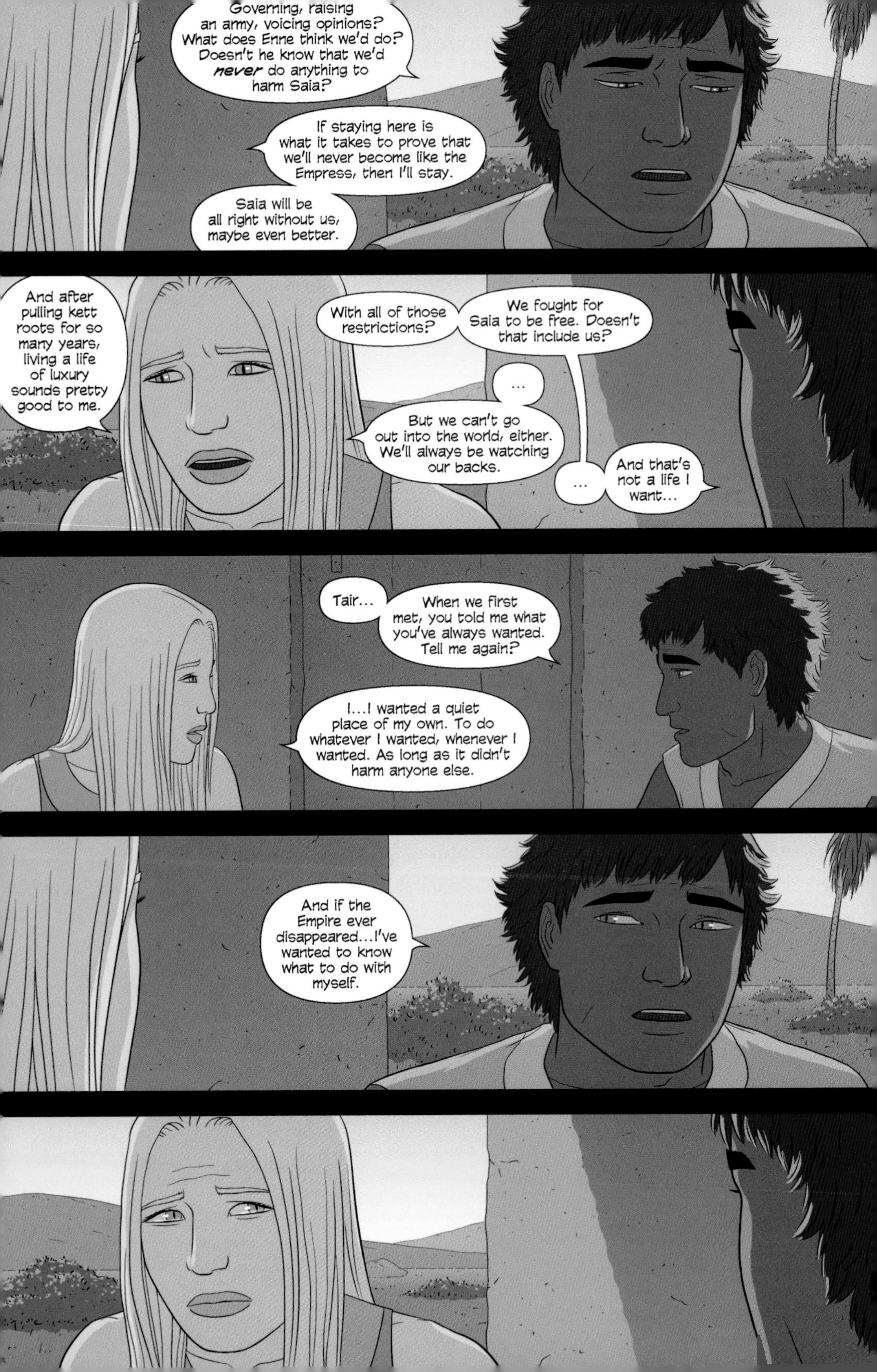

Governing, raising an army, voicing opinions? What does Enne think we'd do? Doesn't he know that we'd *never* do anything to harm Saia?
If staying here is what it takes to prove that we'll never become like the Empress, then I'll stay.
Saia will be all right without us, maybe even better.
And after pulling kett roots for so many years, living a life of luxury sounds pretty good to me.
With all of those restrictions?
We fought for Saia to be free. Doesn't that include us?
...
But we can't go out into the world, either. We'll always be watching our backs.
...
And that's not a life I want...
Tair...
When we first met, you told me what you've always wanted. Tell me again?
I...I wanted a quiet place of my own. To do whatever I wanted, whenever I wanted. As long as it didn't harm anyone else.
And if the Empire ever disappeared...I've wanted to know what to do with myself.

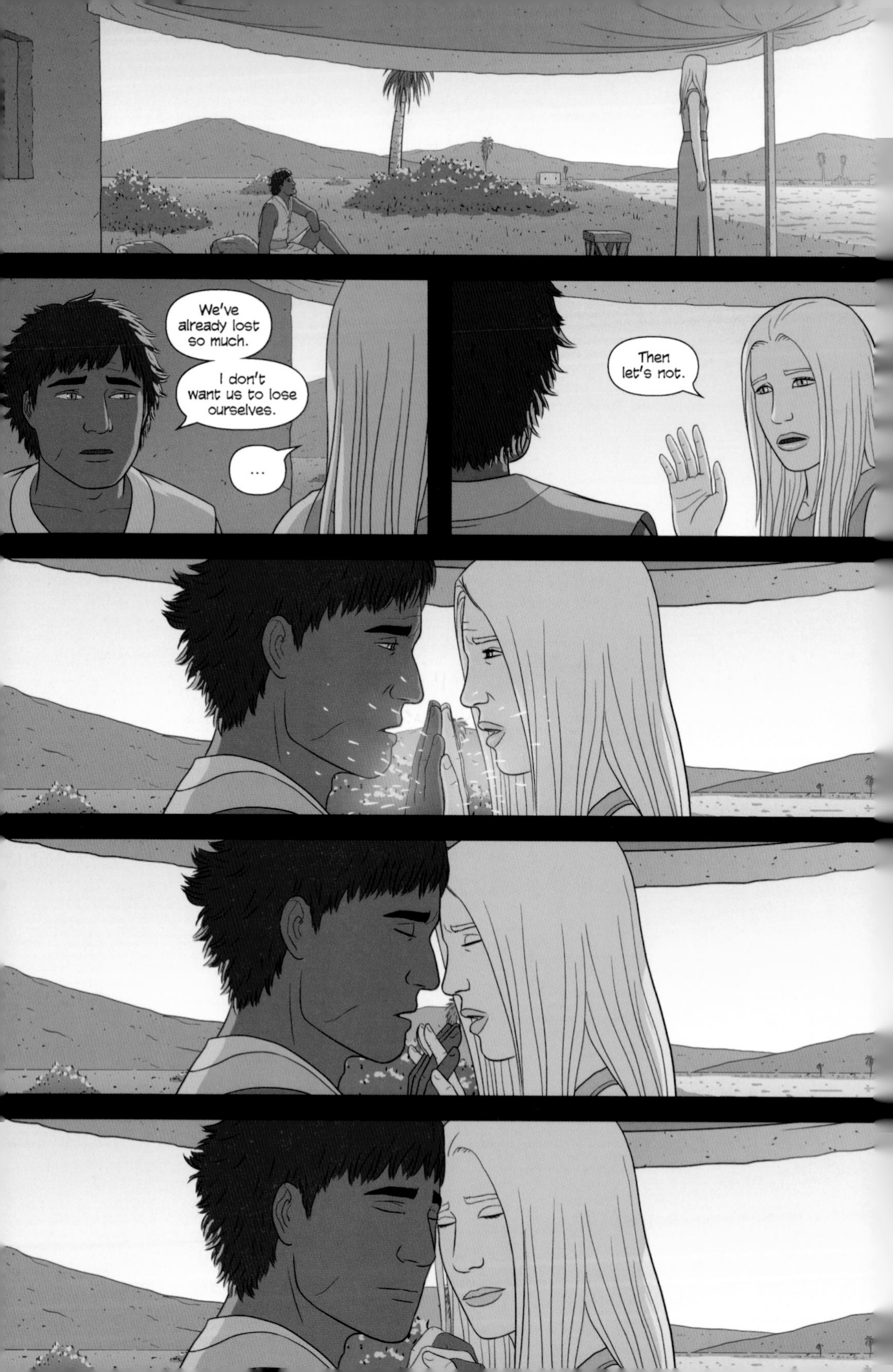
We've already lost so much.
I don't want us to lose ourselves.
...
Then let's not.

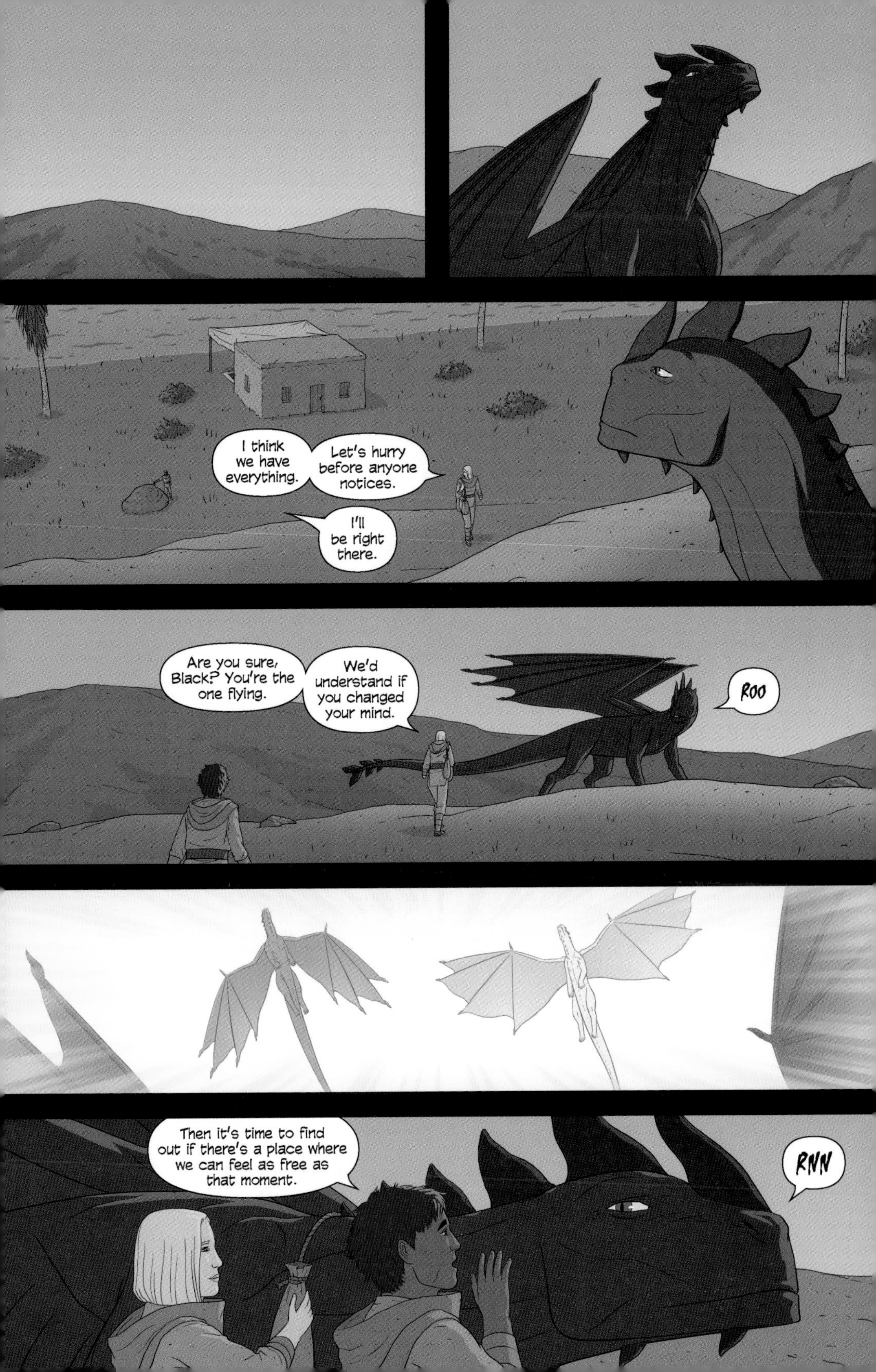
I think we have everything.
Let's hurry before anyone notices.
I'll be right there.
Are you sure, Black? You're the one flying.
We'd understand if you changed your mind.
ROO
Then it's time to find out if there's a place where we can feel as free as that moment.
RNN

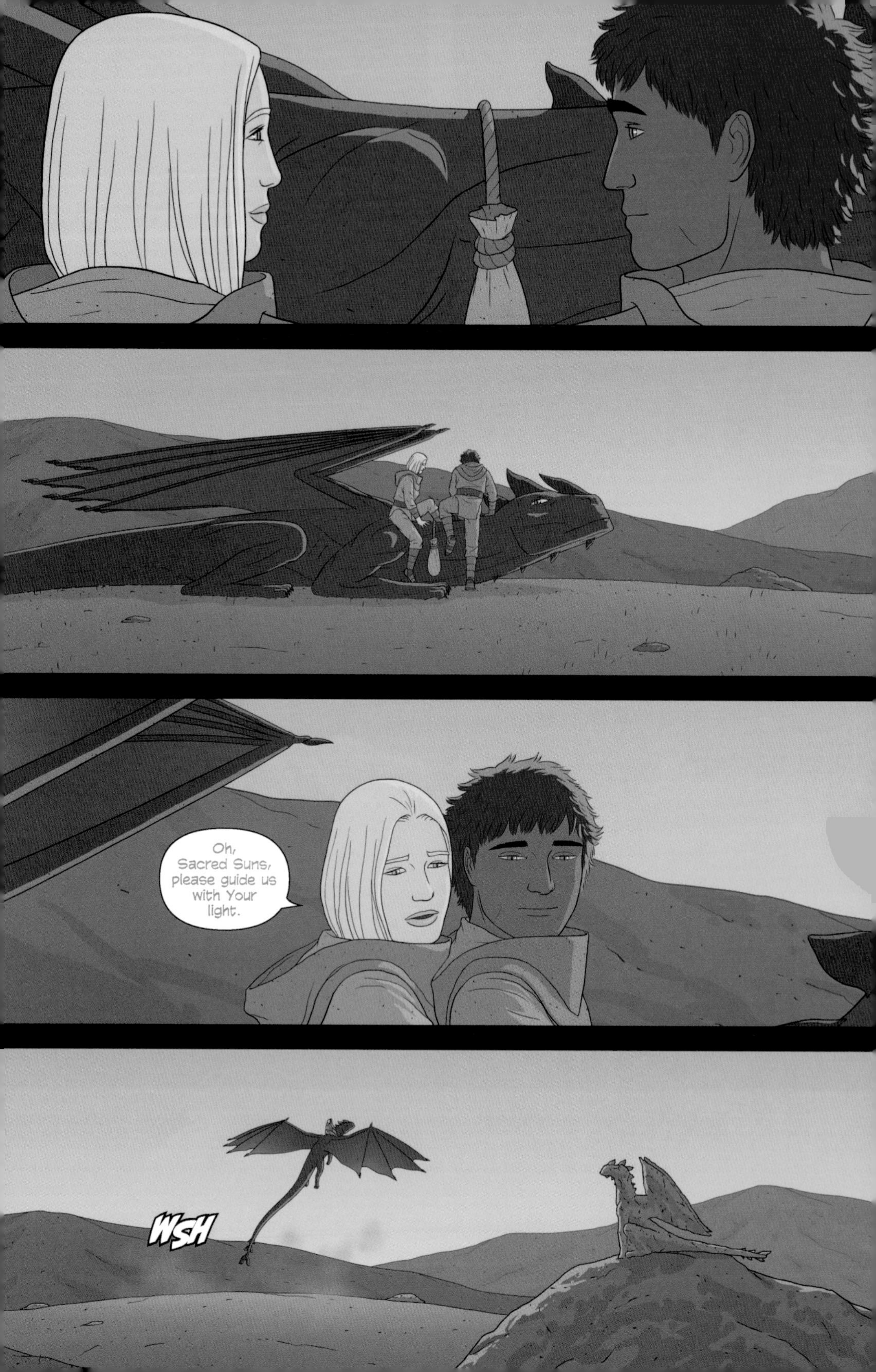
Oh, Sacred Suns, please guide us with Your light.
WSH

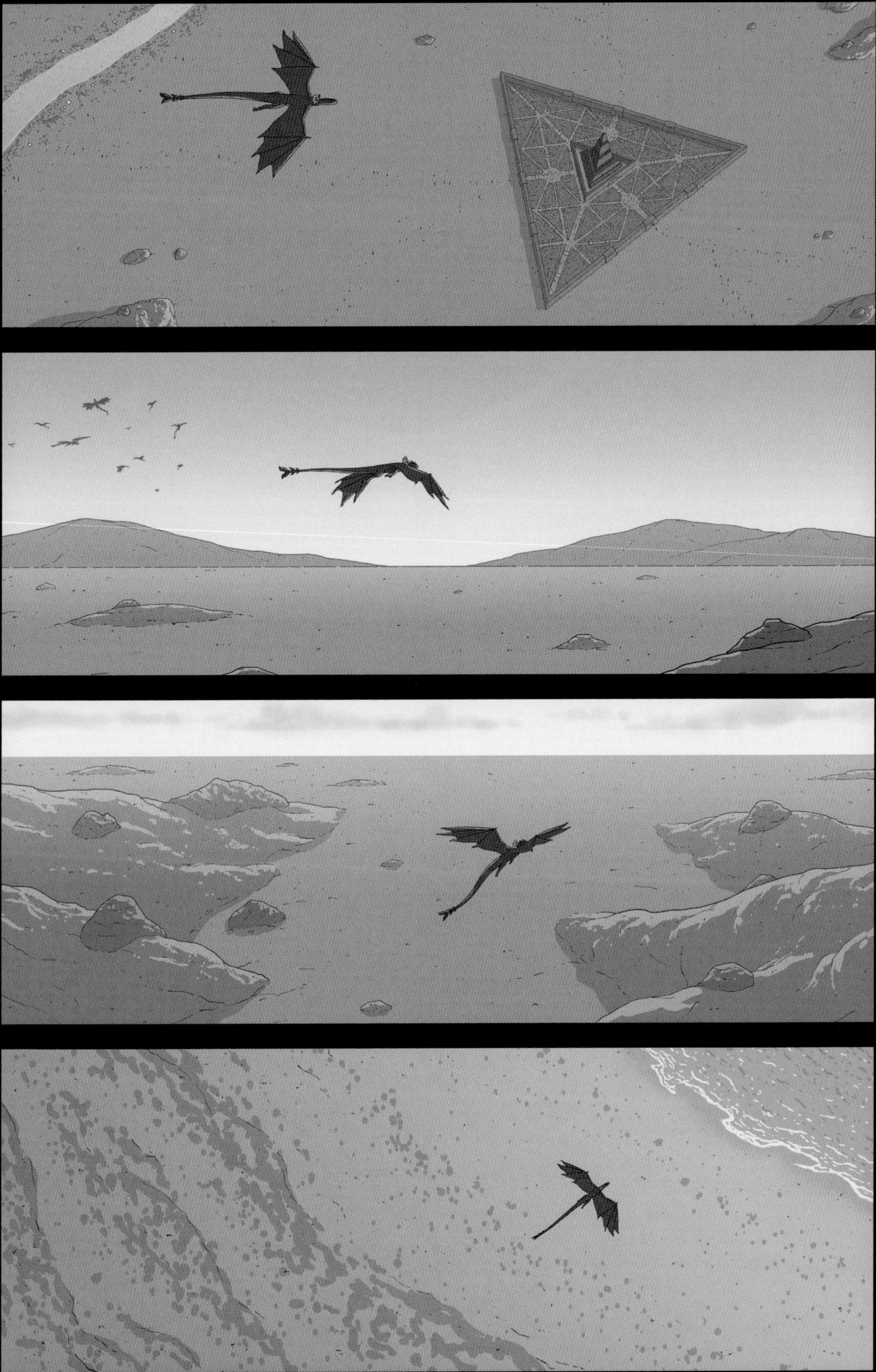

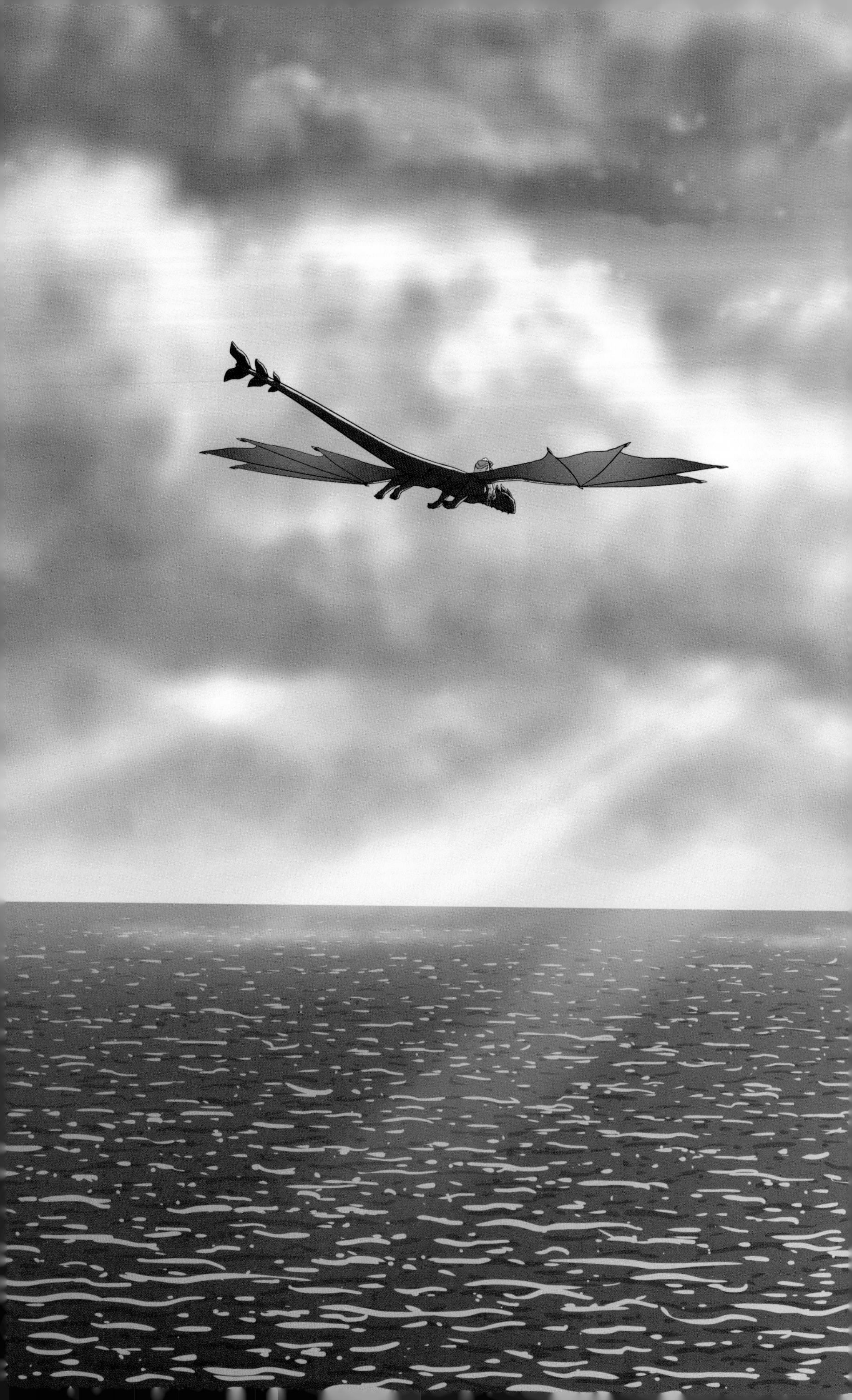

A NOTE ABOUT THE SUNS

The changing configuration of the suns is an important element of ETERNAL EMPIRE. They may seem random, but every configuration is intentional. We wanted to display the suns (and moon's phases) in the most accurate way possible, so Jonathan and 3D-animation friends, Tim Ingle and Rommel Calderon, mapped out an extensive calendar of their movement.

There are numerous factors that go into the changing configuration of the suns:

1. The location of the viewpoint on the planet
2. The rotation of the planet
3. The tilt of the planet's axis
4. The revolution of the planet around the red sun
5. The revolution of the blue and yellow binary suns around the red sun

In ETERNAL EMPIRE, the suns' positions can appear to change drastically, even in one day. In this case, the rotation of the planet is the most contributing factor.

Because of the rotation of Earth, stars in the night sky can appear to spin as a whole. This "spin" also applies to the daytime with Earth's sun, and to the suns in ETERNAL EMPIRE. The "spin" of the suns in one day is not related to the revolution of the binary suns around the red sun--only to the rotation of the planet.

The diagram below gives an example of the "spinning" of the suns, showing three configurations at different times on the same day. At sunrise, the binaries are positioned at the top-left of the red sun. At midday, the binaries are at the center-left. At sunset, the binaries are at the bottom-left.

- Jonathan and Sarah

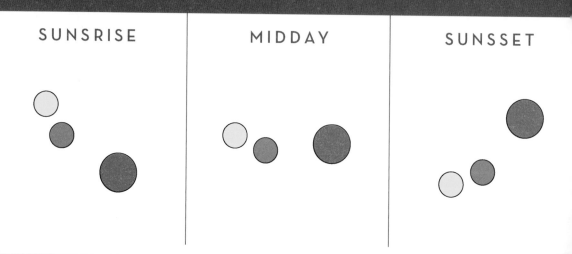

SUNRISE   MIDDAY   SUNSSET

ALEX + ADA

Jonathan Luna and Sarah Vaughn

ALEX+ADA
JONATHAN LUNA
SARAH VAUGHN
VOLUME 1

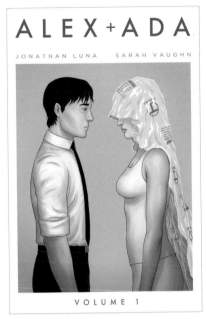

Volume 1
Trade Paperback
$12.99
ISBN: 978-1-63215-006-6
Collects #1-5
128 Pages

ALEX+ADA
JONATHAN LUNA
SARAH VAUGHN
VOLUME 2

Volume 2
Trade Paperback
$12.99
ISBN: 978-1-63215-195-7
Collects #6-10
128 Pages

ALEX+ADA
JONATHAN LUNA
SARAH VAUGHN
VOLUME 3

Volume 3
Trade Paperback
$12.99
ISBN: 978-1-63215-404-0
Collects #11-15
136 Pages

ALEX+ADA
THE COMPLETE COLLECTION
DELUXE EDITION
JONATHAN LUNA
SARAH VAUGHN

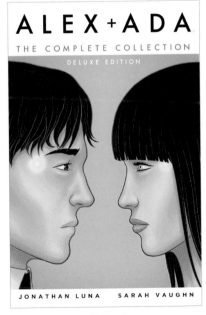

The Complete Collection
Deluxe Edition
Hardcover
$49.99
ISBN: 978-1-63215-869-7
Collects #1-15
376 Pages

To find your nearest comic book store, call: 1-888-COMIC-BOOK

 IMAGECOMICS.COM

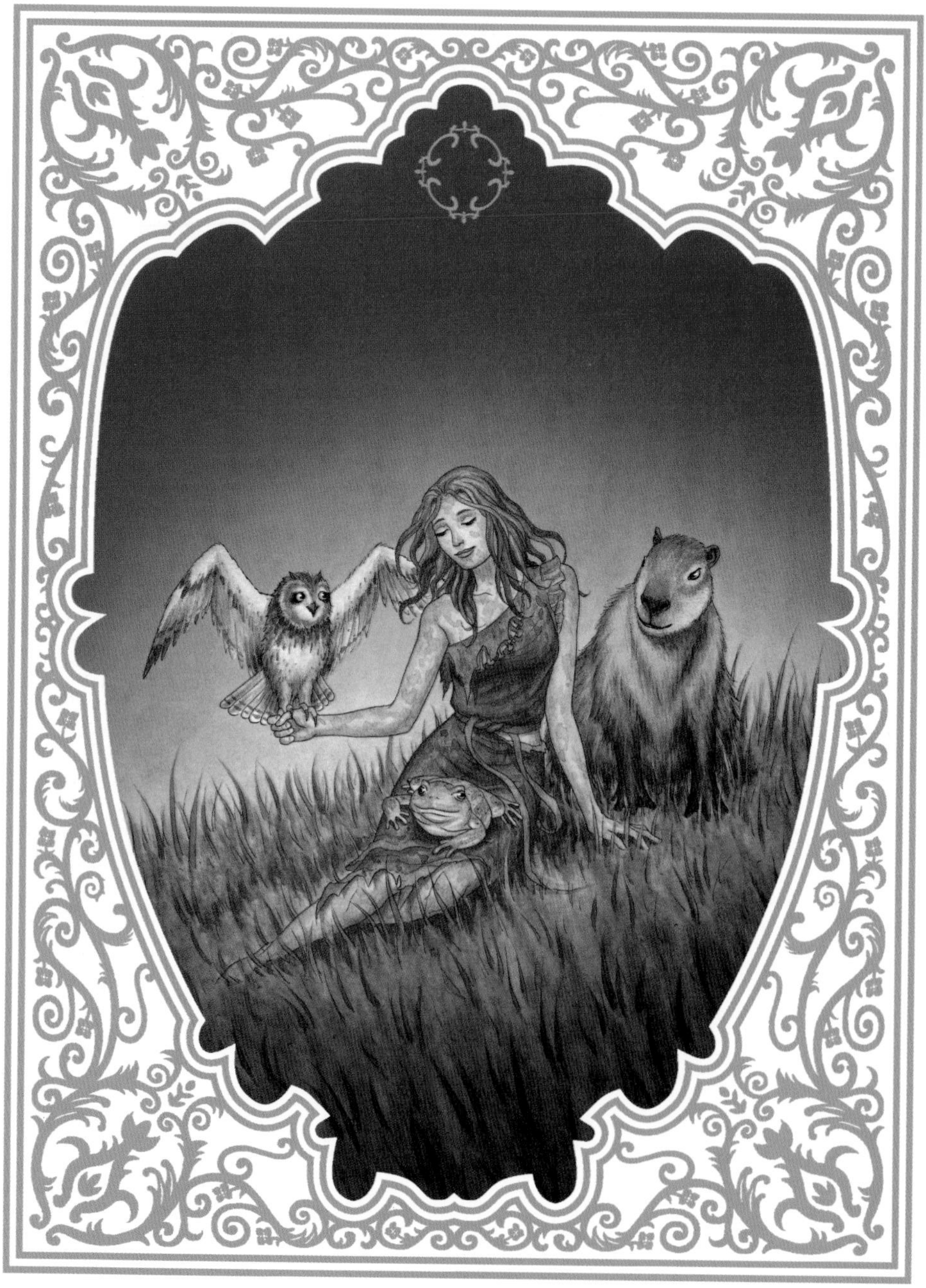

GREAT IMAGE COMICS FROM
THE LUNA BROTHERS

THE SWORD
Vol. 1: FIRE
Trade Paperback
$14.99
ISBN: 978-1-58240-879-8
Collects THE SWORD #1-6
152 Pages

THE SWORD
Vol. 2: WATER
Trade Paperback
$14.99
ISBN: 978-1-58240-976-4
Collects THE SWORD #7-12
152 Pages

THE SWORD
Vol. 3: EARTH
Trade Paperback
$14.99
ISBN: 978-1-60706-073-4
Collects THE SWORD #13-18
152 Pages

THE SWORD
Vol. 4: AIR
Trade Paperback
$14.99
ISBN: 978-1-60706-168-7
Collects THE SWORD #19-24
168 Pages

THE SWORD
THE COMPLETE
COLLECTION DELUXE HC
$99.99
ISBN: 978-1-60706-280-6
Collects THE SWORD #1-24
624 Pages

GIRLS
Vol. 1: CONCEPTION
Trade Paperback
$14.99
ISBN: 978-1-58240-529-2
Collects GIRLS #1-6
152 Pages

GIRLS
Vol. 2: EMERGENCE
Trade Paperback
$14.99
ISBN: 978-1-58240-608-4
Collects GIRLS #7-12
152 Pages

GIRLS
Vol. 3: SURVIVAL
Trade Paperback
$14.99
ISBN: 978-1-58240-703-6
Collects GIRLS #13-18
152 Pages

GIRLS
Vol. 4: EXTINCTION
Trade Paperback
$14.99
ISBN: 978-1-58240-790-6
Collects GIRLS #19-24
168 Pages

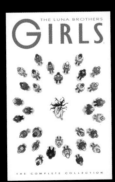

GIRLS
THE COMPLETE
COLLECTION TPB
$49.99
ISBN: 978-1-60706-466-4
Collects GIRLS #1-24
608 Pages

ULTRA
SEVEN DAYS
Trade Paperback
$17.99
ISBN: 978-1-58240-483-7
Collects ULTRA #1-8
248 Pages

ULTRA
SEVEN DAYS DELUXE HC
$74.99
ISBN: 978-1-60706-452-7
Collects ULTRA #1-8
248 Pages

To find your nearest comic book store, call:
1-888-COMIC-BOOK

JONATHAN LUNA

co-created and illustrated ALEX + ADA (Image Comics) with Sarah Vaughn, and THE SWORD, GIRLS, and ULTRA (all Image Comics) with his brother, Joshua Luna. He also wrote and illustrated STAR BRIGHT AND THE LOOKING GLASS (Image Comics), and illustrated SPIDER-WOMAN: ORIGIN (Marvel Comics), written by Brian Michael Bendis and Brian Reed.

Jonathan was born in California and spent most of his childhood overseas, living on military bases in Iceland and Italy. He returned to the United States in his late teens.

Writing and drawing comics since he was a child, he graduated from the Savannah College of Art and Design with a BFA in Sequential Art.

He currently resides in Northern Virginia.

www.jonathanluna.com

SARAH VAUGHN

is a writer, currently in Washington D.C. After living in various parts of the United States, she graduated from Saint Mary-of-the-Woods College with a degree in Sequential Visual Narration.

She is the co-creator of SLEEPLESS (Image Comics) with Leila Del Duca, writer of DEAD-MAN: DARK MANSION OF FORBIDDEN LOVE (DC Comics), co-creator of ALEX + ADA (Image Comics) with Jonathan Luna, and co-creator and writer of the Regency romance comic RUINED (Rosy Press) with Sarah Winifred Searle.

www.savivi.com